The SHAUGHNESSY File

S.J. Garrett

Other Titles by S.J. Garrett

CHRONICLE Series
Chronicle of Destiny
Chronicle of Summer

ETERNITY Series
Ghost Eyes

DESCENDANTS Series
Shadow on the Sea

3rd DISTRICT Series
The Shaughnessy File
The Carmichael File

To all those who believe in happy ever after: this one is for you.

PROLOGUE

There was a place known as the 3rd District.

When viewed from a plane, it resembled a small triangle located in the edge of New York City, New York. From space, it could not be seen. It was not a landmark. It was not a place of great historical import. It was, for all intents and purposes, a backwater area in a bustling city of hundreds of thousands of people.

It was also the place where magic lived. If your life crossed the roads of 3rd District, it was said, you would find true love and live happily ever after. You would find a true faerie tale story.

This story is one of them.

Folder One
AENYA

CHAPTER ONE

"I'll be frank, Mr. Michaels. My daughter is the apple of my eye and my pride and joy. The fact that she has been directly disobeying me is very distressing."

From where he was sitting in Sullivan Shaughnessy's office, Hiro Michaels watched the older man pace back and forth across the carpet behind his desk and decided that was a vast understatement.

Sullivan was moving with the manner of a man who had discovered the world was actually flat and his ships had just sailed off the end. Being a wise man, Hiro decided to remain in his seat and not get in the way. "I was only told the conditions of the offer," he finally said. "Why don't you tell me the reasons behind it?"

Sullivan stopped pacing and took his seat once more. Leaning on his desk, his head in his hands, he explained, "My daughter, Aenya, has aspirations of being a dancer. Not that I doubt her skill, but it's not the sort of career I want my child in. I want her to be able to support herself, or at least *be* supported by a decent husband. I have since forbidden her from going out at night and dancing at clubs, hoping it'll curb her desires."

"Her brother mentioned you lock her in at night."

"Yes." He sighed. "And when she looks at me with those big brown eyes . . . it damn near kills me. She's horribly spoiled. Her mother died in childbirth and Aenya is so like her . . . He got up again and went to pour himself a glass of tea that was sitting on the drink bar. "Anyway, I began to notice lately that her shoe bill was incredibly high."

"Her . . . shoe bill?" Hiro lifted a brow. "How so?"

"A new pair of dancing shoes, every day, for the last six weeks!"

He offered the bill, and Hiro whistled softly through his teeth as he saw the amount. "Exactly my reaction. And the worst part is that she does not leave her room as far as we know. If she was dancing in the house, Taegan would hear her since his room is on the floor right underneath."

"Taegan Shaughnessy, your eldest son." It wasn't a question. Hiro knew as much about the family as anyone would; the Shaughnessy Corporation was very big in society. He was also friends with Kienan Shaughnessy, the youngest son and Aenya's older brother.

"Yes." Sullivan drummed his fingers on the edge of his desk. "Aenya refuses to tell me anything, so I decided to try to force her hand. I arranged a contract that says that if any man can determine within three days where she goes every night, he can have her hand in marriage."

"Then she's not yet twenty-one," Hiro surmised. "How old is she?"

"Eighteen." he sighed deeply. "The law raising the age of majority to twenty-one was a great idea in theory. I actually voted for the damn thing. Now it's just a pain in the ass." He rubbed his forehead. "I didn't expect my daughter to be so . . .."

Hiro hid a smile. "So much like her father?"

He wanted to take offense but he couldn't. It was hard to take offense at the truth. "At this point, I've been hoping she would confess. She has not only held firm, but all potential suitors have completely failed. You're my last hope, Hiro."

Hiro frowned thoughtfully as he looked at the contract. "This contract also offers shares in the company."

"It's a family company," Sullivan explained. "All family members receive shares. I have tried my best to weed out the ones only interested in the company; I do not want my daughter to be in an unhappy marriage. My deepest hope is to find a man she will eventually love, even if it takes a while. Not all love comes at first sight, of course."

Somehow, Hiro got the feeling Sullivan didn't entirely believe it.

There was the slightest of smiles on his lips. "Of course," he responded promptly. Really, what else could he say?

"Are you interested?"

"May I meet her first?" he asked. He smiled. "Hardly seems ideal for me to agree when I'm not certain if I will even like her, let alone wish her for my wife. I know nothing about her other than she is willful, devious, and apparently quite spoiled."

Sullivan laughed at the accurate summation. "Oh, you'll like her. Aenya may be all those things, but she is far more. She's an absolutely wonderful young woman, and more than her doting father think so." He walked over to the intercom and pressed a button. "Shelly, send my daughter in." There was a murmured response, and he walked back around behind his desk. "Don't be startled by her appearance. The family wolf follows her everywhere."

Family . . . wolf? Hiro began to wonder just what the hell he had gotten himself into when the side door opened and he turned his head to see Aenya Shaughnessy walk in, like a princess arriving for court.

He decided that the coffee was spiked. Or maybe he had been in the sun too long. There was no way in hell a mere look at a woman could turn a man's mind into mush and bring every single pulse he had to blinding life. There was no denying Aenya was an exceptionally lovely young woman, mature beyond her years, but a single look at her shouldn't have had his heart pounding so hard it was impossible to breathe.

She was on the shorter side; probably a foot shorter than him, and he was six-one. She had a slender, graceful figure with baby fine sandy blonde hair and large honey brown eyes. She wore a pale pink dress covered in cherry blossoms that should have been a century out of date but looked perfectly at home on such a modern female. It suited her in a way that was more elemental than fashionable.

Her utter femininity and delicate appearance was not marred at all by the slender black and gray wolf sitting by her ankle. The wolf was taller than average and reached just over Aenya's hip. It was also distinctly female, for Aenya had tied a sassy pink bow around the wolf's neck.

The very picture of innocence, she flashed a smile at her father that revealed dimples in her cheeks. "You called for me, Daddy?"

Hiro was instantly on his guard. His calm, analytical brain kicked in and overrode his surprising desire. He wasn't buying the sweetness and light kick. She was intelligent enough to get out of a locked room without being caught, and she was Sullivan Shaughnessy's daughter. She would be a formidable opponent to any who dared test her.

If Sullivan suspected his daughter was up to anything, he didn't show it as she walked over and kissed his cheek. "I did indeed. I'd like you to meet Hiro Michaels. He has come here today to discuss the contract."

Something that was anger and annoyance flashed across her face so quickly that it was nearly gone before it was truly there. Hiro's sharp eyes missed nothing, yet she was all smiles when she turned to him. Her eyes even managed to sparkle merrily. "So," she said after a quick study, "you're another hunter, huh? Well, at least you're young."

"Aenya!" Sullivan scolded gently.

"It's true!" She pouted prettily. "Most of the men who have come through are too old for me. Daddy, can't you rethink this?"

"Tell me where you go," he countered softly, "and the contract is voided."

Hiro found himself holding his breath. On one hand, he wanted her to confess so that she was no longer under this burden. On the other, he wanted her to continue the charade so he had time to get closer to her. This honey-eyed dancer with a modern mind in an old-fashioned dress was *everything* he had ever wanted.

She didn't hesitate. "No."

Sullivan sighed, expecting no less. "Very well. You are excused, little one. And take the wolf. She's chewing on my slippers again."

Aenya giggled, and it was a sound of pure enchantment. "Come on, Stormy." She waved a hand at her pet then shot Hiro a look that was as challenging as it was innocent. For a moment, the guileless brown eyes revealed the wildness inside. "Good luck, Mr. Michaels. If

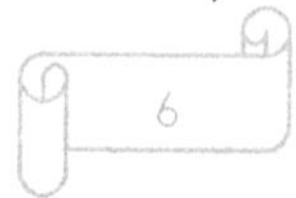

you decide to take this contract, you'll need more than youth on your side." With a dancer's grace, she turned and left the room, Stormy padding along at her heels.

The door hadn't even fully shut behind her before Hiro swiveled on his seat, picked up a pen, and scrawled his name across the bottom of the contract. Something satisfied gleamed in Sullivan's eyes as he watched. "Good luck, son," the older man murmured. "You'll need it."

Since Hiro had come over with a suitcase, just in case, all he had to do was bring his bag up to the door. The Shaughnessy home (mansion, frankly) had servants to help run it. An older butler, who looked more like Michael Gough's version of Alfred from *Batman & Robin,* than Michael Caine's version in *The Dark Knight,* happily absconded with Hiro's suitcase to take it upstairs to the room he would be using.

Bemused, Hiro headed toward the back of the house where he could see patio doors leading to an immense garden. Aenya was sitting on the edge of a pond with her feet dangling in the water. When he was close, she asked without looking up, "Why, Mr. Michaels? Money? Fame?"

He chose his words very carefully. "A . . . vision, I suppose. And call me Hiro, please. I can't quite bring myself to call you 'Miss Shaughnessy' and me using your first name and you not using mine went out of style when your dress was made."

Her smile flickered across her face. "It's a family heirloom. But 'Hiro' it is." She looked up at him. "Nobody seems to understand, Hiro. This isn't a game. It isn't a bit of rebellion because I think I should be an adult and I'm legally not. I don't argue with my father being my guardian. I argue with his trying to stop my dreams. This is my *life.*"

Stormy, lying with her head on Aenya's lap, whined softly. He suspected it was in agreement. The wolf's eyes were far more intelligent than he had ever seen in any animal. "Maybe he wants to protect you," he offered.

"Oh, undoubtedly," she agreed. "I know his motives." She nudged Stormy, then got to her feet. She swung around to smile at him. "You're by far the hottest guy to come through here lately. And just because I think so, just because you know so, don't expect me to lower my guard."

A black brow lifted over pine green eyes. It was one thing to be attractive and know it. It was another to have it blatantly pointed out. How the hell Sullivan thought his baby girl was shy was a mystery to him. "Thank you?" He deliberately made it a question and saw her quick grin. With a shrug of one shoulder, and a matching smile, he said, "Don't expect me to be like the others in any way, shape, or form."

"True," she admitted, "you're already different. You're talking to me as if I'm a human and not a prize. I've had to double-check periodically to make sure there isn't a 'for sale' sign around my neck."

Gravely, he said, "And prime real estate is so expensive these days." He studied her face curiously. "You're still in high school?" he asked.

She sighed. "Yes. And yes, I'm eighteen, and yes I'll be nineteen around graduation. My birthday is in June." It was currently November. "I started school late. My father is a smidge overprotective."

"I hadn't noticed," he murmured blandly.

"He's so subtle, isn't he?" She shrugged one shoulder as she let him help her up the slippery incline away from the pond. "The school has allowed my 'suitors' to follow me around to my classes; I presume you will be doing it as well."

He was fascinated. She truly was very small. She wasn't just short; she was also incredibly slender and fine boned. It took considerable strength not to pull her into his arms and see how well she fit. Stormy's presence helped his control. She looked ready to chew on his ankle.

"You presume right," he decided. With honest sympathy, he

said, "I take it the school is enjoying this."

"Bad enough I'm a Shaughnessy," she muttered, her brows pulling together into a scowl, "but now this. I could punch them all!"

After a thoughtful moment, he decided, "You are cute as hell."

Her mouth fell open. She warily took a step back, her cheeks turning a pink as becoming as her dress. Without a further word, she whirled and fled into the house, nearly knocking over one of her brothers as he sleepily staggered past with a cup of coffee in hand.

That was interesting, Hiro decided. She confronted him head-on about his being attractive, but turned skittish when he indicated he thought she was cute. He would have to see if he could piece together that puzzle at the same time as the others. If anything, today wouldn't be boring.

Aenya didn't stop running until she was safely in her room. She cursed herself as she swiftly changed out of her dress and switched into her school uniform. She *loathed* her school uniform. She understood it was a requirement for a private school, but she *hated* the way the clothes looked and how oddly vulnerable she felt in the knee-length skirt. The sexism didn't appeal to her either.

She had a secret compromise that no one except her brothers knew about. She wore a pair of dancing shorts under her uniform. That way if some jerk wanted to try to flip her skirt, he wouldn't get a peep show. Even at private schools, teenage males were perverts.

She scowled as she looked in her mirror. It hardly seemed fair that she was eighteen and still in school. Okay, she wasn't officially an adult until she was twenty-one, but she wanted to be out of high school and start working on college. She only had three classes; she was bored out of her mind.

With a sigh, she left the room and headed downstairs to the dining room. Hiro was already there and so were her brothers. The only open spot was next to Hiro, so, reluctantly, she went and sat down. Thankfully, she had a brother on her other side.

Peeking at Hiro from the corner of her eye, she felt again that flutter in her heart and somewhere lower in her belly. Attractive? Yeah, he was. Attracted to him? Yeah, she was. And *attraction* was the understatement of the century. She was in so much trouble.

Over a wide yawn, her brother Kienan said, "At leasht we can trusht Hiro."

"Try it without the yawn," the second eldest brother, Mel, said as he squinted at the textbook in front of him.

"Glasses," both his siblings said.

Muttering, he put them on. "I hate math."

"That's why I cram it down your throat," Taegan noted in amusement. He was the eldest at twenty-eight, followed by Mel at twenty-four, Kienan at twenty, and Aenya at the age of eighteen.

Hiro was mentally acquainted with all of them. Part of his job as a private investigator was to find information; before coming over to the house, he had been sure to get all the information he could. Of course, the fact that he had been friends with Kienan for several years helped.

He looked at Taegan curiously. The older man was a math instructor at the college his brothers attended. As the eldest, he had been the next in line to inherit the company, but obviously he hadn't—that duty was currently on Mel's shoulders. And thinking it, he asked Taegan, "Did your dad blow a gasket when you decided not to follow in his wolf-chewed slippers?"

Kienan almost fell out of his chair laughing. Taegan pulled him upright without looking. He tipped his glasses down to study Hiro then smiled. "A little. You know, I must say I'm impressed. You're better than the rest who have come through. You're actually genuinely interested in us."

"If I'm to marry Aenya," he countered calmly, and felt her bristle, "then I ought to know my brothers-in-law."

Mel peered over the top of his glasses, reluctantly intrigued, and impressed by the new male in their midst. "You're cocky."

"Confident." He smiled. "Your baby brother is cocky."

"I'm self-assured," Kienan muttered.

"You're cocky," his three siblings and Hiro retorted.

Aenya said nothing as a lively discussion ensued. She was *not* happy. She didn't want Hiro to win her brothers' favor. She didn't want him to become a part of the family. She didn't want to like him, or be attracted to him. She didn't want to be so aware of him, conscious of even his leg bumping hers. Unfortunately, her wants didn't seem to be counting for much.

When Sullivan walked into the dining room, she was grateful for the distraction. "Morning, Daddy!" she called cheerfully. Her heart fluttered as she felt Hiro's gaze on her face. Eyes that color in a face that handsome couldn't possibly be healthy for women. Why didn't he have a Surgeon General's warning somewhere?

"Good morning, kids." Sullivan sat down at the table with surprising grace. He was still a lean and attractive man in a black suit even though he was creeping into his sixties. Proving it might be more genetics than healthy living, he groaned when he saw the fresh fruit being put in front of him. "Why do I have fruit and you have bacon?"

"Because your cholesterol was far too high when you went to the doctor last," Taegan explained. He sharply rapped Kienan's wrist with a spoon when he tried to sneak their father a piece of the forbidden pork. "We like you healthy and fit."

"My children are tyrants." With a grumble, Sullivan began to eat the fruit.

"Not that they take after their father," Hiro noted.

The four siblings exchanged a grin with their father. No one could deny it. Sullivan Shaughnessy was known for his steel fist in a velvet glove ways; it was practically a family motto.

"What about you, Hiro?" Mel asked. "Kien said you're a private investigator. I remember you saved his ass a few years ago."

Hiro nodded. "It was in high school. I was a senior and he was a freshman. Some other seniors decided that he needed to learn the 'laws of reality' or some such crap. They decided to try to beat him up."

"Hiro decided they wouldn't," Kienan added dryly. "I was left standing there with my mouth hanging to my knees, not a scratch on me. He got a black eye, though. Someone snuck in a punch."

"I didn't duck fast enough." Hiro smiled. "Anyway, it's not a worry now. I understand someone went into martial arts after the incident. And got a black belt."

"Two." Pride filled Aenya's voice. "And he's won tournaments."

"So you naturally want to solve problems?" Sullivan asked Hiro.

"Oh, very much so. I'm the guy who never played Sudoku because it was too easy." He flicked a glance at Aenya who was pointedly staring at her plate. "I'm tenacious and stubborn. When I set my eyes on a goal, I always get it. And I *never* leave a puzzle undone."

"I have to get ready for class." She got to her feet quickly. "Excuse me."

Mel watched her run out of the dining room. He had seen her run from the conversation at the pond, too. He turned back to study Hiro. "Aenya isn't usually like this," he said thoughtfully. "You've really got her nervous. I've never seen her run from *anything*. She's little, but she's spirited."

"Willful," their father muttered.

Hiro agreed with both, but was too polite to say it. Instead, he said, "Maybe because she senses she's met her match." He glanced at Sullivan. "May I take her to school?"

"Normally the chauffeur takes her." Sullivan eyed him. "What kind of car do you drive?"

"I don't."

Taegan quirked a brow at Mel and Kienan then all three looked at Sullivan. Both Taegan and Kienan owned motorcycles, and Sullivan had expressly forbidden Aenya to ride with either because she was small.

Sullivan hesitated then very slowly said, "I will trust you to keep her safe." He sighed. "I'm well aware that I've been . . . harsh about her safety. If she comes through unscathed, then I'll be willing to let her ride with you sometimes, Kienan."

"Geez, finally. Drives me *nuts* when she gives me that big-eyed look and I have to tell her no."

Hiro got to his feet. "In that case, I need to go make sure she doesn't desert me. Please excuse me."

All four males watched him leave the room, then Sullivan turned to his sons. Taegan studied his father then asked quietly, "Are you sure about this, Father?" He wasn't referring to the motorcycle ride, and they all knew it.

"I'm sure. I saw this morning precisely what Kienan suspected I would. I'm *desperate*, boys. Kien, you had better be right about all of it."

"I am." He wasn't being cocky; he was just confident.

On a sigh, Sullivan took a drink from his coffee mug then promptly sputtered. "What is this? It tastes like some sort of fiber supplement. Where's my coffee?"

"Your blood pressure was high too."

CHAPTER TWO

Aenya was sitting on the steps of her house pulling her shoes on when she heard the purr of a well-kept engine. Warily, she looked up to see Hiro sitting on the back of a gleaming white motorcycle at the edge of the long driveway.

Her romantic heart wobbled in her chest. It wasn't quite the image of a handsome prince on a white horse that she had sometimes fantasized about, but it was pretty close. After all, what prince rode horses down the middle of New York City? Any prince worth his salt would choose modern horses. Try as she might, she couldn't shake the image of him as a prince. Did the bike *have* to be white?

She went down the driveway toward him carefully, trying to get her tongue unstuck from the top of her mouth. If she started babbling incoherently, then she would lose more ground than she could afford. As she got closer, she realized his hair was windblown and his shoulders were strong and powerful under his leather jacket. *Dangerous.* This man was completely dangerous.

She had stopped more than five feet away from him. Sensing she was suddenly wary, he held out his hand to her, as gentle as he would be if trying to coax a scared wild animal. And she was wild. All of her family had a wild spirit.

"Want a ride?" He kept his voice as soothing as he could.

She slowly moved closer and looked at the bike in longing. "Daddy said I couldn't ride one because I was too small. I've always been much smaller than everyone for my whole life. Weaker sometimes too."

That was interesting. He filed it for review and investigation later. "You look quite strong to me." Keeping his movements slow and

deliberate, he held out the extra helmet he had borrowed from Kienan. "Your chauffeur was happy for a morning off, and Sullivan had no true issues with my taking you to school. So you either get to ride, or walk."

She put her hand in his and let him draw her closer. She waited patiently while he fastened the helmet on her then her heart flipped up as he lifted her effortlessly onto the bike in front of him. The skirt demanded she ride sidesaddle, but it still rode up as she scooted into place. His hand touched her outer leg warmly and then gently pulled her skirt down and tucked it in where it couldn't be caught in the wind. In that moment, she began to trust him despite the battle they were locked in.

He felt her body relax and let out the breath he had been holding. "Put your arms around my waist and hold on." His eyes danced behind his sunglasses. "I'd hate to lose you. Your father would happily hire hit men."

Her eyes sparkled in return. "We're Irish, not Italian."

"No accents, though," he noted as he walked the bike down toward the street.

"Mmm, no. Not really. Well, we *kind* of do. Mostly it's only noticeable when we lose our tempers. Taegan's is the strongest. I always giggle at him because there are words he says that always have a brogue. Daddy hides his *really* well, but oooh, I used to play games with Kienan under the board table. When he wants to make a point, he goes full Irish."

"I bet you learned some interesting words that way."

Her smile was angelic. "I save them for special occasions."

He was in danger of being absolutely crazy about her, he decided as they made their way down the roads toward the high school. It was the same one all the Shaughnessys and Hiro had attended, and the route was well remembered. He found himself quite impressed with his passenger, too. She held onto his waist with just enough strength to keep her balance but showed no fear. If anything, the delight in her eyes was clear that she was enjoying herself.

She stiffened slightly as they rode into the parking lot, however. A lot of students were standing around, and all were snickering and pointing as they saw her getting off Hiro's bike. She said nothing as she pulled her helmet off. As soon as Hiro removed his helmet, she saw nearly every female present widen their eyes. She really couldn't blame them.

"Wow," one girl said distinctly. She called, "Is he your boyfriend?"

"It's the stupid contract thing again." Aenya concentrated on looking in her backpack for her building pass. The school required all students to carry passes to even get on the grounds.

Hiro's eyes swept over the teenagers in the area. Most were smirking or snickering. He caught more than one snippet of conversation that indicated everyone found Aenya's predicament to be vastly entertaining. Some of the males even watched her with an open lust that objectified rather than admired. He shifted closer to Aenya protectively and narrowed his eyes. The boys were smart enough to sense he was beyond their league. They slunk into the building.

"Savages," he muttered.

Aenya blinked up at him as they headed toward the school office to get him a visitor badge. The office was very amenable to the goings-on. Frankly, they had little choice. The Shaughnessy Corp. had invested much money in the school and kept it afloat when budget crises had threatened.

While Hiro went into the office to get a pass, she stayed in the hall. She just didn't feel like facing the sympathetic secretary. Students passed around her, but they were a blur. To be truthful, her mind was a million miles away. Every minute she spent in Hiro Michaels' company was a minute more that she liked him.

She closed her eyes. It was so stressful! It didn't help that she was madly attracted to him. The entire ride she had been vividly aware of his strong arms around her and his muscular chest right near her face, perfect for leaning against. Whenever his green eyes landed on her, she was tempted to lift up and kiss him.

But she *liked* him, too. He was funny and witty. He didn't object to her personality, and he certainly accepted the wildness inside her that she knew he had seen. Was that why he was so different from the rest? Some others had been handsome, and all had been intelligent in some way. Her dig at his age had been a misnomer. Sullivan allowed no male over thirty to enter the contract.

But when she had seen Hiro . . . her breath had stopped. Her heart had begun racing and she had felt a heat in her blood and body that every female instinct identified. Desire. Lust. *Hunger*. There were dozens of words for it. Just looking at a man shouldn't have been that devastating, but his impact on her was akin to Hurricane Katrina's impact on New Orleans.

She cared about the outcome of this particular contract. She had never cared before. She had felt no guilt for deceiving and destroying the hopes of countless other men. Hiro . . . she hated the idea of deceiving him. She almost wanted to ask him if he would want to date her if there was no contract involved. She was half afraid he would say no, and that alone scared her.

Her heart began to pound harder, and her mouth went dry. Was she falling in love with him? How? She had known him barely three hours! But in those three hours, she had learned he was easy with other people, intelligent, and witty. He was conscious of the difference in their heights and handled her, not as if she was fragile, but with the care that said he knew he could hurt her and didn't want to. He had been a gentleman, not taking advantage of the ride to the school, and he had been open and honest with her.

She was in *deep* trouble. The sooner she got rid of him, the better.

"Hey, Aenya."

The male voice jerked her out of her thoughts, and she looked up quickly. Her shoulders tensed slightly. The young man in front of her was her age, several inches taller, and attractive enough. He was also one of the biggest jerks in the school. "Hey." She kept her voice carefully neutral.

"So when're you going to go out with me?" He flexed one arm

at her. "I could always come apply for the contract. Give the new guy competition."

She sniffed slightly. There *was* no competition. Hiro had more muscles in one arm than Leroy did in his entire body. "You can't even pass Pre-Algebra. What makes you think you can figure out what dozens of other *adult* men have failed to?"

"You think you're so much better than the rest of us because you're a Shaughnessy. Far as I'm concerned, you're nothing but a spoiled bitch that is being sold to the highest bidder." He bit the words out, unaware of the dark shadow looming behind him. "I hope you get used up by some guy. Then you'll know you're no better than the rest of us. Grk!"

She had looked away, but at the odd noise he made, her head jerked around and she discovered Hiro had him by the back of the neck and had lifted him off the ground. Her mouth fell open.

"You know," Hiro said calmly, ignoring Leroy's mad wiggling, "I'm only six or seven years older than you. Technically, we're in the same generation. The era I was eighteen in is identical to the one you're in." His voice dropped to a dangerous octave. "I *never* insulted a good woman because I wanted her more than common sense."

He let Leroy go, but the younger male couldn't get his feet under himself and landed on his ass. That, naturally, made everyone in the area start laughing. Hiro looked at Aenya's face then stepped into the office again for a moment. When he came out, he gently took her elbow and began escorting her to the exit. "Let's go, princess."

She stared at the ground, not looking at him even when he pulled her closer and tucked her under his arm in a manner that was both protective and possessive. She felt humiliated down to her very core. Only when she saw that they were leaving the building did her head come up quickly. "Where are we going?"

"Where do you want to go?" he countered. When she tried to get away, he stopped walking and brought her around to face him. He lifted her chin until their eyes met. "Aenya," he said softly, gently, "I know you see me as your enemy."

"Aren't you?" Her eyes met and held his evenly. "These are my dreams that I'm fighting for. Something I've wanted ever since I was three and told I could take ballet. Ever since I had to work harder than other girls because I wasn't tall enough to reach the barre until I was older. When I had to wear higher than average heels for ballroom because I was that much shorter than my partners. I want this, Hiro. Badly. A husband won't fit in."

He gently tucked a stray strand of hair behind her ear. It was not the time to tell her that he was a trained dancer himself and knew intimately how hard it was to be good when you were of average height let alone when you were at a disadvantage. "Well, you're stuck in this contract unless you want to tell Sullivan where you go at night." She shook her head and he smiled. He wasn't surprised. "Alright. Then you're stuck with me as well. Your father has offered me something I want very badly."

Her lips turned down. "Stocks, just like all the others. Sometimes I wish *our* share of the market would dip just like everyone else's."

"Sadly, your father has too many fingers in too many pies."

"And has yet to find a plum."

"His name is actually Jack Horner? That's not very Irish."

She bit her lip, but a giggle escaped anyway. Even when she didn't want to like him, she did. And it took great power to hide the pain cutting inside her. She wanted him to want her. She didn't want him to look at her and see dollar signs. She wanted him to see a woman he desired.

They had reached the bike. He handed her the helmet and watched her fasten it on. "So, where to?" he asked. "I'll take you anywhere you want to go."

She hesitated then made her decision. "Can we swing by the college? I have a friend who attends classes there. Normally we'd meet after school, but I might as well meet her early. She keeps me up-to-date on what's going on with my brothers' college."

He grinned. "Ah-ha! So you're as possessive of them as they are of you."

She gave him a look as if he was mad. "And you only *just* noticed this? Shaughnessys stick together through rain, shine, snow, and chicken pox."

"Chicken pox."

"All at the same time. I was seven, Kienan was nine, Mel was thirteen, and Taegan was a miserable seventeen." She grinned. "Daddy vowed that if we ever all got sick at the same time again, he was going to quarantine us at a hospital and make us be their problem."

He laughed and lifted her up onto the back before swinging up behind her. "Will your friend know to meet you early?"

"I'll send her a text message when I get to the place where we usually meet." As they began to ride out of the lot, she gave in to the urge to follow her heart. She softly laid her head on his shoulder. He felt strong and secure. He even smelled good, like something comforting and welcoming. His heartbeat was sure and steady. Nothing could ever hurt her if she was in his arms.

When they got to the college, he obediently parked on the other side of the lot from where the fountain was located. "Why am I stopping here?" he asked her mildly.

She shook her head as she quickly texted a message over her cell phone. He could only watch in admiration; he wasn't that fast even on a good day. After the message was sent, she put the phone in her pocket. "You're stopping here because I don't want you to scare Madelyne. She has an aversion to handsome men. Now stay here!"

He quirked a brow as she hurried across the lot. Not that he doubted her, but now she really had his interest. He gave her a good minute head start then began to follow her. He had a natural ability to blend in with the background, something he often used in his line of work. It allowed him to remain less than twenty feet behind her without her even noticing.

When they reached the fountain, he crouched down to watch. She sat on the side of the fountain and swung her feet lightly. After a few moments, she looked up with a genuine and welcoming smile. "Madelyne!"

He shifted his gaze to see another young woman approaching.

Intrigued, he studied her closer. She was, without a doubt, one of the plainest girls he had ever seen. There was nothing extraordinary about her face or figure or coloring. She had hair an unusual shade of dove gray and spirited violet eyes, but he wouldn't have called either attribute overly compelling. She simply was what she was.

When she sat beside Aenya, he couldn't help but feel that he was looking at a nightingale sitting beside a swan. They were markedly different and yet neither seemed to notice. If Madelyne felt discomfort around a beautiful woman, then it didn't show. And if Aenya felt sorry for her plain friend, it also didn't show. He had the feeling that neither had even noticed they were different at all, and it was wonderful.

As he moved closer, he heard Aenya say, "Madelyne, did you bring it? Please?"

"Yes, of course." Madelyne Winters was rummaging in her bag as she spoke. "I'm sorry it has once more come to this, but I have it. I take it you have another suitor?"

"Yes. I need to get rid of him quickly. He's too intelligent. He's a private investigator and he's friends with Kienan." Aenya didn't mention her unfortunate attraction to him, but she was sure Madelyne suspected. She was sensitive like that.

"All things to make it difficult." Madelyne emerged from her bag with a small canning jar. "Here you go. A few drops in something he drinks will knock him out for a full night. No side effects at all. He'll wake up with a good night's sleep." She laughed. "Well, I admit, there have been a few people I know who have complained of odd dreams, but one in twenty is a small margin."

As Hiro watched Aenya tuck the jar into her backpack, a slow smile began to curve his lips. Devious, intelligent, and spoiled. He could also add cunning and slightly terrifying to the list now. She had been drugging her suitors the entire time so that they slept the night away, none the wiser. Naturally, no man would admit such a thing, so there was no way Sullivan would have suspected.

He would just have to avoid drinking anything she gave him if it ever left his sight. Still smiling, he edged back from the scene and headed for his bike. Much to his surprise, he found Stormy sitting beside it with a lump of material in her mouth. Her tail thumped in greeting when she saw him.

"Hey, put that down," he scolded as he bent to tug the material away. She let go instantly and looked at him expectantly. A little shiver went down his back as he met her eyes. This was *not* a normal wolf. "I'm beginning to wonder where you're from," he murmured.

She pawed at the material and he decided to humor her. He obligingly shook out the material to discover it was a large piece of burlap big enough to cover even a larger man. It resembled a painter's drop cloth but the colored splatters seemed more deliberate than accidental. "Okay, now what? Am I supposed to use it to cover my bike?"

He tossed it over the bike as a joke . . . and discovered the joke was on him when the bike promptly disappeared. "Holy shit," he managed to say, looking around sharply to be sure no one was watching. There was no one close, and he cautiously patted for the bike. It was definitely still there, but it was just as definitely invisible. He pulled the blanket off and the bike reappeared. "Well, well," he murmured. He began to grin. "Whose side are you on, girl?"

Stormy cocked her head, gave the wolf equivalent of a smirk, and loped off gracefully. He decided to completely ignore the fact that no one even seemed to realize there was a wolf running around, even a wolf with a pink bow. Some questions were best left unasked. Instead, he folded the blanket and stuffed it into the bag on the side of his bike. It would be quite handy.

Aenya came running up to him a few moments later with a smile on her face. "Okay, let's go."

She was so relaxed and at ease that he immediately began to like Madelyne. Her plain appearance hid a beautiful heart for her to so completely bring back Aenya's cheer. Unconditional acceptance on both sides of the friendship. He hoped Madelyne wasn't really wary of handsome men. He would love to meet her.

"Where do you want to go now?" he asked.

She hopped up onto the bike. "I want to play hooky. I've never

done that before. We can get to know each other. I want to know everything about you."

He plopped her helmet on her head and smiled internally as he sensed her game. "I thought you didn't want to like me."

"I don't," she admitted readily. "A good tactician knows that to defeat an enemy, you need to know an enemy. Isn't that your intent as well? Well, I have the most to lose, so I get to play twenty questions first. Take me out for Chinese, and I'll start asking. I'll even be fair and only ask ten. You get the other half."

He laughed outright and swung up on the bike behind her. "How your father can think you're an angel is beyond me. You're no angel, princess." When she grinned up at him, the wild spirit visible in her eyes, he felt sixteen again and noticing a beautiful girl for the first time. In a way, he felt sorry for Leroy. The impact was devastating at any age.

The place that he chose was a noisy diner several miles away. It served the best Chinese food outside of China but it was nearly hidden between two giant restaurants. Aenya almost didn't see it was there until they were parked and approaching the doors. Once inside, the smell was so heavenly that she took a deep breath in contentment. "Oh yum."

In bemusement, he watched her heap a plate as high as his as they went along the buffet. "Where do you *put* it?" he demanded. "You can't even weigh over one hundred pounds!"

She glowered. "I do too weigh over a hundred pounds!" Not by much, but enough that she felt justified in defending herself.

She blinked when he put down his plate and then gave a startled yelp as he caught her around the waist and lifted her off her feet. He held her for a moment, then put her back down. "One hundred five." He picked up his plate again.

She glared at the people behind her as they snickered and giggled. Bad enough he had checked, but he had been *right*. That burned. "To answer the original question," she said pointedly, "I burn energy very quickly. I can out-eat Kienan, and he's the bottomless pit of the family."

They grabbed a table in a corner where they could squeeze together into a booth. Despite how noisy the place was, the tables were oddly quiet. The diner had been built with custom acoustics that drew sound up from tables rather than dispersing it outward.

"I'm going to come back here with Mel," she decided. "He loves Chinese."

He tilted his head. "Out of curiosity, is Mel a nickname? It doesn't seem to fit in with the rest of your names."

She looked around then lowered her voice. "It's short for Melville. It was our grandfather's name. But Mel *hates* his name, so he only goes by Mel. The only way anyone will ever know is if they look at his birth certificate."

"Gotcha. So, what do you want to know from me?"

She considered things. "Where were you born?"

"Miami. We moved to New York when I was toddler." He stole a shrimp from her plate and nimbly dodged her chopsticks.

Naturally, that meant war. She snitched an eggroll in retaliation. "What's your family like?"

"Small but fun. Mom and Dad co-own a flower shop. It's a family thing, too. They wanted me to take over, but I have absolutely no design aesthetic so it'll probably go to one of my cousins. She's lethal with bouquets." Because he knew she wanted to know, and he didn't want her to waste a question, he offered, "I have no brothers and sisters. And the flower shop is called Belladawn. Not like the poison but dawn as in sunrise." He blocked her from grabbing a meat bun and eyed her chow mien.

Her eyes widened then began to sparkle merrily. "They make beautiful bouquets, yes." When he quirked a brow, she giggled. "Ask me later how I know, when you have your questions."

"Fair enough."

"Where did you go to school and what did you major in?" She smartly rapped his wrist when he made a grab for chow mien. He could have a fair shot at anything except that.

"I went to the same high school as you, obviously, since that's where I met Kienan, but I also went to the college where your

brothers are. I majored in Criminal Justice and got a minor in, er, Performing Arts."

She almost asked what art, but he seemed uncomfortable so she didn't bother. It was probably something 'girly,' she decided, like costuming or such. And, because she was a good sport, she gave him some of her chow mien. She was having more fun than she had ever imagined. It was almost like a date. "Have you ever lived anywhere but America?"

"No, but I've traveled overseas. I've been to England, France, China, and New Zealand. The next place I've wanted to go was Ireland. I'll take you with me; you'd love your ancestral homeland."

She decided to ignore that, not wanting to argue over who would win and who would lose. "What are your likes and dislikes?"

"Be more specific."

"Food for now. Asking anything else would use up all my questions."

"Clever girl." He contemplated his answers. "I like fresh fruits and veggies. I hate white meat of any kind. I will, however, carnivorously devour red meat, particularly hamburgers. I'm not a wine snob, but I could probably identify the minute differences in beer. I'm a Coke person versus a Pepsi person, but I like Mountain Dew. Hmm . . . not picky about desserts at all. If it has sugar, I'll probably eat it. Except fried Twinkies. Ew."

She snickered into her glass of tea. "What sort of sports do you like?"

"Basketball is my game of choice." He gave a little salute. "I never played on a team with your brother because I'm not suicidal. Neither high school nor college, I might add. However, it was kind of unspoken knowledge around campus that I could give Mel a run for his money."

"Shh. Don't let him hear you say that. He's still sore when he loses in family matches. We all play." Pleasantly full, she pushed her plate away. She loved Chinese food, and she was discovering a new hunger. She was hungry to learn everything about Hiro that she could. Every answer made her like him more. Oh, they didn't have entirely matching likes and dislikes, but it was *how* he told her things that she loved. "Let's see . . . favorite color?"

His eyes swept over her face slowly. "Brown," he said softly. "Honey brown. That rich and golden color that reminds me of summer tea and the best of candies. Like your eyes."

Breath lodged in her chest, she tore her gaze away. No one had ever looked at her like that before. "What are your plans for the future?"

The minute the words left her mouth, she kicked herself. She didn't want to hear his answer. She was sure she didn't. She didn't want her family connections to ruin this beautiful conversation. No one before had been so open with her. She had been either a piece of property or, worse, a spoiled little kid. Hiro was different. He treated her like the woman she was and showed respect for her as a person.

For a moment, she nearly considered throwing out the sleeping potion. She could chuck it out, let him follow her, and maybe he would understand. If anyone would, it would be him. But she couldn't risk it. She couldn't! There was so little time left . . .

He considered his words very carefully then decided to answer honestly. "I want a settled life. A family. I want the adventure of everyday life. In my line of work, I've been shot at, slept in cramped cars, and seen some pretty bad things. But . . . I'd give it all up for the right home." His eyes met hers. "The right woman. A loving wife."

Silence stretched. They both knew it was a subtle dig. She didn't want to be married, and that meant she would never be a loving wife. But he was becoming much attuned to his honey-eyed, dancing princess. He was almost positive that she wanted him as badly as he wanted her. And if she did, it gave him a leverage that no other suitor had ever or would ever have.

She decided on the coward's route and took her tray over to the trashcan. "You won't find one with me," she said curtly. "Chase your dreams elsewhere, Hiro."

"You don't want to ask your last question?" he asked softly as he dumped his tray as well.

"I'll hold it in reserve for when I think of something important. If I promise not to ask anything you wouldn't want to tell, would you promise to tell me the absolute truth?"

"Without hesitation," he agreed calmly.

She turned around and found that he was right behind her. He was looking at her so intently that she saw herself reflected in his green eyes. That flutter in her body came back with a vengeance and the urge to touch him was nearly uncontrollable. She hastily put her hands in her pockets.

He just smiled and put a hand lightly on the middle of her back to escort her from the diner and back toward the motorcycle. Her innocence was his best ally because she couldn't hide her physical or emotional reactions. He was as ruthless as she was, fully intending to take every advantage he could.

"Exactly who did you meet earlier, anyway?" he asked casually.

The tension left her shoulders. "A friend. Her name is Madelyne Winters. She's my best friend. She's from 3rd District." She glanced up at him as she said it.

He tilted his head thoughtfully. "I'm not sure I know of the 3rd District."

"Few do." She pulled her helmet on. "It's a small part of NYC. Very small; only a few miles big in all directions. If you Google it, it won't even show up. It's mostly businesses but there are a few residences as well. Enforcers operate out of there."

"Now them I know."

"Most do. Anyway, 3rd District looks old-fashioned on the surface. Old-style buildings from most recognizable periods of history. Everything inside is modernized, naturally, but going there is like going back in time. Madelyne runs an inn there, and lives there." She smiled. "There are rumors about 3rd District, you know."

"What sort of rumors?" He quirked a brow.

"Magic. They say that 3rd District is the home of magic. If you believe in the impossible, then you'll find it. Faerie tales, werewolves, and the like."

He opened his mouth to dismiss it out of hand then changed his mind. He had seen impossible things. He believed in magic. Why couldn't it live in a District where it could be protected from those who would tear it apart in the name of science and civilization? "I believe you," he decided.

She blinked. "That's a surprise. You admit to believing in magic?"

"Of course." He said it so simply that she believed him. "I've seen it and felt it. It's everywhere if you know where to look for it."

She was quiet for long moments then looked at him very seriously. "I don't understand you."

"You will." He tucked a stray strand of hair behind her ear. "You will, I promise. And I'll show you a magic that even your District might envy."

CHAPTER THREE

The rest of the day passed in a blur. Aenya lost track of the places that Hiro took her to see. She hadn't even realized her hometown was full of that many interesting places. She found herself oddly grateful for his sensitivity, too; the first place they stopped was a store where she could buy a new set of clothes to wear instead of her school uniform.

She almost got the first pants and shirt to come to hand, but her feminine side rebelled. Instead, she got a pair of snug jeans that flattered her legs and a junior-tee that was her favorite shade of pale pink. When Hiro smiled at her, she felt truly beautiful. Damn it, why couldn't he be interested in her because of *her*?

It was almost dinnertime by the time they were on their way home. Since she was in jeans, this time she got to ride behind Hiro with her arms around his waist. She felt no less safe and secure. She had picked up the rhythm of the bike and was fully comfortable with turns. The only blip on the happy day was that it *was* a happy day.

It had been a daylong date. She knew it. But though it had been an amazing and wonderful experience for her, she felt certain it had been merely a weapon wielded by her 'suitor'. She was fairly sure he was attracted to her, though, and that helped. She was half-tempted to kiss him, just to see what he would do. Her instincts told her it would be like baiting a hungry tiger with green eyes, but it was still tempting.

They parked the bike in its borrowed spot at the Shaughnessy manor and then made their way toward the front door where Sullivan clearly waited for them. Stormy sat beside his ankle, but she looked vastly more amused than her master did. She even woofed in greeting, the sound odd coming from a wolf of her caliber.

Hiro stopped walking and let Aenya go forward. When she was in front of her father, she lowered her gaze. Sullivan regarded her for long moments then asked quietly, "Did you ditch school, Aenya?"

"Yes," she admitted softly. She offered no excuse.

He ruffled her hair gently. "Good." She looked at him in shock, and he grinned at her. "All students need to play hooky at least once in their life. It's a rule. And anyway," he added mildly, "more than one person felt compelled to call me about the scene at school." His eyes met Hiro's. "Something I'm sure neither of you would have told me about."

"Because you worry too much as it is," she reminded him primly.

"Hurry and wash up for dinner." He headed back into the house, refusing to acknowledge that she was right.

"I thought for sure he'd get a shotgun," Hiro said musingly to Aenya as he stepped up beside her.

"It's not our style. If you ever piss off my dad or brothers, you'll know when a fist lands in your face." She grinned up at him. "And, by the way, that also goes for me. Kienan has taught me how to make a good punch."

"That's because he's smart." He sensed the guardedness coming back long before it reached her face. "Don't worry. I won't assume that today means you'll lower your guard."

"Good," she retorted evenly. "Because even though I would call you a friend now, I'm not going to give up." She turned on her heel and disappeared into the house with Stormy following her amiably.

When she got to her room, she wasn't surprised to find one of her brothers. She also wasn't surprised to find him frowning. It was a favored pastime of Mel's. "Now what?" She disappeared into her large closet to find something more comfortable to wear for dinner. "You're going to have some serious wrinkles by the time you're thirty if you keep that up."

He ignored that and ruffled Stormy's fur as she leapt up onto Aenya's bed to listen. He had taken mercy on her earlier and removed the pink ribbon. It just didn't suit her.

"Look," he told his sister, "I know you think you have no choice about things, but you might want to change whatever tactics you've been employing. I got Kienan to talk about Hiro. You've met your match, sis. And to hear his past clients talk, he's borderline psychic."

She pulled on a yellow sundress then walked out of the closet. She sat down on the bed beside her brother and turned to face him. She fully trusted her brothers' instincts. "Mel, what do you think about Hiro? Honestly. Not just on the basis of what other people have said, but on your own experience."

"You won't hit me?"

"Not this time."

He smiled. That was his sister! "I think he's a great guy. He had a serious reputation at school for sticking up for the underdog. He crammed classes and challenged others so that he got his Bachelor's degree within two years instead of four. To put it the easiest way I can, if these were normal circumstances, I'd be completely encouraging him dating my baby sister. We all would be."

"But things aren't normal." She went over to her mirror and began to brush her hair. "He doesn't want me, Mel." She couldn't quite keep the longing out of her voice. "Just the family connection."

Her brother was a wise man. He covered his mouth to hide a grin. She seemed to be the only person who hadn't realized that Hiro wanted her so badly he could taste it. Every male in the house was dead certain that he had signed the contract for the chance to have Aenya and would have signed it even if stocks weren't involved.

It was Hiro's job to tell her, though. There were some things a brother simply did not want to say to his sister. Still smiling, Mel got to his feet. "Well, be that as it may, you better be careful. Hiro will catch you when you're looking the other way." He ruffled her hair with the same affection he had ruffled Stormy's then left the room.

She sighed and headed downstairs as well. Playing by ear wasn't her strong suit, but she was going to have to try. And it was for that reason that she was nonplussed to reach her chair in the dining room to discover a peach rose sitting on the seat. She picked it up warily and looked around. Most everyone else was already present.

"Where'd this come from?"

Taegan was grading homework and making notes. "It was there when I got here." Bemused, he made a red checkmark. How could a college level student add two and two and get three? The kid probably had a future in politics.

"Me, too." Kienan looked like he was sitting with his head on the table, but the beeping from his area belied that he was playing a Nintendo DS under the table. "Damn it!" He sat up with his game. "He blew me up!" he said crossly. "Oy!" He made a grab as Mel walked past and took the DS. "I was winning!"

"And you overrode my save file for it." He closed the game and pocketed the device as he sat down. He smiled at Aenya. "Ask Hiro. He got here first."

"Magic," Hiro offered. Aenya frowned at him and he gently caught her hand to bring her knuckles to his lips. "It's a gift. No strings attached, no hidden agendas. I may not have flower aesthetic, but I know roses."

"No kidding." She put the rose by her plate as she sat down. She didn't want to accept the gesture because there was an underlying romance in it. Romance had nothing to do with the current events. Yet she couldn't bear to give it back. "I hate my life," she decided on a sigh.

Sullivan walked into the dining room at that point and scowled. "If you're feeding me more vegetables . . ."

"Artfully disguised vegetables," Taegan promised. He pushed his glasses higher on his nose as he smiled. "Father, we like you healthy even if you're not happy. You'll just have to handle our bossiness."

"And you're soooo good at it." Aenya grinned at Hiro. "Taegan's a den mother in disguise. And he's so much older than me that he's really been more like a second dad than a big brother."

"Someone has to keep you in line." Her brother quirked a brow in amusement. "You're too inclined to run haywire." He turned to Hiro as Kienan reached across him for the potatoes. "You're our last hope, you see."

"Hey!" Aenya was not only indignant but also a little hurt. "What happened to family sticking together?" She let tears well in her eyes. "How can you be that mean?"

"Don't make your sister cry." Sullivan probed at the orange bits in his food. He hoped they weren't carrots. He hated carrots.

"Oh, she's just playing." Taegan reached across the table to lightly pinch Aenya's nose. His eyes were the same honey brown as hers, and both pairs sparkled merrily. "She's just putting on a show, and we all know it. If she was really upset, she'd be shouting at me."

"She's loud when she's angry," Kienan apologized to Hiro.

"And spoiled," Mel added. "Did we mention spoiled?"

"Unfortunately," Sullivan said, seeing his daughter's pout, "I am forced to agree with all three of them." She stuck her tongue out at him, and he just chuckled. It was promptly followed by a frown at his plate. "Are there peas in this?"

"No," all his kids said.

It was a fascinating and beautiful family dynamic that Hiro felt privileged to be a part of. No matter how much money they had, no matter how much power, no matter the servants or grand house . . . this was a family. They hadn't been sheltered from reality as they were often accused. If anything, he thought, glancing to the side where a portrait sat in a place of honor, they knew more than most.

Compelled, he got to his feet to go look at the image. It was a family photo of a lovely blonde woman holding three young boys that had to be the Shaughnessy brothers. Since the woman was very pregnant—humorously wearing a shirt saying 'Baby On Board'—he assumed it was from right before Aenya's birth. Taegan was around ten, Mel around six, and Kienan was two. Such young ages to lose a parent.

"Your late wife?" he asked Sullivan softly.

"Yes." Something eternally sad lingered in the older man's eyes as he looked at the portrait. "The only woman I've ever loved. When I die, I'll join her again." Even after nearly twenty years, the pain was sharp. "Aenya favors her most in appearance, but Kienan and Mel have her eyes. Taegan got her kindness, and Mel . . . well, he seems to have inherited her lack of discipline for studies."

"Mom almost flunked high school," Mel muttered. "I've never been that bad."

"No, but you're dangerously close." Taegan's smile looked almost amused. "Your grades continue to drop like this and you might end up with a tutor for general education."

Mel lost some of the color in his face. There was only one general education tutor at the college, and everyone knew her reputation. "I don't study well. It's in one ear and out the other. And you can stop snickering, Hiro!" he muttered. "I may not have your brain, but I can whip you at basketball, punk."

"Hiro says you can't," Aenya offered with a touch of glee. When he glared at her, she shot him a challenging look. All was fair in love and war.

"Ha." Mel's smile turned confident, self-assured, and dangerously beautiful. It was a smile that marked all Shaughnessy males, and Aenya had often said it was their most lethal weapon. If directed specifically at a female of compatible hormones, she lost all ability to think straight. "You wish, Michaels. You want a match?"

"I'm on Hiro's side!" Kienan decided as he grabbed a dessert from the tray being carried past. "Ooh, vanilla!" He dug into the ice cream happily. "I've seen Hiro play. He's *good*, Mel."

"Fine then." Mel looked at his older brother. "You with me, Taegan?"

"Naturally." Taegan nimbly took the pudding his father had grabbed and traded him for another. "Sorbet, Father. No pudding."

"Me!" When Taegan offered the pudding, Aenya took it happily. "So while you guys are all dudes and stuff, am I supposed to just sit on the sidelines and wave pompoms?" Her eyes slid to Sullivan's and he winked. "Okay, then." She sat back with a smile no less confident than Mel's. "Daddy and I will play the winners."

Hiro choked on his water.

"Which concerns you?" Kienan asked with a grin. "Dad or Aenya?"

"Aenya. Sullivan looks like he gets the iron in his diet by eating nails. Aenya barely reaches your shoulder, Kien, and you're the shortest of all of us. She's also got to be at least eighty pounds lighter than you!"

"At least he didn't automatically assume she doesn't know how to play," Mel told Taegan.

"He's smarter than that."

Sullivan was sulking over his sorbet but was glad to comment, "Oh, Aenya can play, Hiro, I assure you. She was on the girls' team for both her freshman and junior years of high school. No cheerleading for my daughter. She went right onto the courts." He grinned proudly. "That's my girl."

After dinner, everyone went into the family room. Since it was Friday, Aenya had no homework and wouldn't have even if she hadn't skipped school. Mel and Kienan had no weekend assignments. The three of them and Hiro, instead, entered into a lively game of Monopoly. Taegan and Sullivan refereed and kept things legal in between doing their own work.

Aenya was vividly conscious of how easily Hiro had meshed into the family unit. He seemed as if he belonged there. She had to force herself to remember that he wasn't simply her boyfriend. *Damn* that stupid contract, and *damn* the reasons she had been caught dancing at night.

It was getting late by the time Kienan won the game. Everyone split up to go to bed. Aenya found herself escorting Hiro upstairs to where their rooms were located. For convenience, he had the room right beside hers. It was, in fact, connected to hers through an internal door. It had never been more than a nuisance before.

A guard was standing outside Aenya's door. Hiro knew he was there as much to keep Aenya safe from any suitor as he was there to keep her inside. He stopped outside his own door and looked at her. "Well."

"Well." She cleared her throat and prayed she wasn't blushing. "You know the rules. And I'd be lying if I wished you good luck, so, good night." She turned on her heel and went into her room, and she only let out her breath when she heard the door lock behind her.

Almost helplessly, her eyes went to the connecting door. She had never before thought that a door could seem so . . . dangerously intimate.

She let out a longer breath and went to where there was a tray with a pot of tea and two cups. She had always asked for tea before bed; it helped her wind down to sleep. It was her own luck that it provided such a convenient way to drug her suitors.

She took her time. She washed off what little makeup she was wearing then changed into the ugliest, dowdiest, most unappealing nightgown she owned. It was practically a flannel tent and entirely concealed anything and everything appealing about her body. She *loathed* that nightgown and only kept it because it was good for body armor she could sleep in.

She went to the tea and poured two cups. She fetched the potion and added a few drops to Hiro's tea before she could change her mind. Then, steeling herself, she picked up the tray and went over to the connecting door. "Hey, Hiro?" she called.

The door opened and she almost bobbled the tray. Her eyes slowly widened until they were pools of honey color. Her mouth went dry. He wasn't wearing a shirt and his pajama pants rode low on his hips. He was as beautiful and sculpted as any statue of a Greek god. Every muscle was defined and alluring. His skin was lightly tanned and the light sprinkling of hair across his spectacular chest seemed to *beg* for her touch. "I . . ." It was all she could manage.

He took the tray from her before she dropped it. Its presence didn't surprise him, but it also held no importance at that moment. He put it to the side then lifted his hands to frame her face and tilt her head back. A flush rode her elegant cheekbones that he knew wasn't entirely embarrassment. Her pulse beat at the same frantic rhythm that his did. "Hi," he said softly.

"Could you put a shirt on?" She closed her eyes to remove temptation from sight.

"Why?"

"Because you're making me very nervous."

The admission made her vulnerable, and he knew it. Out of

respect for her, he released her entirely and pulled on his pajama shirt. As he fastened a few buttons, he studied her intently. A grin tugged at his lips. "That is the ugliest nightgown I've ever seen in my life."

She cautiously opened her eyes and relaxed as she saw that the shirt was mostly buttoned. She had never before been flustered by seeing a half-naked male. Hell, she lived with *brothers.* A handsome male form was hardly foreign. But Hiro . . . in every way, he was different. For one thing, he sure as heck wasn't her brother. For another, he just felt unique to her. Something inside him called to something inside her.

She put it aside to the best of her ability. "I wouldn't want to give anyone the wrong idea."

He decided not to tell her that he found her sexy as hell in everything she wore. "Fair enough." He walked over to look at the tray. "What is this, anyway?"

"Tea. I always have tea before bed, and I thought I'd share." She shrugged one shoulder. "You don't have to have some. It's not a peace offering." She picked up one of the cups and took a sip. "I've had tea with all my suitors. It's like fraternizing with the enemy."

Clever girl. By continuing to play on their competition, she ensured the fact that her opponent wouldn't automatically assume foul play. Defending herself and the tea would raise suspicion. He was not only impressed, he was also quite delighted. He would be bored with a woman who couldn't keep him on his toes. "In that case, I'll have some as well." He picked up the cup and started to take a sip when he spotted a perfect distraction. "Is that Stormy pawing under your door?"

She turned and sighed. "Yes. I have to tell them to let her in. Hang on."

The minute she went into the other room, he swiftly dumped his tea in the plant beside him. He poured a fresh cup and was sipping it when she returned. He had banked on her not spiking the entire pot just in case she needed to pour herself another cup. "Good tea," he told her. "Little stronger than I'm used to, but good regardless."

"I like my tea on the stronger side, sorry." She felt her stomach quiver with guilt and nerves. It was too late now. She quickly finished her tea and put the cup down. "Good night, Hiro."

As she went to lift the tray, his hand closed around her wrist gently. She stopped breathing entirely. She was in deep water, well over her head. If he tried to get physical with her, she wasn't sure she had the will to shout for help.

Sensing the rise of her nerves, he feigned a yawn. "Sorry." He shook his head for good measure. "Will you at least tell me if you like me?"

She felt the tension leave her shoulders. She could pull this off for a few minutes. "Well, yes. I do."

"How much?" He used his grip to pull her slowly into his arms, and he savored the feel of her curves pressing against his aching body. To his immense satisfaction, he discovered he had been right. She did fit perfectly in his arms. He lowered his head and began to trail soft kisses over her jaw. "And in what way?"

Warning bells went off in her mind but she found she had no will to listen to them as his soft breath and kisses stole her strength. His fingers, where they were pressed against her lower back, felt hot. The heat slowly spread through every nerve she possessed. "A lot, I guess, but . . ." She lost her words as his lips touched hers. "Hiro, stop it," she whispered.

"No." Giving in to the urge, he buried his hands in her hair and tilted her head back. "I like you, a lot. Guess how." He didn't give her a chance to answer as his mouth settled heavily over hers. His control wavered violently. He had to kiss her, taste her, more than he needed to breathe.

Her eyes opened wide in shock and she tried to jerk backwards out of his grip. He held her firmly and pulled her closer so that she was forced to put her hands on his chest if she wanted to get away. She did so . . . and the heat of his body made her palms tingle. The kiss was soft, and gentle, as if he was wary of frightening her away. As far as first kisses went, it was a doozy. With an innocent trust in his self-control, she hesitantly kissed him back, parting her lips slightly in response to the pressure of his.

The nuclear bomb on Hiroshima had made less of an impact than that kiss as he took immediate advantage and deepened the embrace, his tongue surging past her lips to tangle with hers. Nerves promptly evaporated in hunger. She moved closer, and her hands lifted to curl around his neck.

He taught her how to kiss, and dragged her closer against his body to feed from her mouth. She even tasted like honey, and the touch of her skin was addicting. Aching, desperate, he caught the edge of the nightgown and drew it up until his hand could rest on the heated flesh of her leg.

She panicked and tore her mouth free to gulp in air. "No, no, bad idea, stop now!" Her entire body quivered as hard as his did, but the first stirring of fear had moved inside her heart. For the first time, she knew just how badly out of her league she was with him. If he tried to push the issue, she had no way of fighting him. She wanted him too badly.

He fought for control and won, but barely. He buried his face in her hair and muttered, "Magic. I told you." He let more of his weight sink against her and felt her stagger slightly as she almost lost her balance. "I'm a little sleepy, Aenya. Guess I was punchy. I'm sorry. Don't be afraid."

"Okay. I trust you." She was only a little surprised to find that it was true. Even having been scorched by his kiss, she trusted him to not take advantage of her. She tried to balance him and turn him at the same time. "Maybe if you lay down for a moment, you'll be okay."

He let her guide him toward the bed, and he forced himself to resist the urge to tumble her down onto it with him. He was walking a thin line; his entire body throbbed with stifled desire. "Whatever you can say about me," his voice was slightly rough, "never doubt how badly I want you."

"I'm not *that* naïve," she assured him, her heart skipping happily in her chest. "I had noticed, I assure you." How could she have missed it? The way they had been plastered together had ensured she felt every inch of his body. There was a vast difference between a physical innocence and a mental one.

As he was dumped onto the bed, he looked up at her. Her soft hair tumbled forward over her shoulders and her lips were swollen from his. On a groan, he rolled onto his side and closed his eyes. "Remove thyself, temptation incarnate."

She found herself smiling as she edged back toward the door. "Don't make any assumptions, Hiro. I just decided I wanted my first kiss to be interesting."

Softly he murmured, "Then give me a scale. One to ten for the first kiss."

She hesitated, then sighed. "A twelve, damn you. Now shut up." She grabbed the tray, went into her room, and shut the door. She leaned against it for a few moments and only relaxed when she heard the soft sound of snoring. Even his snoring sounded appealing, she thought in disgruntlement.

Her eyes went to where Stormy was laying on the bed and she suddenly found herself grinning. "Okay, it was a ninety-six, but I refuse to admit that on the grounds that it would be used against me."

A little spring in her step, she went into her closet and happily stripped off the ugly nightgown. She debated her choices then decided to wear a loose, flowing red skirt and a snug white camisole. Both were specially designed for dancers and she would feel perfectly comfortable no matter what type of dancing she decided on.

As she pulled on low-heeled dance shoes, she had to muffle giggles. She had overheard her father and Kienan talking. Kienan had wanted to know why Sullivan was letting her buy new shoes every day. Sullivan's theory was that since so far they couldn't stop her, he would rather see the shoes have the wear and tear than her feet.

She contemplated her feet for a moment. They were lined with more calluses than Kienan's were, and he was a martial artist. She was proud of every single mark.

She hurriedly put on a light touch of makeup and spread glitter across her face. She put on a few select pieces of jewelry before sneaking over to the connecting door to peek inside. Sure enough, there was a lump under the covers, still snoring lightly. Leaving the door open slightly because it would confound him when he woke the next morning, she dashed over to her bed and pushed it out of the way.

The secret passage hidden in the wall wasn't even known to her father. She had found it purely by accident when she was sixteen. She had been moving her furniture around and Stormy had bumped the wall when she was trying to get out of the way. A little digging had uncovered that the passage had been built back in the late 1800s when the house had been built. Aenya still wasn't sure *why,* but she was grateful.

At the end of the very long tunnel, she opened another door to find a young woman waiting for her. She dressed similarly to Aenya and had the same glitter on her face. "You're late!" she scolded.

Aenya smiled. "Sorry!"

Hands linked, they ran giggling to where a car waited for them. The drive was a short one for 3rd District was not far away, and at that time of night, the traffic was light. The club that they were heading toward sat in the center of the District, but the smaller size of the District made the trip barely noticeable.

The 3rd District. You couldn't research it on the internet. It wasn't in Wikipedia's immense database as more than a set of coordinates. Google and MapQuest didn't even know it existed. Even New Yorkers were mostly unaware of its presence. But it was there, it was alive, and it breathed and pulsed with magic and mystery.

And it was there that the hottest club in New York City was located. They called it the Faerie Club, and it was far from mainstream. You only knew about it if someone told you. If you were compelled by something inside urging you to go, then there was something you needed that you could only find there.

The two girls went into the club with laughter and were immediately absorbed by the gathering of people. Music pounded out of the speakers without being deafening, and dancers crowded the floor. Around the edges of the floor, people of all ages sat playing games or talking. Some younger kids were even doing homework, and the occasional toddler could be seen.

There wasn't a single drop of alcohol on the grounds. Anyone who wanted to smoke had to go at least a block away. No drugs of any shape or form were permitted. There would be no missing the rules; they were posted clearly beside the entrance where a very large man served as a physical deterrent to any who wanted to cause trouble.

Hiro was enchanted as he followed Aenya in his invisible cloak. If this was where she went every night, then he understood completely. In his short career, he had seen places that teenagers should have never known of and yet were going to all the same. The Faerie Club was a breath of fresh, peach-scented, air. It was wonderful.

So was Aenya. He leaned on the rail over the dance pit and watched as she moved across the floor, dancing with different men and women alike. He had seen many dancers. He had danced with many partners. He had still never seen anyone like Aenya. She had the rare grace and perfection that came once in a lifetime to one truly spectacular dancer. She was the Faerie Club's reigning princess, uncontested for her crown.

The understanding didn't come with a blaze of blinding recognition. It didn't send off rockets and whistles like their kiss had done. It was just a quiet little click inside his heart. It made sense of everything, confirmed what he had suspected all along.

He was in love with her.

And because he loved her, he knew he would never be able to keep her. If he kept her secret, he would have to leave. If he told her secret, she would hate him forever. She would never believe that he had done all of this for love. A woman who had been burned was always wary of more flames.

Damned if he did and damned if he didn't, but he still had another day and night to think of something. If he could only build some trust in her! Convince her that he was her ally. Maybe he could get her to tell him about this place, convince her that he loved her. He just needed more information about her. He turned to go toward the stairs, but, softly behind him, he heard a woman say, "Come over here for a while."

Startled, he looked to the side to see a woman sitting in the shadows of a table. Her entire face was hidden from sight except for her piercing yellow eyes. They were eyes that saw everything for they had seen directly through his invisibility. He didn't hesitate to shrug off the cloak, and he was vastly amused when no one even batted a lash that he had appeared out of nowhere. He walked over to the table. "And you are?"

"You're in love with Aenya Shaughnessy." It wasn't a question, nor had she answered his.

Try as he might, he couldn't make out her face. It vexed him because there was something familiar about her. "Yes," he finally sighed. "Tell me, how did she find this place?"

"Eventually, if they need to, everyone finds 3rd District. Even you, Hiro Michaels." The woman reached for her glass of water, and he noticed that her short nails were as sharp as claws. "What will you do with your dancing princess?" she asked.

He turned his gaze toward the floor where Aenya was dancing a jive so fast and expertly that it was a wonder smoke didn't emerge from the floor. He couldn't even see her feet!

"Whatever I can to keep her," he decided as he turned back around. He was alone, though, for the woman had disappeared as mysteriously as she had arrived.

Only vaguely intrigued rather than alarmed, he put his cloak back on and walked over to the rail to watch. He found himself not sleepy in the slightest as he watched Aenya dance the night away and wear through her shoes visibly. On one hand, he wasn't surprised. He hadn't thought any feet could ever move that fast. On the other hand, he felt like she needed a better cobbler. You would think she could afford one.

As dawn began to hint at the horizon, patrons began to drift home. Aenya was driven back to where she had been picked up, and she snuck back down into the passage. Stormy was waiting for her, as always. Quickly, her feet aching, she hurried toward her home and her room, wanting to be in bed if anyone came to wake her up. It was a Saturday, though, so she could sleep in as late as she wanted.

The first thing she did when she got to her room was change back into her nightgown. Only then did she creep over to the connecting room and peek inside. Hiro was still asleep, this time sprawled on top of the covers on his stomach. Thankfully, he wasn't snoring anymore. She muffled a giggle as she bit her lip. She tiptoed quietly into the room to pull the blanket over him.

He really was beautiful, she thought as she studied his face with a hunger she didn't want to examine. Giving in to the urge, she softly touched his cheek, needing to feel his warm skin. He stirred, and she snatched her hand back before whirling and darting into her room. She started to throw her ruined shoes into the garbage then stopped.

She smirked a little and set the shoes just inside Hiro's door so that he would see them when he woke up. Giggling softly, she crawled into her bed and pulled the blankets up to her chin. It was akin to throwing down a gauntlet, but she figured that as long as she could hold onto her control for another day, everything would be just fine.

Stormy climbed up beside her and Aenya draped an arm across her back. She always felt safe near her wolf. Contented, tired, she fell asleep easily.

In the other room, Hiro studied the shoes on his floor and felt his lips twitch. The little witch. She was challenging him, and he had to assume she knew it or she wouldn't have done it. She wanted to make this a battle of wills, and he was more than happy to oblige. The prize was well worth it, and though she didn't know it, he had already won.

Now he just needed to make sure that she didn't lose at the same time.

CHAPTER FOUR

The morning sun was strong through the window when Aenya finally began to stir. With a sleepy mumble, she rolled over and pulled her pillow over her head. She had barely been asleep for two hours. Oh, sure, she was used to it, but she had been having such an interesting dream about a half-naked Hiro and those wonderful hands of his.

"Aenya."

Red color climbed her face as she realized that it was his presence that had disturbed her sleep. He was in her room with her, and judging by the sound of his voice, he was right next to her bed. She hastily sat up and pulled the pillow off her head. Half her hair fell in her eyes, and she swiped at it as she tried to bring him into focus.

He had dressed in a casual denim shirt and jeans, and he stood leaning against the wall beside the bed. A pair of familiar, and trashed, dance shoes dangled from his fingers. She held up a hand to forestall anything he might say. "Please, save all commentary until I have caffeine in my system and my brain returns from dreamland."

It was just as well she needed a moment. He needed several. She looked so wonderfully rumpled and flushed that he wanted to slide into the bed with her and remove the horrid nightgown that marred her beauty. He cleared his throat. "At least admit that you're challenging me."

"Well, you failed one night already." She patted away a yawn and took the robe that Stormy brought her. She pulled it on and slid out of bed. "You didn't stop me from dancing." She gave a long stretch that had his pulse spiking like a thermometer in July. "Day after tomorrow, you're gone."

"We'll just see, Aenya. In the meantime, I have another day to get to know you, and I'd like to spend it with you somewhere other than the middle of the city. Will you trust me enough to go on a trip with me?"

She looked at him warily before deciding it didn't matter. She had promised him ten questions and she had the feeling she would rather have some privacy herself. She didn't trust him to stick with the normal 'getting to know you' bit.

"Okay," she finally said. "Can I wear a skirt, or are we going somewhere that jeans are better?"

He couldn't resist. "I'd prefer a skirt. You've got stunning legs, and I wouldn't mind an excuse to get my hands on them."

"You jerk!" She chucked her hairbrush at him, but he was quick and ducked into his room. The door shut just in time, and the brush thumped against it harmlessly. As she heard his chuckle, she gave a little growl and turned to Stormy. "Men are such idiots!"

Stormy's tail thumped on the bed in agreement, and her canine eyes held amusement. Because Aenya refused to give Hiro the satisfaction, she pulled on a yellow t-shirt covered in sunflowers and a pair of white jeans. Feeling defiant, she went out her now unlocked door and headed downstairs toward the dining room where the morning buffet was waiting.

Hiro was already sitting at the table, and when he saw her, he burst into laughter. Kienan, dragging his feet and his eyes at half-mast, staggered into the dining room and mumbled, "What is so funny at the crack of dawn?"

"It's almost ten, Kien." Because of polite company, he refrained from telling Aenya that he had deliberately manipulated her into wearing jeans because they flattered the hell out of her legs.

Kienan, however, was not blind despite being half-awake. "Stop staring at my sister's ass." He grabbed a cup of coffee and headed for the back garden, hoping for fresh air to aid with waking him up. He hated mornings.

There was a loud splash and a lot of male cursing a few moments later. "That bank is slipperier than it looks," Aenya told Hiro.

"And I'm sure Kienan is much more awake now," he countered dryly in return.

As Kienan stomped soaking wet past the dining room, Sullivan walked in. Aenya smiled. "Morning, Daddy." She walked over to kiss his cheek and nimbly took his coffee mug away. "No."

"Aenya, light of my life and my dearest daughter, have some mercy for your poor father?" He sat down at the table and squinted at the glass of juice she put in front of him. "Oranges?"

"Mangos. You hate oranges." She hugged him tightly with her arms around his neck. "I don't want you to get sick, Daddy. Please? Try to be a good sport? For me?" She gave him a look out of big and pleading brown eyes and he visibly crumbled.

"Alright, alright." He reluctantly began to eat his whole-wheat toast. As he did, he glanced at Hiro. "I saw the shoes on the banister. I assume you did not stop her."

"No, sir. I confess I was very tired last night. I was asleep when my head hit the pillow. But I'm such a light sleeper, it amazes me I did not hear her." He saw the little smirk that crossed Aenya's face and couldn't resist getting a little revenge. "Just so you know, sir," he added casually, "I kissed Aenya last night."

Aenya and Sullivan both choked on their drinks. Mel walked into the dining room, stopped, blinked, then turned around and walked away. Taegan walked in a few seconds later. "Mel is laughing so hard that he's literally on the floor. I presume I missed something."

"I just told your father that I kissed Aenya." Hiro's smile was calm.

Taegan nodded sagely as he saw the bright red on his sister's cheeks. "Since we certainly didn't hear her screaming bloody murder, then she must not have minded much." He was moving as he spoke, and the spoon that she threw at him missed him entirely.

Sullivan cleared his throat. "Aenya, something you want to say?"

She shot Hiro a furious look. "It was *nothing*. It was just a kiss. And it wasn't even that good of a kiss," she lied, turning up her nose. She was going to *kill* him! How dare he mention something like that?

Her father just sighed and rubbed his forehead. "I don't think I'm even going to say anything about this. I'm just going to forget you ever mentioned it." He dunked a piece of toast in his juice and discovered it improved the flavor of both. "What are the plans for today?"

"Aenya and I are going out today. I want to get to know her better. After that, I don't know." Hiro glanced at Taegan. "We ought to have that match this evening before dinner. Might as well get the slaughter over with."

"In your dreams, kid." Taegan pulled his glasses off and put them on top of his head. His smile was almost challenging and hinted that the same wild spirit lurked inside him that was inside all the Shaughnessys. "I'm not such a geek that I can't hold my own on a court." He waved a finger at Aenya as she giggled softly. "Stop that. Just because you beat me one-on-one is no reason to gloat."

"Sure it is." She felt better now that the conversation had gone back to normal. She was still blushing though, and seeing Mel still snickering as he entered the dining room didn't help any. Just wait until she got Hiro alone! Oh he was going to get it!

She got her opportunity an hour later as she stood at the edge of the driveway and waited for him to bring his bike around. He stopped next to her and got off and then promptly ducked as she took a swing for him. She missed entirely and spun around, throwing herself off balance as she fell backward.

Laughing, he caught her under the arms and held her steady. "You deserved that, you little brat! For one thing, you lied blatantly. For another, I don't want your family thinking I'm taking advantage of you."

"I can't believe you said that to my *father*!" she wailed. "How am I supposed to face him? This is so humiliating! First that stupid contract and now this! What will he think?"

Once more, he couldn't resist. "That I'm pragmatic enough to want to know if I can handle bedding my wife should I win?" he suggested. She went still with shock, her mouth falling open, then she began to struggle furiously to get out of his grip. He couldn't help but be pleasantly surprised with her strength; she was much stronger than she looked. "Calm down, honey."

"No! Let me go, and I'll kill you! How *dare* you! You son-of-a—!" Her words were stopped sharply as he twisted her in his arms, bent his head, and took her mouth with a wild hunger that brought her own to life with a blaze of fire.

She gave a little jerk of shock before a soft sound of need slipped past her lips and was muffled by his. It wasn't the gentle initiation kiss of the night before. It was more. It was a detonation. She was helpless in her own desire, helpless to his. She found herself returning the kiss as hotly as it was given, her body beginning to throb and ache as she struggled to be closer.

When he lifted his head, his eyes brilliant green and his breath coming quickly, she discovered she was dangling, off her feet, with her arms around his neck and his around her hips. She was breathing just as hard as he was, her body demanding more and more of his touch, pleasure stinging her nerves wherever they touched.

"I hate you," she managed to say, but her voice was too husky with desire to be believable.

"If you did, then we wouldn't have this problem." His voice was no less rough. He kissed her again quickly and then let her go before he couldn't at all. He swung onto the bike and pulled on his helmet. Conversationally, he said, "I got onto a tear when I was twenty-one and stupid. I was legal, so I promptly went drinking. I had this thing called a 'Nuclear Surprise.' I don't know what was in it, but it went right to my head and exploded. I was nice and happy and fuzzy for several hours. Woke up the next morning and wanted to die."

She pulled on her helmet and got onto the bike in front of him. "What's your point?"

"Your impact is twice as devastating, and so far, I don't have a hangover." He grinned when she started to laugh. "That's better. I'd rather have you laughing at me than threatening to kill me."

"Stop being an ass, then."

"And yet my ass is so cute."

She opened her mouth, then closed it. "No comment."

He coaxed teasingly, "Oh come on, Aenya. You can be honest. I'll be honest. I stare at your ass a lot. It's so nice and firm and those jeans do really nice things for your legs."

She tried not to, but he was being so utterly ridiculous that she had to giggle. "I ought to slap you for that." She didn't, though. She just wrapped her arms around his waist instead and held on tightly. Her hands landed on his waist at the back, and she had to bite her lip to keep from giggling again. Sadly, he was right. He did have a cute ass.

She began to drift lightly as they took off down the road. It felt so nice to be in his arms, and she was so tired from the night before. He was strong and confident, his shoulders just right for resting her head on. His heartbeat was still uneven and it thrilled something inside her soul. It was powerful to know that she could deeply affect such a strong man.

That strength was one of the biggest lures to her. He made her feel safe and cherished. She had never really liked being small, but she loved it when she was in his arms. She loved being in his arms, period. The next time he kissed her, there was no telling what might happen. The only reason either of their kisses had ended was because of his control, not hers. Knowing that, oddly, only made her trust him more.

"Aenya," he murmured sometime later. "Wake up, baby."

"Huh?" She lifted her head, surprised to discover that she had fallen asleep. She sat upright and looked around. They were riding slowly through a quiet suburb full of well-manicured lawns and people enjoying their Saturday morning. "Where are we?"

"You'll see." He pulled into a driveway and parked. He got off the bike and removed his helmet, and then he helped her off and removed hers. With her tucked under his arm, he headed for the front door of the house they were approaching.

She began to get a sinking feeling in the pit of her stomach as she saw all the stunning flowers growing in the garden. "Hiro . . ."

The front door opened as they got close and a woman with familiar green eyes happily descended the steps to hug him

enthusiastically. "What a wonderful surprise!" She gave him a smacking kiss. "I've missed you like mad! You don't visit enough!"

"Work is busy lately, Mom." He smiled as he hugged her back just as tightly. Still smiling, he turned and held a hand toward Aenya. "Meet Aenya."

Maria Michaels turned and regarded the blushing young woman, and she studied her with a mother's knowing eye. Hiro had never brought a girlfriend over to 'meet his family' before, and that told Maria that her son's feelings were very serious. Aenya's visible embarrassment was evidence that she was as surprised by the visit as Maria. "Hello, Aenya. I'm Maria, Hiro's mother. You're a friend of his?"

Aenya's eyes shot daggers at Hiro's back as he headed into the house. "It remains to be seen." Her manners took over and she smiled at Maria. "I'm sorry for imposing upon you so suddenly. You have a lovely home."

"Stop showing off your etiquette training," Hiro scolded over his shoulder.

"At least I *have* manners, you ass!" The instant the words left her mouth, she went red from ear to ear. She whirled toward Maria in horror with her hands covering her mouth. Maria, however, was laughing too hard to notice. "I am *so* sorry!"

"Oh, no, no! Please don't!" Maria took her hand and brought her into the house. "I think you're delightful! You're welcome in our home anytime, even if you dump Hiro. If he dumps you, I'm disowning him."

She decided it would be too complicated to explain that they weren't dating and that it was more like a betrothal without her consent. Instead, she followed Maria to the family room where Hiro was engaged in a lively argument with a man who had to be his father. They had the same hair color and same build.

"Zeke," Maria said with a smile. "Meet Aenya. She's Hiro's friend."

Zeke Michaels lifted a brow as he looked at Aenya. He looked at his son. "Are you keeping this one? Because you're an idiot if you don't, and I didn't raise an idiot."

"It's a bit complicated." He walked over to Aenya and ran a hand lightly down her hair. "If I get the chance, I'm keeping her, yes. I'll explain later. We're just passing through because I wanted you to meet her."

"Well, it's good to meet you." Zeke studied Aenya curiously. The name was familiar. "Aenya . . . ?"

Very reluctantly, she muttered, "Shaughnessy."

Zeke and Maria's brows lifted almost simultaneously. Anyone who read the news knew about Sullivan Shaughnessy's desperation to find out where his daughter was dancing at night. Reporters were being curiously kind about the situation, writing with more sympathy than one might expect, but they were still telling the tale.

"I see," Zeke said. And he did. If Hiro was involved, then he loved Aenya. It was that simple. "Well, Shaughnessy or not, you're always welcome in our home." He grinned. "Say hi to your dad for me."

She had to grin back. "I will." She stifled a sigh as Hiro began to drag her toward the door. "I can walk, damn it! Stop dragging me or I'll make Stormy chew on your leather jacket! My wolf has sharp teeth!"

"Wolf?" Zeke and Maria both asked as the door shut.

Hiro swung Aenya up into his arms and kept walking, grinning as she kicked her feet in annoyance. "If we'd stayed any longer, they'd have disowned me and kept you." He kept walking and headed past the motorcycle, much to her puzzlement. "Did you like them?"

"Yes, now put me down!" She huffed as he did so, then her heart flipped over in her chest again as he took her hand and linked their fingers together. It felt . . . normal to be walking with him down the sidewalk like that. She gave in to the urge and rested her head on his shoulder. "Where're we going?"

"Just there." He pointed and she saw that they were heading toward a park not far ahead of them in the distance. It was quiet this time of morning and none of the kids had arrived for the day.

It was just a small park with a well-built wooden playground set and sand filling in around it. Flowers bloomed all around the grass

patches, and someone had left a sandcastle abandoned in the middle. A lone basketball sat under the tire swing, and the regular swings squeaked lightly as they swung slowly back and forth in the breeze.

"It's so friendly." She walked over to one of the swings and sat down. She pushed it lightly with her foot. "Well," she added with a wry smile, "I guess this is the part where you get a chance at your ten questions." The setting didn't surprise her. It made her feel oddly safe and secure, and she suspected it made him feel the same way.

"Fair's fair." He leaned on the slide to watch her. "What was your mother like?"

Startled, she looked at him. It seemed a question from left field. "I don't know personally, but my brothers have always told me about her so that I don't feel left out." She rocked the swing gently. "She was always a lady in public but she was seriously temperamental. I guess she and Daddy would always get into arguments that ended with cookies and flowers. Bad cookies," she added on a laugh. "The class she almost flunked was Home Ec. She couldn't cook."

"Flowers." He smiled. "From my parent's shop, I bet. No wonder you knew the name of the place, and Dad said to tell your dad hi."

"That'd be why." She turned her gaze toward the sky and decided to tell him the rest without his asking. "I was born prematurely, Hiro. I was supposed to be born in September."

He went very still. Her birthday was in the beginning of June. Even presuming that she had originally been due at the beginning of September, that was still three months early. "Jesus." His heart clenched in his chest. He knew how hard preemie babies struggled to survive. Those that did were miracles. It was no wonder she was so small.

Softly, she continued, "Mom was coming home from picking up Taegan at school and there was a car accident. He got a broken arm and she had internal bleeding. They got it stopped, but she went into labor, and the bleeding started again." Tears slid slowly down her cheeks. "The choice was her life or mine. They could abort me and stop the bleeding, or they could deliver me and risk her life. She chose mine."

"For a while, they thought she might pull through, but she died a week later. I didn't get out of the intensive care unit for almost four months. Daddy and my brothers fought over me, arguing over who would get to hold me, and who would get to feed me, and who would change me. Even Kienan wanted to take care of me." She smiled through her tears. "I love them all so much."

It explained Sullivan's desperate actions. For a man who had lost his wife and was risking losing his child as well, any action, no matter how desperate, was called for. Her brothers were a little more relaxed, but Hiro had noticed Kienan was very possessive of his sister, to the point he had literally hired him to hopefully help her.

When Kienan had shown up at his office, he hadn't been sure what to think. The situation was, to say the least, outrageous. But Kienan had been insistent, saying that he wanted to give Aenya a chance to find someone she could at least learn to love. He was certain, somehow, that Hiro was that person. Hiro hadn't been so sure himself until the day before when he had seen a pair of honey brown eyes and been hit by lightning. It fried his mind better than that stupid Nuclear Surprise.

Wanting to lighten the mood, he sat down on the swing next to her. "What do you like? What do you dislike? And, yes, that counts as two questions."

She blinked then smiled, grateful for the change of subject. "Turnabout's fair play, right? Let's see . . . well, I like most anything. I'm not a picky eater, but I absolutely *hate* beets. Despise them with a passion. And let's see . . . favorite color is pink. I'm a girly girl," she warned him.

He thought of the bedroom decorated in pink and lace and covered a laugh. "I hadn't noticed."

"I dislike stupid things. Not just people, but things. Like . . . letters mailed two days after they were written. Stuff like that." She cocked her head slightly. "Some stupid things amuse me though. Like men."

He applauded her lightly. "Have you ever been traveling?"

"Like out of New York? Sure. We go to Florida for a week every summer and Colorado for a week every winter. It's awesome." She snickered. "I've been forbidden from wearing a bikini until I'm twenty-one though. I almost caused someone to drown."

He thought of the elegant and slender body she possessed and sighed wistfully. "I can imagine why." Sea sirens only wished they were as beautiful as his princess. "How did you meet Madelyne?"

She smiled. "Stormy ran away from home and we were trying to track her down. I ended up wandering into the 3rd District and got lost. Madelyne found me, and when we got to her inn, Stormy was there. Madelyne had found her and was going to call the number on the tag when she found me instead. We became friends." It had been Madelyne who had introduced her to the Faerie Club, she thought wistfully.

"Tell me more about the 3rd District." He watched her face. "When was it built?"

"Well, according to Madelyne, it was built in 333 B.C. I know," she winced wryly when he lifted a brow, "that's well before America was 'civilized.' But there were indigenous tribes here even then. Heck, I think it was when some Norsemen came down to the area that the District was built as some sort of haven. And every nation that ever encountered the District has left it alone. So it's evolved along with society, always one step behind and one step forward.

"I love it there. I feel *normal*. But then again, by their standards, I *am* normal. I've met some . . . amazing people there. The stories are unusual to say the least. And the Enforcers operate out of there, so they have some pretty interesting stories, too. I think that's part of the reason no one has ever tried to change 3rd District. No one wants to take on the Enforcers because no one is really sure how much power they have."

She got up and wandered over to where the basketball was sitting. She took aim at the basket and made her shot. It went in with nothing but net from almost thirty feet away.

"Holy hell," Hiro murmured. "Did you really play basketball?"

She turned to laugh at him. "Yes, really. Everyone so hyped on me to be a cheerleader when tryouts came around that I tried out for the team just to spite everybody. Not only did I end up as captain for two years, but I led our team to both championships those years. And won." She climbed up into the tower of one of the structures. "You're down to three questions," she teased him.

"Okay, so here's a random question like yours about color. What's your favorite song?"

"It's not one you'll hear on a radio." She leaned on the rail. "It's a song Madelyne wrote. It's about magic and faerie tales. And her voice is *amazing*. You wouldn't think a voice like hers would come out of someone so plain. Susan Boyle has *nothing* on Madelyne."

He moved closer and asked very softly, "What are your dreams, Aenya? Why do you dance every night?"

She went very still. Then, finally, she gave a soft sigh and sat on the top of the slide. "I was waiting for that," she admitted. She tilted her head back and closed her eyes. "I want to dance, Hiro. I want it with everything I am. If I couldn't dance, it would destroy me. When I started this year of school, I told Daddy that I wanted to go to a special dance school instead of college. I told him I had been offered an internship with a large company. He refused."

"He worries about losing you," he said quietly. "He just wants you to be provided for."

"If he'd give me a chance, he'd see that I've got what it takes to make my dreams a reality. Our entire family company is built around that very concept, and he doesn't even realize I've got as much potential as his favorite small businesses." She opened her eyes and stared at the sky. "I just want to be free. If I can just hold on till my twenty-first birthday, I can do whatever I want . . ."

What right did he have to destroy her dreams? Heart sinking, he held his hands up to her. "Come down and we'll go back, Aenya."

She said nothing as she let him help her down. She could sense his withdrawal and it hurt her deeper than she had ever imagined. She didn't blame him. Who wanted to be caught in a contract that would force him to marry a woman who would always want something else?

Yet something had changed. She felt it as she walked with him

back toward the bike. If, somehow, she lost this battle, then she would never have the will to make his life hell. She would hurt, and she would suffer, but she would take whatever affection she could get from him. She had done the stupidest thing possible. She had fallen in love with a man who would never love her. Unable to help herself, she asked, "Would you have ever asked me out if things were normal?"

He hesitated for long moments. Truthfully, he would have skipped the dating stage and gone straight to her father to ask for her hand. He would have used every weapon at his disposal to convince the woman he loved to give in. Dating? It would have never crossed his mind. "I don't know," he finally hedged.

Pain blossomed inside her heart and stayed there as they retrieved the bike and began to head back toward the city. Any way she looked at it, she was doomed to be miserable. If she let him win, then she would lose her dreams and would have to suffer marrying a man who, at most, felt affection for her. If she won, then she would never see him again.

And what if she did win? Another suitor would come through. Then another. Then another. What if she didn't manage to trick them all? What if someone was immune to the potion? She would really lose then and be forced to marry a man she hated. She wasn't hopeful enough to think it would be a marriage in name only though her stomach churned at the thought of letting any man but Hiro touch her.

And yet . . . her mind began to move quickly. Hiro wanted her. He wanted her as terribly as she wanted him. Maybe that could be turned into love. Maybe if she gave him everything she could, she could make him understand her better. Maybe he would love her. Maybe he would let her have her dreams.

Maybe.

Maybe.

Maybe.

It was all maybes. There were no positives except for one: she absolutely would have no man other than Hiro Michaels for her first lover. She straightened up and moved as close to his ear as she could. "If I asked you to be my first lover, what would you say?"

He almost dumped the bike. He swiftly pulled off the road and stared at her in shock. What in the *hell* was going through that terrifyingly sharp mind? "Alright, please repeat that when I'm not worried that I'm going to crash us."

She couldn't quite meet his eyes as her cheeks turned red. "I wanted to know what you'd say if I asked you to be my first lover."

"I'd say . . . why?" He kept his voice even with effort. She had thrown him for a loop, and it was hard to fight his deepest instincts. He had been resisting the urge to carry her away ever since he had met her. "I thought you didn't want to like me."

"I didn't. But I do. And I don't like how we've been forced into this situation. To be honest, I like you more than I've ever liked anyone else. There's something about you. I'm drawn to it. And . . . it occurred to me rather blindingly that someday I might mess up and be forced to marry someone that I loathe. I don't want to give them the satisfaction." Her eyes lifted to his. "I want to make one decision for myself for once. And I want you to be my first lover. I know you want me, and I know you said you liked me. That's enough." For now, she added mentally.

He ran a thumb over her lips, tempted to remove her helmet so he could get his hands in her hair. "I want you like I've never wanted anything before. But I'm not going to let anything keep me from my goals. You can't seduce me into walking away."

"I'm not trying to. I just . . . I just want my first time to be with someone I desire. If it's the only time I ever feel real desire for a man, then I want to have the memory to cling to." She let out a breath. "We can both go into this with our eyes open. We know it will change neither of our minds."

He fought with himself violently. In the end, he realized he could refuse her nothing. If things ended badly, he too wanted to cling onto this memory. He still hadn't figured out how to give them both what they wanted. She liked him. It was a start. Perhaps the explosive hunger between them could help fan flames even more elemental.

He started the bike up again and turned for another road. She remained silent as long as she could, but when she saw they were heading away from her home rather than toward it, she felt her heart begin beating harder. When they stopped at a light, she asked, "Where are we going?"

"My apartment. I'm not taking you to a hotel. You deserve better than that." He could feel the trembling in her body and it matched the trembling inside his heart. He was terrified of hurting her, or losing her, or ruining the trust she was giving him so generously.

As they pulled into the parking lot of the apartment complex, her eyes went wide. "This is not an apartment," she said decisively. "It's a condo. And it's an upscale condo. In fact, I think Daddy invested in this complex." As he lifted her off the bike and she pulled off her helmet, she asked warily, "You're rather well off, aren't you?"

"I get by." He possessively held her closer as they headed up the stairs toward where his apartment was located. It was the corner one, and on the top floor so he had a lot of privacy, which he much preferred.

She loved it the instant she walked inside. It was light and airy and he hadn't cluttered it with a ton of furniture. There was a giant oversized couch that she couldn't resist going over to and sitting down on. It promptly tried to swallow her up.

"Is this a couch or a bed?" she asked him laughingly.

"Both. Sometimes I'm working too hard and fall asleep where I'm sitting." He hung up his jacket before walking over to kneel in front of her. "You said you trust me. Do you mean it?" She nodded and he let out a little breath. "Good." Watching her eyes, he reached out and unfastened her jacket for her.

She let him remove it and half expected him to go for the edge of her shirt right after. Instead, she made a startled sound as he lifted her into his arms and carried her down the hall toward his bedroom. Her heart was beating so hard that she wondered how he couldn't hear it. "Hiro, if I panic, I'm sorry. I'm just nervous."

"If you panic, we stop." He stopped beside the bed and slowly lowered her to the top of the covers. Her hair tumbled around her shoulders and across the sapphire-colored pillowcase. His breath came in sharply. "No matter how hard it is," he added huskily. "At least I'll try. God, Aenya, do you have any idea how badly I want you?"

"Teach me." Her hands reached for his and their fingers laced together. His head lowered slowly and their lips met, softly at first then with growing passion as nerves gave way to their hearts.

Unspoken between them, their feelings welled up and swept them both away. It was like a dance just for the two of them. His fingers skimmed lightly down her side then slipped under the edge of her shirt. Unlike the night before when his hot hand had touched her bare flesh, this time she didn't panic. Her fingers lifted and framed his face, holding him closer to her as she willingly sank into the promise of his kiss. He tasted like lemonade. As if he had just eaten a piece of lemon candy. It was an addicting flavor and she made a sound of disappointment as he eased her back.

When she realized he was slowly removing her shirt, she blushed. She didn't stop him, though, and her arms came up to shield her breasts as he tossed the top to the side. She was wearing a bra, but she still felt almost horribly exposed.

He forgot how to breathe. "Yeah," he murmured thickly, skimming a knuckle over the top curve of her breast, "I feel for the poor sap who almost drowned. I'd gladly drown for you, too." His hand cupped the back of her head and he dragged her against him again for another hungry kiss. His teeth nipped at her lower lip teasingly.

A soft moan was her only answer and she forgot to shield herself as her hands went to the buttons of his shirt. Her fingers were trembling almost too hard and she finally dropped them into her lap. His free hand lowered and caught her hands, and then lifted them again to hold them against his chest until the trembling eased. "It's alright," he murmured, trailing kisses down the side of her neck. She tasted like honey and summertime. He hadn't known it would be so addicting.

Taking a slow breath, which was all she could manage because it was hard to breathe when his mouth was planting hot kisses along her shoulder, she began to unbutton his shirt again. She got it open and spread her hands across his chest slowly, feeling again that tingling in her palms. "Hiro," she whispered softly, her head falling back.

He shrugged out of the shirt and tossed it aside. He then slowly lowered her to the bed again. His hand ran sensuously over her bare stomach. She trembled, and he smiled as he kissed her again. Against her lips, he asked, "Scared?"

She shook her head. "No." She wasn't, not really. She was a little nervous, but not scared. She did gulp a quick breath of air, however, as his fingers unfastened her jeans. As they slowly slid down her legs, she clutched his shoulders for balance, her head spinning. His fingers trailed over her legs, and the skin was suddenly so sensitive that it seemed as if she felt every line of his fingerprints.

He knew the exact instant her hunger overrode her nerves. Tension shot into her muscles, and she twisted against him as if to follow his hands. Delight made him light-headed. He rolled her underneath him and caught his weight so that he didn't hurt her. Eagerly he ran kisses over the top curves of her breasts, his lips tugging at the lace that covered them.

On a shudder, she caught her fingers in his hair and held him closer. She felt too hot, as if she was going to go up in flames, and she could barely breathe in the thick and heavy air. Her breasts ached and so did between her legs. Everywhere she had a pulse, she could feel it pounding with the drugging rhythm of a drum.

Lifting her slightly, he unfastened her bra and then dropped it over the bed as well. His mouth went dry, and he softly ran the back of his hand down the outside curve of her breast. The nipple tightened and flushed and he couldn't resist the temptation to bend and cover the point with his mouth.

She couldn't stop a soft cry as lightning scored her insides. It was pleasure almost unbearably strong and her dazed mind accepted the fact that she had gotten herself in further than she was going to be able to safely emerge from again. Gripping onto him tightly, her nails digging little crescents into his shoulders, she arched against him in a plea for more.

Her eyes flew wide with sudden shock as she felt his hand on the bare skin of her inner thigh and slowly moving upward. She was naked, she realized, and she buried her flaming face against his shoulder. "Where'd my underwear go?" she managed to ask.

"Magic," he told her, his free hand tilting her head back. He kissed her hard, then his lips curved. "And besides, there were little ribbons on the hip. You looked like a really nice Christmas present. The best ever."

"Don't be a pervert!" The last word was a gasp as his knuckles brushed over her in an intimate caress. Her legs came together protectively and trapped his hand against her heated flesh. She moaned softly as he teased her with his fingers, finding all the sensitive places on her body. Places she hadn't even envisioned owning. "Stop."

"Are you scared?" He held her closer protectively. He was shaking with stifled desire but he wanted to see her go completely wild in his arms. He wanted to pleasure her until she knew beyond a doubt she belonged to him. "Hold onto me. I'll keep you safe."

"Hiro, stop." She squeezed her eyes shut as her body shook with hunger, pleasure making it impossible to breathe. Breathing wasn't important. Nothing was important but Hiro. She would have cried out, but his mouth sealed hers shut, his tongue dueling with hers hungrily. His fingers were insistent, and she twisted against him desperately.

The terrible tension snapped. Ecstasy swept over her entire body, pleasure consuming her until she couldn't think or breathe. All she could do was hold onto him wildly, finding him to be her only anchor. Even when the wave ebbed, she couldn't let go of him. The strength drained from her body and left soft ripples of satisfaction fluttering inside.

The best she could manage to say was, "Wow."

He felt no less shaken. He was suddenly out of his depth, too, never daring dream of finding someone like her. His hunger for her

was a living thing inside him, his body tight and desperate for relief.

"Aenya." He tilted her face up so that he could kiss her again. Even as his hands moved over her again, awakening her senses once more, he didn't release her from the kiss. He couldn't get enough of her. He didn't think he ever would. "Let me love you," he said against her lips. "I need you so badly."

"Yes." She reluctantly released him as he slipped out of her arms and she watched him curiously as he stripped off the rest of his clothes. She realized a bit distantly she was no longer embarrassed, no longer nervous. It was as if everything inside her had finally embraced this decision she had made. Why had she ever been nervous to begin with?

With immense curiosity, she rose to her knees on the bed and looked at him eagerly. She wanted to run her hands over him and explore him, especially where he was so obviously aroused, but she didn't quite have the courage for that. Not yet, at least. Her eyes shifted to his stomach and she sucked in a painful breath as she saw something she had been too flustered to see the night before.

There was a scar across his lower stomach; a nasty looking mark that spoke of a painful wound. She knew, somehow, that she was staring at a bullet wound. Stricken, she looked up at him. "Hiro."

"It's okay. I'll explain later." He lowered her to the bed again and forced his hands to be gentle as they skimmed over her curves. He wanted her wild again, so hot for him that any pain was brief. It was hard to restrain himself, and he prayed for an outcome where he would someday be able to see if he would ever be sated with her. He strongly doubted it.

She gave up her innocence without hesitation, winding her arms around his shoulders and gripping her fingers into the sweaty slopes of his back. He watched her face as he slowly took her and saw the way her breath hitched. Instantly he stopped. "It's okay. I'm sorry." His mouth rushed over her face to comfort and he tasted her tears. "Aenya, damn it, don't cry."

"Then don't stop! I want you, Hiro. Just you. Please. It doesn't hurt that badly." It was more a burning than a pain and her body somehow knew there was something behind it. She couldn't control the arch of her hips any more than she could stop her own heart. She *craved* him.

On a low groan, he stopped fighting and surged into her in a single stroke. She gave a strangled little yelp, and he froze, terrified he had hurt her, but her feet hooked behind his thighs and she pressed herself closer against him. It was just a little gesture but it broke his control. "I'm sorry," he said into her hair as he began to drive into her with more power than precision.

She wanted to tell him it was okay, she didn't mind, but she couldn't speak. That terrible pleasure that demanded release from its pressure was climbing again. This time she eagerly embraced it. Her breaths became whimpers and her nails dug into his shoulders. When the release came, it was harder and hotter than before, ripping a cry from her throat that she muffled against his neck.

The ripples of her inner muscles were too much for him to bear. Shuddering, he could only hold onto her fiercely, ecstasy unlike any before consuming him, emptying his heart and soul in her as deeply as it did his body. He had told her he would show her the magic, but she had shown him instead. And he knew, knew beyond a doubt, that this was a magic that they would only find together.

He wrapped her protectively in his arms and rolled onto his side. He stared over the top of her head at the wall across the room as she snuggled close. Even if he had to steal her, she belonged with him, and he would not let her go. There had to be a way for him to win the contract and for her to have her dreams too. There had to be!

CHAPTER FIVE

They slept for a while, tangled together with a sheet haphazardly thrown over them. When Aenya stirred and sat up, it roused Hiro enough to reach for her. "Where're you going?" he murmured drowsily.

"Nowhere."

The soft muted pain in her voice brought him fully awake. He opened his eyes to find her sitting beside him and looking at the scar on his stomach. "Aenya."

She gently reached out to put a hand over the old wound. Her fingertips trembled. "Where did you get this?" she asked softly. "It looks so horrible."

"I was in junior high. I had the unfortunate timing of being at a bus stop when a member of a gang was there. His rivals happened to drive by and open up fire. I, and an old woman, were innocent bystanders. She didn't survive the trip to the hospital. The bullet only went across my stomach, not directly in, so I somehow made it. The cops who got there before the ambulance . . . they saved my life."

Tears welled in her eyes. She could have lost him before ever knowing he existed. Needing to feel his arms around her, she lay down and put her head on his shoulder. He immediately turned and pulled her close. "Is that why you went into criminal justice? You wanted to give something back? Or was your name going to your head?"

"Hush you." He snuggled her closer. "It was probably a combination of both. I never really questioned my path after that." He glanced over her head and sighed as he saw the clock. "It's getting late. We should head back to your house if we want to have our basketball game." He sat up and looked at her lying so naturally and comfortably in his bed. "Regrets?" he asked softly.

"No." She turned her face into his hand as he cupped her cheek. "No matter what happens, I can say that my first time was special."

"You still think that I won't win?"

"I'm positive." Try as she might, it was getting harder and harder to remind herself that she had to play things out. She wanted nothing more than to crawl into his arms and tell him that she loved him and didn't want him to go. She couldn't even tell anymore what she wanted most: him or her dance.

Pushing it aside, she sat up and swung her feet over the side of the bed. She promptly winced. He was at her side in a flash and lifted her into his arms to carry her into the master bathroom. "You need a hot shower," he told her. "I'm not putting you onto the bike if you're sore."

"I'm not *that* sore. Just a little bit." She couldn't resist taking a shower anyway. It was just so intimate to be bathing in her lover's bathroom. But was he actually her lover? It was just a one-night stand, right? Or a one-day stand, as it were.

One *hell* of a one-day stand, she decided as she stood under the shower spray. She felt as if she was glowing, and there was no embarrassment as she washed away the evidence of their lovemaking. It was only as she did so that something finally occurred to her belatedly. She wasn't on birth control, and he hadn't used protection.

She rushed through washing her hair and drying it. She hurried out of the shower and wrapped herself in a towel as she went into the bedroom. A calendar sat on the dresser. She swiftly counted days. She was *very* regular with her periods, so she could be sure on timing. Unless the gods really were pissed off at her, she should start her period in a matter of days. She should be safe.

And yet . . . realizing it, made her immensely sad. Having known Hiro's passion and her own, she couldn't bear the idea of ever being in any other man's arms, let alone having his child. She wanted Hiro. Wanted a family with him. Shaughnessys *needed* family.

She kept the knowledge to herself, knowing that nothing was

foolproof and the gods knew she had been enough of a fool over Hiro lately. Instead, she got dressed and headed for the living room. When she got there, she was amused to discover he was reading a romance novel. "I wasn't expecting that."

"There are no laws against men liking romance." He put the book up on a shelf and got to his feet. "Have I sufficiently sacrificed my manly image?"

She giggled as she let him help her with her jacket. "I don't think your image can suffer too badly." She considered that, then added impishly, "At least not until I whip you on the court. When you're crying like a baby, *then* your manly image will be SOL."

He laughed outright as they reached the parking lot. He exuberantly swung her up into his arms and in a wild circle. He was absolutely crazy about her. Knowing she wouldn't believe him, he said only, "You make me very happy, Aenya. I hope you know that."

It wasn't the same as love, but it was the beginnings of hope. She hugged him tightly. If she was wrong and she found she was pregnant, then she would run away from home and force him to go with her. Eventually he would have to love her. She was a loveable type, or so said her brothers.

They found Kienan waiting on the driveway at home with a basketball in his hands. He had a sixth sense for Aenya and had known she was almost home. "There you are!" he called cheerfully. "We're ready to play if you are." He watched Hiro help her off the bike, and his eyes narrowed sharply and dangerously. She looked at him and he was promptly all smiles. "You should put something better on, sis."

"Okay." She kissed his cheek and then jogged into the house.

As soon as the door shut, his fist slammed into Hiro's jaw. Before the older male could recover, he had grabbed him by the shirt and slammed him into the garage wall. "You son-of-a-bitch!" he snarled. "I *trusted* you, Hiro! You think I'm an idiot?! I saw how Aenya looked!"

Hiro didn't bother to try and fight his way loose. Kienan may have been two inches shorter but he was much stronger and vastly better trained. The fact that Hiro's jaw was throbbing but not swelling was evidence of that.

"No," he said evenly. "I don't think you're an idiot. I knew you'd all notice even though Aenya doesn't seem to think so." His eyes narrowed sharply. "And I'm going to tell you something I don't dare tell her."

"And that is?" Kienan challenged.

"I'm in love with her. But she'll never believe me because of this fucking contract."

Kienan stared into his eyes with an oddly piercing gaze and then released him and stepped back. "I had hoped you would. That's why I went to you. When I described you to my brothers and Dad, they were all in agreement with me that you were perfect for Aenya. That's why I hired you."

"As to that . . ." He pulled out his wallet and removed the check inside. He handed it to Kienan. "I'm firing myself. Nothing personal."

Kienan's grin came lightning quick across his face as he tore up the check. "And that's why I trusted you," he said simply. Something dangerous flickered across his eyes. "But I don't want my sister hurt. If you hurt her . . ."

"I'm doing my level best not to. I'm going to make her as happy as I can, Kien." He eyed his friend. "Just don't go hitting me again or I'll hit back and break your pretty nose." He caught movement from the corner of his eyes and turned his head to see Aenya jogging toward them in a pair of jean shorts and a sports bra. His pulse spiked through the roof. "No wonder you forbid the bikini," he murmured.

Kienan snorted. "The dork swam into a pier and knocked himself cold. Even the lifeguard was laughing almost too hard to save him."

"Okay, let's go." Aenya frowned as she saw the slight swelling on Hiro's jaw. "What happened?"

"A bee stung me." He grinned over her head as Kienan flipped him off behind her back. He glanced down at her with a smile. "Are you hoping to distract me with the shorts?"

"Hardly. I'll be moving so fast you won't get a chance to see my legs." She waved at her other two brothers and her father as she saw that they were on the court already. It had been built into the backyard when she had joined the team and the whole family used it whenever they could.

Mel and Taegan were wearing loose tank tops so Kienan and Hiro both stripped their shirts off. Aenya felt a slight blush warm her cheeks. She cleared her throat and sat on one of the benches, her eyes following Hiro helplessly. She had been held by that body, and underneath it. She shouldn't be blushing at seeing it again. But, damn it, he was too sexy! Her fingers itched to run all over him.

His reputation as a player was not exaggerated. He was definitely just as good as Mel, and her brother was lethal. Taegan and Kienan were equally matched in skill, so it really was down to Hiro and Mel and who could outwit the other. The score remained consistently tied and that meant the deciding factor would come down to time.

"Go Mel!" Aenya shouted. When Hiro glared at her, she blew him a kiss impishly.

"Thirty seconds!" Sullivan called.

Kienan had control of the ball. He shot around Taegan and made his way toward the basket. Mel tried to get in his way but Hiro intercepted, forcing Mel to pull up short before they collided. Kienan made the shot and the ball bounced off the rim and into the air. Everyone watched with their breath held as the ball flipped into the air. When it came down, it went through the net.

"Time!" Sullivan called. "Hiro and Kienan are the winners!" Mel said something distinctly unpleasant under his breath, and Sullivan just laughed. "Now boys, let's be good sports."

Kienan flexed the muscles in his arm. "So, Aenya, ready to get your ass whipped? No offense, Dad, but you're getting old."

The way Sullivan went down the short stacked bleachers to the court, no one would have ever guessed his age. "I'll show you old," he said mildly. Oh, it was harder to catch a breath lately, but that didn't mean he couldn't keep up with his kids on a court.

"Kick his ass, Dad," Mel muttered. "Gloating bastards." Despite the cool weather, he was hot from the match. He dumped half his bottle of water over his head rather than drink it. Aenya had better

marry Hiro so that Mel had a chance at a rematch. He wasn't going to settle for being punked by a non-team player.

Taegan watched as the match began, the stopwatch swinging lightly from his fingers. The look on Hiro's face was absolutely priceless when he realized how good Aenya was at the game. Her height, which was her greatest disadvantage, was also her greatest weapon.

"Did you notice?" he murmured when Mel sat next to him.

"What, am I blind?" Mel sighed and rubbed the back of his neck. "On one hand, I want to be an outraged big brother and kick his ass for touching my baby sister. On the other hand, I know Aenya. She wouldn't have let him touch her unless she wanted him to. And it was definitely a mutual decision. The way they look at each other . . ."

"And she thinks we won't notice." Taegan shook his head.

"What the hell is she going to do if he fails?" Mel wondered quietly.

"I get the feeling that Hiro hasn't been playing all his cards. He knows something. I'm positive of it. This morning . . . something rang false in what he said. And I've always been sensitive to lies, so . . ." He sat up straighter and added calmly, "I'm willing to trust him with my sister. I will, however, have to hurt him, regardless, for his lack of honesty with her."

"Hit him on my behalf too," Mel offered.

He grinned briefly and then picked up the stopwatch. He had been calculating the points automatically even during the conversation. Numbers were his specialty. "Thirty seconds!" he called. "Aenya's team has a three point lead!"

Hiro said something explicit and rude under his breath. He couldn't get a hand on Aenya because she was so small, and she was so ridiculously agile that she was like a flash across the court. And how in the hell could anyone that short make a basket from that far? "Hold still!" he almost snarled.

She laughed in his face and ducked around him. She whirled and shot the ball at her father. Hiro was blocking the goal and it was time to show her stuff. She wouldn't want him to think he was the only one with tricks. "Daddy, rim it!"

"Hell!" Kienan whirled as his father shot the basketball. "Hiro, grab her! Tackle her! Do *something*!"

Hiro tried, really he did, but she ducked and slid between his legs. Before he could turn, she sprang to her feet and leapt into the air. The ball bounced off the rim and she caught it to dunk it through the net.

"Time!" Taegan called. Beside him, Mel was laughing so hard he couldn't breathe. With a grin, Taegan said, "The Rim Dunk is Aenya's specialty. No one expects her to be able to jump that high. She has all the agility of a gazelle. And she's so small that she can duck through most opponents' legs."

Aenya was holding onto the rim of the basketball net and let go to drop down into Kienan's arms. He hugged her fiercely, then ruffled her hair. "I hate you! I never want to talk to you again!" He gave her a smacking kiss. He was so proud of her that losing didn't really matter.

She got free of his grip and went over to hug Sullivan tightly. They exchanged a high five, and then she turned and gave Hiro a triumphant look. "Your manly image is officially forfeit, Michaels. You just lost a match to a woman half your size."

Everyone, Hiro included, began to laugh. Mel hoisted Aenya up onto his shoulders as they made their way back toward the house. "Make way, make way!" he called, and had the servants laughing as they cleared a path. "Her highness has royally trumped the invading knight."

Dinner was lively that night, as was normal, even though it was later than usual since they had all needed showers. Hiro was still nursing a sulk over dessert and so was Mel. That, naturally, amused everyone else immensely.

"Oh don't be such spoilsports," Aenya scolded them teasingly. "Honestly, you're too much alike in some ways."

"We are not," both males groused.

She just shook her head. It didn't surprise her that she had fallen in love with a man who was that much like her brothers. With a large stretch, she got to her feet. "It's late and I'm tired. I'm turning in early." She walked over to her father and kissed his cheek. "G'night, Daddy. Good match today."

Everyone remained silent as they heard her going upstairs. Only when the door shut did the Shaughnessys turn to look at Hiro. All four, nearly identical, pairs of eyes had varying levels of annoyance and warning.

Hiro held up his hands. "I'm in love with her. She asked me to be her first." The frustration filled his voice for a moment. "How in the name of hell was I supposed to say no?"

"If you do not find where she dances by morning, you must forfeit the contract," Sullivan reminded him quietly. "And if you forfeit the contract, you are not eligible to attempt a second time. Until the terms of the contract are met, it remains active."

Hiro looked at him evenly. "Come hell or high water, Mr. Shaughnessy, Aenya will be mine. I could care less about your company. In fact, you can take your shares and burn them. I have no need for your money. Do I, Taegan?" He shot the question challengingly across the table.

Taegan quirked a brow. "Most don't find me digging in their history."

"You cover your tracks well, particularly since you have a third party assisting you, but I do this sort of thing for a living—and I was expecting it. Why don't you tell your family what you found?"

Taegan removed his glasses and put them on the table. "To put it simply, Hiro's grandfather was a very intelligent man. He ran a fairly sizable investment fund for many years. When he saw the potential downturn in the market, he cashed out and put the money into savings. Upon his death last year, Hiro became the sole heir."

"Which investment fund?" Sullivan asked curiously.

"Archway Financial."

"Well." That was about all Mel could say.

"I see." Sullivan leaned back in his chair and studied Hiro. A man who was the heir to the fortune of what had once been one of the top five biggest investment houses certainly didn't need additional money, even from Shaughnessy Corporation. "The contract is still binding."

"With loopholes so big I could drive a bus through them." Hiro got to his feet. "And I will take advantage of every single one as needed. Now, if you'll excuse me, I'm going to turn in as well." He looked at Taegan. "Feel free to hit me at your leisure. Kienan already did."

"I'm holding it in reserve." Taegan watched Hiro leave the dining room and remarked to no one in particular, "Am I the only one of us with an image in their mind of two bulls yanking different directions on the same rope without realizing they're on the same side?"

"No," his brothers and father decided.

Upstairs, Aenya indulged in a long bath. All the bedrooms in the house had their own bathroom, which was much to their advantage. She would hate to share a bathroom with one of her brothers. They were all meticulous in their organization, and she left stuff all over the counters.

Because there was no need to keep up the farce—she absolutely did *not* want to confront her lover if she was wearing that horrible nightgown—she instead opted to wear the prettiest pair of pajamas she owned. They were pale peach in color and made of soft, silky material. They hugged her body and flattered every curve.

As she picked up the potion to add some to Hiro's tea, her fingers shook. The trembling came from the inside out and could not be controlled. Cursing herself, she grabbed for her courage and added the potion to the tea. Then, bracing her shoulders, she picked up the tray.

He was waiting for her when she knocked lightly on the door. He opened it instantly and smiled when he saw the tray. His lover was nothing if not an incredibly strong woman. "Ah, a midnight snack." As she put the tray down, he realized what she was wearing. His body heated and tightened with greedy hunger. "Well."

"I couldn't bring myself to wear that ugly nightgown for you," she admitted.

"I'm going to tell you something." He tugged her into his arms and ran his hands up under the back of the shirt. "Even in it, I thought you were the sexiest woman alive." He lowered his head and nibbled along the line of her jaw. "Of course, I like you naked even more. Think I could seduce you into staying home tonight?"

Her knees went weak as heat rose swiftly. Shivering in delight, she tilted her head to give him better access. "It would delay the inevitable." She still didn't resist when his lips claimed hers. Her arms wound around his shoulders and she rose onto her toes to improve their fit. She loved how he kissed her. That alone was pure pleasure.

When they slowly drew apart, their eyes met. Unspoken words seemed to flow between them. She took a deep breath and released him to step back. Casually, she handed him his tea. "You're far too good at that."

He smiled at her. "I'll take that as a compliment." He gave a grimace and rubbed his jaw. There was barely any swelling from where Kienan had hit him but it still ached.

"I can grab you an icepack," she offered. "All the bathrooms have first aid kits."

"Thanks." The instant she had gone into the bathroom, he dumped out his tea and poured fresh. When she returned and handed him the pack, it looked as if nothing had changed. He held the pack to his chin with one hand and sipped his tea with the other. "Out of curiosity, what's your dance of preference?"

"That's a hard one." She considered things. "I've tried and trained in several styles but for the last few years I've really concentrated on Latin." She gave him a sheepish grin. "I always feel really sexy but don't you *dare* tell my brothers. They already have problems when they see me in class or performance."

"I'm surprised your father hasn't stopped you entirely." He added a yawn for punctuation.

"He loves me," she said simply. "He wouldn't take away dance from me entirely. He just doesn't want it to be more than a hobby." She covered a smile as she saw him starting to sway a little. "Maybe you should lay down, Hiro. I think you're coming down off the adrenaline of the match. I once saw Mel fall asleep into his dinner plate."

"I'm telling him you're blabbing his secrets." He obligingly lay down on his bed and turned on his side away from her. "I'm not looking at you," he murmured, deliberately slurring his words, "else I might pull you into this bed with me."

Her body clenched with heat and hunger and love. It was a deadly combination that nearly overrode her control. Somehow she held on long enough to hear him beginning to snore softly. Strangely, he hadn't snored when they had slept together. Maybe he was just conscious of bed partners. It was oddly endearing.

She took the tray back into her room and went into her closet. It was Masquerade Night at the Faerie Club. Because she felt defiant and miserable, she pulled out her sexiest dancing dress. It was deep rose with beads and lace, and the silk material clung to every curve of her body. It split to the hip on her right side and the material was very stretchy to accommodate anything she might do. The neckline plunged daringly in the front, and slender but strong straps held it up. The supportive bra that went underneath was nearly invisible, giving the impression she could fall out anytime.

Her mask was an elaborate confection of white and pink, something that covered the entirety of her face except for her lips and eyes. In the light of the Club, even her eyes would seem invisible. She artfully pinned and piled her hair up high, and only wore lipstick since the mask covered everything else.

She pulled on her shoes, fastened them tightly, and decided against jewelry. Even as she was hurrying down the passage toward her ride, she was still miserable. She didn't want to go to the Club alone. She wanted to go with Hiro. She had seen the way he moved and was suspicious he might know how to dance. If so, she *really* wanted to dance with him just once, even if she was better.

Her mood didn't improve when she reached the Club. There was a sign in the front that clearly said 'For Sale by Owner.' On a panicked sound, she rushed into the Club and to where the owner was tending bar. "Please, please, tell me it's not this bad!" she pleaded. "Grandma, please!"

The owner was in her seventies and had no one to inherit. Everyone called her Grandma, no matter who they were. Because she had no family, she had been slowly bowing under the pressure of running the place alone. "I'm sorry, honey," she said softly. "I can't manage the bills anymore. I'm getting too old. I'm praying to find a good buyer else we'll close entirely."

"Can't the Enforcers do anything?" Aenya felt desperate.

"When I spoke with Rhianna Taber, she said she had already tried something and could only wait for the results." Grandma sighed and looked around the room at all the people laughing and enjoying themselves as they attempted to identify each other behind masks. "The Faerie Club was built for people like you who have nowhere else to go. People who need to feel normal. If only I could afford decent advertising to bring in more people and a good manager to keep us running exactly as we are."

"I'll think of something," Aenya vowed. If she had to, she would get together a collection. There had to be *something* that could be done. She swung around to head for the dance floor and walked right into someone. "Oomph!" She looked up quickly to find herself staring at a tall man in a mask that covered his entire face. Something was . . . familiar about him, and it was a little intriguing to see that he wore an outfit that matched hers. "I'm sorry."

Hiro felt his stomach relax when she didn't recognize him. He had been intending to do his invisibility bit, but when he had gotten to the club, Stormy had been sitting outside with the mask and a bag of clothes. He was *seriously* beginning to suspect that wolf.

Because he was fairly sure Aenya would recognize his voice, he deliberately spoke in French. "My apologies as well, miss."

She didn't bat an eyelash. "Mutual apologies are the best," she answered, her accent and speech as fluent as his.

"I'm new here," he said as he took her elbow to escort her to a table. "I don't suppose you can tell me about this place."

She sighed and dropped down onto a bench. "The Faerie Club is a place for people like me who have dreams and want to live them. We come here to dance and talk anonymously, to forget that in real life most of us are for some reason or another pushed out of normal society.

"There are no drugs here. No alcohol. Everything that we eat here is healthy and the drinks are all fruit based. They have a papaya fizzy water that's to die for. It's a family place because kids come here too." She lowered her head and rested her cheek on her arms. "But because it's not mainstream, we can't pull as many people in as we need to stay afloat. Now they have to sell," she whispered. "If someone buys the club who doesn't understand . . . it'll all change."

So that was why. His heart ached for her and for all those present. They knew their dream would end and were driven to enjoy every minute they could. It made sense; Aenya was smart. She could have bided her time until she was twenty-one and then changed her career without her father's refusal. Taegan himself had done it successfully. Aenya had been so blatant, though, that everyone had known, and now she was trapped.

"What if someone you trusted bought the place?" he asked her softly.

Her laugh sounded sad. "Oh, I know someone who could afford it. In fact, it wouldn't even make a dent in his finances. But he doesn't want me to dance, and I don't want him to know about this place."

"It's a pity. I saw you last night and you were amazing. I'm a trained dancer myself, in fact." He stood and offered a hand to her as the music changed to something drugging and slow, an invitation for lovers to move together. "Dance with me."

It wasn't a request, but she found no will to refuse. Her hand slipped into his and she let him draw her down to the dance floor. Her body was already finding the rhythm of the dance, swaying with a seduction that transcended age and gender. Everyone watching was entranced.

As her partner turned her into the dance, she found herself trusting him implicitly and without question. He knew her body, and his touch was familiar. She closed her eyes, trusting him further, feeling as if she was falling into a dream. It was Hiro with her. Her soul and body knew it even when her eyes did not.

"Just dream," he murmured in her ear, and his voice was suddenly Hiro's voice. "And I'll dream with you."

They dominated the floor. Everyone else pulled back to give them plenty of room, not wanting to miss a moment. Aenya's eyes never opened but she never missed a step. Hiro was always there, handling her body with a gentleness that added to the romance and seduction of their dance.

When the music ended, there were no dry eyes in the club. Even the children were spellbound, watching with rapt adoration. They loved Aenya. Everyone knew it was her. No one danced like she did. Her partner was a mystery, and a stranger. Yet there was no question in anyone's mind that he loved the woman he had danced with.

Aenya opened her eyes slowly and turned around. Her partner was gone. Even her mind now insisted it was Hiro, but it made absolutely no sense. And if it wasn't Hiro, what was she supposed to do? She felt seduced by the dance and it felt as if she had betrayed Hiro. Yet, at the same time, it *had* to be Hiro because no one else knew her body so well. It was too confusing!

She pushed it off and away to the best of her ability. She lost herself in the rest of the night by dancing with some of her favorite people. Some were really good dancers. Others were really bad. She had fun with each and every one. She even joined in an energetic circle dance with a bunch of the kids.

As dawn was beginning to creep near, everyone was shocked to hear Grandma give a loud gasp. Everything came to a stop as they all turned to look at her. She was on the phone and talking excitedly, her hands waving in the air. When she hung up the phone, she promptly burst into tears.

One of the young men nearby helped her into a chair. Aenya hurried over and knelt beside the old patron that had given them all a home. "What's wrong?" she asked urgently. "Is something wrong?"

"No, no!" Grandma took a deep breath. "It's wonderful! We're saved! I just got off the phone with a businessman who saw the sign outside. He said he's been watching the Club for a few days now and he would hate to see it go under. He's going to pay off the debts and bring in a new manager to make sure the Club never changes."

A resounding cheer rose throughout the room. Aenya found herself grinning. "That's wonderful! Do you know who it was? We'd all love to thank him!"

"He didn't actually give me his name, but he said he would be coming by tomorrow morning with the check. We'll have the first dance tomorrow night in his honor." Grandma got to her feet. "Now then, all of you scat and go home. We'll never have to worry again."

Aenya floated almost the entire way home, giddy with happiness. She wouldn't have to dance all night anymore. She could go back to being more secretive and go for only a few hours each night. Her father wouldn't have to use the contract anymore because he would assume she had stopped.

Contract.

Hiro.

Pain exploded inside her chest as she stood in her bathroom getting ready for bed. The second night had ended, and Hiro would have to fulfill the terms of the contract in the morning. If he didn't, then he would have to disappear from her life forever.

At least she had the Faerie Club, she thought fiercely. At least she still had her dreams. Maybe her partner would come back and dance with her again. Maybe he could make her forget Hiro.

Even as she thought it, she knew it was hopeless. She would never forget Hiro. Her dreams were cold comfort when she looked at the long and lonely years ahead without the man she loved. Her hands went to her stomach. In that moment, she prayed with everything she was that the timing was wrong.

Trembling, she took her shoes and left them just inside Hiro's room. She then crawled into her bed and curled up. Stormy climbed up next to her, and Aenya hugged her tightly as she buried her face in her fur. And giving in to the pain, she cried herself to sleep. Why was life always so unfair?

CHAPTER SIX

Stormy woke Aenya a few hours later by nudging her insistently. At first, Aenya didn't want to wake, but then she became aware of the utter silence in the room beside hers. She scrambled out of bed and pulled on her robe. When she went into Hiro's room, it was empty. Every sign that he had been there was gone.

Heart pounding in her throat, she changed clothes as fast as she could, yanking on the first jeans and shirt to come to hand. Her door was unlocked once more, and she rushed downstairs toward her father's office. Hiro's suitcase was outside the door. She threw the door open without knocking.

Sullivan looked up and found a smile for her. "We were waiting for you. Have a seat, Aenya."

On rubbery legs, she walked over to the second chair and sat down. Hiro was sitting in the first and he wasn't looking at her. "So," she said as evenly as she could. "This is the third day."

"Yes, it is." Sullivan looked at Hiro. "You know the terms. And I can tell from these shoes that you did not stop her last night, either." It wasn't a question, for the shoes he referred to were sitting on his desk.

"No, I didn't." Hiro's voice was both calm and even.

"Do you know where my daughter dances every night?"

"Yes, I do." He didn't look at Aenya even when she leapt out of her chair in shock. "Twice now I have followed Aenya to a place known as the Faerie Club in the 3rd District."

Sullivan slowly rubbed his chin, not yet looking at his daughter. "I have not heard of it."

"No, I imagine not. It's a good place, sir. It's oriented toward

people of all ages and maintains a family atmosphere. While I was there, I did not hear a single objectionable song, unless you have something against polka. The drinks are all fruit based and there is no alcohol on site, nor are there drugs of any kind. I witnessed no fights, no bad language. It was like a dream come true for parents, honestly. I wish I had found it myself and sooner. Aenya dances there and rules the floor. I've never seen anyone better." He did look at her then and saw the soundless fall of tears down her cheeks. "She lives her dream there."

Sullivan studied his daughter. "Is this true, Aenya?"

She closed her eyes and nodded tightly. "It is." She opened her eyes, her lips trembling. "I've been dancing there for almost two years; you just didn't know until recently. The Club was in danger of closing and we were all so desperate to spend every minute there we could. It's a wonderful place, Daddy, I swear. Please . . . please don't make me stop going!"

"It's no longer my business," he said quietly. "Hiro has fulfilled the terms of the contract. You will be his wife."

"No!" She shook her head furiously. "I won't marry a man who does not love me!"

"Aenya, the contract is binding and I am your legal guardian. You like Hiro. You gave yourself to him," he added in a hard tone. When his daughter's eyes flared with shock, he nodded curtly. "Did you think I wouldn't know?"

"I hoped you wouldn't." She straightened her back, her eyes fixed on the wall across from her. "I hope you're happy, Hiro. You've got the rich bride you wanted. And obviously if you wanted to stop me from dancing, you can. I didn't fool you at all."

Hiro got to his feet. "I don't want to stop you from dancing. Do I look like that much of a bastard? I *saw* you. I *saw* how much you love to dance." He took her hand and placed a slip of paper in it. When she looked at it, he said quietly, "The Faerie Club is yours, Aenya. This check will pay off its debts, and you will be its new owner. You will be its new manager, and I know you'll keep it alive. You can dance as much as you want. And . . . ." He looked at Sullivan. "As per the stipulations in the contract, having fulfilled its terms, I am free to reject the reward. I am doing so. Aenya may make her own decisions about her life. She can marry whomever she wants and go wherever she wants."

Aenya was staring at the check in such shock that she didn't hear him leave until the door shut behind him. She looked up sharply and took a step toward the door. Her hand tightened around the check. "Why?" she whispered. "You were so sure this was what you wanted."

"He never wanted the shares, Aenya," Sullivan said quietly. "He wanted you. It was only after he saw you that he signed the contract. Last night, he told me and your brothers that we could burn the shares for all he cared. This morning, he told me that he knew you'd never believe him if he told you he loves you. You've been so badly burned by this whole ordeal. But he does love you, baby. I know he does."

"He never told me!" Her breath hitched as she held the check against her heart. "I wanted him to love me so badly . . . I would have believed him."

"Did you tell him that?" He got to his feet. "Unless you go to him, Aenya, you'll never see him again. Kienan told me that Hiro has put his condo up for sale. He's making arrangements to leave the city entirely."

A horn honked outside the window and she looked over in surprise to see Kienan on his motorcycle. "Hey!" he called through the open window. "I know where he's heading! Let's go drop off your check then track him down!" When she hesitated, he snapped, "I'm not letting my hard work go to waste! You need to grow up, Aenya! What good is a dream if you don't fight for it? You fought for your dancing. Now fight for Hiro!"

She whirled and ran from the room. She stopped only long enough to yank on sneakers and rushed outside to where he was waiting. She stuffed the check in her pocket and pulled on her helmet. She climbed onto the bike behind him and grabbed his waist. "Hurry!"

"You got it!" He took off quickly and proceeded to cut through traffic as he headed for the 3rd District. "You know," he called over his shoulder, "I was sure you were going to completely mess everything up."

"What do you mean?" she called back.

"I hired Hiro. I'm the one who told him to come and take a shot at the contract. I was pretty certain that he would fall for you once he met you, and vice versa." He winced as she hit the back of his helmet. "Ow!"

"You jerk!" she shouted. "I wouldn't have worried so much if all of you had been more honest with me!"

"And like you were honest with us!" He winced as she hit him again. "I knew that Hiro was well off. He inherited a serious chunk of change from his grandfather. He doesn't need any part of our company, kid. He only wanted you."

"I have to admit, I'm not entirely surprised." She thought about his condo and motorcycle. Few private investigators could have afforded both. Both were also owned outright and that meant he had paid cash. "I hope it's not too late."

The Faerie Club was quiet at that time of morning. She hurried around to the back where Grandma had a small apartment attached to the club. Most people in 3rd District lived in places attached to their place of work. Grandma cried when she got the check, and Aenya didn't blame her. "I didn't know last night," Aenya admitted. "I didn't know that someone would buy the Club for me. I promise I'm going to make you proud!"

"I have no doubt in you." Grandma waved a hand. "Come in and talk."

"I can't," she apologized. "I have to go find someone."

"Your partner from last night? He's in the Club. He came by a little while ago and asked if he could say goodbye. I guess he's on his way back home."

She frowned. "You speak French?"

"He spoke English with me."

Warning bells went off in her mind. "I think I had better go have a word with him." She turned to go back to the front of the Club, and, no surprise, Kienan was nowhere in sight. Eyes narrowed slightly, she went into the Club. A man in a mask sat studying the dance pit with his back to her. Gee, interestingly, his hair was black.

"So," she asked in French, "you speak English?"

"I speak many languages," he countered in the same without turning. "I hear you're no longer engaged."

"Funny." She walked closer, arms crossed. She switched to English on purpose. "I don't recall anyone here knowing I was engaged. But as it happens, you're right. It's only temporary, though. I'm going to chase my former fiancé down. He's an idiot."

"He seems to think so, too." Hiro got to his feet and turned around. He pulled the mask off and dropped it on a table. There was a darkening bruise on his jaw, and his eyes were haunted, but his stride was deliberate as he walked toward her. She held her ground and he caged her against a table. "Why are you chasing after your idiot fiancé?"

She closed her eyes. "I decided I wanted to ask my last question. We made a promise, you see." When he cursed and paced away, she opened her eyes. "We promised that if I didn't ask anything you wouldn't want to answer, you would answer me truthfully."

"Yes, we did." Impatience gnawed at him. He had laid it all on the line and she wanted to ask him a stupid question. "So ask," he shot at her.

Very quietly, she asked, "Why did you sign the contract, Hiro?"

He went very still and slowly turned around. Understanding had filled her honey eyes. She already knew the answer, and she was giving him the chance to tell her. She would believe him. He slowly walked toward her, longing for her with every fiber of his being. "Because I loved you the moment I laid eyes on you. A dancing princess. I was helpless against you."

Tears slid down her cheeks. "Then don't go away," she whispered. "Stay with me. Screw the contract. I love you, Hiro. So much so it's been destroying me. You gave me my dream and it means nothing without you."

On a low sound of need, he snatched her into his arms and held

her fiercely. "Thank god," he muttered over and over again, his lips rushing over her face, memorizing her with painful hunger. "I was doing everything I could to make you trust me. To make you love me. When you asked me to be your first, I was praying it would help bind you to me. But you seemed so practical!"

Her laugh was almost a hiccupping sob. "Practical? I was desperate!" She took a deep breath, her hands running compulsively over his arms, needing to feel him close. "I'm not on birth control."

"I know." His voice had roughened. "Timing?"

"Poor, but I was praying." Her lips trembled. "I realized it last night. I'd run away if I found I was pregnant. Then I'd find you and make you stay with me until you loved me."

"Too late. I'm already mad with loving you." He shot her a dirty look. "You are never allowed to dance like that with any man but me, by the way. I will very happily be your partner for any future dances that involve scraps of silk and lace and highly seductive music."

"Yes, as to that." She eyed him. "How did you follow me? I can assume you knew about the potion and avoided it. But how did you follow me without my seeing you?"

"Like this." He took a step back from her and picked up the material he had dropped near his suitcase. He twirled it like a matador, then said, "Now you see me," and pulled the cloak over his body. "Now you don't!"

She rubbed her eyes, stunned. He had completely disappeared right before her eyes. She warily took a step forward and shrieked as she was unceremoniously caught around the waist and tumbled onto the floor. "Hiro!" The yelp turned to laughter as he tucked her underneath him. "Okay, when'd you learn to dance?"

He pulled off the cloak and tossed it over the railing out of sight. "I've been training most of my life," he confessed. "I didn't tell you because I didn't want you to think I was using dance to get to you."

"It's an absolute waste of your talents," she decided. "You need to give up being a private investigator—or at least the dangerous parts—and help me win lots of competitions that will produce much publicity for my Club so that it never worries for patrons."

"I need a better offer than that. And I recall we aren't engaged anymore."

"Then ask me to marry you. Or I can ask you. I'd get on my knees but I seem to be pinned to a dance floor."

"You look very lovely on a dance floor in any fashion." He lowered his head until their lips were a breath apart. "Will you marry me, Aenya Shaughnessy? Will you be my partner in life and in dance? Help me raise bunches of tiny terrors to drive your father and brothers crazy with?"

"Yes, Hiro Michaels. I will." As he kissed her, she started to frame his face with her hands, but he sucked in a breath and reminded her that he had a bruise on his jaw. "Oh, I'm sorry!" She blinked and squinted at the mark. "What happened? You didn't have that this morning."

"Taegan slugged me for walking out," he muttered. "I should have believed you about the hitting when angry thing. I've been hit or nearly hit by all of you Shaughnessy siblings except Mel."

"When did Kienan . . ." Her voice trailed off and she rolled her eyes with a smile. "A bee sting. Sure. No more fighting with my brothers, got it?"

"Not even at the bachelor party, before the strippers arrive?"

"No! Pervert. No strippers."

"You're going to be a demanding wife, aren't you?"

"Yeah. Scared yet?"

"Shaking in my boots." He smiled and kissed her again lingeringly. Demanding or not, she was absolutely perfect for him in every way. Everything had worked out exactly as it was meant.

Back at the Shaughnessy house, Sullivan was still at his desk staring at the contract in front of him when it suddenly glowed and the word 'Complete' appeared on the top. Grinning, lightheaded with

relief, he folded it and handed it to Stormy who was sitting beside his desk. "Return it with my regards."

Like a gleeful cherub, he got to his feet and hurried to the door to call for his housekeeper. He had a wedding to organize! He couldn't wait to see his daughter dancing at her wedding. She had always taken his breath away. He couldn't be any prouder of her.

CHAPTER SEVEN

The red haired woman looked up at the knock on her door and smiled when she saw who was entering. On a chair next to her was a neatly folded swath of burlap. "Ah, there you are," she said. "Got something for me?"

She swiveled around on her chair and took the contract that Stormy held out to her. She opened it and smiled in satisfaction. "Beautiful." She scrawled her notes across the bottom, and then tucked it into the open folder on her desk. As she closed it, it also reflected the word 'Complete' and she slid it into a drawer that said 'Shaughnessy' on it. There were close to one hundred files in there already.

"Only three left, isn't it now?" She reached for a blank contract on her desk. "Let's get to work, shall we? Oh, and remind me to send a nice wedding gift with you. I have some music that they're bound to simply love."

Status: File In Progress
Analysis: To catch a dancing princess, you only need to know the right steps.

Folder Two
KIENAN

CHAPTER EIGHT

The fighting and cursing could be heard from across the house. In fact, it was probably heard from the street even though the house was set back from it by a large driveway and vast front garden.

Hiro was walking past the front door of his future father-in-law's office when he saw his fiancée suddenly rush out the door, slam it, and lean back against it. Her cheeks were flaming red. He coughed. If there was anything he had gotten used to in the week he had resided in the Shaughnessy household, it was that the family did everything loud and large.

"Bad morning?" he offered.

She glowered at him. "*You* go in there and try to be a mediator. Kienan's either going to blow a fuse or Daddy's going to have a heart attack." She blew out a hard breath that stirred her pale bangs. "I need a distraction. Distract me please."

He smiled and swung an arm around her shoulders to escort her away from the door. He wasn't stupid enough to go in there when he could hear both Shaughnessy males shouting. "Gladly."

Inside the office, Kienan leaned across the desk to get in his father's face. He had never been one to back away from a fight. "You're being unreasonable, Dad!"

"Unreasonable!" Sullivan leaned equally across the table so he was eye to eye with his son. "Just because I don't want my children to throw their lives away, I'm unreasonable!"

"You let Taegan do what he wanted!"

"That's because he didn't tell me his plans until he was twenty-one! Damn it!" Sullivan sat back in his chair. First Aenya, now Kienan. Thank *god* Mel was both of legal age and levelheaded.

Kienan's chocolate eyes were tinted slightly red, evidence of his flying temper. Though no red hair marked the Shaughnessy bloodline, their tempers were pure, one hundred percent Irish. "I'm tired of pretending to care about my linguistic studies! I just want a *chance*! You're letting Aenya have a chance!"

"Ha! There was no letting involved on my part! She's Hiro's problem now, and I have every confidence he can catch her if she falls." Sullivan raked his hands through his hair. Why the hell did his kids have to be so much like him? They dreamed big and chased those dreams with all their soul.

As Kienan dropped back down into his chair, Sullivan contemplated the slender wolf sitting beside him. Stormy had been with the family longer than he remembered. In fact, he was fairly sure she had been there before even he was born, and he was climbing into his sixties with every day. Whenever she decided to attach to someone in their family, they rose up and fought harder for their dreams. There was more as well, but he was wary to examine it too closely until he was more certain. It was, to say the least, a very odd situation.

It had been a nice and normal morning until Kienan had walked in and dropped his bombshell. He had plopped down into one of the chairs and announced he was changing his major from Linguistics to Music Composition and Performance.

Sullivan didn't doubt his son's talent. Kienan had an amazing voice and a brilliant talent with most any instrument he chose to pick up. In fact, everyone in the family had some sort of musical skill. Aenya was a dancer, of course. Mel could play on a piano any piece of music after hearing it once. Taegan played several instruments.

However, Sullivan wanted his children to be able to support themselves. God only knew that they refused to accept anything more than an allowance from him, but even Kienan was the only one still receiving that. Taegan had his pay as a teacher. Aenya now received money from the club she owned. Mel drew a paycheck from the Shaughnessy Corp. where he was already working.

Aware that Kienan was watching him, he rubbed his forehead.

"Why can't you just get hired at Aenya's club? You could do it as a side job, and then have a regular job to support yourself."

"For one thing, I don't want to work for my sister. I love her, but she's a Shaughnessy, too. She's just as good a businesswoman as you and Mel are businessmen. We'd kill each other. And anyway, I want more. I want to have the world hear my voice."

"It's a hard world to break into," his father warned him. "It's even more stressful than my company. I just want to make sure you're taken care of, and, damn it, I'm still your guardian for almost another full year."

"Was that a general curse or just 'cause you're tired of me?"

"Both, you brat."

They glared at each other, then the younger grinned cheekily. "I'm adorable, and you love me, Dad. You're just a pain in the ass."

"My son takes after me," Sullivan retorted. He found himself thankfully diverted by his phone ringing and Stormy pawing at the drawer beside him. He picked up the phone when he recognized the number on Caller ID. "Shaughnessy." There was a long silence as he listened to whoever was on the other end of the line. He looked down and opened the drawer Stormy was pawing at.

Stormy walked back over to Kienan, and he bent down to scratch her head. Ever since Aenya had gotten engaged to Hiro, Stormy had been hanging around Kienan more. Not that he minded. He had always liked the family wolf. She had always seemed like a big sister or parental unit when he was kid. He even had a vivid memory of her carrying him by the seat of his pants to keep him out of the pond when he was two.

Sullivan was still listening to whoever was on the phone. He was reading over the papers he had pulled out, and he had even put his glasses on. That meant he was serious. Kienan idly leaned back so his chair was on two legs and propped his feet on the edge of the desk. He didn't mind if business interrupted the argument. His dad kicked ass in the corporate world.

"Since everything went so well before," Sullivan finally said, "I will trust your judgment yet again, Ms. Taber. Do I want to know how

you arrange all of these things?" He listened, then laughed. "No, I didn't think I did. Good day." He hung up the phone and pulled his glasses off with a sigh. "Alright, Kien. I want to make a deal with you."

"'sup?"

"If you're willing to dedicate a weekend to music and come up with one original song with sale potential, I will help you arrange a chance to sell it."

Kienan fell out of his chair with a thump. "Ouch!" Stormy promptly began licking his face and he sputtered and shoved at her. "Damn dog! Let me up!" She obligingly moved and he flipped gracefully to his feet, his martial arts training long ingrained after many years. "Thanks for the shock, Dad."

"You're welcome." Sullivan slid the contract across the desk as Kienan righted his chair. "Here. If you're worried I'll renege, it's all here in print. Read it for yourself."

Kienan didn't have Mel's vanity; he didn't mind wearing reading glasses. All the men in the family wore them. He pulled them out of his pocket and stuck them on his nose as he sat down. He picked up the contract and began to read.

He was, in his heart, his father's son. It didn't take long for him to skim over the details. The contract was oddly clear of the legalese that was common in the business world. It stated, rather plainly, that he would be given a full weekend to concentrate solely on music. Should he return with a song with sale potential, to be determined by an independent party, then Sullivan's contacts within the Enforcers would arrange said sale. The Enforcers were possibly one of the biggest companies in America. It didn't surprise Kienan that they would have music contacts.

In fact, there was only one thing that puzzled him at all. He dropped the contract to tap a finger on the last line. "Here. 'This contract is considered complete only on the basis of the signee's dreams coming true. If they do not find what they are seeking, this contract is considered null and void.' That's a bit vague, isn't it?"

"It's in all Enforcers' contracts. It was, in fact, in your sister's contract as well." Sullivan tugged the contract back and twirled it around so he could see it. "Lodgings have already been arranged for you since it is very difficult to find a place with the correct atmosphere for an artist of any type. As such, you will be staying at an inn within the 3rd District. The Enforcers know the owner and have booked the entire place for the weekend. It will be just you and the innkeeper."

Kienan frowned and crossed his arms. "I'm getting a really good deal here. Where's the catch? There's always a catch."

"Not this time." Sullivan sighed. "Kienan, I don't want to demolish your dreams. I just want to be certain you are provided for. If that means I go to some very strange extremes, then so be it."

"Strange is the understatement of the year," he muttered.

"It's not as easy as it sounds," his father warned him. "You have to come back with a unique, sellable, song. Otherwise you have to continue with your Linguistics studies." Kienan was fluent in nearly ten languages and had been headed toward a job as a translator with the Shaughnessy Corp. They had worldwide contacts.

As he watched Sullivan sign the contract, Kienan drummed his fingers on his arm. "So, in other words, I put a gamble on this weekend. I risk it all for a chance at my dreams. Hell, it's more of a deal than Aenya got. She never even had a choice. And yet all that went well, so I guess it's not such a raw deal. What the hell. Gimme a pen."

While he scrawled his name across the bottom of the contract, Sullivan spotted a strangely satisfied look on Stormy's face. It made him wonder just what his son would really be finding at the Gentle Brook Inn. That he would find his dreams was a given. It was just a question of whether his dreams would be the same when he left as when he arrived.

Dreams could, after all, change very quickly.

CHAPTER NINE

Taegan stood in the doorway of his baby brother's room and watched with a slightly lifted brow as Kienan packed a suitcase. The facts were slim at the moment. All he knew was that Kienan had come out of the office with a glint in his eye and a determined stride.

He had always known Kienan was a musical time bomb and had, in fact, expected an explosion much sooner. That Kienan had waited this long was the impressive part. Then again, after the events with Aenya, perhaps he felt he had a chance. Taegan propped a shoulder against the door and asked, "What's the story?"

"Dad offered me a deal." Kienan straightened up with a shirt over his shoulder. "He offered me a contract, which is more than he did for Aenya. I accepted the offer, so I'm off for a weekend to concentrate on my music."

Taegan walked over to sit on the bed and Stormy jumped up next to him. He gently ruffled her fur and companionably kept a hand on her back. She was too alone sometimes. She needed family as badly the Shaughnessys did. "Where's the catch, Kien? Father wouldn't just give in like this. You know how stubborn he is. You should have just waited a year."

"I have to take the chance *now*, Taegan." He looked at the guitar case leaning against the wall. "Somehow, I'm absolutely certain that if I don't take a chance now, I'll miss out on something that could define my life and give me everything I ever wanted." On a sigh, he shut the suitcase. "The basic deal is that I go away for a weekend to concentrate. If I come back with a sellable song, I get my chance. If I don't, I continue on as I am."

"That's risky, Kien." Taegan frowned slightly. "Doesn't that mean that even when you're twenty-one, you'll have to continue Linguistics? You wouldn't be able to take another chance just because you're an official adult."

"Yeah. But I'm going to try."

"You've never composed a song in a weekend before," his older brother noted softly.

"I've never tried. If I get the right inspiration, I can do anything. When I come home, I'm going to have one of the greatest songs you've ever heard."

Taegan was silent for long moments, his eyes lingering on Stormy, then he smiled and got to his feet. "I'm looking forward to it. If you make it a love song, we can convince Aenya to let you sing at her wedding."

"Wouldn't take much convincing." He smiled ruefully. "I think I've already been blackmailed into it. And is it weird to be the bride's brother *and* the groom's best man?"

Taegan laughed. "Not around here." He ruffled first Stormy's fur, then Kienan's hair. "Take the sidecar and bring Stormy along. She'll be good company."

"If she wants to go." Kienan smiled at her. "Want to go?" She wagged her tail happily and he laughed. "I figured. C'mon, girl. Let's get going. You'll like riding by motorcycle. It's the kind of thing I think you'll appreciate."

With the wolf at his heels, he headed downstairs and out to the large garage where all the vehicles were kept. He, Taegan, and Hiro owned motorcycles. Sullivan had a sleek little hybrid. Mel had a restored 1970 Mustang that he doted on. Aenya didn't have a car yet, but she was contemplating a motorcycle too. Kienan grinned. He loved his sister.

There was one sidecar that everyone with a bike shared. He attached it and stuck his suitcase in. Stormy jumped in as well and he made sure she was securely fastened in.

As he was looking at the map to Gentle Brook Inn, Aenya suddenly came running into the garage. She skidded to a stop and smiled. "Don't forget to say hi for me."

He blinked, then remembered. "Oh, yeah. One of your friends works at the inn I'm going to. I forgot about that. If she's there, sure, I'll say hi. Her name is Evelyn right?"

"Madelyne!" She poked him in the chest. "She's wary of handsome men, so be nice to her, got it?" She frowned when he leaned over to kiss her forehead. She knew he would never do anything to deliberately hurt anyone, let alone a woman, but she absolutely felt as if the warning was important. "Promise me."

"Of course I promise." He pulled on his helmet. "See you on Sunday afternoon." When she had moved, he fired up his bike and backed down the driveway. Once on the street, he took off for the familiar roads leading to the 3rd District. He had been there several times lately, mostly to visit Aenya's club. He liked it there as much as she did. In many ways, he wasn't surprised that it was where he was being sent for the weekend.

The District was mostly small businesses. The people who worked there also lived there, with very few exceptions. Most businesses were attached to apartments or small houses where the owners lived. There was a very small residential area, but it was mostly run down. Deliberately, he thought, to keep outsiders from hustling in. He was fairly sure a computer teacher from college lived there.

The Gentle Brook Inn was less than four blocks from the Faerie Club. The Inn was a popular resort location due to the fact that it possessed at least three different hot springs, all naturally fed from a brook that ran beside the inn. The brook was from an underground vein; it had never run dry.

Bamboo trees and ferns of all shapes and sizes lined the front of the inn, and the walkway was covered in a riot of flowers blooming in every color. There were flowers that he was certain he had never heard of, let alone seen, before. There was a gentle, relaxing feel to the inn and he felt the tension in his shoulders disappear without his having really known it was there to begin with.

He spotted a small parking lot and rode slowly over to park. As he was pulling his suitcase out of the sidecar, he heard Stormy give a happy bark and take off running toward the inn. There came a startled feminine yelp that almost immediately turned to a laugh, and the woman said, "Easy, girl! Down now!"

His stomach quivered with a sudden and shocking longing. Sheer heat seemed to surge in his veins and every nerve in his body revved at the same time. In bemused understanding, he stood there and realized he was attracted to the owner of the voice. It was a little puzzling. Oh, the voice was powerful and beautiful, but he had never before encountered such a ferocious lust before, and certainly not just because of a *voice*.

More than a little intrigued, he turned around to see who or what Stormy had found. When his eyes fell on the young woman with Stormy, he felt the ground move under his feet even as his heart began to beat harder. It was the last thing he would have expected to happen for the young woman was potentially the plainest girl he had ever seen in his life.

Her hair was dove gray and pinned up on her head in a thick coil of braids. Her eyes were slightly tilted at the corner but not enough to be considered exotic. The color was of violets just starting to open, neither rich nor blushing.

She stood at slightly taller than average height with a slender frame, but there was nothing extremely spectacular about her figure either. Her legs were only a little longer than normal, and her hands were graceful. There was nothing about her that was designed to inspire lust or attraction in the general populace.

And yet, he realized in fascination as he walked toward her slowly, he was enthralled. Attracted. The hard fist of lust had punched in and left him with the most powerful urge to taste her smiling lips and feel her soft-looking skin. More still, his heart ached even harder. Lust was really longing and the longing was as emotional as physical.

The birds hadn't stopped singing and the sun still shined, but he felt cushioned in a pocket that only contained the two of them. He had known beautiful women. He'd had one or two for a lover. He couldn't remember their faces anymore. They had been wiped from his mind for all time by this plain nightingale in an old-fashioned gray dress.

"Welcome to the Gentle Brook Inn." She held out a hand. "I'm Madelyne Winters, the owner and keeper." As he continued to stare at her with a fascinated look on his face, she blinked in bemusement. Most people, men in particular, passed right over her. "Mr. Shaughnessy?"

He shook his head quickly. "Sorry. I was off somewhere." He took her hand and was delighted with her firm handshake. He was also fascinated by her soft skin. It felt like down feathers. "It's nice to meet you, Madelyne. I'm Kienan." The name registered finally. "Oh! *You're* Madelyne! Aenya told me to tell you hi." His eyes sparkled merrily. "Hi."

Aenya was going to burn in hell. Madelyne was going to kill her friend when she saw her next, because she had neglected to mention that Kienan was by far the most beautiful of her brothers. Madelyne had seen Mel in passing at college and she was currently in one of Taegan's classes. Kienan smoked them both.

Men that gorgeous should have had sirens go off when they were near helpless females. He was the shortest Shaughnessy brother, but that didn't make him short. He was barely shy of six feet tall with a strong and muscular body designed to inspire feminine heatstroke. He moved with predatory grace like a large cat, light and agile on his feet. His golden brown hair flopped into his chocolaty brown eyes. They were an artist's eyes, full of dreams and visions.

And she was hopelessly outmatched. She always was when faced with beauty, especially men. She slipped her hand free of his and retreated into professional mode. "The Gentle Brook Inn is yours for the weekend, Mr. Shaughnessy," she told him as she walked inside. "We have four hot springs, two for each gender. Unfortunately, the men's springs are currently broken as the heater decided to fall apart right before winter. You can still go into the spring, but it'll be a smidge cold. Your room is on the first floor, second on the left down this first hall."

She even walked like a lady. He followed her but didn't really listen to her words. All he could hear was the beautiful, melodic sound

of her voice and it danced over his skin like invisible fingers. He really didn't need the encouragement. Though the dress muffled her figure, his deft eye suspected she had some very lovely, if subtle, curves under her unflattering clothes. He had never been interested in overly curvy girls anyway.

She started to turn, and he hastily lifted his gaze to smile. "I guess this is a little unusual. Having just one guest. I hope you're being fully reimbursed."

"Oh of course. The Enforcers look after me very closely. And anyway, one or one hundred, I treat all guests the same." She smiled as she handed him his key. "Dinner is at six, but if you're hungry at other times, you can ring the bell. Small my inn may be, but we assuredly have room service."

"Even at midnight?" he teased.

Laughter filled her eyes and took his breath. "Yes, even then. I'm mostly nocturnal." She turned her gaze toward the window where the morning sun was streaming in. "I follow the nightingale's path."

"Nightingale?" He glanced up from signing the register. "What nightingale?"

"It's one of the many legends of the 3rd District." She knelt and ran a hand over Stormy's head. "Do you believe in legends, Mr. Shaughnessy?"

"It's Kienan. My father is Mr. Shaughnessy." He leaned against the counter and cocked his head slightly. "I suppose I do," he finally said. "I don't dismiss them out of hand but I always think they need to be taken with a grain of salt."

"A wise attitude to have, Kienan." She glanced up at him, her violet eyes bottomless with mysteries and secrets. "Especially around this area of town. We all protect our legends."

"Tell me about the nightingale then," he offered. When she tilted her head slightly, he smiled and reached out a hand to help her up. "Your voice is beautiful. I like hearing you talk. So, talk to me. Keep me company while I unpack."

"If you like." She fell into step beside him as they went down the hall, Stormy padding by her ankle companionably. "The

nightingale's legend is a sad one, as most are. Once, a long, long time ago, a swan fell in love with a human. In order to become human himself, he needed to sacrifice something great. So he gave up his beauty and was turned human. His love, however, was afraid of him.

"One night as he sat lamenting his sorrow, a small bird hopped into his lap. It was a plain, very ordinary bird. The human was going to turn her away, but she offered to help him win his love if only he would offer her a home. He decided that it couldn't hurt to accept such a deal and agreed. To his amazement, the little bird began to sing.

"The nightingale, you see, is a bird whose only beauty comes from its voice. In the dark of the night, when it sings, you forget how plain it is. Needless to say the man won his ladylove and his beauty was restored. The nightingale asked to be granted her home; none else would have her for she was so plain.

"The man refused. Now that he had his lover and his beauty, he did not want such a plain little bird hanging around. He turned her away, telling her that only when she was beautiful would he ever allow her entry into his home." She fell silent for a moment, aware Kienan was listening avidly. She continued softly, "After a while the man felt guilty and decided to seek the nightingale out. He found her wounded in a forest, pierced by a hunter's arrow which had been aiming for another swan.

"As she died, she told him she did not blame him for his ways. He blamed himself instead, and in his grief, he built a curse upon them both. Only when the nightingale finds herself a home will he be free. They say that at night, the nightingale can be heard singing her songs of sadness, always seeking the home she cannot have. Sometimes, too, you can hear the hunter who has always cursed the little bird that kept him from his prize."

Kienan's breath unraveled. There was a painful hitch inside his chest as if he had experienced every pain the characters in the tale had. "Maddie, have you ever considered a career as a storyteller or bard or something?"

The nickname briefly startled her. She brushed it off with a laugh and decided to accept it. He was obviously an informal type of man. "I'll take that as a compliment." She walked over to the window in the room and opened it to let in sunshine and fresh air. She took a deep breath and turned around. "The nightingale can be heard singing near here every night, you know. Maybe you'll hear her."

"Have you ever looked for her?" He watched her intently, memorizing her face. There was . . . just something about her. Something he couldn't get out of his mind. Every minute in her company made him want her more. Need her more. He was beginning to think he needed her more than he needed air.

"No, she likes her privacy as much as I do." Her mouth went dry as she saw the way he watched her intently. She had never been stared at like that before, as if she was absolutely vital to someone. Unnerved, she took a little step back. Red color climbed her cheeks. "Is something wrong?"

"No, actually." He walked slowly toward her, not wanting to frighten her. Aenya's warning rang in his head. Not to his surprise, Madelyne backed up until she bumped into the wall. He moved even closer and placed a hand on the wall to keep her trapped. Instinctively, he turned so that his body cut off everything around her. "There's nothing wrong. I just have this odd situation."

She had to clear her throat to find her voice. He smelled like wild, wicked danger and the promise of happily ever after. "And that is?" Her voice belied her feelings, sounding huskier and longing. The ferocious desire for him was, to say the least, a problem.

"I'm attracted to you, and I don't even know why." Her eyes widened with shock and her mouth fell open. He grinned. "It struck me that way too, actually. But I've decided to go with the flow. I just figured I ought to warn you since I'm going to spend an inordinate amount of time staring at you."

"Don't joke around!" She pushed him aside and ducked toward the door. Her heart raced furiously in her chest and there was a pain underneath. "Men like you don't want women like me. I don't appreciate the joke, Mr. Shaughnessy!"

"My name is Kienan." He linked his hands behind his head in the picture of casualness, but his body tensed slightly like a tiger ready to pounce. Something wild shifted in his artist eyes. "You better use it instead of my last name."

"Why?"

"Because otherwise I'll do something drastic." His smile turned slow, wicked, and outrageously beautiful. It was the smile that marked all Shaughnessy men, and he used it deliberately as a way to catch the woman he wanted.

Her color rose as her entire body flushed with heat. A smile like that made a woman feel as if she had just been stroked in every sensitive place on her body. "Drastic?" Her voice came out nearly breathless despite her best efforts. "Like what?"

His smile turned into a masculine challenge. "Why don't you call me by my last name and find out?"

She gave in to the coward's urge and fled the room so fast that the door slammed behind her. Her entire world had just flipped inside out and she felt like Alice falling down the rabbit hole. Hearing him clucking his tongue at her softly wasn't enough to make her dare going back into the room.

Her eyes fell on Stormy at the end of the hall. The wolf's eyes seemed guileless, but her tail wagged happily. Madelyne's eyes narrowed. "I absolutely hate you." She turned on her heel and stalked away down the hall, her skirts swishing around her ankles. She wasn't surprised when Stormy followed her with a little smirk on her face. Nothing fazed her.

Kienan gave Madelyne plenty of room; he knew he had made his point well enough. She needed room to breathe and he gave it to her. Instead, he stayed in his room and fiddled with his guitar. There was a melody in the back of his mind. Snippets of words flashed through his thoughts but wouldn't form lyrics. Nothing could seem to make it to his fingers to be captured. In frustration, he launched into a rousing rendition of Yankee Doodle.

Laughter made him look up in surprise to see Madelyne standing in the doorway. Her eyes sparkled merrily. Politely she said, "Dinner is ready, but if you'd rather keep playing, please do. I could make you some macaroni."

"Oh, be quiet!" he groused as he got to his feet. He put the guitar aside and followed her as she headed toward the dining room. As if he wasn't hungry for all knowledge about her that he could have, he asked casually, "How old are you, Maddie? You seem a bit young to be an innkeeper."

"I'm nineteen," she offered. "I go to the same college as you." She gestured him in to the dining room.

As he sat down, he considered her words. "I never noticed you before."

"Most don't." There was no sadness in her voice. Just a simple acceptance of the truth. She put a plate in front of him, and then headed for the door to the kitchen. She felt his curious gaze and smiled over her shoulder. "You're a guest, Kienan. I don't eat with the guests."

He contemplated the door as it shut behind her. Unless he was mistaken—and he highly doubted he was—this was a woman in some serious need of TLC. Her loneliness was practically visible, and his reliable sixth sense told him that she had become so used to rejection that it was automatic to assume more. It appalled him to think that so many would judge on basis of appearance. Her warm and open personality should have drawn droves of people. Even if he hadn't been attracted to her, he would have liked her and wanted to be her friend.

And she really wasn't that plain. Every time he looked at her, she somehow got more and more lovely. Whether it was because her very plainness was appealing or because her personality was shining through, he didn't know. Frankly, if beauty was measured by a person's heart, she would be exquisite.

Decision made, he picked up his plate and went into the kitchen.

She was in the process of wiping down a counter and looked at him in surprise. "Is something wrong? Too much garlic in the sauce?"

"It smells *amazing*," he told her sincerely. Then he lied without compunction, "I'm used to eating dinner with lots of people. I figured I'd eat in here with you. Besides, you're good company." He sat down at the counter across from her and scooped up a big bite of pasta. As the flavor exploded on his tongue, his eyes nearly rolled back. "Holy jumping Christ on a motorcycle." He stared at his plate. "Promise you'll marry me and cook for me, please?"

A giggle escaped before she could stop it. "You're so different, Kienan. But it's in a good way." She leaned on the counter and watched him with a smile. "You and your sister have much in common."

"She's an incorrigible brat," he said around a mouthful.

Her eyes danced. "Well . . ."

He nearly choked, then began to laugh. "You're terrible!" Content with her humor, for it was much like his own, he looked around the kitchen. It was a gourmet chef's dream, but there was only one apron hanging from the hooks. There was no sign that anyone other than Madelyne lived or worked there. "May I ask what happened to your parents? I mean, obviously you're alone here."

"They were killed when I was ten. Some psycho was high on something and decided he wanted to rid 3rd District of its witches. Among the casualties were my parents. A few others lost family members that day as well." She ran a hand over the stainless steel countertop. "I thought I'd have to move and be adopted, but the Enforcers bought the inn and said that because they knew I wanted it, they wanted me to have it." She smiled suddenly. "Rhianna Taber is the closest thing to a mother I have. She's my legal guardian, and she and her partner have raised me. If you want to see something amusing, watch a businesswoman slap on an apron over a five hundred dollar suit and start mopping."

Stormy made a sound suspiciously like a snicker. Kienan ignored it. With a smile, he pushed his plate across the counter. "That was wonderful. What's for dessert?"

"You really are a bottomless pit just like your sister." She smiled. "Dessert is a soufflé."

As she started to go past him to retrieve the dish from the oven, he caught her by the wrist. "What," he asked softly, "if I wanted something plainer?" She went very still and he drew her steadily closer as he stood. Pointedly, he caged her between his body and the counter. "You didn't believe me when I said I wanted you."

Her heart was beating fast enough that it was impossible to breathe. His body gave off waves of heat that urged her to simply lean forward and rest her head on his broad shoulder. She could, she thought distantly. She could lean on him, and he would hold her. She hadn't been held in so long . . .

She stiffened her spine and stared at his collar. It was safer than staring into his velvety eyes and sinking into him. "Why should I believe something like that? I own mirrors, Kienan. I know what I look like. And I know what you look like. Men, especially handsome men, do not want a plain woman like me."

"Mirrors only show what's on the surface," he countered with a slight shrug. "They don't reflect my desire for music any more than they reflect your tenderness. And that sort of a thing, Maddie," he caught her chin and tilted her head back, "would appeal to the right man a lot more certainly than any amount of beauty. Besides," his head lowered and his lips skimmed along her jaw, "the longer I look at you, the more beautiful you are to me."

She couldn't breathe and couldn't think, her entire body beginning to tingle as if it had awakened just for the first time. "Don't lie," she whispered.

"I don't lie," he whispered back, his lips teasing hers. He watched her eyes darken to purple, like the most powerful of storms, and his lips curved slightly. "Better get your soufflé."

She gasped and wrenched herself free from his grip. She rushed to the oven, but it was too late. The top had already collapsed entirely, and the edges were beginning to burn. Resigned, she dumped the soufflé into the garbage; she would not serve something that had burned. Instead, she got out the ice cream she had been intending to serve with it and scooped some into a bowl.

As she set it in front of Kienan, he gave her a quick grin. "Vanilla was always my favorite."

Giving in for the second time to her coward's urge, she hurried to the doorway. "Good night, Kienan. Breakfast is whenever you wake up so just ring me so that I know. Oh," she added over her shoulder, "remember to watch out for the nightingale. You would probably scare her. Any sane female would be scared of you."

He watched her go before thoughtfully taking a bite of the ice cream. It was homemade and had little bits of real vanilla in it to give it bite. It was just like its creator. It was unassuming and plain until you got close, then it became irresistible and made everything else seem overdone and over-the-top. As vanilla had been his favorite flavor for his entire life, he thought it entirely fitting that he wanted a woman who was vanilla incarnate.

He just had to convince her that he wouldn't be swayed away by the soufflés of the world.

CHAPTER TEN

As Kienan laid in bed that night and stared at the ceiling, he was unable to fall asleep for the thoughts whirling through his head. He had come here to chase his dreams of music, to take a chance, to have everything he had always wanted. All that had gone flying out the window the instant he had seen Madelyne. How could he even think about music when his thoughts were consumed with her?

There had to be another reason why she was careful to keep people away. It couldn't be because she wasn't lovely. Hell, five minutes in her company and anyone with half a brain would realize what a wonderful person she was inside. Even in a superficial world, people wanted to be near others who made them happy. She brought sunshine and smiles to a very gloomy world.

There had to be something more. And everything inside him, every instinct he owned, tore at him with a fierce vengeance, insisting that he protect her from everything. He had to shelter her from those who would try to hurt her. He was a protector by nature, but this went deeper than that, and he knew it. This urge came from his very soul.

On a wry sigh, he got out of bed and went to the window where the garden beyond was shrouded in shadows and moonlight. Really, he wasn't too surprised. He had been expecting it when he had turned around and felt the world stop as he looked into violet eyes. He, the flighty and irresponsible one, was in love.

Hiro had once said that realizing he loved Aenya had felt like a click in his heart. Kienan hadn't heard a click. He hadn't heard anything. It had all slammed into him like a fist from a gauntlet. It left him reeling and wobbling, his breath gone and his senses dazed. And there was pain, too, thinking of how hard it would be to help heal

Madelyne so that she believed he loved her. Thank *god* Aenya had warned him else he might have really ruined things.

With a sigh, he opened the window and closed his eyes. The night was calm and quiet. Then, slowly into the stillness, he began to hear something. He couldn't identify it initially, but as he listened harder, he realized he could hear someone singing. It belonged to a woman, and the lonely haunting melody made goose bumps rise on his skin. He had never heard anything that incredible before. It didn't sound human.

When the purple moon is high in the sky, I walk through the heat of a savannah

His heart began to thud dully in his chest as he straightened and stared out the window intently, trying to see if he could spot anything. There was nothing but the swaying of trees in the night wind and the shimmering of the moon above. No indication that anyone was in the garden, anywhere.

When the pain is too much for my heart, my nightingale's melody soothes my tears

Was it really the nightingale singing? He didn't care. He simply closed his eyes and let the music wrap around him. He felt something nudge his hand and looked down to see Stormy watching him, her canine eyes filled with grief. She walked over to the guitar leaning against the wall and pawed at it lightly.

After a moment's hesitation, he got up and walked over to pick up the guitar. As he sat at the window again, he felt the soft breezes blowing around him. They should have been cool but they were warm as he lifted the guitar. He didn't know if he could possibly soothe a nightingale's pain, but he wanted her to know she wasn't completely alone.

It wasn't hard to pick up the melody. He began to play along after a few beats. There was more there, he thought. So much more that the song could say. But, for that moment, he simply lost himself in the joy of the music, sharing the night with the lonely ghost singing outside his window.

When he heard light knocking on his door a few hours later, he was barely cognizant. He had stayed up the entire night playing with the nightingale. As the first light of dawn had appeared, the voice had disappeared as if afraid of facing the light of day. He had put his guitar away and fallen into bed.

It was now ten o'clock and he had severely overslept. With a distinct curse in Spanish, he rolled over and pulled the blankets up to his chin. Mornings were good for nothing except sleeping. Or snuggling a vanilla flavored nightingale, but despite her knocking on the door, he doubted she would get into bed with him. Damn it.

When there was no answer beyond the curse, Madelyne opened the door slightly and peeked inside. She bit her lip to hide a snicker as she saw the lump under the blankets. She had been expressly ordered by her own role in the contract to make sure that he was awake by ten in the morning so that he had ample writing time. On a sigh, she opened the door and walked in.

He was more sensitive than she had given him credit for. She stood beside the bed and studied his sleeping face with a hunger she didn't want to admit, let alone examine closely. He was wonderfully beautiful, and her fingers itched to touch him. His hair always fell in his face, and this time she couldn't stop herself from gently brushing the strands back.

She had heard him the entire night. He had true talent; not many could pick up a song he had never heard before and play it for hours without sheet music. She sighed and skimmed her fingers down his cheek. What was she going to do with him?

To her surprise, his fingers suddenly closed around her wrist. Before she could catch her breath, he had tumbled her across him onto the bed and turned to pin her beneath his body.

He was half-naked, and the sight of his strong chest made her mouth dry. He was almost unbearably hot, his body giving off waves of heat that sank into her and touched the wounded parts of her that had seemed frozen solid. If she put her arms around him, he would hold her, and she caught herself as her hands were lifting.

He had thought it would be a nice way to teach her not to pet him while he was asleep, but the plan had backfired. Now he knew how she fit in his arms, her soft curves molding perfectly against his body. Her skin felt as soft as down feathers and was smooth and fragrant. Her scent, apples and vanilla, went to his head.

Her hair was already pinned up and he wanted to see it down. He deliberately began to remove every pin he found and tossed them over the side of the bed where they bounced on the wood floor. The sheer number of pins was staggering, and he combed his fingers through her hair to make sure he had not missed one. When he was sure, he leaned back and lifted her so that she wasn't lying on her hair and holding it in place.

Her hair came down eagerly and stole his breath. Unbound, her hair had to be at least as long as she was tall and it spilled across the bed to fall over the side. It was the same fragrant scent as her skin and just as soft. As fine as silk but incredibly thick with no hair products to detract from its presence.

He buried his fingers in it with a sense of wonder. "Why do you hide it?" he asked softly. "It's incredible."

"It's a vanity," she managed to say. She felt exposed and vulnerable with her hair down. He was seeing something that nearly no one else had ever seen. "I keep intending to get it cut."

"Don't you dare!" He drew her closer and buried his face in her hair to seek the gentle curve of her ear. When he found it, he nibbled gently and heard her breath break softly. The little sound sent licks of fire through his entire body.

He lifted his head to see her face and studied her intently. Now used to her features, his eyes began to pick out little details, like the fact that her lips were a little fuller than average and just right for kissing. Her lashes were long and thick and smoky gray; she probably never had to wear any sort of makeup. He knew nothing about her

face had changed. It was his eyes that had changed. He saw her with the eyes of a man in love, and because he loved her, he found her completely and utterly . . . "Beautiful," he said softly.

Her startled gaze lifted to his. "Don't be ridiculous," she said curtly. "No matter how badly you might . . . might want to get laid, don't assume I'm going to buy something stupid like that."

His eyes danced. "Well, I definitely want to get laid," he conceded, "but it's not because I woke up horny. I want *you* and only you. Morning, noon, or night. Deal with it." Before she could argue, he lowered his head and kissed her. A shudder rippled through his strong body at her flavor. She was soft everywhere, her lips the perfect shape to mold to his. He would never get enough.

She tried to stiffen her body and keep her lips tightly sealed but she had no more resistance to him than the sun did to the dawn. On a low moan, she lifted her hands and curled them around his neck, holding him closer even as her lips parted to let him in.

The kiss turned wild and carnal as his tongue tangled hotly with hers. His hands lowered and in a single sweep went entirely over her body, leaving her feeling as if he had just branded her completely. Still kissing her, unable to get enough of her, he began to unfasten the front of her dress. He felt desperate for the feel of her skin.

He did stop kissing her as he felt the dress open, and he levered himself up so he could see. Delighted, he skimmed a knuckle over the top curve of her breast gently hidden behind a lace bra. "Who'd have thought?" He lowered his head and trailed his lips over where his fingers had gone.

She flushed both with embarrassment and desire as his lips left a wake of heat behind. "Well," she said, "it's my underwear. Who's likely to see it?" The last word was a gasp as his mouth found the hardened peak of one nipple and tugged lightly. Pleasure spread from her breasts outward, and she realized in a sense of panic that if she didn't stop him, he wouldn't stop at all. "No," she gasped and lifted her hands to cover herself as he deftly opened the front of her bra.

If he had thought it was just nerves, then he would have just loved her past them. He glanced at her eyes to gauge her emotions, and he saw genuine fear. He took a deep breath to get a hold of himself. It wasn't an easy feat when he was so desperate for her that he felt as if he was going to explode, but he would be *damned* if he hurt her.

Because he didn't trust his self-control, he rolled to the side, onto his back and put an arm over his eyes. She scrambled up quickly and his breath hissed in as her hair dragged across his skin like silken fire. He warily opened one eye to see her standing a few feet away with her arms defensively crossed.

He stopped breathing entirely. Curtained in her hair, which did indeed touch the floor, her entire being spoke of unconscious sensuality. No, she wasn't beautiful, but *damn* she was sexy. Even behind her arms he could see the gentle curve of her breasts, and his hands burned to touch her. Roughly he said, "I don't care what you call it, but I want you until I can't think."

She began to button her dress with shaking fingers. "I'm not what you think I am," she said quietly. "I'm not a virgin, Kienan, scared by the unknown."

He thought of her stunned response in his arms and the shock in her eyes as she had felt pleasure for what was clearly the first time. "Why?"

"Why what?" She didn't look at him and cursed her clumsy hands that she couldn't finish fixing her clothes.

He got to his feet and brushed her hands aside to button the dress for her. "Why aren't you a virgin?" he asked calmly. "Because the asshole who was your first, clearly didn't teach you anything about what a woman should feel in a decent man's arms. Mind you, it wouldn't be anything compared to what is between us, but that's because I'm *the* man for you, and that's a big difference."

She flushed. "This is hardly an appropriate conversation to be having."

"I'm the man who is going to be your lover. Therefore, any conversation between us is appropriate." He gently settled his hands on her shoulders and pulled her against him. She gave in after a moment and rested her forehead against his shoulder. "Tell me,

Maddie. And give me a name so I can kill him."

She just sighed. "It was two years ago; it's in the past. But . . . well, to make a long story short, he was the most popular guy in the school. He suddenly asked me out and began to date me, and I was flattered. I was stupid," she amended softly. "When he asked, I was stupid enough to agree. It was unimpressive and hurt." She shrugged one shoulder. "I figured it took practice."

"Let me guess." He kept his voice even with effort. "He did it on a dare."

She looked up at him in surprise. "Yes, how did you know?"

"I know my gender, ashamed of it as I am sometimes." He caught her chin in his hand. "There's a big difference between him and me, Maddie. For one, I have a higher respect for any woman than that. For two, I happen to be head over heels in love with you." He gave her a hard kiss on her startled lips, then released her entirely. "So when's breakfast?"

She made a little sound of frustration. "You confuse me. What is it you want from me, Kienan? You could have your choice of women. Why *me*?"

"I don't know. I just looked at you and knew you were mine." He watched her flee toward the door and added softly, "And if you put your hair back up, I will most definitely take it as a challenge, honey. In ten seconds, I will have your hair down and you naked in my arms." He smiled slowly and lethally. "And then I'll teach you what that idiot should have back then."

With a little gulp, she ducked out of the room and fled down the hall to her bedroom. She swiftly brushed her hair, removing the signs of his fingers in it, then reached for her hairpins. She hesitated, however, her fingers hovering over the little jar. She *knew* he wouldn't have said it unless he meant it, and she knew she had an alarming lack of control around him. Compromising, she tied her hair at the base of her neck with a ribbon. At least it would be out of the way.

Now knowing the bottomless pit he could be, she then went into the kitchen and began to make breakfast. Stormy was on her

heels and she shot the wolf a fierce glower. "I'm going to murder you, and then I'm going to go explain to Rhianna why her prize 'pet' is gone. I'm sure she'd sympathize!"

Stormy snorted lightly and laid down on the floor under the table. Madelyne sighed faintly and got to work. She had just transferred a huge stack of pancakes onto a platter when Kienan walked in fully dressed. Unfortunately for her heart rate, he wore a sleeveless black shirt that let her see every muscle in his arms. There were a good many to see.

Distracted, she accidentally grabbed the metal part of the skillet and burned her hand. "Ow!"

He moved instantly to her side and ushered her to the sink. As her hand was held under the cold water, she glared up at him. She didn't need to see the little smile at the corner of his mouth to know he had done it on purpose. "Damn you."

"I just wanted to be sure you appreciated what you're getting." He nuzzled his nose into her hair. As long as she didn't confine all that glorious gray silk, she could do anything else with it that she wanted. "I want you to want me, Maddie."

That should have been the least of his worries. She was as subtle as neon, and he knew it! Still, her heart fluttered when he lifted her hand to his lips and kissed the burn mark. He was incredibly gentle with her, always sensing when she felt off balance. It was as if he knew that her vulnerability to his beauty was paired with her fear of it.

He released her and wandered over to sniff at the pancakes. "Is this homemade?"

She dried her hands. The burn barely hurt anymore. "Why use a mix when homemade is better?"

He gave her such a charming and boyish grin that her heart flipped into her throat and stayed lodged there even as her stomach quivered warningly with heat and hunger for something other than pancakes. Trying to ignore it, she walked into the dining room and set down the syrup, butter, and jelly. Aware he was watching her, she carried out the pancakes as well.

She had no sooner gotten back into the kitchen than he was

following her with the pancakes again. Exasperated, she put her hands on her hips. "Out, Kienan. You are a guest and should be treated as such."

"Nuh-uh." He sat down at the kitchen counter, a stubborn set to his chin. "I wanna be with you." He pulled his best puppy dog expression and looked so pitiful that it startled a laugh out of her. He grinned and lavishly poured syrup over his pancakes. "You're too alone all the time."

She gave up with a sigh. "Alright, alright." She kept an eye on him as he ate breakfast and she went about cleaning up the kitchen. It was a novel concept to have someone wanting to spend time with her. She still couldn't even figure out why he wanted her. That he did want her, she didn't doubt. As she had said, she wasn't innocent. It was the 'why' that had her all confused inside. What *did* he see when he looked at her?

He suddenly came up behind her, and his arms stole around her waist. He rested his chin on her shoulder and looked out the window they were facing. It looked out into the rest of 3rd District, and children ran everywhere. Despite herself, she felt something inside eagerly soaking up the feel of his arms. "Kienan?"

"Hmm?" He turned his head to brush his lips over her ear. "You needed cuddling, and I felt compelled to give you some. And I won't argue that I'm enjoying it, too." He slowly released her so that she could turn around to face him. "Would you show me around the area? It looks wonderful outside."

Puzzled, she tilted her head. "You're here to write, not play tourist."

"But I need inspiration. Please, Maddie?" He skimmed a finger down her cheek and then across her lips. "You're supposed to be tending to your guest's needs, right?"

Her lips tingled and she tried to press them together to stop it. "Within reason, Kienan. I'm not a harem girl."

He swallowed hard as she licked her lips. Beautiful? No. Attractive? No. Sexy? *Hell* yes. And she had absolutely no idea of her devastating impact. If she had been doing it on purpose, he wouldn't have been able to stop himself from tumbling her down onto her kitchen floor. "So," he had to force his tone to remain light, "then it's reasonable to show me around, right?"

Her sigh was internal this time as she gave in and headed for the door. "Let me go change clothes."

"Put jeans on," he called after her. When she eyed him, he grinned. "What? I want to see your legs. I can't tell you how beautiful they are if I can't see them." He had to snicker as she said something rude under her breath in French, and he whistled lightly as she disappeared out of the kitchen. Try as she might, his elusive nightingale was not a gentle innkeeper.

Nightingale.

The little click in his mind put together many different puzzle pieces. Her voice, even just her regular speaking voice, carried a very potent power. It was tangible power likely able to bend reality. Hey, she was from 3rd District, after all. And the nightingale he had heard singing the night before had sung with the exact same type of power unleashed. Was Madelyne pretending to be the nightingale's ghost?

No, that didn't make sense. She had no reason to playact in such a way. There was something more going on. Something that he felt oddly pulled into. His hand slowly went to his lower right hip and covered a mark he'd had since he was born. He didn't believe in coincidences, and 3rd District was the home to magic. Everything had to be connected.

Upstairs, Madelyne studied her closet, then sighed and pulled out a long skirt and blouse. She simply didn't own any jeans or pants of any kind. At least, none she would wear outside. She had some that she wore solely for cleaning. And as she studied her closet, she was forced to accept that she owned nothing trendy. Her clothes suited a woman thrice her age.

It was why, when she got downstairs and Kienan clucked his tongue at her, she retorted, "Cluck, cluck, yourself. I don't own jeans."

"Pity." He linked his hands behind his head as he followed her out of the inn. "Were you born here?"

She hesitated, then admitted, "Yes. My family has lived here for centuries." She glanced at him to see him smiling. "It doesn't bother you? There are . . . interesting stories about this place."

"I think it's amazing. And to be honest, I love it here. When I'm here, I feel like I belong." He was quiet for a few moments. He had never admitted it out loud, but he wanted her to know. "I'm not exactly normal either. I'm . . . sensitive to some people's energy. My sister is one of them. You would be another. I always know when Aenya is close, and I swear I can sometimes read your emotions, Maddie."

That explained a lot. She looked up at his face. "Your whole family is special, Kienan. I could feel something inside Aenya, too. I don't think it's fully manifested yet. It might be her age. And Professor Shaughnessy is definitely sensitive to emotions too. It's obvious to me at least. What about your other brother?"

"I'm not sure," he admitted. "We're all wild spirits, but his is . . . volatile, I guess. He's very, *very* careful to control it. Whatever his 'gift' is, it might be connected." He smiled suddenly. "Think we have an ancestor from 3rd District?"

"Do you want there to be?"

"If it would make me belong here? Absolutely. I can *breathe* here, Maddie. Those kids waving and smiling at me? They're doing it because they see a stranger they want to meet. They're not doing it because I'm a Shaughnessy. I love it here."

"You're an amazing man, Kienan Shaughnessy." Her heart skipped a beat as he took her hand and laced their fingers together. It felt natural to be walking down the sidewalk with him. Most people from outside the 3rd District looked and felt like outsiders, but he didn't. He looked and felt like a resident.

"Madelyne!" A little girl came running up and grabbed onto her skirt. Her face was streaked with tears. "I promise I was watering it and giving it sunshine!" She hiccupped on a sob. "But it *died*! I really tried, Madelyne! Make it better!"

"Wait here," she told Kienan. "I'll go see if the plant can be saved."

"Sure." He waited only long enough for them to go around the corner before he followed. He moved just close enough to hear what was going on, and by looking in a window across the street, he could see the events clearly.

There were a few other children gathered around what looked like a miserably dying flower of some kind. The bulb was brown and drooping, no signs of color or life. Madelyne knelt and gently cupped her hands around the bulb, and a soft wind began to blow. Her voice rose with haunting cadence to sing a song of morning and rebirth. And when she opened her hand, the bulb bloomed and unfurled into a brilliant sunflower. Flushed with life and health, it seemed to glow in the sunshine.

Heart pounding, Kienan leaned against the building behind him. She had definitely been the singer he had heard the night before. But *how* had she done that? It was one thing to say that he thought her voice could bend reality, but *seeing* it was doubly intriguing. There definitely had to be a good reason for why she sang at night with such pain and grief. It made him wonder where in the legend of the nightingale she belonged.

It also made him wonder where he belonged as well.

CHAPTER ELEVEN

When Madelyne rejoined Kienan, he was watching kids play hopscotch across the street. Absently he said, "When I was seven, Dad gave me and Aenya a box of chalks to draw on the driveway with. Within a few minutes, Mel was drawing too. And shortly thereafter Taegan was involved. We covered the entire driveway in loops and squiggles and flowers and aliens."

She smiled. "What did your dad say?"

"Before or after he stopped laughing?" He turned to smile at her. "Our chauffeur was terrified to drive any vehicle over it. Everyone wanted to keep it intact. So in the middle of the night, us four kids snuck out and washed it away. In the morning we swore it was gremlins. After that we were really careful to keep our chalk drawings to places where they wouldn't be trampled."

"You're all so close. You're so lucky, Kien." Her breath caught as he once more linked their fingers together. This time he brought her hand to his lips. "I always wondered what having siblings must be like."

"Riotous," he decided. "But fun." He tucked her close as he began walking down the sidewalk. Since she wasn't inclined to mention the event he had witnessed, he asked, "Will it live, doctor?"

Gravely, she answered, "It will need much care and love but it should play the piano again."

"Piano playing flowers. Man, 3rd District definitely has some interesting flora. The fauna won't suddenly, you know, break into musical numbers, right? I'm not sure I could handle walking through a Disney movie."

This time she couldn't stop the giggles. "You never liked

Bambi?"

His grimace was not entirely joking. "It hit a bit too close to home. Dad rented it without thinking when Aenya was six or so. We got as far as Bambi's mom getting killed. It then took Taegan and Dad a solid hour to get me and Aenya, and Mel, to stop crying."

"Oh, Kienan." Hurting for him, she brought his hand up to her cheek. "I know how much it hurts to lose a parent. And you must have been just a baby."

"Two. But we had Aenya. She helped fill in the holes. If we'd lost her too, the entire family would have fallen apart." He found a smile. "Let's talk about something else. Tell me about the kids."

"Many of them are orphans who didn't fit in at any other shelter. Rhianna keeps a shelter here in 3rd District for kids like them. A friend of mine, Audra Alexandrios, serves as a tutor so that they get the full benefit of schooling without the censure of public schools."

His eyes widened slightly. "She's a professor at college, isn't she?"

She slid a smiling glance at him. "She is."

"She has an . . . interesting reputation."

"That she does. But her heart is good."

"What about that guy?" He indicated a man who was hanging up colorful tapestries for sale in front of a small shop.

"He's a tailor and weaver. A few of the blankets at the inn were made by him. His blankets are very special. They can bond with owners to aid with healing when sick or to do other things." She pointed to a young couple pushing a stroller with twins down the other side of the street. "He made them a blanket to help them have a child when they'd been trying for years."

"And they got twins." He smiled. "I like that."

It was evening by the time they got back to the inn. She had never enjoyed a day so much. He was *hungry* for knowledge. He had asked questions about everyone and everything, showing only fascination for the stories that bordered on fantastical. He had even played a short game of basketball with several kids and showed them how to make proper baskets.

It was such an oddity to her. She had always seen beauty as carrying a certain disregard for intelligence. Most of the beautiful people she had known had never looked past the surface. But Kienan, for all his amazing physical beauty, seemed to be just as beautiful on the inside.

The entire District probably thought he was her boyfriend. He had held her hand the entire time and had stolen more than one quick kiss. When one little girl had exclaimed with delight that he had kissed Madelyne, he had promptly scooped the girl up and given her a smacking kiss on her ice cream streaked cheek 'just to be fair to other pretty girls.'

Unfortunately, for all her enjoyment of the day, Madelyne was exhausted. The mental and physical war she was waging inside had taken their toll. Her days were always long, and she had been under other stresses lately as well. The broken heater was just another in a line of problems lately.

Kienan, showing his sharp sensitivity, followed her into the kitchen. Before she could grab her apron, he lifted her up into his arms and carried her over to a chair. She hastily grabbed his shoulders for balance. "Kien! What are you doing?"

"I'm going to make dinner. Mind you, it won't be fancy, but you're drained, Maddie." He knelt and studied her face intently. "When was the last time someone took care of you?" Her silence was an answer and it broke his heart. He framed her face with one hand, his touch and eyes equally tender. "Just say the word, and I'll take care of you forever."

"No." It was getting harder and harder to say just that one word, as if her resistance was slowly crumbling. She didn't know what he wanted, but she didn't expect it to last. She had reached for the stars twice and both times she had hit the ground so hard she had nearly shattered. She refused to try for three.

"I'll make you change your mind eventually," he said softly as he stood. "But, for now, you stay right there."

It felt odd to be sitting in her own kitchen while someone else cooked, but she knew there was no stopping him. With a little sigh, she folded her arms on the table and rested her head. She was careful not to fall asleep. He wasn't above kissing her awake, and she didn't trust her control. She was fairly sure she didn't have any at all.

What was it about him that called to her? Was it because he might very well be 3rd District descended? Maybe in part, but it was more than that. He was funny and witty, brilliant and sensitive. He *felt* so much. There was a bright light inside him that expanded out and lit up everyone around him. What was wrong with her? It wasn't just the desire for him, though god only knew that was only getting worse.

A plate was suddenly set in front of her and she straightened up in surprise. As she blinked at the plate, she felt her lips quivering. "You made me a peanut butter and jelly sandwich."

He sat across from her with two of the same. "I told you I can't cook. I can make a killer PB&J, though."

He had no way of knowing, she thought, tears beginning to well in her eyes. He had no way of knowing that her parents had always made PB&J sandwiches for Saturday dinner. They had called it their special feast because no one else would eat such a thing on a Saturday night. In her mind, PB&Js had become synonymous with a loving family.

In a blind sort of terror, she realized finally what was wrong with her. She was in love with him. In barely twenty-four hours he had become a vital part of her life and her heart. That stupid sandwich had been the final straw. He had known, subconsciously, what to give her to make her happy and he had done it.

Terrified, she pushed the plate away. "Thank you, but I'm not hungry."

He frowned as she ran out of the kitchen and the door swung wildly behind her. He had been positive she would like a PB&J for dinner. Yet there had been tears in her eyes and fear underneath them as she had looked at him. He wanted to go after her, to cuddle her and promise to make everything better. The only thing that stopped him was the knowledge that she might claw at him like a wildcat if he tried.

Stormy whined softly as she stopped next to his chair. He sighed and rubbed her head gently. "I know, Stormy. But sometimes it's best to give her space. Trust me, I want to comfort her. I think it would just make it worse right now."

He finished his own dinner and dumped the uneaten sandwich in the garbage. He put the plates in the sink and headed down the hall to his room. It was the second night. He was due to go home the next day and have a presentable song for his father. What the hell was he going to do?

He tried to fiddle around with his guitar but the only tune he could bring to mind was the song the nightingale had been singing. He let his mind drift as he thought about songs and love and dancing. The basic beat of the nightingale's song began to throb in his blood, and he grabbed sheet music to write out the rhythm playing in his mind. He grabbed more music and built a harmony with a guitar and piano.

Inspired, he completely forgot the time and began to add more instruments, building a full set to compliment the singer's voice. He wasn't fully conscious of what he was doing until he actually sat back and read the lyrics he had written. He had written a love duet. A song of seduction and love and music. He had written a song for Madelyne to sing with him.

His concentration broke. He sighed and leaned back in his chair as he pushed his glasses up to rub his nose. His chances of getting her on a stage or in a studio were slim to nonexistent. She was a reverse snob. She had been burned so many times that she assumed everyone else would burn her too.

If he burned her with anything, it would be with desire. He burned to have her in his arms again, to taste every inch of her impossibly soft skin. She burned too. He knew it. She just had no more of an idea how to control things than he did, and her reaction was to retreat.

A little stiff from sitting too long, he got to his feet and went to the window to stare across the garden. It was almost midnight and the moonlight complemented the landscape perfectly. It seemed to call to the wildness inside him, and it stirred something inside his soul, so that he wanted to go outside and walk in the midnight garden.

When the purple moon is high in the sky, I walk through the heat of a savannah

When the pain is too much for my heart, my nightingale's melody soothes my tears

He went very still, his mouth going dry as he heard the soft singing. Without giving himself a chance to think, he turned and yanked on his jacket as protection against the cold night air. He started to pick up his guitar, and then changed his mind and left it. He wanted only to confirm what his heart was telling him.

I want to regain the innocence of my youth

But there are no more hopes for me to cling to

Heart pounding, he hurried down the hall and toward the back of the inn. He didn't see Madelyne on the way, nor was there any light under the door that he suspected was her bedroom. He paused a moment, eased the door open, and looked inside. She wasn't there, but it was clearly her room for it smelled of apples and vanilla.

He headed out the back. He tried to be as quiet as possible as he went down the worn pathways of the garden. He could hear the whispering of the hot springs and realized he was drawing close to the women's springs. It had to be the women's side because there was steam lifting in the air to curl like ethereal wisps in lamplight.

His stomach tightened with sudden hunger. If Madelyne was bathing, he had no idea if he could control himself and keep from going to her side.

In the night, the nightingale sings, bringing a change in the wind

He pushed aside an extremely large fern and held his breath as he ducked down. He almost cursed as Stormy ran past him, but he was able to maintain his hidden position. He wasn't breathing. He didn't think he would ever breathe again.

Madelyne was indeed at the spring but not bathing. She was sitting on the side with her feet dangling in the water and her long hair loosely fluttering behind her in the breeze. She sang softly, her voice carrying all the millions of cadences that hundreds of thousands of people struggled to learn one by one.

She had wings.

In the night, the nightingale prays, bringing a change in my dreams

He swallowed hard, but his mouth was dry as a bone. Extending from her back was a pair of brown wings. There were flecks of red within them, and little bits of white. As far as wings went, they weren't extremely beautiful. The color wasn't lustrous, nor was it abundant in variety and shape. They were simply wings of a smaller size that indicated she probably couldn't fly.

It explained a lot. She wasn't a ghost: she was a flesh and blood woman. Yet she *was* the nightingale in the legend. Whether she had existed for all those centuries, or she had been reborn, he couldn't begin to guess. He wanted to change the story. This one would not end in tragedy. If his stubborn nightingale would open her eyes, then she would realize there was a home right in front of her.

Once more he lightly touched the mark on his hip. His suspicions were growing. As quietly as he could, he eased out of the bushes and went back to his room. His mind was going millions of miles per second. He had his song. He definitely knew it was sellable. He just needed Madelyne to be his partner. It wouldn't be as good as a solo, it needed to be sung as a duet. He had deliberately written the woman's part to take advantage of her brilliant voice.

He needed to find a way to finagle more time to convince her to be his partner, not just in music, but in life, as well. He tried to remember the details of the contract. There had to be a loophole in there somewhere. There had to be a way for him to have everything he wanted and give the woman he loved everything she needed.

He awoke the next morning to light knocking on his door. He tried to convince himself she would come in, but he knew she was too smart for that a second time. He muttered under his breath and got out of bed. When he opened the door, all he said was, "Yes, it's morning. Unless you're getting into bed with me, go away."

She cleared her throat. She was more tempted by the offer than she wanted to admit. He was shirtless again, and his pajama pants were low on the hip. He looked like an invitation to break a few commandments. "It's eleven in the morning," she informed him. "You're scheduled for check out at noon."

"Crap. Right." He eyed her intently. She had her hair up again, and he was tempted to pull the pins out. He simply didn't have the time for what he wanted, and she knew it, if the smug look in her eyes was any indication. She had deliberately waited to wake him up. "If you think that my checking out will make me forget about you, think again!"

She blinked as the door shut in her face. He clearly wasn't a morning person. She shook her head and went to the lobby to finish up the paperwork. Despite what he thought, she had no doubt in her mind that once he was away from the District, he would completely forget her. A face like hers didn't linger in anyone's memory.

It was a painful and sobering thought. She sank down to her knees, wrapped her arms around Stormy's neck, and buried her face in her fur. "Why did you bring him here?" she asked in despair. "It's so hopeless for the both of us!"

An hour later, Kienan walked into the lobby and over to the desk. He was wearing his jacket and sunglasses and carrying a suitcase. Putting on her best innkeeper smile, she took the key he was holding out to her. "I hope you'll stay here again, Kienan. I like seeing return visitors."

She stood behind the desk on purpose in an attempt to keep things impersonal. To her shock, he yanked his sunglasses off, dropped them on the counter, and then cleared the top in a single graceful leap. He yanked her into his arms before she could say a word. One hand gripped the back of her head and the other splayed across her lower back. "You will not," he snarled softly, "make this seem so unimportant, nightingale!"

His mouth came down on hers, hard and hungry, and try as she might, she couldn't control her response to him. Even as his head slanted to deepen the kiss, her lips were parting to meet his passion head on. Her fingers lifted and slid into his hair, curled in and held on. She felt hot and wild and breathless with need, craving the drugging delight of his touch.

He turned and trapped her against the wall. Her body pressed to his, and he felt incredible. Small sounds of pleasure slipped through her lips only to be muffled by his. He shuddered, craving her with a force that was painful. He wanted nothing more than to drag her onto the floor and show her how serious he was, but there was no time, damn it!

As suddenly as he had grabbed her, he released her and backed up a step. Her entire body was weak, trembling with desire, and she had to brace a hand against the wall to hold herself up. Her first lover had never gotten even a fraction of a response like that from her, especially not with a single kiss. She swallowed hard as she grabbed for control. "Goodbye, Kienan."

He stared at her for long moments before cursing softly in French. As he went around the counter again and scooped up his glasses, he shot over his shoulder, "This is not the end, nightingale. You better get used to having me around because hell, high water, or curses, you will be mine."

As the inn door shut behind him, she had the sharp sensation that it was less a threat than a promise.

Aenya was waiting for Kienan on the porch when he got home. Dragging his suitcase as he went, he tried to ignore his sister as she fell into step beside him. "Well?" she demanded. "Did you get anywhere? Do you have a song? Did you see Madelyne? Wasn't she awesome?"

He turned his head to snarl at her and then slammed his bedroom door in her face. She could only stare at the door in utter shock. He had *never* lost his temper with her before. Not like that. She heard someone clearing their throat and turned her head to see Hiro trying his best not to smile. "What is wrong with him?" she demanded.

Hiro, having had a similar experience when trying to win her,

had a strong feeling he knew precisely what was wrong with the youngest Shaughnessy brother. Trying to find a delicate way of phrasing it, he finally said, "I think he met Madelyne. And I think he liked her a little too much."

She was anything but slow and her mouth formed an 'O' silently. She considered that for a few moments. Carefully, she finally said, "I told you that Madelyne distrusts beautiful men. Kienan's handsome. I can see this is not going to be easy."

"Something tells me the entire weekend was not easy on your brother." He heard the door moving and pulled her back a step so they were out of Kienan's way as he emerged from his room. Since discretion really was the better part of valor, neither Hiro nor Aenya said a word.

Kienan started to walk down the hall, and then paused. He turned around to say to his sister, "I'm in love with Maddie. I also tried to seduce her. Anything you want to say?" His tone made it a challenge.

A bit weakly she offered, "Good luck?" She winced slightly as he stomped down the hall. Now that she was actually looking, she was fairly sure she saw steam coming from the top of his head that had nothing at all to do with temper. "Oh boy," she said on a sigh. "Here we go again." She glared toward where Stormy was following Kienan. "I'm beginning to suspect that wolf."

Hiro was, too, but said nothing as he remembered a woman with yellow eyes at the Faerie Club. Some things he didn't want to understand.

Sullivan was fighting with his computer as Kienan walked into his office. Giving up on the stubborn program for the time being, he swiveled in his chair to smile at his son. "Well, how was it?" The smile began to fade as he saw the determined glint in the corner of Kienan's eyes. "Kien?"

"One," Kienan leaned forward and planted his hands on the desk, "I have a song. But I need the time to polish it and get a partner. A week, tops. By the talent show at the college, okay? I'll perform it there and you can make your judgment then. The contract says that an outside party has to review the song, and it's best if they see me under pressure."

"That sounds fair enough," he conceded. He wasn't surprised Kienan had caught that little detail. He picked up his tea and studied his son curiously. "What's the other thing?"

"I want permission to get married."

He choked on his tea. Gasping, he set the glass down and grabbed a tissue to blot at his eyes. After a few moments he was able to breathe again, and he stared at Kienan in utter shock. "In a weekend, less than forty-eight hours, you come back with a song *and* a future bride?"

"Future bride if I can get her to agree. She's stubborn as hell!" Kienan threw himself down in the company chair and swung his legs over the side. "She's the innkeeper at the Gentle Brook Inn, and Aenya's friend. I just looked at her and knew."

Sullivan drummed his fingers lightly on the top of his desk. Oddly, now that the shock had passed, he found himself unsurprised. His eyes lowered to Stormy briefly, then lifted to Kienan again. "Tell me about her," he finally decided.

"She's an orphan. She's run the inn her whole life, with help from the person in charge of the Enforcers, I guess. She's got an incredible sense of humor and has more than a bit of a temper. She tries to come across as being very reserved and elegant, but she's not at all. Oh, she can definitely be elegant," he added wryly, "but it's more a polish than a real finish. She's got more kindness and gentleness than anyone I can think of, and she needs some serious TLC from the right guy, especially because she's been burned. That guy is going to be me."

Sullivan thought it was very telling that he had yet to mention what Madelyne looked like. Hormones alone were not a strong basis for a relationship. A good helping hand, certainly, but they were useless without something deeper. "And what does she look like?"

"She's about five-seven, slender. Extremely long gray hair and violet eyes. From an objective standpoint, she's very plain, very ordinary. I guess she'd be the kind of girl you'd pass over in a crowd, but five minutes in her company—hell, two—and you can't mistake how beautiful she is inside. Every time I look at her I can't stand to look away. In my eyes, she's perfect." His voice was simple, but completely sincere.

With a soft sigh, Sullivan accepted the inevitable. "Alright. I hereby extend the contract for a week to allow you the time to prepare and perform at the contest. As for your Madelyne, I also give my blessings and my advice as well. Women who have been burned, especially intelligent ones, are very cautious of being burned again."

"I'm aware of that." He hopped to his feet. "I've told her how I feel, but she doesn't want to listen. So, I've decided to go on to plan B and show her that I'm completely serious."

"And how are you going to do that?"

"You still got the number for that flower place you always got bouquets for Mom from? You know, the one run by Hiro's parents. And do you think they'd give me a discount because I'm Hiro's future brother-in-law?"

CHAPTER TWELVE

The college where Madelyne attended school was the same one that all the Shaughnessy males attended. It was an hour's trip from the 3rd District and required multiple bus transfers. It was the best university in the area, though, and she refused to waste a dime of the generous tuition that Rhianna gave her.

It was a delicate balance that she walked. She couldn't always attend classes physically because of her inn. Sometimes she had to stay at home to take care of guests. Rhianna had thankfully worked out an arrangement with the college, and Madelyne was able to do her work online when she couldn't be there physically. So far it had been working.

She was majoring in Business Management with a minor in Music Composition. She was in one of Taegan's math classes—Advanced Calculus—and had been enjoying him as a teacher all semester. After the weekend she had just had, however, she found herself tempted to skip class for reasons that had nothing to do with the inn. How in the world was she supposed to face Professor Shaughnessy when his baby brother had just spent the better part of forty-eight hours trying to seduce her?

She had never considered herself a coward. She told herself to grow up and walked into the classroom as if her life hadn't changed. She waved when others waved at her and smiled at everyone. It actually took her a moment before she realized there was a lot of giggling going on. Her stomach sinking, she slowly turned to look at the desk where she always sat. A cheerful bouquet of sunflowers greeted her.

Her bag fell on the floor with a thump as she lost her grip on

the handle. She could only gape at the desk. She was so shocked that she jumped when a girl grabbed her arm enthusiastically. "It's so romantic!" the girl said happily. "Madelyne, it's wonderful! Who is it from?"

She spotted a card in the bouquet and plucked it free. The handwriting was instantly familiar to her, but the message read *'To a nightingale from an adoring swan.'*

"You idiot," she whispered softly. Did he know what she was?

"Madelyne has a secret admirer!" the other girl called happily to the rest of the class.

"No! No! I don't!" She waved her hands quickly. "It's got to be a mistake! No one would give me flowers!"

"Professor Shaughnessy brought them in himself. They were left on his desk with a note that specifically had your name on it." One of the boys grinned as he leaned on the top of his desk. "I don't think there's a mistake, Madelyne, and why would there be? You're so nice that you absolutely should have an admirer."

"My boyfriend was telling me the other day," one of the other girls commented, "that he sometimes wished I was more like Madelyne because she's so open-minded and fun to be around. I couldn't even get mad because he was right," she added on a laugh.

Feeling woefully out of step and wondering what had happened to the world, Madelyne sank down onto her chair and buried her face in her arms. First Kienan and now her classmates. Had everyone suddenly gone blind? Or was she the one who had been blind all along? Oh, it was all too confusing!

When Taegan walked in, she couldn't bring herself to meet his eyes. "Morning," she mumbled.

"Madelyne, I'd like to talk to you after class." His voice was gentle and calming, a hint of a brogue softening the words. "It's nothing serious; don't spend an hour worrying." He got to the front of the class and began to take roll. He was smiling inside. She had always been one of his favorite students anyway. He would like having her for a sister.

When class was done, she waited by the door for him, and then fell into step beside him as they headed toward his office. She carried her flowers to put them in her art locker until she could figure out how to take them home. They were really beautiful. If he had given her roses, she could have easily thrown them away!

As they walked into the office, she asked, "What did you need to see me about, Professor?"

He shut the door with a sigh and walked over to sit behind his desk. He pulled off his glasses and dropped them on the table in front of him. "I'm not speaking to you as a teacher," he admitted ruefully. She went very still, and he gestured to the chair across from him. "Sit down, Maddie." The use of her nickname was deliberate.

She warily sat down and he studied her intently. He had always been saddened to see how much she held herself back from others. Her classmates idolized her, and she had never had a clue until that morning. Kienan's methods, blunt as they were, were at the least helping her see her own worth. If he ever found who had hurt her so badly, Taegan would very happily help him deal with the offender. "Maddie, I think you should transfer to another math class."

She sighed. "I was afraid of that. It'd look bad on both of us if your brother's current interest was in your class. But it's just fleeting, Taegan, really. It'll fade." Taegan had insisted on informality outside of the classroom, wanting to be available for students to talk to if they were having trouble, academic or not. She had never before felt comfortable calling him by his first name but things had definitely changed.

Bemused, he leaned back in his chair. "You haven't heard what Kienan did when he came home yesterday?"

"No . . ."

He cleared his throat. "I believe he went into our father's office and demanded permission to marry."

"He did *what*?!" She leapt to her feet and her bag fell on the floor with a thump. "What is *wrong* with that man? I said no to an affair and now he's talking about marriage?" She made a disgusted sound. "Did someone drop him on his head too much when he was a baby? There's something not firing right in his brain!"

He coughed but couldn't quite disguise the laugh. It had suddenly become quite obvious why Kienan was in love with her. She would be an absolutely perfect addition to their family, and she was strong enough to keep Kienan in line. Their father was going to adore her. "Well, I know he had some interesting escapades, but I think his brain remained intact. That being said, I love Kienan very dearly, and I wanted to make a pitch for him. He doesn't know about this," he added.

She slowly sat down again and folded her hands in her lap. She stared at the front of the desk rather than at him. She felt horribly embarrassed and couldn't help but wonder if he would still be so accepting of her if he knew what she really was.

He considered her for a moment before leaning back in his chair. "Kienan is an unusual young man," he started slowly. "I suppose some boys who grew up without a mother might lean toward being very casual and harsh with women. Whether it was Aenya's presence or something inside Kienan naturally, he's always been very protective of everyone, especially women. He would sooner die than hurt anyone, and he's a fierce defender. It was such a terror helping Father raise him because of that very thing. He's easily hurt."

She looked up quickly. "He never indicated anything like that to me."

"He wouldn't, not if he wanted to protect you, which he most definitely does." He went around the desk and knelt to put a hand on hers. "I love him very dearly, and I can see how much he loves you. All I ask is that you try to open your heart to him. He won't betray you, Maddie. When Kienan is serious, he's serious for life."

Her lower lip trembling slightly, she whispered, "He just doesn't understand. The novelty will wear off and everything will be normal again."

He got to his feet with an odd smile on his lips. "I can see you've got a lot to learn about men in general, and men in love in particular. Speaking as a future big brother, I'd start sewing your wedding dress."

"Thanks a lot!" She got to her feet and snatched up her bag. She slapped the sunflowers down on the desk, her eyes snapping sparks.

"Tell your brother to keep his flowers. I don't want them."

As the door swung shut behind her, he grinned slightly to himself. He knew full well what his brother had been up to all morning.

It didn't take long for her to figure it out herself. Her next class had another bouquet of flowers, another note from a swan, and another giggling room full of students. She gave the flowers to one of the other girls and tried to ignore everyone for the next hour.

It was to her folly that it was Monday and all of her classes met on Mondays (with them falling on other days the rest of the week). She found more flowers at her next class, delivered by a teacher so that no one knew who was behind them. Even the teacher wasn't sure since the flowers had arrived anonymously at his office. Rumors were flying and fingers were being pointed. She was sure that Kienan was deliberately having fun with the entire school.

It came to a head while she was sitting at a lunch table in the cafeteria. The other people at the table fell silent suddenly and she looked up to see Kienan approaching with a single yellow carnation. The entire room went quiet as everyone noticed him. Red color slowly climbed her face.

"Special delivery!" he told her cheerfully as he reached her side. "I caught the teacher at the door and decided to save him a trip."

If she hadn't been sure that he was behind it, she would have never suspected him. She warily got to her feet and took the carnation he was holding out. The card was blank and she blinked at it. "It's not signed." What *was* this maddening male up to?

"It's not?" He peered at the card. "How are you supposed to know who it's from then? Ah! Wait. I bet this will help." He reached into his pocket and pulled out a pen. Before she could stop him, he had taken the card and scrawled his distinctive signature across it. "There. That ought to do it."

"Oh my god!" a girl in the back of the room blurted excitedly. "Kienan Shaughnessy is *courting* Madelyne Winters!"

The entire room erupted into an excited buzz. It was the most interesting thing to happen in a long time, and definitely the most romantic thing to happen *ever*.

"No!" Madelyne said hastily, trying to wave her hands in the air for attention. "No, he's not! Kienan," she pleaded, looking at her 'admirer,' "tell them the truth!"

"What truth?" He grinned. "I am courting you, nightingale." He was quick enough to dodge the punch she threw, but he wasn't quick enough to escape her other hand. It came up and threw the contents of her glass of tea in his face. He swiped the liquid out of his eyes in time to see her sweep out of the cafeteria with all the grandeur of a queen.

Everyone else watched her leave as well. The door shut behind her, and all eyes turned toward him expectantly. He shook the tea out of his hair and said musingly, "Plan C it is." He swiftly headed for the exit.

He left behind a clamor in the cafeteria. Everyone was absolutely certain they were going to love every minute of this scenario. Bets were made, and Kienan led the margin by an almost unanimous decision. It wasn't a question of whether he would win; it was merely a matter of *when*.

By the end of her second-to-last class, Madelyne was ready to go home and never emerge again. Kienan was still delivering flowers to her classes by way of the teacher but he had started signing his initials. Now everyone knew. It was enough to drive a sane woman crazy, and she felt the urge to throw a tantrum growing quickly.

At her wit's end, she ditched class for the first time in her life. She left the campus and hurried toward the bus stop down the street. It sat in front of a cheerful salon known for hiring college interns. Even with photos of glamorous models in the windows, she had always felt oddly comfortable there.

As she was passing by, however, she was surprised to hear a young woman shout, "Hey, hang on! Yes, you with the awesome gray hair!"

She had to assume the voice was referring to her since no one else was around. She turned around to see a nearly frighteningly beautiful young woman hurrying toward her. She was shorter than Madelyne, but not as short as Aenya, and had thick black hair that was artfully curled and piled on top of her head. Her eyes were the same smoky black, nearly doe-shaped, and her lashes seemed long and lovely. Her body was graceful and well curved in a way that surely stopped traffic.

As always, Madelyne felt horribly out of her league. "Who, me?" she asked warily.

"Of course!" The woman came to a stop beside her and smiled. "I'm Kalliope, or Kally if you like. I work in the salon here. Please, please, *please* will you let me style your hair?" She clasped her hands together and winked. "I'm working on my degree and I love makeovers! You've got such *amazing* hair. It deserves an amazing cut!"

Madelyne could only gape at her. "I'm sorry?" she finally managed to say. "Surely you're mistaken."

"Me? Mistaken about hair? Not a chance." Kalliope flicked a finger at her own curls. "I know my stuff, hon." She began to circle Madelyne slowly. "I admit, you're not the belle of the ball, but you've got something a lot of people wish for."

"I do?"

"Sure. Here's some advice." Kalliope leaned closer. "The grass is always greener on the other side. Therefore, people who are plain want to be beautiful. And those who are beautiful sometimes wish to be plain." She shrugged one shoulder. "I've wished to be plain sometimes myself. When you're beautiful, people demand things of you. After a while, I learned to use it like a weapon if needed."

Madelyne was fascinated not only by her attitude but her entire manner. "And you stopped me because . . . ?"

"You have major potential. Your face is normal, but we can give you a different kind of appeal with makeup to play up what you have. And your hair is completely your best feature. I can't wait to style it.

Also, far as I can see you've got a nice, regular figure. Some flattering clothes would really show it to its best advantage. 'A bird may not change its color, but it can change its feathers.' Right?" She smiled.

Madelyne wanted to laugh. Her new friend had no idea how eerily accurate she was. She didn't give herself time to debate; she just took a breath and said, "Okay. Where do we start?" She got her answer as Kalliope caught her wrist and dragged her into the salon. "Whoa! I'm Madelyne Winters, a freshman at college. You're . . . ?"

"Oh, I'm sorry. Tavoularis. Kalliope Tavoularis." Kalliope urged her toward the washing station. "I'm the heiress to Tavoularis Industries. I guess we could be considered associates, considering what Kienan Shaughnessy is up to." She smiled innocently as Madelyne groaned. "I'm a senior at college. Because of my major, I hang out with Mel Shaughnessy a lot, and I have one of Taegan's classes. I hear things."

Madelyne sat down on a seat with a sigh. "It's a fleeting fancy."

Kalliope looped an arm around her shoulders. "Hmm, don't think so. Let's try it from a different angle." She went around and knelt down to be on eye level with her. "Madelyne, do you love Kienan? Ah!" she added, waving a finger in the air. "No lies or denials. Just yes or no."

"Yes," she whispered.

"Then let me have a chance to make you over, and I'll show you how to use every weapon nature gave us as women in order to make him yours."

It was more for Madelyne's confidence than anything. Mel was one of Kalliope's friends, and he had, rather subtly, indicated some of his suspicions regarding the difficulties of the relationship. Having seen some of the day's events, Kalliope was fully onboard to help Kienan get his lady. They were *perfect* for each other.

"I guess we could try," Madelyne conceded reluctantly. "It hurts to fail though."

"Then don't fail. If I want something, I go after it until I have it. It's just the way I am." She removed all the pins in Madelyne's hair and whistled softly as the length came down. "Okay, I am *so* not cutting this! Maybe some feathering . . ."

It was with some morbid fascination that Madelyne found her hair being fully scrubbed clean before she was escorted to a styling chair. Kalliope turned her away from the mirror so that she couldn't see what she was doing, and she could only bide her time by mentally chewing on her nails. She had never let anyone do anything to her hair before. It had always seemed like putting pretty pillows on an unattractive couch.

"Well, talk to me," Kalliope coaxed. "I've never seen someone your age with gray hair. You spend your time worrying as a career *and* hobby?"

She had to smile. "No, it's genetic. All children of my father's bloodline are fully gray by the time they're preteens. Our hair just doesn't hold onto its color. I *think* I was once a brunette. I really don't remember. I'm so used to having gray hair."

"It totally suits you." Kalliope began to trim more than split ends. "And it's so *soft*. I feel like I'm cutting feathers. People don't have allergic reactions around you, right?" She was rewarded with a laugh, which was exactly what she wanted. Madelyne's voice was wonderful to listen to, and she looked like she was in dire need of a friend. Kalliope knew how it felt; she needed a friend too. Maybe that was another reason Mel had nudged her. He was good at that stuff.

"Hair goop or hair spritz?" she offered as she was getting ready to use the hair dryer.

"Neither if possible. I'd just have to wash it out."

She sighed. "You poor neglected child. Has no one taught you the nuances of hair care and beautification? Style virgins are so vexing sometimes." She worked quickly and expertly, brushing out Madelyne's hair in a way that it didn't need product.

"Are you sure about this, Kally?"

The note of worry in her voice made Kalliope give her a hug with her free arm. "Of course! You're going to look cute and sexy and knock Kienan Shaughnessy on his attractive ass." She twirled the chair around toward the mirror. "Voila! My masterpiece!"

Taking a deep breath, Madelyne opened her eyes and looked in

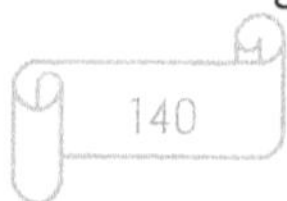

the mirror. Her eyes slowly widened and she looked harder. She was still no raving beauty, but the feathered effect had shortened the hair around her face and made it steadily longer until it reached the back and her ankles. It softened the lines on her face and made her sort of appealing somehow. "How did you *do* that?"

Kalliope blew on her nails. "Magic. It's like decorating a plain couch. You put some pretty pillows on it and suddenly everything looks good." She blinked when Madelyne gaped at her. "Did I say something wrong?"

"Something *very* unnerving, actually." The exact same analogy but with different reactions. That, more than anything, told her that perhaps it was time to change her way of thinking. She took a deep breath. She had money in her savings account. It was supposed to go toward the heater repair, but she could put it off for another month or two. Tourist season hadn't started yet. "Do you have any advice for clothes shopping? I think you can tell I'm hopeless."

"Untutored," Kalliope corrected, "not hopeless. Hey, Ben!" She began to gather up her station. When an older man peered around the corner of the back room, she grinned at him. "I'm going to take off early. I don't have any appointments."

"Can you do that?" Madelyne blinked as she was ushered out of the salon. She felt as if she was being carried along by an unstoppable wave. "I mean, can you just walk out for the afternoon?"

"Sure! Cosmetology is just a minor; my major is Business Management like yours. I want to take my daddy's company." She grinned as they reached her bright blue Camry. It looked as sleek and stylish as its owner. "Mind you, he told me I couldn't have it until either he dies or I give him a grandkid. Considering I've said I won't marry for less than love, I suppose It'll be a while." Madelyne had to laugh at that and she took a quick bow. "So," she asked as she slid into the car, "where to? What's the budget?"

"Reasonable, but a small splurge wouldn't hurt."

"Well of course there has to be a splurge! Where's the fun without it? Besides," she continued blithely, "you're coming to my birthday party and it's going to be amazingly fancy. You need a dress.

Something in a blue tone to bring out your eyes. Or red, just to drive Kienan crazy."

Madelyne liked the idea a little too much for her own sanity. "Has anyone told you that you're a bad influence, Kally?" she asked.

"All the time." Kalliope grinned at her and then gunned the engine so that they sailed off down the road. All Madelyne found herself capable of doing was laughing and holding on for dear life. She was enjoying herself so much that she didn't recognize the sound of her cell phone when it began to ring.

Kalliope glanced down at her bag. "That's you, not me. Mine plays Metallica."

She *really* liked Kalliope, Madelyne decided, and pulled out her cell. She didn't know the number and answered warily, "Hello?"

"There you are, nightingale! You ran away from me!"

Pure instinct had her snapping the phone closed almost before Kienan stopped speaking. When Kalliope slowly lifted a brow at her, she said a bit weakly, "I think I just hung up on a short-tempered Irishman."

"Oh, *nice* one." There was more admiration than censure in Kalliope's voice. "Give him ten seconds and he'll call back breathing fire." She snickered as the phone began to ring rather insistently. "He dials faster than I do."

"He doesn't have those nails."

Kalliope admired her well-manicured nails and their rich green color. "We'll have to get yours done too."

Suspecting that arguing wouldn't sway her new friend, Madelyne gave in before there could be a fight. She cautiously answered her phone, "Hello?"

"That was NOT funny!" Kienan wasn't breathing fire, but he was definitely annoyed. "You hang up on me again, and I'll come hunt you down in person." He huffed out a breath and then suddenly sighed. "However, I guess I can't blame you. What will it take to convince you that I'm serious, Maddie?"

"I don't know." She stared out the window but didn't see anything except a blur. "Kienan, I've been down this route before. I just . . . I just don't want to risk everything again. I lost a lot when I did before."

"Give me a chance." His voice was soft and firm. "Just a chance, nightingale. Give me a chance to show you how much I love you. I'll make it as public as possible. I'll tell everyone. Just give me a chance. Please. If you wanted me begging, here I am."

She closed her eyes. "You ask too much," she whispered.

"I want everything. And I'll give you everything in return. Somehow, I'll prove it." He gently hung the phone up.

She let go of the phone and it dropped into her lap where it closed itself. She became aware that Kalliope had stopped the car and was looking at her expectantly. "It hurts," she whispered. "I hate this! I want him, so badly, but I'm so afraid! It destroyed me before! I still haven't recovered!"

"Recovered from what?" Kalliope murmured softly.

"The curse." The words were out before she could stop them and she looked at Kalliope swiftly.

Kalliope examined her nails but she was watching Madelyne under her lashes. "I'm beginning to think you're less afraid of him not loving you, than you are of his loving you and being hurt to protect you. Or should I say that you might die protecting him . . . again?" She smiled when she received a sharp look. "One hears legends in the 3rd District. I go to the Faerie Club a lot."

Madelyne took a deep breath. "I just can't take the risk."

"You know, if it comes down to it, I think Kienan is smart enough to know how to change the past. The cycle can be broken." She got out of the car and gestured to the mall in front of them. "Let's start here. Start with the things you can change. They're like ripples in water. Eventually they spread."

Madelyne got out of the car, hesitated, then said slowly, "Kally . . . thank you. I hope you find that true love you're waiting for."

Kalliope smiled, but there was a touch of sadness in the corner. "Me too. Now, let's shop. Forget the stuff about men. Let's focus on us women, okay?" She caught Madelyne's hand and drew her along toward the mall. "We definitely need to get you stocked up on a combination of casual and professional clothes. I mean, you're an innkeeper. You need to have that old world charm but modern elegance combination."

Madelyne eyed the store she was being dragged into. "I'm leaving myself in your knowledgeable hands for I am completely out of my league here. I don't even own any jeans other than the ones I wear to clean in."

Kalliope looked up from a rack with such a look of horror on her face that Madelyne burst into laughter. All eyes in the store swung toward her and instantly everyone was smiling. Her laughter seemed to demand it. She lit the entire store with it.

"Thank god that I found you," Kalliope said fervently. "You were on a path to complete disaster."

"What's going on?" a saleswoman asked as she approached.

"She doesn't own any jeans. Not a single pair of pants to show off her legs."

A look of horror not dissimilar from Kalliope's crossed the saleswoman's face. "Alright then," she said. She nodded decisively. "You're in good hands, my dear. We're going to make you look like a million dollars."

"I'd settle for a hundred," Madelyne admitted.

"Never settle." Kalliope held a sassy shirt up in front of Madelyne to check her coloring. "Rule One of being a woman. Never settle for less than the best." She winked mischievously. "It's a rule I was sure you knew. You picked Kienan, didn't you?"

Oddly, she found she couldn't argue with that. Bemused, she found herself being shoved into a dressing room while Kalliope and several merry saleswomen helped pick out an entirely new wardrobe. She could have sworn the full moon wasn't for another two weeks. The entire world had gone nuts in three days.

CHAPTER THIRTEEN

Madelyne found herself highly bemused by her new friend. Kalliope had dragged her through ninety percent of the stores in the mall, ruthlessly taking advantage of sales and discounts (and her company's clout) to ensure that Madelyne got a full, complete wardrobe for the lowest cost possible.

She had then driven Madelyne home, dropped her off, and promised cheerfully to drive her to campus the next day. Madelyne had ended up carrying a dozen bags into her room and unpacking them on her bed. Jeans, slacks, skirts, shirts, blouses, tank tops, camisoles, dresses . . . they had gone slightly overboard. She had clothes for all seasons, not just the winter the city was happily diving into.

There was one additional item that was in its own box. She left it to the side as she emptied out all of her old clothes and dumped them into the now empty bags. Kalliope had promised to find a thrift store they could be taken to, so they didn't go to waste.

Once her closet was empty, she began to hang up her new clothes. Meticulous as always, she sorted them into casual, work, and school, then by type. She took delight in all the colors and textures as she did. Apparently her skin tone and hair color had made her perfect for pastels. There were only occasional bright splashes of color; most everything was soft and soothing.

She couldn't help but blush slightly as she also unpacked her new underwear and lingerie. It was another 'grave offense' in Kalliope's book that any woman over sixteen didn't own at least one pretty nightgown or piece of lingerie to hide under her clothes. The important thing, she had said, was to make yourself feel good. It didn't matter if no one else ever saw it. It was so you stopped and looked at yourself in a mirror and felt happy.

She had then blithely helped pick out a scrap of purple and black lace and silk that was designed to do nothing except seduce. It was to be Madelyne's secret weapon against Kienan if she ever felt he was close to walking away. Any man who walked away from a woman in a teddy like that was not worth keeping, or so she said.

Once everything was put away, she turned her attention to the lone box. It had been the single most expensive item, but it hadn't been paid for out of her pocket. Kalliope had discovered that her birthday was only recently past and felt honor bound to get her friend a belated gift. It was also to Kalliope's advantage because it was the perfect thing for Madelyne to wear to Kalliope's upcoming birthday extravaganza.

The ball gown was violet silk in a color that was nearly identical to Madelyne's eyes. It was cut with a princess bodice to best frame her slender bust line. The sleeves were spaghetti straps lined with small glittering beads that traveled down along the edge of the bodice. The silk was covered by sheer, shimmery lavender material that also became a train in the back where it fell all the way to Madelyne's ankles.

The matching shoes were low heels in violet color and covered with more beading. There was a hairpiece for it, and she was under strict orders to see no one, except Kalliope, to have her hair done for the party. As if she would trust anyone else!

After a quick shower to wash away the strange day, she decided to start as she would go on. She dressed in a pair of slim jeans that flattered her legs and a pale yellow camisole with lace straps. And, looking in the mirror, she actually felt as if she might be kind of cute. Oh, she would never look like Kalliope or Aenya, or a lot of the girls at school, but there was definitely something, finally, appealing about her looks.

The front bell rang and she tilted her head. Because of her school schedule, the inn didn't book walk-in travelers unless there was an emergency. Everything was by reservation. There was no one scheduled for check-in for at least a few weeks.

"Coming!" she called as she walked down the hall. To her surprise, she saw a man in a work uniform standing at the front desk. "Hello, I'm the owner. May I help you?"

He turned to smile at her. "Miss Winters?" He glanced down at the clipboard he was carrying. "Broken water heater on the men's springs? I'm here to fix it."

"Oh, I can't afford it right now! I was going to arrange for this next month. I didn't already send in an order without thinking, did I?" She suddenly got a sinking feeling in her stomach. "Wait. Who ordered this?" Her violet eyes began to snap.

He coughed. "I was just asked to fix the heater. It was paid for ahead of time. I was told not to say who had arranged it." Judging by the temper in Madelyne Winters' eyes, he was beginning to understand why. "The springs are out back, right? I'll just go take care of things." He grabbed his toolkit and made a hasty exit toward the back garden.

She said nothing for long moments, then, smiling a little to herself, she grabbed a phone book. She skimmed the pages for the number she wanted and calmly dialed the phone. When the other side was answered, she said sweetly, "Mr. Shaughnessy? Hello, this is Madelyne Winters with the Gentle Brook Inn. I do appreciate the gesture of good will from your youngest son, but I would much prefer a business gesture. Perhaps we can make a deal?"

Ten minutes later, she hung up the phone and felt quite satisfied with herself. The fax machine under the counter began to spit out some documents and she read over them lightly. Content, she signed them, then faxed them back. She began to log the repair and the deal into the computer as she started counting mentally.

The phone rang just as she got to one hundred. He was getting slower. She smiled and picked up the phone. "Gentle Brook Inn."

"You are NOT funny, nightingale!" Kienan was audibly annoyed. "It was a *gift*. How dare you call my father and make it a business arrangement?" Clearly quoting from memory, he bit out, "'In return for the repair of a broken water heater, Aenya Shaughnessy and Hiro

Michaels may spend their two-week honeymoon free of charge in one of Gentle Brook Inn's large honeymoon suites.'" His breath huffed out. "Damn it, Maddie, you know why I did it!"

"I know, Kienan," she agreed gently. "And you know in your heart why I can't accept it. Though your heart guided you, and though my heart would like to accept, I have pride as well. And sometimes pride is more important than hearts." She softly hung up the phone.

The repairman walked back into the lobby and cleared his throat. "Everything is taken care of, Miss Winters."

She sighed and smiled at him. "I won't lose my temper with the innocent messenger. Am I correct in assuming that a warranty was included so that if something else happens, I just call and it'll be fixed?" His color rose slightly. "That man," she said in exasperation. "Well, thank you. If you're ever in the area on a weekend, swing by. There are always extra cookies around."

He smiled at her. Gentle Brook Inn's owner was as appealing and calming as the place she operated. "I'll take you up on that." He tipped his hat. "Good evening, Miss Winters."

Once he was gone, she got out a clipboard and began to continue her examination of the inn. It was a project she had been working on for a few weeks. The inn was up-to-date electrically with properly grounded outlets wherever they needed to be, and the plumbing was as modern as possible. Those had been critical needs and they had been taken care of by the Enforcers as a birthday gift for her. The inn had many other things that should be done as well. It was a two-story building with a total of seven regular rooms and three honeymoon suites. Technically, 'inn' was a misnomer since it was more of a bed and breakfast.

The only place with updated décor was in the kitchen, which had almost been a 'have-to' as well. Everything else needed to be updated. She didn't want to change the style of the inn; she just wanted to make it fresh and new. Some rooms needed to be renovated entirely. She wanted to remove the carpet and put in hardwood floors. Some walls needed to be moved to make the rooms more uniform in size. And if it meant sacrificing one of the small rooms, she would love to put in a small elevator, so the inn would be handicap accessible.

Her list was growing by leaps and bounds. By the time she went to bed, she was well aware that the amount of money needed to bring Gentle Brook Inn up-to-date, so that it was true competition with bigger places, was potentially beyond her reach.

She would need an investor. She could think of two companies, three potentially, that might be willing to invest because they knew her personally, but she didn't want that. She wanted to prove she could make things work. Maybe Kalliope could give her some advice. Certainly the older woman had changed everything else about Madelyne's life. She was going to be dangerous when she took her daddy's company.

The next morning was no less daunting than the night before, but she decided to keep her chin high. She pulled on another pair of jeans, a white sweater with a scoop neck, and pretty white sneakers. She left her hair down and used a little bit of gel to keep it styled out of her eyes. And having been tutored quite carefully, she was even able to use her new makeup kit to enhance her eyes and lips. "Why," she complained to her reflection as she felt her heart beating, "is this so nerve-wracking?"

A cheerful honking horn caught her attention and she picked up her backpack. She locked the doors to the inn and then went down to get in Kalliope's car. As always, the black-haired heiress looked as if she had stepped off a runway. Oddly, Madelyne didn't feel that outmatched anymore. "Am I supposed to be nervous?"

Kalliope contemplated that as she navigated traffic. "Yes," she decided. "Because it means you feel you look good and you want verification from other members of the species. Some people will look at you oddly, I'm sure, because you've done a total one-eighty. But most people are going to either accept it without comment or be ecstatic because they will feel like you're approachable now. The ones with snippy things to say are the ones who would have been snippy even if you were being your normal self."

"You taking Psych 101?"

"Cosmetology. Stylists are notorious for reading their clients. It eventually turns into an ability to read people in general." She eyed Madelyne's hair. "Not bad, kid. For a newbie, you did that pretty good. If you comb out the excess next time, it won't feel as tacky to your fingers."

Madelyne stopped fiddling with her hair. She smiled. "You're amazing, Kally."

"Ain't I? Don't forget we're having lunch together. You promised to bring enough for both of us. I've heard rumors about your cooking."

She patted her backpack. "Plenty for both of us. I'll meet you at the fountain." Her confidence felt higher than ever as she walked toward her art locker; she had a watercolors class first on Tuesdays. Kalliope's unquestioning support was doing miracles.

Her friend proved herself to indeed be astute. By the time she got to her locker, she had collected more compliments than she had ever heard in her entire life. Once more she was Alice tumbling down the rabbit hole. Again, wondering if the moon was full and just pretending it wasn't, she slammed her locker and found Kienan on the other side. She leapt backward on a yelp. "Kien! Don't *do* that!"

He could only stare at her, barely breathing. In wonder and delight, he reached out to run his fingers through her hair. It looked even softer and more alluring. Her body was perfect to his eyes, shaped *just* for his hands. Her hips and breasts were rounded just enough to entice his fingers into touching. She had done some strange female thing, and her eyes looked large and sultry. Beautiful? Had he thought she was beautiful? She was *exquisite*. "Nightingale."

The word was little more than a husky rumble of male desire. His brown eyes smoldered as they swept over her. His fingers, when he cupped her cheek, were hot. A soft tremor seemed to be going through his entire body. To think she made such a powerful creature weak enough to tremble . . . Almost helplessly, she found herself swaying toward him, the heat spreading through her as well. If he didn't kiss her, she was going to die.

His breath hitched and his head lowered. Despite the hunger in

both their bodies, he kissed her with a tenderness and generosity that was more seductive than a thousand wild embraces. Her hands fell weakly to her sides in sheer bliss.

He sensed the surrender and slowly eased back until there was barely a breath between their lips. He only distantly heard students giggling as they went past. His world had narrowed so that it only included his nightingale. "I love you," he vowed with all the conviction in his soul. "Please, believe me."

"I do." The words slipped past her guard before she could stop them.

When had it happened? When had it finally sunk in that this incredibly beautiful man truly loved her? She couldn't even question herself, not when she saw the brilliant joy slowly lighting his eyes. It blazed from the depths of his heart and soul, illuminating her in his love.

Unfortunately, believing him didn't change one critical fact: she was cursed. She had been cursed for centuries. Curses didn't go away when you died. They just came back more vicious than ever. More than once over her life, she had felt the slimy sensation of being watched. The hunter was out there, lurking in his new life. He would never rest until he killed the one she loved.

The one she loved was a protector. He would sacrifice his life for hers without hesitation. If the hunter learned it, realized that Kienan's weakness was his incredible depth of emotion, then none of the Shaughnessys would be safe. Madelyne wouldn't be safe. And Kienan would die. For his own sake, she had to keep her love inside. No one could know how badly she loved this man.

"What's wrong, Maddie?" He brushed his lips over her forehead to remove the lines forming there. "You're frowning. You feel so sad." The largest hurdle had been cleared. She believed him. Now he just needed to make her fall for him in return. "I can't bear it if you're sad."

"Not sad," she lied. "Embarrassed. You're making quite a scene."

"Yeah." He eased back and grinned. "You're entitled to a few." He stole a quick kiss and snatched her portfolio and books up before she could get to them. "Allow me, my lady." He gave a courtly bow and almost dropped everything. He caught the books quickly and gave her a sheepish grin.

She bit her lip but couldn't quite hide a snicker. "You're an idiot." She fell into step beside him as he headed down the hall. "Thank you, by the way."

He knew to what she was referring. "You're welcome." Softer he added, "I am sorry. It never occurred to me that it might wound your pride. I just wanted to do something for you." He shot her a sour look. "You told on me, to my dad, damn it. I got a lecture!"

She smiled and took her books at the door to her class. "Serves you right, doesn't it?" She firmly shut the door in his face and walked over to her seat. A low wolf whistle made her look over in surprise and one of the boys winked at her. Surprised, she could only blink.

"What?" He grinned. "It was meant sincerely, promise. You look kinda cute today. Wear your hair down more. I'd hit on you, but Kienan would thrash me soundly, and he has a black belt."

"He . . . he does?" Her eyes widened. "I didn't know that." It wasn't entirely unexpected, however. And it certainly explained why his body was spectacularly corded with muscle. Her pulse fluttered just remembering how all that delightful weight had felt against her.

At lunchtime, she met up with Kalliope at the fountain in the quad area. "Hungry?" she asked her friend as she sat down.

"Famished!" Kalliope took the sandwich being held out. "Is this homemade bread?"

"And homegrown veggies. The meat is from a deli near 3rd District. Closest thing to homegrown that you can get in NYC. I made the dressing, too." Madelyne happily bit into her own sandwich. "You said you liked turkey."

"Gobble." Kalliope bit in and rolled her eyes. "Oh man. No wonder Kienan wants to marry you. You cook like a goddess. How much would I have to pay you to get you to cater my birthday party?"

Madelyne laughed. "Thanks."

"No, seriously." She smiled. "I'm asking sincerely. I haven't settled on a caterer yet. And I can afford the best so I absolutely want it. We can make it a business deal if you like so that our friendship doesn't get in the way. It'll be a lot of food, and I know it'll take a lot of your time. And I absolutely want to pay you as you deserve."

"I'll make you a deal." Madelyne finished off her sandwich. "You can hire me to cater the regular food, but your birthday cake will be my gift to you."

"Done!" She pulled out her iPhone and began making notes on one of the applications. "I'll talk with my dad tonight. We'll do some research, find the proper rate, then make the deal official." She glanced up as she heard the quad beginning to buzz. She grinned. "Incoming stud at nine o'clock, and he's carrying a wrapped package."

Madelyne bit her lip to hide a laugh and turned to see Kienan approaching. He was indeed carrying a gaily-wrapped package in his hands. It wasn't very large and he was carrying it with visible gentleness. "Kien," she said warningly when he was close.

He just grinned and put the package in her hands very softly. "Be very careful," he warned. "It's very fragile, and I can't take it back."

She stifled a sigh and began to unwrap the paper. Expecting to find something very expensive and outrageous, she was stunned speechless as she lifted the lid on the top of the box to find herself staring at a bed of material and a sleeping kitten.

It was no bigger than the palm of her hand and it was probably the most mismatched kitten she had ever seen in her life. It was no purebred, that was for certain. Its nose was kind of scrunched, and its fur was on the shaggier side. Its base color was off white and it had stripes and splotches in every shade of brown and orange possible.

"You gave me a kitten," she whispered, reaching into the box and gently lifting the baby out. It fit in her palms and opened its eyes slightly as it gave a pitiful sounding mew. Its eyes were almost peridot in color and its nose was pink. "Kienan, it's a baby."

"A baby girl, in fact." He crouched down so he could see her face. "When I went to the shelter, there were purebreds and beautiful kittens as far as the eye could see. This little lady was hiding in the back of the cage. Apparently she was from an accidental pregnancy, and the owner had thrown her out. The people at the shelter figured she had little appeal and kept her out of sight.

"Thing is," he continued softly, "she reminded me of you. She may not be part of the norm, she may never win any prizes, but to the right person she would be absolutely perfect. She doesn't change. She doesn't *have* to change. The eyes looking at her love her for everything she is. With enough time, maybe she'll see how much value she has."

She lifted the kitten to her cheek and closed her eyes as tears spilled down her face. She had always wanted a pet but she had never been able to find the right one. "She's so tiny," she whispered, gently lowering the kitten to her lap where it curled up to sleep.

"She'll need someone to take care of her." He gently covered her hand and the kitten both, his hand enough larger that both were protectively sheltered. "She'll need you, Maddie."

"No one's ever needed me." Her startled gaze lifted as his free hand softly cupped her cheek. "Kien . . ."

"I need you," he said softly. "But not just in my heart. I need your voice." When she blinked at him, he smiled. "I found my inspiration in you, Maddie. That last night, I stayed up late writing a song for us. I know it's the song that will give me all my dreams. I just need you to sing with me. Together we can show everyone at the talent show that I've got what it takes. Please. Help me."

"I can't." She lifted her hands and framed his face, for the first time touching him of her own will. "Kien, there are so many things complicating this. I want to sing with you, but it's too dangerous. I don't dare sing in public. Please understand." She gave away all her emotions when she sang, and anyone hearing her would know she loved him.

He was silent for long moments and then got to his feet. "I wonder if the swan felt this way," he said quietly.

"Swan?" She looked up from where she had been putting the kitten back in her nest.

"The swan the nightingale gave her life for." He looked at her intently, his eyes darkened to almost black. "I wonder if this was the way he felt, watching the one he loved sacrifice herself for him. No matter what his family or anyone said, he would have wanted just her."

Kalliope watched him walk away. She murmured softly, "Somehow, I think he knows what you are, hon."

"I think so, too." Madelyne smiled sadly. "That reincarnation thing is a real bitch, isn't it?" She got to her feet and picked up the box with her kitten. She was going to have to ditch again, but she really couldn't regret it much.

When Kienan arrived at the inn much later, it was just turning into evening. He wanted to coax Madelyne into going on a date with him and was looking forward to seeing how she and her pet were getting along.

He got his answer for the second question when he walked into the lobby and heard her exclaim, "No, stop wiggling!" Something splashed loudly and she groused, "I will never be a mother."

Trying not to laugh, he left Stormy to guard the door and wandered toward the kitchen where he had heard the sounds coming from. Not to his surprise, he found Madelyne trying to bathe her kitten. He leaned in the doorway and grinned as he watched. "She's just playing."

"I noticed." She caught the kitten in a towel and began to gently dry her. "She got into the plants and was filthy. Scatterbrained little scamp."

"You should name her that." She quirked a brow, and he quirked one back in amusement. "Scatterbrain. If the name fits and all."

"If that was true, you'd be named Troublemaker!" She rubbed her cheek against the kitten's fur before setting her gently down on the floor. "Scatterbrain it is." Leaving the kitten to her own devices, she began to clean up the spill of water on the floor. "What are you here for, Kienan? Don't tell me you're actually going to try and ask me out. That's a little silly at this point."

"Well, a man could hope." It was time to take one of the biggest risks of his life. He glanced down the hall. The kitten was walking toward Stormy fearlessly and the wolf was eyeing the small creature as if it was poisonous. She wasn't especially fond of cats, but when the kitten cuddled up close, she sighed and laid down. She was a protector at heart. Kienan had every confidence that Scatterbrain would be well protected.

Madelyne was wringing out the washcloth in the sink when his hands settled on her hips. Her heart gave a dull thud in her chest even as heat seemed to spread from his fingers outward and made it hard to breathe. "Kienan?" she whispered.

She still wore the low cut sweater, and it was wonderfully easy for him to lower his head and press his lips to the curve of her shoulder where it met her neck. She even tasted like vanilla, but with the crispness of apple. The taste went to his head. "Let me touch you," he whispered, his arms sliding around her waist to pull her more firmly back against him. "Let me love you."

She trembled as he began to trail soft kisses along the line of her neck. She could almost literally feel her strength fading, and her head tilted unconsciously to the side to give him better access. "I'm scared," she whispered. "If I gave myself to you and you walked out while I was asleep . . ."

Fury made his fingers tighten on her hips and his voice was equally tight as he said, "I will kill him if I find him. That's something no decent man does to any woman." He turned her in his arms and used his free hand to tilt her head back. "I would *never* do that to you," he vowed fiercely. "You couldn't make me leave if you tried!"

She closed her eyes for long moments. A small and hurting part of her cynically suggested that this would be a good way to find out if he was really serious. Another part tried to tell her that she might be able to keep him if she gave him what he wanted.

In the end, what made her choose was the memory of his gentleness and the look in his eyes as he watched her. Her heart

craved his closeness no matter how long it lasted. If this ended horribly, at least she would know she had belonged to him. She loved him. She could do nothing less than give him everything.

"Okay," she finally whispered in a trembling voice. She lifted her arms to wind them around his neck. "I trust you."

Relief almost made him lightheaded and he caught her closer against him, so tightly she almost couldn't breathe. He swiftly released her only to scoop her up into his arms. "I swear you won't regret this," he promised softly as he carried her out of the kitchen and down the hall.

Astonished at his strength, her heart quivering in her chest, she could only manage to bury her face against his shoulder and hold on tightly. The room spun dizzyingly around her head and she took a quick breath as she felt him lowering her to the top of her bed. "Turn the light off," she pleaded.

"Hell no." His fingers moved with confidence to the edge of her sweater and he quickly pulled it up and over her head. As her hair fluttered and slowly drifted down around her body, he sucked in a sharp breath, desire fisting into his stomach and gleefully holding on. He was literally aching fit to burst, desperate to feel her skin under his hands. "You're beautiful."

"Liar." Her breath caught as his knuckles skimmed over the top of her breast bared by her low cut silk bra. She felt too hot, her skin ready to burst into flame. Her wings ached restlessly. That alone was frightening for she had never before encountered a feeling that consumed her entire body.

"Mm, you'll just have to trust me. I'm the one looking at you." She was soft skin and slender curves, and he wanted to ravish and plunder. Hands shaking slightly, he drew her toward him until her hands lifted and flattened against his chest. "I want to be gentle," he whispered as he brushed soft kisses over her face. "Give me a few moments to find some control before I go after you like a chocoholic on a sundae binge."

A shudder went through her body. She had never wanted anyone like this. She had never *been* wanted like this. Throwing caution to the winds, she took a deep breath and began to unbutton his shirt. She pulled the edges apart and slid her hands inside where she could smooth her palms over the hot skin of his chest. "Dessert's on," she said huskily.

He gave a rough laugh and then dragged her closer, his mouth capturing hers. Her lips parted instantly, and he curled his tongue around hers. A shudder wracked his body at the taste of her. For the life of him he couldn't get enough of her taste, as if it had been centuries since he had last held her.

His hands rushed over her swiftly, learning every curve, and the feel of her was somehow familiar. He knew how her body felt, how she was sensitive on the inner curve of her hip. He knew that a little pressure in the middle of her back made her arch fluidly toward him.

He hungrily caught the edge of her bra in his teeth and dragged it down even as his fingers found the clasp and opened it. She could only moan softly as his mouth captured one nipple and tugged sharply, sending the same tug echoing through her body. Mindless, willingly losing herself in the wildness of his passion and her own, she yanked his shirt down his arms until he shrugged out of it impatiently.

The sight of his golden skin tempted her. She reached for him to run her hands eagerly over his muscles. She had never before known that sort of freedom, and the desire to know him completely was new. She reveled in it, and in understanding for the first time what it meant to be a lover—a true lover. There was power in knowing she made such a strong creature weak.

His lips covered hers again, and she held him closer, where he could not escape. She felt his fingers trying to unfasten her jeans but they were trembling too much to do any good. "What, are you nervous?" she teased. She nipped at his ear and enjoyed the way he shuddered.

"You terrify me. Any sane man would be terrified." His lips raced over her face wildly, hungrily. "I'm so scared I can't run away. You'll have to keep me. I'm housebroken." He kissed her in between every word. "And lots of fun."

She started to laugh but it turned into a gasp as he got her jeans open and ran his knuckles across the skin of her lower stomach. Lightning sparked from his touch. She twisted against him and lifted her hips so he could remove her jeans entirely. Her underwear went with them but she felt no embarrassment.

And for the first time in her life, as she felt his hot gaze raking over her naked body, she felt beautiful. She didn't know what quirk of fate had made him different, that he would see so differently, but he was there. She would fight the devil himself to hold him. "I love you!" she whispered fiercely as she threw her arms around him.

He went still for a moment. On a low sound of need he sank into her arms and kissed her as deeply as he could. "I love you," he whispered against her lips, over and over again, as if the words had been kept inside him too long to be bottled anymore.

His hands skimmed down the outside of her hips then up again, sensitizing her skin almost unbearably. Still breathing his love with every kiss, he shifted down her body, his lips trailing over her breasts, teasing the little birthmarks along the sides that almost looked like the outline of feathers.

Before she could catch a breath, his hand had slipped between her legs and his palm ruffled the gray curls at the apex of her thighs. The feel of his fingers teasing her was maddening, and she clung onto his arms tightly. She was being shaken apart by the pleasure taking her over. It had to stop somehow, eventually, because she couldn't take it anymore . . .

His weight left her suddenly, and her eyes opened in shock. "Kien?" she managed to ask. He had left her so tightly knotted with desire that she could barely breathe. She would kill him with a dull knife if he was leaving.

"I'm not going anywhere," he promised as he quickly shed the rest of his clothes. He pounced, much like a great cat, and caught her in his arms to roll with her over the top of the bed until she was breathless from laughter as well.

The laugh changed to a strangled cry as he tucked her underneath him and his hard flesh began to sink into her body. She grabbed his shoulders desperately and held on tightly, the lash of pleasure sharper than she had thought.

He stopped moving and she dug her nails into his shoulders, "What're you doing?" she managed to ask.

"I thought I hurt you." His entire body trembled with the strength he exerted to stay still. She felt like hot silk and he was wild to bury himself inside her as deeply as he could, until they were completely one and nothing separated them. One thought glaringly burst in his mind and he gulped air. "Tell me you're on birth control."

It had never even occurred to her. She knew the risk that they were taking and knew that if she said 'no' he would somehow find the strength to stop. She didn't want him to stop; she wanted to feel him inside her, to be his entirely in a way she had never been anyone else's. "Yes," she lied, her voice barely a whisper.

He kissed her deeply on a low groan, his tongue tangling with hers even as he thrust into her completely. Her startled gasp was muffled by his mouth, and he broke the kiss to rain kisses over her face softly. "Am I hurting you? You're so tight."

"No." It had never felt like that before. More powerful, more intimate, and far more wonderful. She slowly twisted underneath him to savor every sensation.

"Stop wiggling," he muttered into her hair, clinging to control with his teeth and toes. She fit like a glove, and he could feel ecstasy beckoning, his skin prickling with the electric tension. His breath hissed out as she clenched her muscles around him. "Maddie!"

"Then do something!" She wrapped herself around him as tightly as she could and held onto him with desperate strength as he began to drive quickly in and out of her body. Heat drowned her, and her breath was almost a sob as she tried to endure the pleasure gripping her body. It snapped with a suddenness that took her breath and unbearable ecstasy swept over her senses. She could only hold onto him fiercely as he buried himself one last time inside her and shuddered as his release consumed his entire body.

He was heavy, but she didn't mind. He felt wonderful as a blanket, and his heat sank all the way inside her soul. She felt sated and replete, contented all the way to her soul. He groaned suddenly, and it made her smile with smug satisfaction. She had worn him out as much as he had worn her out. She would have been happy to stay that way, but he rolled off her to the side and onto his back. The look on his face made a chill ripple through her. Try as she might, she couldn't stop her sudden terror.

He didn't even look at her as he threw an arm over his eyes. "You lied, nightingale."

She gulped softly. "No, I didn't."

"The hell you didn't. Why would you be on birth control? You were convinced you'd never catch a lover." He lowered his arm to eye her. "I might have made you pregnant."

She closed her eyes as despair rose inside. "I'm sorry," she whispered. She sat up, intending to leave the bed, but quick as a snake his arm shot out and wrapped around her waist to hold her in place. "Kienan?" she asked hesitantly.

"You're not going anywhere." He firmly drew her down until she was lying beside him. He turned onto his side and anchored her with an arm around her waist. "When was your last period?" he asked softly as he ran a hand slowly over her body. She blushed at the question and he skimmed a knuckle over her stomach. "When, nightingale?"

"It ended only yesterday," she finally admitted. "We should be safe."

"No wonder you were so crabby!" he muttered. He winced as she hit his shoulder. "Well, damn it, you were! I swear the nicest girls can become downright shrews! My sister isn't worth talking to when she's on her period. She'll snap your head off! Not that I begrudge you guys that, but don't take it out on the innocent bystanders!"

She glared at him. "Innocent bystander, my ass!" Her breath caught as his hand slid between her legs. "Cut it out!" She tried to wiggle loose but only trapped his hand more firmly. "Kien, we can't! Once is stupid, twice is asking for trouble."

"I have protection in my jeans; I just forgot it," he admitted. "It was how I convinced myself to take a gamble. But as soon as I had you in my arms, nothing else seemed to matter. I knew, at the back of my mind, that you weren't on birth control. And I wanted that. I didn't want anything between us." He lowered his head to trail his lips over her shoulder.

"Me neither," she admitted a bit breathlessly.

He lifted his head and framed her face gently with a hand. His brown eyes were as soft as velvet. "Tell me now," he urged softly. "Tell me now when your mind is in control. I need more than something given in the heat of the moment."

Her eyes closed helplessly. She couldn't lie about something that important. "I love you," she admitted achingly. "But it changes nothing, Kienan. You don't know what I am."

"Then tell me." His free hand smoothed slowly over her body, the calluses on his fingers scraping deliberately.

"I'm afraid. You'd never understand." Her breath caught as his fingers slid between her legs once more, unerringly finding where she was most sensitive. "Kienan!"

"I understand that you're the woman I love." He began to shift slowly down her body, caressing and worshipping every inch. "That's all that matters, nightingale. The past doesn't matter. Only the future. You're my future. I'm yours." His lips curved against the swell of her hip. "If you have to explain, save it for the honeymoon."

Any protest she wanted to make was lost as his lips and hands incited her senses to riot. She was drowning in him, unable to resist his tenderness any more than she could resist his passion. But, even then, she knew she had to tell him. Not telling him was a lie by omission, and he deserved so much more. He deserved more than a plain innkeeper, but she couldn't let him go yet. That would come in the morning. Right then he was hers, and she held onto him with all the love in her heart.

CHAPTER FOURTEEN

Kienan awoke around midnight and realized he was alone in bed. Scatterbrain was curled up asleep on his chest. He gently lifted her off and put her on the pillow as he sat up. Madelyne was nowhere in the room but her side of the bed was warm so she had only just left.

He knew where she had gone. He got out of bed and pulled on his jeans quickly. Not that he minded walking around naked, but he had a feeling she might be annoyed. She had an adorable prudish streak.

A prickle went down his back and he turned sharply toward the window. He was being watched. His regular sight told him there was nothing outside the window except the garden and moonlight. He didn't need his eyes, though. He felt it through his sixth sense, and the gaze was volatile and deadly.

When the purple moon is high in the sky, I walk through the heat of a savannah

When the pain is too much for my heart, my nightingale's melody soothes my tears

He went very still as he heard the singing. He yanked his shirt on without buttoning it and hurried out of the bedroom and across the empty lobby. Stormy was sitting at the back door, whining to go out, and he opened the door for them both.

I want to regain the innocence of my youth

But there are no more hopes for me to cling to

The hot springs whispered and murmured as if to play the melody of the nightingale's song. He knew he wasn't breathing, but didn't care as he went as quickly down the path as he could. He still felt as if he was being watched and it was stirring every protective instinct he owned. Madelyne was in danger.

In the night, the nightingale sings, bringing a change in the wind

In the night, the nightingale prays, bringing a change in my dreams

As he drew close to the women's hot springs, he slowed his steps to make as little noise as possible. He crouched down and eased aside the ferns to look into the bathing area. His breath came in sharply as he saw Madelyne wading through the hot spring. She wore nothing but her loose hair and her wings.

When my wings are unable to fly anymore, I can still soar the skies on the notes of a song

And when I cannot see the way out of nightmares, my nightingale's melody becomes my light

There was no place on her body that he hadn't touched or caressed, but fresh desire still prowled through his blood as he watched her. Even now, she could be carrying his child. He wanted her to be pregnant. He wanted to watch the life growing in her, knowing that they had created it together. He had never really thought of himself as a future father, but now that the idea had settled in his brain, it was very appealing. Family was as critical to him as breathing, and he wanted to start his own with Madelyne.

He straightened and pushed aside the bushes to walk toward the hot spring. She stopped singing and turned toward him sharply, her arms crossing defensively across her chest. Terror beat hard in her chest as she watched him. He would turn away from her now. She was sure of it!

He smiled at her, and the terror went away. He held out a hand, his eyes soft. "Come to me, nightingale." When she had hesitantly crossed to him, he reached down and lifted her with easy strength out of the hot spring. "You're beautiful," he murmured. "Why didn't you tell me?"

"I was afraid." Her lips turned down. "Most men would think themselves seduced by a . . . a witch or something."

"I," he decided after a moment of thought, "would be a most willing participant if you decided to seduce me. But if you're going to

use potions for it, please, refrain from putting an IX on them."

She bit her lip and tried not to giggle. "You're ridiculous! I'm not a witch!" Her breath caught as he skimmed a knuckle down the curve of her breast where the birthmark was located. "I'm her. In the legend. I'm the nightingale. This is my second life."

"I know." He drew one of her hands up to rest over his heart. "I've known for a while. And there's something I haven't told you, Maddie." He shrugged out of his shirt and put it around her shoulders. He then stepped back and waited.

She ran her eyes over him and wondered what she was supposed to be looking to find. She found it quickly and her breath caught in her chest. With his jeans riding low on his hips, the little birthmark on his lower right hip was very visible. It was the mark of feathers, and it was nearly white against his golden skin. Most would think it was a tattoo, but she knew better. She didn't know how she hadn't noticed it before. "It was you," she breathed. "You were the swan I saved."

"It came to me rather blindingly the other night." He began to gently fasten the shirt for her. She had started to shiver. "It had been nagging at me for a while, your legend of the nightingale. You'd never explained what the second swan's role was and why he was there. It seemed a bit odd for him to just somehow be there with the nightingale, in a place where poachers often were."

"I never knew. Not then and not now." She didn't resist when he pulled her over to a bench and sat down with her on his lap. She couldn't bring herself to meet his eyes. "It's fuzzy from back then. It comes as hazy vignettes of emotions and brief words. All I know for sure was that I loved you. Somehow, despite being betrayed by one swan, I loved another. I wanted only to protect you. That's why I . . . I did what I did."

"I started having vignettes of my own yesterday. And I'll tell you what happened." He framed her face with his free hand. "I saw you flying through the trees. You were so sad, so lonely. I was drawn to you. I loved you. I decided to leave my flock and go with you anywhere. It was dangerous, yes, but it didn't matter to me. When you died for me . . . I had nothing left to live for." His voice turned quiet and firm. "I flew into the sun."

She took a sharp breath and shook her head quickly. "No. No!" Tears burned her eyes. "How *could* you?! What did I die for if you didn't live?"

"Do you honestly think any life is worth living without you?" he demanded roughly. "Would you live on without me if I was dead?"

Her eyes closed as the tears spilled down her cheeks. "No," she finally whispered. "I couldn't bear it." Her eyes opened then, intent and fierce. "Knowing all this, you must understand why I can't sing with you. Why I can't let anyone know I love you. We were reborn *and so was he*!"

"He?"

"Oh, god." She stared at him through her hands, stricken. "You didn't realize? I'm *cursed*, Kienan! It's not the swan's curse that keeps him from resting until I have a home. There's something else, something more. When the swan built the curse on us both . . . the poacher was there. And he bound himself into the curse. He will never rest until he destroys any chance I have at finding a home."

He could only stare at her. Didn't she see what was really going on? The answer was right there in front of her. Determination filled his heart. "I think I know how to break both curses, but you're going to have to trust me more than you've ever trusted me before."

Before she could form a response to that, they both heard the rustling of bushes. She scrambled to her feet and ducked behind him as he stood. The shirt covered her decently enough but she had to wear it low on her arms so that it went underneath her wings in the back. She felt very vulnerable.

A man walked out of the bushes with all the casual grace of someone walking into a restaurant. He was dressed regularly enough in slacks and a shirt, but there was a long and wicked knife in his hand. It was held with the competence of someone who knew how to kill. "Good evening," he said pleasantly.

Kienan's shoulders tensed slightly. "Trespassing isn't exactly a good thing around here," he said curtly. "The Enforcers take their

District seriously. And I take this inn very seriously. Kindly leave."

"Afraid I can't do that. I believe you're a Shaughnessy, aren't you? Ah, of course you are. Everyone knows the youngest Shaughnessy 'prince' has been smitten with a common peasant." Something dark and malevolent flickered across his face.

Madelyne recognized it even as Kienan did. Despite her best efforts, everyone knew she was in love with Kienan and he with her. It had drawn out the poacher with violent fury and deadly intent. It tore at her as she felt Kienan's body tense. She knew her lover. He would risk himself to protect her. She couldn't bear the idea of his beautiful body covered in blood.

"And what if I am?" Kienan's voice stayed calm. "You have a problem with the Shaughnessy Corp?" He looked closer and realized why the face was familiar. "Ah. I recognize you. Dad and Mel were talking about you, I believe. Let's see . . . I think it had something to do with illegal bookkeeping. You inflated your own stock so that people paid for something with no value. Dad helped the police set you up so you hung yourself with your own rope. I thought you were in jail."

"That's what bail is for." He suddenly sprang forward with almost unnatural speed, something mad in his eyes. The knife was lifted high and curved to hit Kienan directly.

Without thinking, Madelyne knocked Kienan aside and left herself in the path of the knife. She knew only that she couldn't let him die again. He fell over the bench and tried to get his feet underneath himself. "Maddie!" he screamed.

A wild and vicious growl rose on the air with all the force and fury of a guardian wolf enraged. Stormy lunged from the shadows and leapt directly into the path of the knife. It raked across her face, split skin and fur, and sprayed blood. The blade's path continued and struck her in the flank. It remained there and yanked from the attacker's hand as she went through the air. She landed several feet away and did not move. Blood pooled slowly under her body.

"Oh god!" Madelyne flew toward the wolf as fast as she could.

The attacker took a step after her, but Kienan leapt over the top of the bench and lunged forward. Before the would-be killer could block, Kienan's fist slammed into his jaw and sent him flying. He spun around with his heel but the man caught his leg and tried to throw it away. Kienan had trained too long to fall for that. He turned the throw into a flip and his other foot got the man in the chin with bone-shattering force. His opponent was unconscious before he hit the ground.

"Stay with her," Kienan ordered Madelyne. "I'm calling the cops and a vet." He ran down the path quickly, his bare feet slapping against the tile.

Tears streaming down her cheeks, she ran her fingers over Stormy's fur gently. She could feel the rise and fall of her breath, shallow though it was. "You idiot," she whispered. "Damn it, why'd you do it? For him, for me? If you die, you'll never be free. Don't die, please!"

A groan caught her attention and she looked over to see the attacker stirring. Fury rose inside her and she walked over to look down at him. His eyes opened blearily and she knelt down beside him. Quite firmly, she pressed on his broken jaw. His eyes rolled with pain and knocked him out once more. "I ought to kill you here, you bastard," she said fiercely. She folded her wings away as she stood once more. "If she dies, there will be nowhere you can hide. I will be *your* curse!"

Police and medics arrived minutes later. Kienan told them what had happened as Madelyne and a paramedic tried to stop Stormy's bleeding while they waited for the vet. To Madelyne's surprise, the vet arrived with a familiar red-haired woman in tow. "Rhianna!" She leapt to her feet and hugged the shorter woman tightly. "Rhianna . . . she . . ."

"I know." Rhianna Taber held her surrogate daughter tighter and rocked gently. Her gaze when she looked at the vet was fierce. "Take her back to headquarters to treat her. And if anything happens to her, you're looking for a new job."

"Yes'm." The vet had Stormy lifted onto the ambulance and they took off down the street with sirens blaring even as the attacker

was loaded onto the other truck and taken the other way.

Kienan warily approached where the two women were standing. He had never met Rhianna Taber before, but he knew of her. He knew she had been the force behind his sister's contract as well as his own. He knew she was connected in some way to Stormy since the wolf served as courier. He knew she was a co-owner of Enforcers and had been for at least three decades. She had to be in her fifties, at the minimum, but she barely looked out of her twenties.

Rhianna looked him over once before holding out a hand. "So you're the youngest Shaughnessy male. Your father is a shark, and I very much enjoy working with him." The Enforcers had alliances with dozens of companies, including the Shaughnessy Corp. Not quite a merger, not quite a partnership. It was more like a mutually beneficial relationship for all.

"Thanks." He shook her hand, still wary. She was Madelyne's adopted mother (legal guardian, his ass), and he was sleeping with Madelyne. "I intend to marry Maddie," he finally said. "I want your permission."

"Kienan!" Mortified, Madelyne released Rhianna and glared at her lover. "This is hardly the time!"

"There won't be any better." He held Rhianna's black eyes intently. "I know what she is, and I don't care. I love her, and I want her to be my wife. My father is in agreement."

Rhianna said nothing for a few moments and tapped a scarlet fingernail against her hip. She was in casual clothes but still every inch the businesswoman. "And if I refuse?" she finally asked calmly.

His face tightened. "I'd take her away. I love her too much to let her go, even when she is fighting me. I won't let anyone hurt her, ever again. So, please." He bowed deeply, stunning Madelyne. "I ask again. Give me permission to marry Maddie."

Rhianna smiled. He was just the same as any other Shaughnessy she had ever met. A wild spirit with a generous heart and a willingness to fight for love. "You're one hell of a kid. Yes, you have my permission, and my blessings." She touched Madelyne's face gently. "The rest is up to her now. Good luck, both of you. I'll call when I find out what

Stormy's condition is."

"Thank you," Madelyne whispered. She turned her face into Kienan's shoulder as Rhianna walked away. "Kienan, just because she said . . . it changes nothing. You saw what happened. Stormy might . . ." Her voice broke, unable to bear the very idea.

"Maddie, take a chance." He brought her hand to his lips. "I know you've suffered under your curses, but there's a way out of them both. You said it yourself that they were connected. You'd see the answer if you'd just open your eyes." He let her go slowly. "Saturday is the contest. I'm going to lay it all on the line there. If you don't sing, I won't. I want you more than my music, and if I go big without you, I'll never have you. I'm laying my dreams and my heart at your feet, nightingale."

She felt cold as he walked away toward the inn. "Where are you going?"

"Home." He looked over his shoulder. "I've done everything I can. You have to fly to me of your own will, Madelyne." He smiled suddenly even though it was strained around the edges. "How do you hide those anyway?"

"They push in and out of the skin on my back," she whispered. "It's genetic. They get smaller when they go away, and grow when they come out."

"They're beautiful, you know." He gently shut the inn door and she wrapped her arms around herself. She felt cold all the way to her bones. She simply didn't know if she was strong enough to give him what he wanted and what she so desperately longed for herself.

As soon as everyone was gone, she went into the inn and to her room. Except for the shirt she was wearing, there was no sign that Kienan had been there. Or was there? A sheaf of papers sitting on her dresser called her attention, and she walked over to look at them. Her heart leapt. It was music. It was the song he had written.

She found herself pouring over every note, memorizing every word. It shook her. He had written this for them, for her. She could see where his understanding of her skill had driven him to give her the harder notes, the higher pitches. Her voice would blend with his as naturally as their bodies had come together.

Feeling very cold, she heaped extra blankets on the bed. Scatterbrain snuggled against her, but gave little comfort for the moment. The phone rang two hours later and brought the news that Stormy would be fine, but scarred for life. It nearly broke Madelyne. She was almost crying when she called Kienan's cell phone. She wasn't surprised when he answered immediately.

"She'll be fine," she said without greeting.

He let out a ragged breath. "Thank god." He was silent for long moments then added softly, "A lonely bed is a cold one, Maddie, no matter how many blankets you have. You'll always be warm in my arms, though." Softly, he hung up the phone.

She stared at the blankets and felt fresh tears burning her eyes. How had he known? Holding his shirt tight because it carried his scent, she curled up and closed her eyes, wishing with all she was for the strength to reach for her own dreams. She just didn't know what to do.

By the time Saturday came around, the betting pool was higher than ever. Madelyne was avoiding Kienan, and every time he looked at her, he watched her with a longing that made nearly everyone on campus wildly envious. Even when they began to pester Taegan and Mel, who lived with Kienan, and Kalliope, who was Madelyne's best friend, no one could get a straight answer as to what was going on.

The talent competition had pulled people from all over the city, even Rhianna from the Enforcers, Kalliope's father from Tavoularis Industries, and Sullivan. The Shaughnessy patriarch was clearly waiting for his son's performance; he held the contract they had signed a week prior. Madelyne, watching him from the back of the room, felt her stomach quiver.

Kalliope leaned against the wall next to her suddenly and

murmured, "What holds you back?"

"Ever loved someone so much you'd die for them?" she asked starkly.

After a momentary pause, Kalliope said softly, "No."

"When you do, you'll understand." She pressed her hands to her eyes, but pulled them down quickly when she heard Kienan's name announced. Her heart began to beat in her chest. Surely he would reach for his dreams!

His keyboard was already set up and he walked over to it with his lethal and beautiful stride. As he hit the first chord, he opened his eyes and met her gaze across the room. She knew the music intimately, and she was stunned when the verse started and he did not sing. The room began to shift nervously, and Sullivan frowned.

"Speaking as someone who knows what it's like to long for true love," Kalliope said quietly, "it's very foolish to throw it away when you have it. You're not a fool, Madelyne Winters, and stronger than you think. No curse can stand up to love, hon."

On a shuddering breath, Madelyne stopped fighting. Kalliope was right. Kienan was right. And if he could take a risk like this, then so could she. She waited for the music to come around again and began walking toward the stage, her stomach clenching in nerves as she lifted her voice.

Even when I'm alone I can feel the beat inside my heart

An excited buzz raced through the room as everyone began to murmur excitedly. No one had realized her lovely speaking voice was only the tip of the vocal iceberg that was her incredible talent. Kienan's eyes lit with delight. He kept playing and picked up the next line in the song.

So even when you're apart from me we can dance together

The stage was too high to climb onto and the only stairs were backstage. Before she could figure out how to get to him, Taegan stepped forward and caught her around the waist. He lifted her up gently and made it easy for her to climb up onto the stage. She smiled at him as Kienan continued to sing.

The brush of your body against mine, the scent of your perfume

The touch of your hand on my own, the heat of your skin

Her eyes met his and he inclined his head with a smile toward where the microphone stand waited. She ignored it and walked over to sit beside him on the bench. She pulled the mic down where they both could use it. She smiled as well, and he let out a soft breath as she picked up her part in the lyrics.

Come with me into the darkness where the light is hiding
Come with me where seduction itself is another dance

The audience cheered loudly. Kienan's entire family was grinning. Kalliope all but jumped up and down at the back of the auditorium. Rhianna, from where she was watching, couldn't help but grin as well. She needed to go to her office and make a call or two. She got to her feet and walked out of the auditorium silently as she heard the voices behind her meshing into a perfect harmony.

No matter how the music changes around us
The music in our hearts will never change

Even when I'm alone I can feel the beat inside of my heart
So even when you're apart from me we can dance together

Swaying like the falling stars as you fall into my arms
Spinning like the colorful turrets on a merry-go-round

Come with me into the night where the moon sings high
Come with me where the nightingale practices her scales

No matter how the world around us changes the times
The time in this dance will always be one on one

Even when I'm alone I can feel the beat inside of my heart
So even when you're apart from me we can dance together
Even when I'm dreaming, I can feel the memory of this dance
So even when you're sleeping far away, we can dance together

They didn't win. The winner was a sophomore who could fiddle a medley of recognizable rock hits in under two minutes. Even Kienan and Madelyne felt she had earned it. While Madelyne congratulated her backstage, Kienan went looking for his father.

Sullivan was still sitting in the audience and smiled as Kienan sat beside him. "You far exceeded my expectations, son. I'll do whatever I can to make sure you get that sale. You'll have your musical career."

"I don't want it." He had thought long and hard about it. "I want to record this song with Maddie and sell it, yes, but I don't want to go into music as a career. I'm going to keep my major. Being fluent in many languages will help Madelyne with the inn. We could draw in foreign tourists to help turn a nice profit."

Sullivan contemplated that for long moments and then finally asked, "What changed your mind?"

"Maddie. She belongs in the 3rd District and so do I. I realize that now. The inn needs serious renovations, though. Someone needs to invest." A determined look in his eyes proved that he, too, was a Shaughnessy businessman at the core. "I'm going to go over things with Maddie and we'll write a proposal for you to consider. After all, the Shaughnessy Corp. is about investing in dreams and making them come true."

"It is indeed," Sullivan agreed. "And I will give your proposal for the inn the same consideration I'd give any other. I won't let family get in the way. If it isn't sound, I'll tell you so." He, too, understood pride. "If I accept, what will you do?"

"Start the renovations. Maddie and I can live at home until they're completed and move in just before Aenya's wedding. I know she and Hiro are waiting until she's out of high school, but I'm not waiting for Maddie. She needs family, and I need her."

"Your mother would be proud of you," Sullivan said quietly. "As

I am. And I will be very pleased to call Madelyne," he paused, then corrected himself deliberately, "call Maddie my daughter."

He smiled. "Thanks, Dad." He got to his feet and headed backstage, following his sixth sense for his lover. It was sharper than ever. He always knew when she was near or far, and even how much distance there was between them. He found her sitting just outside the backstage, perched gracefully on the railing of the stairs like the wild little bird she was inside. He walked up beside her and leaned against the rail. "I turned down the offer for a music career."

She stared at him. "But why? It was what you wanted all along."

"I want you." He smiled up at her. "You're not a jetsetter. You're the kind who likes to nest. So I figure we record and sell just this one song and let it provide supplemental income. And we'll get your inn into working order so it gives some of the bigger chains competition. You'll never have to worry in the middle of the night again. And," he added, "if you do, you can just roll over and punch me, and make me worry with you."

She had to smile. "You're that confident, are you?" She sighed and held her arms out to him. "Alright, I give in. I give up." She went into his arms, and her head rested on his shoulder where it had always belonged. "I'll marry you, and we'll run an inn and raise pets and kids."

"Kids?" He stared at her. "Are you . . . ?"

"No, I don't think so." She smiled up at him. "But I'm hoping."

His breath sighed out softly, the tension and pain fading as he pulled her into his arms. "Come home with me, nightingale," he said softly.

"I'm already there." She knew it was true, felt it as his arms closed around her. The curses, both of them, were gone. "That's all I ever had to do," she said softly. "I just had to trust in you and the home you offered. It was always that simple." She lifted her head to look at him, and her violet eyes were soft and beautiful. "Take me home, Kienan. I've been waiting for you for so long."

Inside the auditorium, Sullivan saw the rest of his family waiting for him and got to his feet to go join them. As he did, the contract fell onto the floor. He picked it up just in time to see the word 'Complete' appear across the top. He smiled.

Stormy carefully limped up beside him; she was bandaged but clearly well on the mend. He knelt and ruffled the fur on her head gently before handing her the contract so that she could carry it in her teeth. "Thank you," he said softly, and sincerely. "But you're part of the family too, so you can't go dying on us. Take that to Ms. Taber, but then take care of yourself for a while."

As he watched her head off and he himself headed toward the door, he regarded his two oldest sons and had to wonder just who would be next.

CHAPTER FIFTEEN

Rhianna studied the contract sitting in front of her. This one had been personal, and she was well pleased with the results. She added her notes to the bottom, smiling as she did, then slipped the contract into the open folder waiting on her desk. The folder glowed as the word 'Complete' appeared and she added it to the end of the Shaughnessy folder.

As she shut the drawer, she glanced across the room. "You took too big a risk," she said quietly but firmly.

The voice that responded was also feminine, but it was huskier and held a note of steel. "I'm risking everything this time. If I don't succeed . . . well, we both know what that means, so let's not go there, shall we? Life or death. Right now they mean the same to me. All I care for is freedom."

"As I see." As she always had, she decided as she pulled out two blank contracts from her desk.

"Two?"

"Mmm. You'll see. Let's get to work, shall we?"

Status: File In Progress

Analysis: The nightingale who has a home always sings a love song.

Folder Three
TAEGAN

CHAPTER SIXTEEN

Among the big businesses in New York City, several names were known to one and all. Like modern day kingdoms, these businesses were handed down through family lines. Unlike more traditional kingdoms, the 'kings' and 'queens' usually put the happiness of their families before anything else. There was never any pressure on an heir to inherit. If they chose not to inherit, then a solution would be reached. It was that easy.

In the world of advertising lived the Viani and Dease families. In the world of investment lived the Shaughnessy and Tavoularis families. Shaughnessy Corp. and Tavoularis Industries were not dissimilar in their operations. Shaughnessy Corp. focused on helping small businesses get up and running. Tavoularis Industries stepped in to keep small businesses from bending under the pressure of large markets without sympathy.

Tavoularis Industries was owned and operated by Jiles Tavoularis. He and his wife had inherited the company from his father and mother, who had in turn inherited from his father's mother and father. It had always been passed down from generation to generation within a short time of the selected heir's marriage. There were extenuating circumstances just in case of deaths and surprise births, but it was generally understood by one and all that an heir could not normally inherit until they were married.

Kalliope hated rules. And she *really* hated rules that dictated she couldn't have one thing without the other. She refused to marry for less than love, and that meant she was still unmarried. Her father refused to let her take control of the company until she was at least engaged. It made for some interesting Saturday mornings.

Some loud ones, in fact.

Even across the mansion, Mara Tavoularis could hear her husband and daughter shouting. She ignored them as she always did. She absolutely refused to take sides in the issue. On one hand, she did agree that Kalliope should be less picky. But on the other hand, she also agreed that she deserved to wait for love. The safest thing for Mara to do was to eat her breakfast and ignore the shouting. So she did.

In Jiles' office, Kalliope paced back and forth in front of her father's desk, her pale legs nothing but a blur under the edge of her short denim skirt. She hadn't had time to do her hair and it tumbled around her back in a wave of black curls. She had been rather unceremoniously ordered to her father's office, and she distinctly resented it.

She planted her hands on the desk and leaned forward. "I am an adult," she snapped. "I am capable of making my own decisions! And I *refuse* to be part of a Cinderella plan! You are not going to ruin my birthday, damn you!"

Jiles rubbed his forehead and bemoaned a fate that had given him a headstrong and stubborn daughter for his heir. This was a fight that had been three years in the making. "Kally," he said as calmly as he could manage, "it's not a Cinderella plan."

"Oh the hell it is!" She straightened and began to pace again. "You're planning to invite all of the eligible bachelors in the vicinity to my birthday party in the hopes that I might pick one. If that's not a Cinderella plan, I don't know what is. If I find a *single* name on that list that I didn't specify, I'm going to make you regret it!"

He grimaced. He knew what she was threatening him with. The simple fact was that he loved his daughter and worshipped the ground she walked on. And as she knew it as well, she knew her most potent weapon was to start crying and make him feel guilty. He couldn't help it. Whenever he saw her tears, he was driven to do whatever he could fix things. It was just vexing that she knew it too. She was a businesswoman to her core. "Kally, let's be reasonable."

"I am being reasonable. You're the one with the issues!" She tossed her hair back as she turned toward the door. "And besides, it would serve you right if I went along with things. You've got this mental hang-up about our position in society. You want me to marry someone of a similar standing. Gee, as I recall, the prince in the story found himself a commoner. It would be your just desserts if I fell for someone who was blue collar." Her black eyes fired with a temper that was nearly regal. "Mark my words, Dad. I. Am. Not. A. Prize!"

The door slammed so hard behind her that a vase sitting on the nearby shelf jumped and fell onto the floor where it shattered and sprayed water and flowers everywhere. On a groan, Jiles lowered his head and began to beat it steadily against the top of his desk. Why couldn't she be happy with a nice business marriage? The Shaughnessy heir, Mel, was only a few months older than she was. It would be a good arrangement. The two companies had flirted with the idea of a merger for a few years. Mel seemed nice and levelheaded. He would be perfect for Kalliope.

Certainly, Mel was levelheaded compared to his little brother and sister, but he was by no means an idiot. Sullivan was on a tear, convinced that since the two youngest of his children had gotten married or engaged, then the oldest two should be as well. Mel was much his father's son. He knew a hostile takeover when it reared its paternal head. He locked himself in his room and announced he was studying. Since his grades bordered on the cusp of no hope, no one went near his door.

Unfortunately, Taegan was another story entirely. He had been enduring Sullivan's not so subtle efforts to get him married off for seven years. He still wasn't sure if it was Sullivan's revenge for his decision to become a teacher instead of inheriting the company.

He sighed and looked at the doorway to his bedroom. Stormy sat there waiting for him. She had been sitting there for ten minutes with all the patience of a saint. He knew he couldn't outwait her and finally put down the pen he had been grading papers with. He was summoned, and he knew it.

He walked over and knelt down to study her. Though he couldn't quite understand the 'how' of the situation, let alone the 'why', he knew very well the 'who.' He had a gift, as most of the Shaughnessys did. His was to recognize energy in and around other living beings. Stormy's had always been familiar.

He gently ran his hands over her side to check on the healing wounds. It had been two weeks since she had been wounded defending Kienan and Madelyne, and she was doing amazingly well. She would always carry the scars, but she would soon be strong and healthy once more.

"You're a strange one," he murmured softly as he studied her face and intelligent yellow eyes. "If I asked you what you really were, would you answer?" Her response was to lick his hand and he smiled. "If you really are who I think you are, that was a very flattering kiss."

She snorted lightly. He got to his feet and dropped his glasses on the desk with a sigh. "C'mon then. You can hang around me all you like." He gave her a wry smile, well aware of what her presence had led to lately. "But I'm afraid I'll be a harder mark than my baby brother and sister."

When he got downstairs, he saw the same brother and sister peering around the corner of the hall and watching Sullivan's study door like one might watch a ticking time bomb. They spotted him, and they both began clapping. Aenya even had a pair of pompoms—god only knew where she had gotten them—and she waved them in encouragement.

On a laugh, he said, "Go away."

"Spoilsport," Kienan groused.

Aenya took his hand in sympathy. "Come on. Let Taegan deal with Daddy. Maddie made breakfast this morning." When her brother perked up, she shook her head. "I still say she spoiled you by marrying you so fast. It went to your head."

"Yeah." Kienan just grinned. "But how else would I have gotten

her to cook for us?"

Taegan couldn't argue that the entire family had gotten the benefit of Madelyne's amazing culinary skills. He also couldn't argue that she had spoiled Kienan. He just happened to think that Kienan spoiled her just as much, just as they ought to do.

With a little sigh, he opened the office door and held it long enough to let Stormy in. He then walked in himself and shut the door. "You wanted to see me, Father?"

"Have a seat, Taegan."

Mentally bracing himself, he sat down in one of the chairs. Stormy sat down beside him and firmly aligned herself on his side. He was oddly grateful for the support.

Sullivan took a deep breath. He knew he was in for a fight but he felt compelled to plead his case again. When he had seen Stormy suddenly attach herself to Taegan, he had been ecstatic, sure that his prayers would be answered. The wolf was a good spirit of some kind. He was sure of it. "I'm sure you know why I called you in here."

His son grimaced slightly. "I have a feeling I can give your speech for you." He sighed. "Father . . ." He trailed off as Sullivan held up a hand. Under his breath, he muttered, "Here we go again."

"You're twenty-eight years old, Taegan," Sullivan began. "It's time you considered finding yourself a wife. I was very lenient with your wishes to become a math instructor even though you knew full well I had always expected you to take over the company."

Taegan had to smile at that. "I don't have a head for business. Mel does. He's a much better choice, if he ever gets his grades up. And you really had no chance to argue as you did with Aenya and Kienan. I didn't tell you my plans until I was an adult." Because he loved his father, he willingly admitted, "I would have told you even sooner if the law hadn't changed. I never wanted to get your hopes up, but I knew you would have stopped me."

That law had been a pain in Sullivan's side for several years, though, oddly, he was suddenly looking on it with a kinder eye. It had become almost an aid rather than a hindrance when it came to the happiness of his family. "I can't argue that," he admitted. "And I'm proud of you, Taegan, never doubt that. You got a four-year degree and teaching credentials in a third of the time it takes others. But it's always been tradition . . ."

" . . . Tradition in the family that the eldest marry by thirty and carry on the family name," he finished. He rubbed his forehead. "I have two years left, Father, thank you. I already feel old inside. You don't need to help."

Sullivan knew the feeling, and he knew Taegan had been forced to grow up much faster than normal. He had been only ten when his mother had died, and yet he'd had to step up to help Sullivan raise a newborn Aenya, two-year-old Kienan, and even six-year-old Mel. There was no one who respected Taegan more than Sullivan.

And it was because he loved his son that he said, "Taegan, answer me honestly." He leaned back in his chair. "You haven't dated a single woman since you were twenty-four. If you're gay, I'd appreciate you just saying so."

Taegan could only sigh. "No, I'm not." He rubbed his hands over his face. "There's a reason for it, really. It's just complicated."

Sullivan sighed internally. He had hoped he was right if only because it would be easy to reassure his son that anyone he loved would be welcome, and he could again start looking for the one for him. Shaughnessys needed family. It was part of who and what they were. "Well, what's the reason then?"

Taegan got to his feet and walked over to the window to stare out across the landscape. He had only ever admitted the reason in his mind. It had never come to his lips. "I fear that I am a victim of my own romantic heart." His smile turned sad and wry. "I have the misfortune to be in love with the one woman I can never have. I've loved her for four years. I'll love her until I die. And if I can't have her, I don't want anyone else."

Sullivan looked at him for long moments and then turned his gaze to Stormy. She was watching Taegan too, but when she felt Sullivan's gaze, she turned her head to meet his eyes. She tilted her head a little but it was clear she understood what he was trying to convey. She woofed softly in agreement.

Taegan heard the woof and turned with a smile to kneel and run his hands over her head teasingly, with all the affection he would ruffle his siblings' hair. "She seems to have been a lucky charm lately, so maybe something might change." He looked at his father. "But don't get your hopes up. It's bad for your heart."

Sullivan scowled. "There is nothing wrong with my heart!" He watched the door shut behind his son and the wolf before letting out a sigh. He turned in his chair and looked out the window at the rolling gardens. He didn't know who had captured Taegan's heart. No contract from the Enforcers had mysteriously arrived to help gently nudge things along.

It made him wonder just what this story would be and how it would end.

CHAPTER SEVENTEEN

Taegan taught several different levels of math classes at college, though none that his siblings took. The college frowned sharply on even the slightest hint of impropriety. That didn't stop him from acting as a tutor at home for his younger siblings, of course, but that was under the table.

As most teachers did, he had a few favorite students among all his classes. One was a young man who couldn't do basic math to save his life but could unravel Algebraic equations in his head. Another was Kalliope.

In Latin, she would have been the *decorus procer*. She even looked like a 'beautiful princess' and held one of the best reputations on campus. She was unrivaled for valedictorian, her GPA was a solid 4.0, and she had been voted Homecoming Queen every year she had been at college. She had two courses of study; a major in Business Management and a minor in Cosmetology. She had been tested and retested, and her scores tipped comfortably into the genius range every time.

It was for that reason alone that he realized something was wrong on Monday afternoon. He had always felt particularly attuned to her, and he had known from the moment she arrived that she was out of sorts. Her concentration was absent and she couldn't even add whole numbers, let alone integers.

While everyone was writing down notes from the board, he stopped and knelt next to her desk. "Kalliope," he said softly. "Wait for me after class. I'd like to talk to you."

"Yes, sir." She watched him as he went back to the front of the class. Not that she was the only one. Every female in the class watched Professor Shaughnessy. In fact, the class was mostly female, as were all his classes; it was a phenomena quite well known around the campus. Kalliope could vouch for it personally. She had been in all of his classes.

He was at least a foot taller than she was, and he was strong and muscular. His thick black hair fell into his eyes and clung to the back of his neck. It was never styled and instead left to its own devices, serving a lure to any female with a sense of touch in her fingers. His eyes were honey brown with little flecks of yellow. His face was sheer perfection. He was, without question, the most attractive professor on campus, and one of the three most attractive males over all. The other two were his younger brothers.

He wore glasses to read and was known for sometimes forgetting they were on top of his head. He had the slightest hint of a brogue in his voice, more a flavor of Ireland than an outright accent. Most assumed he had a temper—his brothers certainly did—but he was unfailingly gentle with everyone. He was open and friendly, always ready to lend a hand or an ear, or whatever was needed by anyone.

And she had been in love with him for four years. She acknowledged it inside her heart though she had never spoken of it to anyone, not even Madelyne. She pushed it down where it couldn't be found and acted the same around Taegan as she did anyone else. Never mind that she wanted to run her hands through his hair. Never mind that she longed to feel his hands on her body.

She could even pinpoint the exact moment she had fallen for him. It had been her first day at the school. She had been so nervous that she had found herself bumping into things. One of them had been Taegan. He had smiled at her and told her that he was nervous too because it was his first day as a teacher. She had made sure to take all of his classes ever since. She didn't necessarily love math, but he made it worth it. Even if she hadn't loved him, he would have been her favorite teacher.

After class, she waited by the door for him as he spoke with other students. He wasn't an official campus counselor, but students always went to him first with problems. And he listened. He listened and gave advice. It was for that reason alone that she found herself glad he wanted to talk to her. Maybe he would be open to listening to her, too.

"I'm sorry," he apologized with a smile as he joined her. "Shall we?"

He walked beside her, close enough that he was still with her, but not so close that she felt crowded by his height. She adored that about him. She was short and she knew it, but she hated men who had to point it out. "How tall are you?" she finally asked. She glanced up at him. "I mean, I barely reach your shoulder."

"Six-three." He smiled. "You're not short, Kalliope. You're just . . . compact. Like your car."

She eyed him, but she was smiling. "Let me guess: good things come in small packages? I thought men didn't believe that."

"Only about some things." His smile was as teasing as hers as he held his office door for her. "I like small cars." And the small woman walking beside him, but he didn't say it out loud.

"You'd never fit in one." She dropped her bag on the floor and sat down on the edge of the chair. Her skirt was just short enough that she worried she would stick to the leather seat.

He saw how she was sitting and immediately shrugged out of his jacket. He pulled her up to her feet and put the jacket down on the seat. "Here. Sit comfortably."

"Oh. Thank you." A little flustered, she sat again and settled back in the chair. She tried to keep her gaze as casual as she could while she watched him sit behind his desk. The plain white shirt he wore made his shoulders look even wider. She wanted to cuddle in rather badly. "So what did you want to talk to me about? I know, I was off today."

"Only a little. And as I've never known you to be off about anything, it had me concerned." His eyes darkened as he studied her. "It's obvious something is on your mind, Kalliope. And it clearly has you upset. I thought maybe you might want to talk to someone."

She chewed on her lower lip while she thought about it,

unwittingly causing knots of desire to coil inside his body. He had loved her for four years. He had wanted her with a growing obsession to where her laughter alone could turn him on. He had watched her blossom over four years into a woman whose body was his every fantasy and whose mind always kept him guessing and intrigued.

He was patient. As long as she was in his classes—and she had been rather innocently tormenting him by being in them all—he didn't even dare contemplate crossing any lines. Impropriety would ruin them both. But if he could just wait until she graduated, then he might yet have a chance to win her heart.

Of course, graduation wouldn't remove the problem of her father. He was well aware that Jiles Tavoularis wanted his daughter to marry another businessman. Taegan was a Shaughnessy, but he wasn't in line to inherit the company anymore. He didn't want business. In fact, there were only two things he had ever truly wanted. Teaching . . . and Kalliope.

She made up her mind to tell him everything and lifted her gaze to meet his eyes. Her heart instantly skipped a beat. Heat pooled low in her body. She wanted to tell herself she was imagining things, but she was sure, *positive*, that there was desire in his eyes as he looked at her. "Taegan?"

The look was gone as he blinked at her. "My mind was wandering," he apologized. "So, what's troubling you?"

"My father." She propped her chin on her hand. "He's being a pain in the ass. He wants me to get married." Frustrated all over again, she got to her feet and began to pace. Pacing was how she worked out her anger and he wisely stayed seated. "I keep telling him I want to be in love when I marry, but he won't get a clue!"

"What has he done lately to make this rant different than the others?" he shrewdly asked. He was *well* acquainted with the same exact rant from his own father.

She snorted lightly. "Do I look like a prince?" She turned toward him, hands on her hips.

He studied the distinctly female body in front of him, chicly shown in a short black skirt and a partially unbuttoned cream-colored blouse. There was a black scarf around her neck and silver loops dripped from her ears. "Hardly," he said dryly. "A princess perhaps."

"Gee, thanks." She huffed and dropped into the chair again. "My birthday party is coming up in a few days. He wants to change *my* guest list and invite all the bachelors in the nearby vicinity."

He ran his tongue over his teeth. "I see."

"I am NOT a prince in a Cinderella story!" She shook a fist at him. "And stop snickering at me, you brute!" She crossed her arms on a huff as he laughed outright. "I'm going to watch that guest list like a *hawk*. I'm making the invitations personally. Oh, you're invited, too," she added.

"Well, thank you." He leaned back in his chair with a wry smile. "If it's any consolation, my father has been after me for seven years for much the same. It's driving me insane."

She blinked in surprise. "How old are you, Taegan? Only seven years seems a short time. Aren't you in your thirties?"

"Not yet." He smiled. "I'm only twenty-eight. Just turned recently, as a matter of fact."

"Oh!" She suddenly felt less guilty about her feelings. "You're only four years older than me; I turn twenty-four in a few days. I guess I was assuming you were older because you've been teaching for four years."

"I graduated early. I had to," he added ruefully. "My father wasn't entirely happy when I decided not to inherit the company. But the simple fact is that it isn't for me. Mel's much more suited for it than I am. I just don't want to run a company."

"I do." Her gaze was drawn to a photograph of San Francisco that hung on the wall. She didn't need to see the artist signature in the corner to know that he had taken it. It was as beautiful as its creator. "I want to run Tavoularis Industries. I like being in charge, and there's so much we have the potential to do. Daddy doesn't think big enough. I do, and I can make what I think happen."

She sighed and shrugged her shoulders. "It's just a little lonely, I suppose." She smiled wryly. "Maddie's the first real friend I've had in a long time. Usually I get treated with kid gloves by girls, and the boys

either want to get into the company, or my pants. None really look at *me*. What I wouldn't give for a normal day, just once!"

The decision, for Taegan, was an easy one. "Do you have any more classes today?"

"No. I usually go to the salon for a few hours."

"Good. I'm also free for the rest of the day." He shut down his computer and smiled. "Why don't we both have a normal day? Let's go have some fun. We both need to pretend for a little while that no one expects anything of us."

She began to smile. "I think I'd enjoy that." She got to her feet and picked up his jacket for him as he came around the desk. As she handed it to him, she rose on her toes to kiss his cheek. "You're a good man, Taegan Shaughnessy."

"I do my best." But it really stung in moments like that when the woman he loved viewed him only as a friend. He would have happily killed to have her look at him as a man, desire in her beautiful black eyes.

"Are we taking your car?" she asked as she followed him out into the afternoon sunshine. It was bright, so she pulled out her sunglasses and slid them on. As she did, she saw him exchanging his regular glasses for sunglasses, and her heart gave a wild thump in her chest.

No math teacher should have looked like that. It was going to be an image stuck in her head whenever she was in class. He was wearing a suit but he had taken off his tie and exchanged his suit jacket for a leather one. He suddenly looked his actual age, and he was attractive enough to stop traffic.

"Hoo boy," she said under her breath. Down girl.

"I don't actually have a car," he was saying. He led the way toward the faculty lot. "I have a bike." His smile turned wry. "I can't afford a good car. Teachers don't make very much, and I refuse to accept anything from my father."

A motorcycle. She managed a weak smile. "As long as you have an extra helmet, I don't mind." Yup, she saw, it was a motorcycle. It was also a *red* motorcycle that gleamed and shined. Her entire view of Taegan had changed very sharply, and she tried to reconcile the two sides of him. "By any chance," she asked, "were you a bad boy in high school?"

He flashed her a grin that was pure wicked danger. It was confident and self-assured and so outrageously beautiful that it made every pulse in her body begin beating all at once. She had heard rumor of the Shaughnessy smile, but rumor had vastly understated its potency. He seemed oblivious of its impact.

"I was a paragon," he assured her, but there was laughter in his voice.

"You were a bad boy. I *knew* it. I knew you weren't that different from your siblings. Kienan and Aenya are obvious about their wild spirit, and Mel does his level best to tame it, but can't wholly hide it. You hide yours the best, but it's definitely there! You're a walking oxymoron." She pulled on the helmet he handed her, and then her heart gave a wild thump again as he swung her up onto the bike in front of him.

He reached around her to turn on the bike and the scent of his skin and cologne curled into her lungs. Really, it should have been her first clue. He smelled wild and untamed, a sharp and romantic scent that made her think of swordsmen and heroes and being carried away for happily ever after.

"So where to?" he asked.

"Well, there's a good movie playing. But it's a chick flick," she warned him.

"Here's a secret that my brothers, and future brother-in-law, will deny unto death. We're all suckers for romance. We all read novels and watch movies. Kienan has been known to cry, but he'd kick my ass if that got out. He has a black belt. It would hurt." He glanced down at her with a smile to see her grinning. "Besides, I hear you're known to watch action flicks."

"Most of them have half-naked men with muscles." She smiled serenely. "I'm a healthy woman, what can I say?" She eyed the masculine arm that was in front of her. He would sell a fortune in movies to women if the arm under the sleeve was even half as built as implied.

She felt oddly safe and secure in his arms as he navigated traffic. His body was angled close to hers as if trying to keep her safe and sheltered. In a way she wasn't surprised. She knew he was as much a protector by nature as Kienan was.

When they parked at the movie theater, she couldn't help asking, "What happened to your mother?" Sadness seemed to move through his eyes and she shook her head quickly. "Never mind. That was personal."

"It's alright, Kally." He used her nickname without thought as he pulled his helmet off. He smoothed a hand through his hair as he considered his words. Then, finally, he said it as simply as he could. "My mother died in childbirth with Aenya. We were in a car accident, and it brought on labor too fast. I ended up with a broken arm and a concussion. When I finally woke, it was to the news that my mother was gone, and my sister was three months premature. We couldn't take her home for months."

"Oh, Taegan." She pulled off her helmet, wanting to hold him and take away the pain in his eyes and voice. Resisting the urge was the hardest thing she had ever done. "What was she like?"

"She hated school." He found a genuine smile. "Her grades were always horrible. But she was kind and friendly, and everyone loved her. She was stubborn to a fault, but you could never hold it against her. I've been told I have her gentleness. I try."

She said nothing as he lifted her off the bike. She looked at where his hands were on her hips firmly but without hurting her. "You are gentle," she said. "You know your strength and can control it. That's gentleness. And you care about everybody so much. That's gentleness, too. I bet you're hurt easily."

He thought about denying it, but knew that she wouldn't believe him. She was too intelligent and far too intuitive. "Yes," he admitted. "I don't make friends easily. I envy Aenya and Kienan for that."

"So . . ." She took his hand as he lifted them quickly, only just realizing how long he had been holding her. "Can I be your friend, and you be mine?" She smiled. "I think we have more in common than most would believe."

"Isn't that like the princess mingling with a commoner?" he asked her.

"You're anything but common, and you know it. So, what do you say, Professor Shaughnessy?" She used the title deliberately with a teasing smile.

"I say you don't call me that unless we're in class, and you have a deal." He couldn't resist lifting his hand and touching her cheek lightly. Her skin was as soft as it looked. He dropped his hand quickly before she could take offense, and he began to walk toward the ticket booth. "My treat," he said over his shoulder.

She touched her cheek lightly before letting out a little breath and following him. If only she wasn't in his class, she thought with a little despair. She would have seduced him in a New York minute. To hell with her father's wishes; she wanted Taegan. But since she was only going to get friendship, she might as well take what she was given and not quibble the details.

Two hours later, however, she was annoyed with him as they walked out of the theater. "She was a moron, I swear! I don't care what your romantic brain thinks, Taegan, she was a moron!"

He glowered at her. "You're being cynical and cynicism means you pay for dinner. Pay up, princess."

"Ass." She went over to a vendor and ordered two giant hot dogs. She slapped one into Taegan's hand. "Doctor it yourself." She slathered hers with everything and took a huge bite. Debates always made her hungry. Around a mouthful she said, "She had a fabulous guy, so why would she run off with a dork like the male lead?"

"Her dork was the prince of her dreams," he reminded her as he ate his own hot dog. "It was supposed to be a romantic star crossed lovers' tale. You said it was supposed to be good, and it was."

She waved a hand at him. "If I had someone, I wouldn't run off just for excitement! I'd stick with him through all the times, even rough ones. If your life is boring, it's because you yourself are boring. Get a makeover, go on a second honeymoon; I don't know. I will never have a midlife crisis."

He grinned at her quickly. The smile then faded and turned gentle as he saw the smear of mustard on her chin. "Hold still." He grabbed a napkin and stepped closer to gently wipe the smear away. Her scent, strawberries and cream, went to his head, and he almost gave in to the urge to kiss her.

Catching himself, he stepped back and tossed the napkin in the garbage. She took a quick breath and listened to her pulse rattling in her body. She had been certain he was about to kiss her. If *Mel* had had this effect on her, she would have leapt at a chance for a business marriage. She would have then dragged him off on a honeymoon to make him forget the business part and made him as mad over her as she was over him.

Unfortunately, the only Shaughnessy she had ever wanted was Taegan, and watching him walk toward his bike, she was forced to accept that he was also the one she would never be able to have.

She let out a little breath and followed him. "Well then," she said. "If you could take me back for my car, I'd be much grateful." She carefully kept her voice light. The evening was suddenly beginning to feel dangerously like a date.

"Of course." His voice was as light as hers for he also sensed the suddenly intimate atmosphere.

Despite it, he couldn't stop himself from keeping her as close as possible on the ride back to campus. The scent of her skin teased his lungs and the heat of her body was a haunting lure. It was self-inflicted torture, and he couldn't stop it.

He took her to where her car was parked rather than drop her at the gate. She gave him back the spare helmet and unlocked her car, aware he was waiting to leave until she was safely inside. She gave him a genuine smile. "Thank you, Taegan. You were right. I needed this afternoon badly. I feel more stable once more. We'll need to do it again."

"I agree."

"G'night, Taegan."

"Good night, princess."

The words were nearly a caress. This time she knew she wasn't mistaken by the desire in his voice. His brogue had softened and thickened, turning such a simple nickname into an intimacy between them. Before she said or did something stupid, she got into her car. She watched him ride out of the lot and slowly rested her head on the steering wheel. If he wanted her in more than just a knee-jerk 'pretty girl with boobs' manner (something she was sadly familiar with) then she was going to have to get rough with him. She *always* got what she wanted.

And she wanted Taegan. It was that easy.

CHAPTER EIGHTEEN

If there was anything the college thrived on, it was rumors. They always started innocently but ended up blowing well out of proportion. A simple rumor about someone with a runny nose could become a Swine Flu outbreak by noon.

Kalliope found herself painfully reminded of the wagging tongues the next day. It started innocently, as it always did, when she found Mel waiting for her outside her English class. "Hey, Mel." She fell companionably into step beside him as they walked down the hall together. "What's up? You're looking a tad blue there, Gibson."

Since he refused to tell where the name Mel had come from, she had taken to associating him with Mel Gibson. He had finally gotten used to it. "Well, my father called yours this morning." When she groaned, he smiled wryly. "That would be my exact reaction. I didn't hear the conversation, but we both know what they're hoping for."

"Yeah." She sighed. "Mel, I love you, but only as a brother. I don't want to date you let alone marry you. It would be immoral in my brain. I mean, I'm Greek but not *that* kind of Greek. That sort of thing went out of style when the Pantheon was built."

"My studies may not be the best, but wasn't the Pantheon in Rome?"

"Good boy! Yes, it was, but they borrowed our gods. Remind me to show you the family crest. It has Zeus on it. It's pretty groovy." She bumped his shoulder with hers. "You know, we could always try pulling a fast one on our parents. We could humor them. Let's pretend to date for a while. Hell, let's get engaged. We'll give it a month then call it off. They can't blame us if we tried, right?"

"That's not a bad idea," he conceded. His sense of humor rivaled his siblings', and he couldn't resist giving her a courtly bow. As sincerely as he could, despite the laughter in his eyes, he asked. "Would you marry me, Kally?"

"Well, okay. Since you asked nicely." She spotted a girl staring at them with her mouth hanging open and felt a sudden wariness. She had almost forgotten the entire college had been expecting the same thing as Jiles and Sullivan. "It's a joke," she stressed. "*Joke*." She sighed as the girl ran off. "Oh boy, here we go."

"Eh." Mel shrugged one shoulder with a wry smile. "What's the worst that could happen? We were going to trick our dads anyway. When nothing comes of it and we don't act all lovey-dovey then it'll blow over—with everyone. The winds around this school change faster than the industrial average."

With that image in her mind, she was nearly giggling as she walked into her math class. Taegan walked in not long after, and she couldn't stop her smile. Just seeing him made her happy sometimes. "Morning, Professor Shaughnessy." She said it deliberately, hoping for a secret smile.

What she got was a look that froze her to her core. His brown eyes were hard as they flicked over her face and he barely spared her a glance. When he looked at anyone else, he was the same gentle Taegan. When he looked at her, she felt blasted by waves of anger and betrayal.

It *hurt*. She had to curl her nails into her leg under her desk to fight back tears. She couldn't imagine what she had done to make him furious with her. What if he had found out that she was in love with him? Did he hate her now? She could handle anything but that.

Somehow she held onto her control until after class. She gathered her courage and went to his office, needing to know. When she knocked on the door, she could see her hand trembling.

"Come in," he called, and his voice sounded like the normal Taegan.

She opened the door and walked in, and his face shut down as his eyes went cold. It was terrifying. "I don't suppose you could tell

me why you're so angry with me," she managed to whisper.

"You neglected to mention yesterday that you and my brother were seeing each other." He felt betrayed in the most horrible way possible. His own brother had stolen her from him, and she hadn't had the courtesy to at least tell him that she was seeing Mel. He lifted a sardonic brow. "You indicated that you were single. That seems to be a lie, doesn't it?"

"I hate you!" The tears welled in her eyes and her outburst startled her as much as it did him. "I'm not seeing Mel!" she shouted, her hands curled into fists. "It was a *joke* we were talking about because of our dads. How *could* you believe something like that? How could you accuse me of lying to you of all people?!" Her voice caught on a sob as she whirled and ran out of the room.

The door slammed behind her violently. He felt worse than slime as he sank down in his chair with his hands pressed to his eyes. He had been jealous, and in that jealousy he had been blind. Because he had been hurt, he had lashed out to make her hurt. So much for him being the mature one in the family. He didn't look up as he heard the door open. "It's a bad time right now."

"I imagine it is," Mel bit out, his voice carrying a brogue clipped with fury. His accent was always fainter than Taegan's, but when he was truly angry, it could be just as thick. He crossed around the desk, grabbed his brother by the collar, and gave him a sharp shake. He was a few inches shorter but he wasn't any smaller overall. "You asshole!" he snarled. "What did you say to Kally? She was crying!"

"I accused her of lying to me." Taegan shoved him back and slumped down in his chair once more. "I let myself believe those stupid rumors. I was cold to her, and when she asked me why, I just accused. I didn't even listen to her." He buried his face in his hands. "*Damn* it!"

Mel fell silent. For long moments he studied his big brother. He eased a hip onto the edge of the desk and crossed his arms. He supposed he should have noticed it sooner. It seemed rather obvious now. "How long have you been in love with Kally?" he asked quietly.

Taegan couldn't deny it, not to his family. "Since I met her."

"Taegan, you idiot." He rubbed a hand over his face. "Kally's like a sister to me. She's my friend and nothing more. This morning, we were talking about our fathers and how they want a business marriage to cement the merger they're considering. We were joking about pretending to be engaged then calling it off to show it wouldn't work, and someone overheard us. They got the wrong idea and the rumors spread."

Feeling even worse, Taegan got to his feet and grabbed his jacket. "I need to go apologize to her."

Mel watched him intently. "You could tell her how you feel."

"No." Taegan's eyes were bleak as he looked at him. "She's my student, Mel. If I crossed any lines then we'd both pay for it. And . . . she deserves someone a lot better than me. Her dad is right about that. Besides, all she wants is friendship from me. So, that's what I'll give."

Friendship didn't make a woman like Kalliope Tavoularis cry as if her heart had been broken, but Mel kept that to himself. "Are you still going to her birthday party? You could steal a dance. No one would think that odd."

"No. My ability to control myself is thin around her, as I'm sure you've just noticed. And anyway," he smiled wryly, "I have papers to grade. I wouldn't want my students to think their grades are as bad as yours."

"Thanks a lot!"

"It is true, though." He shrugged into his jacket. "Keep this up and you'll get a tutor in General Ed."

Mel's skin took a pale cast to it. There was only one general education tutor in the college and there wasn't a single student who wasn't deathly afraid of her. She had to be, beyond a doubt, one of the scariest women anyone had ever known. She rarely left the computer room and even her computer sciences students were in a sort of terrified awe of her. "Don't be evil."

"I'm being honest. Lock the door behind you." Taegan pulled on his sunglasses and made his way as quickly off campus as he could. He knew that the salon where Kalliope worked was only just a block

away from the campus. Both his sisters got their hair done there, and, in fact, it was Kalliope who was their stylist. He just hoped she gave him a chance to apologize and didn't come at him with a pair of clippers.

Kalliope knelt behind the counter and organized receipts. She didn't feel like working, but she absolutely needed to get her mind off things. Her manager had been amazingly quiet even though he had seen she was upset. He had simply given her tasks to do and let her be.

She dashed at the tears in her eyes furiously. She hated crying. She hated Taegan for making her cry. She hated that she loved him enough that he could make her cry. She wouldn't have called him an idiot but he had actually *believed* . . . It hurt worse than she had ever imagined. A heart couldn't physically break, but she certainly felt as if there were broken shards inside her chest.

When the bell over the door rang, she was almost pitifully grateful. "Just a second!" she called and swiped at her eyes again. "Can I help you?"

"I don't suppose," Taegan's soft voice asked, "that you have a cure for foot-in-mouth?"

She stood up quickly, the pieces of her heart beating out of rhythm with each other. "It doesn't work on men," she countered waspishly. Her eyes burned with more tears at the sight of him. How dare he look so windblown and gorgeous? Why did he have to look as miserable as she felt? "What do you want? You want to call me a liar again?"

"I need to apologize." He wanted to hug her but knew she would come after him with her nails hooked like claws. "I can't even give you an excuse. I thought I had been lied to, and it hurt. So I hurt you in return. It was childish."

She looked down at the counter. "I thought that I had done something wrong," she whispered. "You were so cold to me. It hurt, a lot."

He studied her long moments before reaching out a hand and lightly cupping her cheek. "I'm not the only one who is easily hurt, am I?" he asked quietly. He softly brushed away the tears that kept welling in her eyes. "I'm so sorry, Kally. Let me be your friend again."

She couldn't stop herself from turning her face into his hand. There was a trembling in his fingers that matched the trembling in her heart. "Always," she said softly. "I forgive you, Taegan. But don't ever assume again. I couldn't marry Mel. He's like a brother to me."

"So he said, too. I thought he was going to hit me when he stormed into the office after you."

She found a smile. "Has he done that before?"

"Once. I was babysitting him and the other two. He wanted to test me, since I was only sixteen and he was twelve—he was obviously far too old to need a babysitter, you know." He found a smile as well. "I tanned his hide, then locked him in his room. Needless to say, he didn't test me like that again."

"He idolizes you, you know." She was sure of it. She was also the tiniest bit envious of the Shaughnessy family. She had always wanted brothers and sisters but she had never gotten them.

"I know." He slowly released her. "What do you want for your birthday present?"

"Pick something out and surprise me. Bring it to the party." When his eyes moved away, she felt her stomach sink. "You're not coming." She had been looking forward to dancing with him, to pretending that he could love her a little.

"I'm sorry, princess." His heart ached as he saw the pain in her eyes. "It's just not a good idea."

"Why not?" She grabbed his arm before he could leave. "Give me one good reason why you shouldn't come. We're friends, aren't we? And what's wrong with a teacher attending a student's party?"

She deserved the truth after the pain he had already caused her. She needed to know why he had to force distance between them.

"Because this teacher happens to be attracted to his student."

Her eyes widened, and he felt a bolt of panic as he realized he could not bear to see what lay beyond her surprise. Anger or fear would destroy him. A mutual desire would make it impossible to keep things platonic. Rather than risk hurting her—again—he turned and walked out swiftly.

He found Stormy waiting for him outside. He sighed as she fell into step beside him. She never wore a leash but no one had ever seemed to notice. He had always assumed it was part of her gifts. "You don't need to meddle. I seem to be getting in over my head all on my own." He knelt and ran a hand over her head. "You can't fix everything," he said softly. "No matter how you try. Kalliope's no more a prince than I am Cinderella. Magic doesn't turn pumpkins into coaches and commoners into royalty."

Stormy almost smiled. She wouldn't have bet on that.

The day of Kalliope's birthday party arrived and the entire Shaughnessy household wasn't sure what to do about Taegan. They had been taking turns all day trying to convince him to go, but he had finally stopped listening to them entirely and started locking his door. Not even Aenya could get through to him, and he had *always* listened to her before.

"What is *wrong* with him?" she demanded from Mel as she followed him across the house. The shimmering white skirts of her ball gown swirled around her ankles as she turned and followed him the other way. "I know you know!"

"Alright, alright!" He gave up and stopped trying to escape her. The others came over to join them and he rubbed the back of his neck. "Taegan is in love with Kally." He didn't feel the need to expand on it. It seemed to sum up everything.

"Oh boy," was Kienan's response.

"In other words, he figures he can't have her, so he's not even going to try." Hiro lifted a brow ever so slightly. "I expected better out of him."

"Daddy," Aenya took her father's arm as she saw the musing look on his face, "would Mr. Tavoularis really dislike Taegan? He's not just a teacher. He's still a Shaughnessy. And he's one of the best men around."

"I think," he said slowly, "that Jiles only wants his daughter to be happy. Just as I feel for my children. If Taegan and Kalliope wanted to be together, then Jiles wouldn't stand in the way." He glanced at Stormy who was napping by the doorway. He had a feeling he might finally know where things were going. "It's Taegan and Kalliope's decision about what to do," he finally decided. "They're both adults."

Even when they met up with Madelyne in the 3rd District, Aenya still didn't think Taegan was being smart about things. She shoved it out of her mind, to the best of her ability, as she helped her sister-in-law unload the rental truck they were using to carry the food that Madelyne had made for the party. The catering job hadn't just turned formal, but it had also opened up a whole new set of possibilities for the inn for Madelyne and Kienan.

The party was being held at a place called the Glass Shoe Palace. It was a formal ballroom, converted from an old manor, and could be rented for a few weeks at a time for parties and formal conferences. Kalliope's party was a full-scale formal masquerade ball. All the men wore tuxedos and tails and all the women were in ball gowns. Everyone wore masks.

Everyone except Kalliope. It was as deliberate as the fact that she had requested that everyone wear pastels—it was her birthday, and she deserved to stand out. No pale colors for her; she wore emerald green. The ball gown bodice clung to her body perfectly and the full skirts had emeralds at the point of every tier. She wore emeralds around her neck and dripping from each ear. Her hair was artfully piled high with a delicate coronet of emeralds and silver perched on top.

She didn't make an immediate appearance as people were

arriving. She was busy in a dressing room with Madelyne to help her friend get ready. Madelyne's gray hair was exceptionally long but Kalliope took the time to curl all of it so that it hung loosely and vibrantly. That done, she helped her with makeup. "Kienan will fall over."

Madelyne smiled. Somehow Kalliope and Kienan made her forget that she was supposed to be plain. "That would be funny."

"But well deserved." She leaned back. "You, Maddie, are one lovely nightingale."

Madelyne looked in the mirror. She really did look appealing. She *felt* lovely. "And I still say you're a miracle worker."

The door opened and Aenya slipped inside. "We're here," she announced. "The guys are all doing the mingling thing and Kienan told me to come find you." Her eyes met Kalliope's and there was understanding in her gaze. "I'm sorry, Kally. We couldn't convince him to come."

Kalliope looked away. It hurt to look at Aenya sometimes. Her eyes were identical to Taegan's. "Am I so obvious?" she asked achingly. "Is he the only one who doesn't realize I love him?"

Madelyne opened her mouth but closed it when Aenya shook her head. The blonde walked around to look into Kalliope's face. "I think we only noticed," she said carefully, "because Mel told us how badly you were hurt when Taegan was cold to you. You're not a woman who cries easily, but he made you cry." Her smile turned wry. "Been there, done that, as they say."

Kalliope let out a little breath. "That makes me feel a little better. Come on. You can be my ladies-in-waiting and keep the hordes at bay." She walked over to the doors and opened them to sweep into the ballroom with a princess's grace and flair. Madelyne and Aenya followed her, but it was as much to make sure she actually enjoyed herself as it was to keep overly avid suitors off.

It was only their presence that kept Kalliope from slinking away into a corner to hide. It was the party of her dreams, and she was utterly miserable. She danced with everyone who asked, even Kienan and Mel, but it made no difference. She let Aenya teach her a complicated waltz pattern, but the enjoyment was short lived.

Finally at her wits end, she slipped into the gardens for fresh air. With all her heart she wanted the man she loved to be there. She wanted to see him even if only for a little while. If she was to make a birthday wish, it would be simply to have Taegan. He made her entire world so much better by being in it.

A sound made her turn and she was surprised to see a wolf sitting at the edge of the fountain. Since it wore a collar, she wasn't worried it was wild and would attack. She crouched down and held out a hand and then smiled as the wolf rubbed against her fingers. "So you wanted to come to the party, too? Well, it's our secret."

She turned her gaze toward the party in full swing behind the glass doors. "He never even gave me a chance," she murmured softly, "to say how I felt. And now he won't come near me because it could ruin us both. But . . . I don't care. I want to see him. Even for a little while. Silly of me, isn't it? You can't wish someone into being."

She patted the wolf once more then let it be as she got to her feet and braced herself. With a smile that she didn't feel, she swept into the ballroom once more. "So when do I open presents? And if one of them has a spring-loaded pie, there better be enough for everyone."

Taegan didn't unlock his door until the house was quiet. He had finished grading the papers hours ago but he hadn't wanted to give his family ammunition to use against him. He only felt guilty for losing his temper with Aenya. He owed her an apology.

He wasn't hungry, but he forced himself to get something to eat. The servants had been given the weekend off, and he savored the knowledge that he was completely alone. It happened very rarely. Not that he didn't love his family, but right then, he couldn't bear talking to anyone.

It was a stupid fate that made a man fall in love with a woman so beyond his reach that all he could do was suffer. For the first time in his life, he questioned his decision to become a teacher. Would things have been different if he had inherited the company? Really, no, they wouldn't have. If anything, he might never have met Kalliope and gotten to see her smile every week.

His room was on the bottom floor and had doors that opened into the garden. He opened them for fresh air but didn't turn on any lights other than a small lamp as he sat at his desk. In despair, he rested his head on his arms. "Tennyson was an idiot. It isn't better to love and lose than to never love at all."

"Enough with the pity party," a woman's cool voice said suddenly from the patio doors. "It's so unbecoming in a man your age."

He turned sharply, astonished that she had snuck up on him. She stood just outside the doors, leaning against the jamb with a predator's casual stillness. She was cloaked in shadows and he couldn't see her face, but her long black hair fluttered in a light wind.

"You frightened me," he accused. "You should have knocked."

"You'd have told me to go away." She waved a hand in the air. "Well then, Taegan Shaughnessy. How badly do you want your princess? Enough to make a deal with me?"

He said nothing for long moments. He knew who she was. In fact, he had begun to suspect he knew the 'what' as well. He also knew that her word was gold. If she made a promise, then she kept it. She always carried through with anything she said. "What sort of deal?"

"Open your desk."

He did so and discovered a neatly written sheaf of papers. As he skimmed them, he realized it was a contract. It said concisely that she would provide him with the means to disguise himself and attend the party, but he would have to leave by midnight. Bemused, he asked, "Midnight?"

"To be honest, I'm not supposed to be doing things this way. I can only cover my tracks until midnight. Take it or leave it, Taegan. It's

your life you're wasting."

"As always, the soul of tact." He looked at the contract again and his lips curved. "I guess this makes me Cinderella and you my faerie godmother."

"Don't *even* go there," she retorted with a bite in her voice that sounded like bared teeth.

"Yes'm." He didn't give himself time to think. He was tired of thinking. For once he just wanted to follow his heart. He grabbed a pen and scrawled his name across the bottom of the contract. As he did, he caught sight of her signature. Seeing it, he asked, "Doesn't your name mean . . . ?"

"Yes." Her tone was dry.

"Whose sense of humor gave you your 'nickname'?"

"Rhianna's. She's twisted like that." She reached into her jacket and pulled out a mask. It looked like a rather plain and ordinary thing, but as light rippled over it, it seemed to glow with magic. "Here's how this works. This is from 3rd District. It's called the Mask of Illusion. When worn, it changes the appearance of the wearer to whatever they wish. It acts as a . . . glamour shield of sorts. Only a very few people would ever know who was behind the mask. So if you wish for blue suede shoes and a new tux, everyone will think you're Elvis."

"My sister is the professional dancer, not I." He got to his feet and walked over to take the mask. He tried to study her face but it was well hidden. "Are you really doing well?" he asked quietly.

"I heal fast. And risks are taken by everyone when love is involved." She flicked a finger at the mask. "Hurry up, handsome. Time's wasting and you only have until midnight. Oh, and Kalliope is wearing emerald green."

He paused as he was about to put the mask on. "You saw her?" The longing couldn't be kept from his voice.

As always, it softened her heart. "Of course. I had to be sure that you two matched. Now, hurry up, the limo is waiting." She turned away, then glanced over her shoulder. He could have sworn she was smiling. "It's a modern pumpkin, if you like. Now, Cinderella, let's go. Your princess awaits. And," she added under her breath as he put the mask on, "don't be an idiot."

The clock was only just ringing eleven o'clock when Kalliope began to have serious thoughts of escaping. She had opened gifts, they'd had Madelyne's outrageously delicious cake, and the party was due to continue for another two hours. She was ready to go home and crawl under the covers until the urge to cry went away.

Quite suddenly, she realized she was being stared at. Her heart began to beat harder as she felt the oddest sensation of déjà vu. She slowly turned around to look at the banister and stairs leading to the entrance of the grand ballroom. Her breath caught in her chest as conversations around her slowly began to die.

A man stood at the top of the stairs, staring at her with a heat in his gaze that burned her from across the room. Though she could not see the color of his eyes, his hair shimmered stark black under the chandeliers. She *knew*. Without a word, she slowly crossed the room toward him. She was only distantly aware that everyone moved out of the way.

He slowly came down the stairs toward her. He wore a tuxedo no different from the other men present, but there was a green waistcoat under his jacket that perfectly matched her dress. Emerald cufflinks kept his sleeves tidy. His mask was elaborate and sculpted, hiding all but his mouth and eyes from view. A bit of a haze of some kind seemed to cover him but she saw through it for she saw with eyes that loved.

All eyes in the room were fixed on them. Mel, at the back of the room, tried to get closer to see what was going on. Because he, too, loved Taegan, his eyes saw through the glamour. He was positive it was his brother descending the stairs. The *how* was what eluded him. The 'why' was obvious.

When Taegan stopped in front of Kalliope, he lifted her hand to his lips and bowed elegantly. "I came to ask for a dance, princess," he said softly.

Only one man had ever called her princess in that tone of voice. Only one man had ever made her pulse flutter with just a touch of his hand. The eyes watching her so unguardedly, so filled with love, were the same honey-colored eyes she had longed for all along.

Her lips trembled as she accepted the gift she was being given. "I would be honored," she whispered, and some inner instinct had her sinking into an elegant curtsey.

Aenya scrambled over to the orchestra. "Waltz!" she hissed at the conductor. "A waltz!" He jumped and turned to the orchestra, and she turned around to look at the dance floor. Her eyes were shining with tears as she clasped her hands together. "It should always be a waltz first." She knew who it was, too.

Everyone had pulled back to give as much room as possible. Kalliope twirled gracefully into Taegan's arms, delighted that her heels made her the perfect height for him. His hand was warm on her waist, and his other hand curled around hers possessively. Even before he stepped her into the dance, the room was spinning around her head.

It was magic. She felt it as they whirled around the floor. Somehow she had known he would know how to waltz. Of course he did. Just as she knew how. Because it was the moment to know, they did. It was that simple.

When the music swelled to an end, they were left in the middle of the floor. Everyone applauded and cheered but she heard nothing except the beat of her heart. When he bowed and moved as if to leave, she grabbed onto his wrist. "No way, Cinderella," she scolded warmly. "You owe me at least until midnight. It's a rule."

He reluctantly let her lead him toward the gardens. Most of the room tried to follow, wanting to know who he was, but they were brought up short as Kienan and Mel got in the way and planted themselves in front of the doors.

"Kally deserves some privacy," Mel warned, his voice soft but very hard. "Don't you think so?" Both brothers' eyes were a

challenging shade of chocolate brown, and the crowd backed off hastily.

Kalliope considered her options as she walked in the garden with Taegan. She could play off the charade and pretend like she didn't know who he was. She could tell him she knew and throw caution to the winds. Or she could let him know, and they could pretend as if they didn't. Still contemplating what her preference was, she said sincerely, "Thank you, Cinderella. You showed up at the right time. I was ready to run away from my own party."

She was so beautiful that she took his breath away. She seemed impossibly radiant, too good for a mortal man. His fingers burned to feel her skin, to have her under his hands, to feel her body pressed against his. "I hadn't considered myself Cinderella." He put humor into his voice. "I came in a limo, not a pumpkin."

"A modern carriage is vastly superior to smelling like pumpkin pie for a week. You're not leaving at midnight, are you?"

Her sense of humor was a frightening match to his 'faerie godmother's.' He reached out and skimmed his thumb over her cheek. "I have to," he apologized. "I don't want to get my godmother in trouble." He smiled. "And besides, what kind of Cinderella would I be if I didn't?"

"Would you take your gloves off?" she asked softly. Once he did, she took his hands and lifted them to where she could see them. She knew these hands. They were frequent visitors in her deepest fantasies. "You know," she said carefully, "your hands are familiar."

He went very still. "Are they?"

"Yes, they remind me of my math professor." She released him and walked a few steps away. "I would know, you see, as I've spent the better part of four years fantasizing about his hands. And his eyes. And his lips. Actually, I think there's very little that I haven't had a fantasy about." She turned to look at him and his eyes burned as they watched her. "He said he was attracted to me then walked out before I could answer. I think he's a coward. What about you?"

"Maybe he was," he said softly, longing for her so badly that his hands curled into fists at his side and his entire body trembled.

"Maybe he feared your answer."

"Then he's an idiot. Even his own family realized how I felt about him." She moved a step forward. "There's a wall between us. No matter how I love him. No matter how badly I want him. He doesn't think it can be climbed right now." She paused, then added softly, "But it would seem to have chinks in it big enough to allow us a forbidden dance in a magical garden."

Silence fell around them. Even the night creatures were quiet. The music of the ballroom was distant and far away. He very slowly reached out toward her, terrified it was a dream. He was going to wake up and it would have never happened. She made a soft sound of pain and surged forward to press against his chest, her arms stealing around his waist. He closed his arms around her as tightly as he dared, knowing that this, too, was stolen. "Don't cry," he whispered achingly.

"I don't cry!" Yet the tears were sliding down her cheeks and she knew it. She eased back enough to smile up at him. "My mascara is waterproof just in case. I was worried someone might have given me a crank gift."

He gently brushed at the tears clinging to her lashes. His fingers lingered and warmly framed her face. The temptation of her trembling lips lured him in, and he bent his head to softly brush her lips with his. It was nowhere near what he needed, but it was still more than he had dared dream of having. It would have to be enough.

Her lashes fluttered closed and she waited in an agony of need for him to deepen the kiss in the way they both desperately craved. He eased back instead, leaving her with just that faint brush of his lips. He released her entirely, and she opened her eyes to see him watching her longingly. That unfailing gentleness inside him kept him from pushing for more than he thought she wanted to give, and she knew it. The ball was in her court.

She took a deep breath. "How silly of me. The prince is supposed to make all the moves. I had forgotten." She moved forward before he could move back, and she wound her arms around his neck. She rose up onto her toes to kiss him as deeply as she needed. A shudder rippled through her body as she realized he tasted just like he smelled. Danger. Wonderful danger. Her geek was a bad boy at heart, and her bad boy was gentle. "Kiss me, damn you," she muttered against his lips.

His control collapsed in a wave of searing heat. He couldn't resist her any longer. He caught her against his aching body with one arm and used his other hand to tilt her head back, parting her lips for him further. Hungrily he kissed her, tangling his tongue with hers until she made a little sound of pleasure in her throat and her hands fisted into the material of his jacket. Her body arched and strained to press closer, as hungry and aching as his.

Drunk on her taste and scent, he released her lips only to bury his own against the curve of her neck. Breathless, her head spinning, she managed to tease huskily, "Don't leave a mark I can't explain. My daddy owns a shotgun."

It was too damned tempting. He carefully lifted his head and set her back from him about a foot. It removed temptation from reach if not from sight. "You're better than a good wine for going to my head," he said by way of apology.

"They always said my personality was bubbly." She took a deep breath and waved a hand in front of her face lightly. "Have you considered registering your kisses as lethal weapons?" Her eyes closed helplessly as his hand lifted and skimmed over the top curves of her breasts. "That's not fair."

He took a quick breath and put his hands in his pockets. She responded so perfectly to his touch that it drove him mad. He wanted to lower her to the ground, to have her where they were with the moon above and the garden all around. Nothing but them, wild and free. Only this woman had ever called up the wild spirit inside his soul. It was as if years of control meant nothing near her.

Her breath caught as she saw the wicked passion in his eyes. It called to her and reached past all veneers of civilization to the hunger for life inside her soul. She had been waiting for her entire life for someone to look at her and see her for what she was. Now that she had found him, she couldn't even keep him.

She heard the bell tolling midnight and went very still. "You're leaving." It wasn't a question. "Don't. Please." She reached up for his mask, wanting to end the charade, but she heard rustling behind her and instinctively turned. She whirled back on a curse, but it was too late. He had already disappeared.

Lonelier than ever, she started to enter the ballroom again when Aenya and Madelyne descended on her. They firmly escorted her around the crowd and into the bathrooms. Startled, she asked, "Is something wrong?"

Aenya cleared her throat delicately. "You tell us." She pointed at the mirror behind them.

She turned and groaned softly as she saw the distinct mark on her neck. She sank onto the vanity chair and buried her face in her arms. "Damn him," she whispered. "He didn't even leave a glass shoe for me to follow."

"Do you know who it was?" Madelyne made it a question, but she already knew the answer. She had been expecting it. Stormy had been hanging around Taegan, and she, more than any other, knew who and what Stormy was and why she was there.

"Yes." Kalliope took the powder compact Aenya held out to her and began to competently hide the mark on her neck. Her eyes burned with determination. "I'm not letting him get away from me. If he thinks he can kiss me like that and just walk off, he's going to be learning a lesson himself, damn it."

"Good," Aenya muttered.

"Maddie." Kalliope met her friend's eyes in the mirror. "I'm sorry if I was harsh with you about Kienan. But I knew. I knew how much you would continue to hurt. You had a chance I would never get. I wanted you to take it."

"I know. I knew as soon you'd done it, that it was exactly what I had needed." Madelyne hugged her tightly. "You taught me to see value in myself. Now you're just going to have to teach my child the same when you're his or her godmother."

"Well I suppose I . . ." She trailed off and whirled on the seat to stare at Madelyne even as Aenya covered her mouth with her hands.

"Does Kienan know?" she demanded.

"Not yet." Madelyne smiled. "I'm saving it for his birthday next month. I only just learned."

Aenya laughed happily and hugged Madelyne tightly. Kalliope got to her feet and hugged her as well, but for the first time she felt an emptiness inside herself as she realized she had lied to Taegan. She didn't want just her daddy's company. She wanted her own family. A husband and a child. She wanted it all. If it would take a fight to get it, then that's just what she would damned well do.

CHAPTER NINETEEN

When they got home, all three Shaughnessy siblings went racing down the hall to Taegan's room. They eased the door open and looked inside, but their big brother was sound asleep in bed. His glasses were on the bedside table next to a book. There was no sign in any shape or fashion that he had gone to the party. Wondering how or what had happened, especially how, they all went to their individual rooms for the night.

Sullivan stayed awake for a while and sat in his study to look out the window at the moon in the sky. It would be full in three weeks. Somehow it felt like a portent of possible devastation. It was a long time before he could shake it off and go to bed.

Taegan awoke the next morning to someone shaking his shoulder and simultaneously waving coffee under his nose. Cursing sleepily in every language he knew, he sat up and pushed the covers aside. He blearily eyed his brother. "I love you," he yawned, "but I'm going to kill you."

Mel didn't bat a lash. "Drink." He put the coffee in his brother's hands and glanced around the room once more, trying desperately to find evidence for what he strongly believed. All he saw was Stormy sleeping at the foot of the bed, the healing wound on her face finally beginning to fade to a normal scar. He owed her so much for saving his baby brother and little sister.

After a few sips, Taegan finally began to feel human again. He raked a hand through his hair. "What do you want? Is this about your grades? Seriously, it could have waited."

"It's not that." Mel frowned. "It's about Kally. How'd you do it, bro?"

"Do what?" He ruffled Stormy's fur gently as she climbed further up the bed to lie beside him with her head on his lap. "I graded papers, read a book, went to sleep." He had also danced with a princess in a magical garden, but that didn't need to be mentioned. Things were complicated enough.

"Pity. You should have seen Kally. Red is really her color."

"She was in green." The words were out of his mouth before he could stop them. As Mel slowly arched a brow and began to smile smugly, Taegan sighed and set his coffee aside. "I knew I should have kicked you out until the caffeine actually circulated in my system."

"Don't suppose you'd be willing to tell me how you managed that. It seems like only our family realized it was you. Seriously. Everyone thought you looked different. Some people thought you were short and others thought you were blond. It was *weird*."

"Umm . . ." His smile and tone were equally rueful. "It's a little complicated."

"Y'think!?" Mel sighed and leaned over to hug him tightly. He hated to see his invincible big brother brokenhearted. "I don't like this. I really don't."

He smiled and ruffled Mel's hair as if he was five again. "There's nothing to worry about. I didn't leave any clues to follow, let alone a glass shoe that only fits my foot, so she can't suddenly come knocking on the door."

"That doesn't mean she won't try." Mel smiled wryly. "She's a very, *very* smart woman."

Kalliope was also a very, *very* pissed woman as she paced back and forth in her room. She was already dressed in jeans and a turtleneck, and she was just waiting for her father to call her down and demand to know what was going on.

Damn, damn, *damn* him. Damn that sneaky, sexy Cinderella!

She looked into the mirror and pulled down the edge of her top to see the mark that was visible against her pale skin. She didn't mind its presence as much as the fact that it was all that had been left behind. It wouldn't be enough to track down the man she wanted. She knew where he was but had no ammunition to make him admit it or make her father accept it. Pity he wasn't a vampire. She could use dental records in lieu of a shoe.

There came a light knock on her door and she turned quickly. "Yes?" When she saw her mother peering around the edge, she sighed and sat on the edge of the bed. "Hi, Mom." As Mara sat beside her on the bed, she turned and pressed her face against her mother's shoulder, comforted when her arms went around her. "I wanted to fall in love," she whispered. "I never thought it would be this difficult."

There were no secrets between mother and daughter. Mara knew full well what man had taken her daughter's heart. She whole-heartedly approved. Kalliope was so headstrong that she needed a man as strong as Taegan Shaughnessy. He was old enough to be able to match her where other men her age would fall behind. Jiles would just have to come around. "You looked beautiful together," she offered, rubbing a hand over Kalliope's back.

"Yeah. And he's one hell of a kisser." She smiled wryly and pulled the edge of her top down to show the mark. "Unfortunately, it wouldn't be easy to explain this."

"Hmm, no. I recall a few times I had to hide your father's antics from my own." Mara's eyes danced. "The right man is worth the extra makeup."

"Thanks for that insight." It was more about her parents than she really needed or wanted to know. She sighed and got to her feet to pace again. "If he wasn't my teacher, it would be fine. But if I drop the class, my GPA will suffer. It's too late to drop a class without penalty. And if my GPA drops, I'll lose my place as valedictorian. Dad would be furious."

"Your dad will understand."

"Oh, yeah, I can see me explaining that one. 'Gee Dad, I dropped the class because I wanted to seduce my teacher.' He'd

freak!" She raked her hands through her hair and groaned as she heard her father's voice calling her name. "Oh boy, here we go. Will I go to hell for lying to my father's face?"

"Nah. A few white lies for his own peace of mind are sometimes good. As long as he eventually learns the truth, it's fine to fib now. Good luck, honey." Mara watched her daughter leave the room, an ache in her heart. Much as she wanted to, there was nothing she could do to make this easier. Her baby had grown up.

Kalliope smoothed down her hair and braced herself before she went into Jiles' office. "You called?" she asked.

He looked up from where he had been going over the guest list. "Yes, have a seat. Did you have a good time last night?"

"After a while." She smiled at him wryly and decided to play it by ear. "You won, by the way. Your mysterious Cinderella caught my attention."

He coughed and cleared his throat. "Yes, well, I'm afraid that's where I'm confused. I didn't invite anyone else. I asked the guards from the doors and they said that everyone who entered had an invitation. And neither could give me a straight answer as to what he looked like. In fact, I'm still rather puzzled myself."

"So . . ." She made her tone thoughtful. "Whoever he was, he had to be someone I invited. But I could have sworn I knew who everyone there was. I'll have to do some investigating and see if I can find out." She smiled. "I didn't know any of the men I knew were that appealing. He's got my attention, that's for sure."

"Good luck, honey. Let me know who he is, will you?" He was impressed himself, not only with the manner with which the mysterious man had carried himself, but also with his cunning in getting Kalliope's attention.

"Oh I will," she murmured. There were a few things to do first, though, before she considered fighting for her father's agreement. She knew that deep down he just wanted her happiness.

The first step was getting Taegan to even admit he had been there. She had nowhere to move without that, no grounds to use against him. Even though he had refused the company to teach, there

was no denying he was still a businessman. She knew she was in for a hostile takeover.

Monday morning brought a new wave of rumors. Everyone was still talking about the party and fingers were pointing. No one could piece together a clear description of the mysterious man. Some thought he was tall, others thought he was short. Some said red hair, others said blond.

Anyone who asked Kalliope couldn't get a straight answer either. She told them all the same thing: she didn't know who he was but she was looking. She wasn't overly fond of lying but felt justified in her reasons. She was biding her time. She needed ammunition and the best way to get information was to talk to an insider.

Mel didn't realize he was about to be kidnapped until he swung around a corner and someone jumped on his back. "Jesus!" Heart pounding, he swung his head around to find Kalliope dangling from his shoulders. "Are you trying to kill me, Kally?"

"March. I need to talk to you. Let's go, Gibson." She held on tight. "I'm not letting go until you spill the beans."

With a sigh, he diverted and stepped into an empty classroom. Once inside, he shut the door. She immediately let him go and hopped off his back. "I can assume you already know the answers," he told her wryly, "but feel free to force them out of me so I don't feel guilty."

"Oh, I can do worse than force." She let her eyes well with tears. "Mel?"

"Gah!" He covered his eyes. "Okay, that's just playing dirty! Ask, you foul creature."

"Was it Taegan at my party? Was he the one who danced with me?"

"Yes. Are you still crying?" He peeked through his fingers and saw the tears were gone. He let out a relieved breath. "How did you know?"

"Well, for one thing," her smile turned a little taunting, "I recognized his hands."

"TMI, thank you."

"Well, that was part of it." She closed her eyes. "I've only ever loved one man, Mel. And when I saw him last night, masked though he was, I knew it was him. I fell in love with a slightly geeky math teacher and was seduced by a bad boy in a mask. Your brother is a walking paradox!"

"Yeah." He had to smile. "He's always been like that. He had to be responsible so early because of Aenya and Kienan that he just sort of bottled up the wild spirit we all have. It's genetic, I'm afraid," he apologized.

"Thanks for the warning," she sighed. She pressed her hands against her eyes tightly. "I love him so much, Mel. It's destroying me. Please, just tell me one thing. Is the only thing that keeps him so distant the impropriety? Does he stay back because he loves me too much, or not enough?"

"It's because it's too much," he admitted quietly. "You could both be ruined if word got out. At this point, whether you stay in his class and risk people knowing, or drop the class to catch him, you could lose your place as valedictorian, and if you do that, your dad will never forgive you or Taegan."

"So it comes down to whether I can wait or not. Either way, I'm going to make my dad mad." She took a deep breath. "I can't wait, Mel. I can't." The tears that lurked in her voice were this time very real. "I've waited so long already, and I can't shake the feeling that if I don't do something now, then nothing will ever be done."

"Then go to him." His voice was simple. "You know the Shaughnessys will stand behind you, no matter what."

"Thank you, Mel." She hugged him tightly before hurrying out of the room to head across campus to the building where the math and computer sciences classes were held. If Taegan wasn't in his office, then she would wait for him until he came back.

As she was passing through the computer wing, she was surprised to see the door to one of the labs open. She knew which one it was. She had heard the rumors too, but she wasn't precisely frightened. She knew how badly things always got exaggerated. More curious than anything, she peered into the darkened room. It was lit only by the light from a computer monitor across the room. The only sound was that of keys clicking as someone typed.

Compelled, somehow, to stop, she asked, "Hello?"

"Hello." The typing stopped as the woman spoke. Her voice sounded cool and calm as if she was never ruffled by anything. There was an oddly welcoming note in her husky voice, though, that made Kalliope relax a little. "Need something?"

"Just curious. The rumors and all." Kalliope walked slowly into the room. As she did, she had the strangest feeling that she had just walked into a room with a predator. She didn't feel threatened, precisely, but the hair on the back of her neck quivered. "You're . . . the computer sciences teacher? Professor Alexandrios?"

"Yes. Audra Alexandrios." Audra leaned back in her chair and regarded the young woman in front of her. Kalliope had a strong mind and will, but she had been using mental compulsions on much stronger people for many years. "You're Kalliope Tavoularis."

"Guess you're not the only one whose reputation carries." Kalliope hesitated then blurted, "Can I ask a question? Hypothetical."

"Hypothetical. Right. Sure, be my guest. Don't expect me to believe you have a friend we're discussing, though. I'm not stupid." Audra began to type again. She was fully able to speak and listen at the same time.

"Well . . . suppose someone is in love with a teacher. Their teacher no less. The teacher loves them as well. Is it worth risking status and reputation to be together?" She realized she was wringing her hands and tucked them into her pockets quickly.

"I've always thought," Audra said calmly without looking up from her computer, "that love was worth risking everything. Take Cinderella, for example. The prince risked his pride entirely by showing the whole world how desperate he was to find the woman

he loved. She risked what little safety she had by going to him in the first place."

She half laughed. "You're very intuitive with that, but I get your point." She walked closer, still trying to see Audra's face properly. All she could see were her piercing yellow eyes. The color was unusual, but it might have been a trick of the computer's glow. "What do you think about Professor Shaughnessy?"

"And hypothetical goes out the window." Audra leaned back in her chair and linked her hands behind her head. "He's atypical of his family in some ways since he dreams big, but he refuses to go completely after his dreams. If he would, it wouldn't be difficult, you see."

"You sound like you've known the family a long time."

"Off and on for what feels like a century." She brushed that aside with a wave of her hand. "He's too old to be able to simply follow his gut. The inclination to think too much that comes with age has sunk in. A woman would need to shake him up a little bit, perhaps push him. He's been in charge of his life so long that no one pushes him—not even his father."

Kalliope thought about that for a few moments. She had been starting to suspect those things as well. She hurried toward the door. "Thanks, Professor Alexandrios." She stopped in the doorway and turned back with a quick smile. "You know, you're not as big a beast as everyone thinks."

Audra just smirked slightly to herself. "You have no idea, honey." As the footsteps faded, she opened her mail client and sent a single, one word email across the building.

Taegan heard the beep from his computer and swiveled in his chair to open the email. It was classic Audra. No body to the message; the subject said it all.

Incoming.

He lifted a brow. What on Earth did that mean? She wasn't usually *that* cryptic. He got his answer as his office door opened, and Kalliope stepped into the doorway. Completely unprepared for her presence, he almost couldn't stop himself from leaping up and snatching her into his arms. His mouth went dry, his palms burned, and he grabbed the arms of his chair for support. She wore a peach colored sundress despite the winter air outside and the threat of snow.

Desire for her roughened the edge of his voice without his control as he said, "Good morning."

Her heart fluttered as she heard the edge, and it seemed to caress her everywhere. With a quick breath, she shut the door and walked over to sit down in the visitor's chair. "I thought you might be interested in hearing about the party." Try as she might, she couldn't keep the soft note of memory out of her voice.

Their eyes met. A nearly tangible electric current ran between them. They both knew. They knew they both knew. It was a game where neither knew the rules but the stakes were high. Taegan sent a response to Audra and shut down his computer entirely. He had a feeling that he might need to make a fast exit before he was over his head. "Go ahead," he finally said. "You have my undivided attention."

"It was a really fun party," she started. She got to her feet to walk slowly around the small office. "Everyone was in formal ball clothes and everyone but me was wearing a mask. It was fun seeing who was who. I kept hoping you'd change your mind," she continued, "but when the others showed up without you, I stopped hoping. Aenya told me they tried to convince you, but that you turned stubborn on them."

She ran a finger lightly over the face of a picture showing him as a child holding a wiggling bundle she assumed was Aenya since it wore a pink ribbon. "We had cake. I saved you a piece; I'll bring it by sometime. Oh, and I had presents." She grimaced wryly. "Lots of jewelry and stuff. Not like I didn't have enough. I like Kienan's best though. A weekend stay at the Gentle Brook Inn when it opens again after renovations. Sounds fabulous."

He smiled. "He's good at that sort of thing."

"I noticed. It's why I pushed Maddie at him." She took a quick breath and turned to look at him directly. "We were dancing again when this funny thing happened. I looked up, and I saw this man watching me. He was masked, but I knew him. We danced together, and he kissed me in a moonlit garden. And then he ran off without even leaving a glass slipper behind. I mean, really, what kind of decent Cinderella does that?"

"Kalliope," he said quietly. "No more."

"No." She leaned toward him, her eyes fierce. "We both knew then, and we both know now, that it was you with me in that garden. God, how could I *not* know, Taegan? You haunt my waking hours and make me burn in my dreams." His eyes shot to hers, hot and wild, and she felt an answering emotion well from somewhere deep inside. "Do you dream of me?" she whispered.

He got to his feet, his control threadbare and growing thinner. He moved to go toward the door, but she got firmly into his path and forced him to look at her. "Tell me I'm wrong," she challenged. "Prove me wrong, right here and now."

"How?"

"Kiss me." She lifted her chin slightly when he looked at her in shock. Determination and desperation mingled inside her. "Prove me wrong. That *mysterious stranger* kissed me. I'll know the difference. Worst thing that happens is you get to kiss a hot woman and me a hot man."

"That," he muttered softly, his hand lifting to fist into her loose hair, "is not the worst thing that could happen! Damn you, princess." He dragged her against him, surprising a gasp out of her, then covered her mouth with his in the kiss he had been craving for the last two days and his entire life.

A low moan vibrated in her throat. She threw her arms around him and met his desire equally, recklessly not caring where they were. "I love you!" she whispered fiercely when he lifted his head slightly. "Admit that it was you!"

"It was." He couldn't deny it any longer, not when she was in his arms again. Despite the difference between their heights, her body seemed perfectly formed to mold against him. He had a vision of simply lifting her onto the edge of the desk and finding every inch of her soft skin to imprint her on his memory. A shudder rippled through his body and he caught her even closer. "Kally."

Ready to demand he admit he loved her, for she was sure now that he did, she opened her mouth . . . and the office door suddenly swung open. A student blithely walked in saying, "Hey, Professor Shaughnessy, I have a question about Tuesday's homework." His words came to a startled stop as he saw Kalliope in Taegan's arms. His eyes slowly widened as red color climbed up his neck. "Oh, shit. Umm, sorry!" He backed out hastily and slammed the door.

As if he had been burned, Taegan lifted his hands sharply. "Shit." While Kalliope sank weakly down onto the edge of the chair, he leaned against the edge of the desk. "Well," he sighed, "there go our reputations. Your status as valedictorian will be revoked at the least."

"Do you think that matters to me?!" she snapped at him as she leapt to her feet. "I want you! I don't want anything else! My grades can go to hell. Oh, god." She buried her face in her hands. "You might get fired. I never wanted this, Taegan. I'm so sorry!"

He gently reached out and drew her into his arms. He pressed her face to his shoulder as she sobbed softly. "I know." He softly ran a hand over her back. "I know you didn't. But you understand now why I said this was a bad idea."

She swiped at her eyes. "I guess I'm still a child in some ways."

"No." He pressed his lips to her forehead. "You're just too quick to follow your heart. Sometimes you need to stop and think." He held her closer, uncaring about the passage of time. He had no classes to go to, and she wasn't afraid to skip. Once word spread, they wouldn't be able to see each other on or off campus. It was his last chance to hold her.

It was noon when his phone finally rang. By then, he was sitting with her curled up on his lap. She reluctantly got to her feet as he just as reluctantly let her go. With a bracing sigh, he picked up the phone. "Shaughnessy." He listened for long moments, then said, "I'll be right there." He hung up the phone and turned to where she was standing with her arms crossed protectively. "The school president and council want to see me. You should go home."

"I'll go with you. I'll tell them it wasn't your fault." She turned her face helplessly into his hand as he touched her cheek. "Taegan, please." She couldn't bear the idea of him going into battle alone. And it was a battle. She felt it. Things would have been easy if he had only had a wicked stepmother. He had the school president instead, and that was eons worse. Private campuses abided by different rules than public ones.

"Go home." He leaned down and softly touched her lips with his. It would be the last time he ever tasted her. And because he felt so sure it was, he gave her the truth he had wanted to give her for years. "I love you."

She could only stand there with tears running down her cheeks as he pulled on his jacket and walked out of the office. Helplessly, she sank down onto the chair and buried her face in her hands. "I'm such an idiot!"

A very gentle hand touched her hair so lightly she almost didn't feel it. When she lifted her head sharply, Audra was standing in the room beside her. The sunlight in the room had somehow receded, and shadows hid Audra's face from view once more. It seemed a curious thing, but Kalliope didn't question it.

Audra leaned against the desk and regarded Kalliope. Things were moving forward just as she had thought they would. "Well," she said.

"Well indeed." Her lips trembled. "Do you hate me as much as I'm sure everyone else will?"

"Why would I hate a woman who took a desperate grab for love?" Audra shook her head. "No, Kalliope, I don't hate you. And I don't hate Taegan. It may not make sense, and you may not believe me, but I care about you both."

Oddly, it did make sense somehow, and she did believe her. "Is there any advice you can give me? My attempts at winging it seemed to have backfired."

Audra cocked her head. "I think your best option is to take a few days off. Go stay at a hotel on the other side of town. Let the air clear and everything blow over. When you come back, I think you'll have a better idea of what to do."

"I like that idea." She got to her feet. "Any recommendations for a hotel?" It seemed another compulsion, as if she had to ask.

"Actually, yes." Audra held out a business card. "It's owned by a . . . friend. They won't ask questions or make you uncomfortable. Promise."

Because it was well known that Audra didn't make promises she didn't keep, Kalliope felt her shoulders relax. "I guess I'll go home and see where I stand with my dad, and if it's too bad, I'll go to the hotel. Thank you, Professor Alexandrios."

"Sure." Audra watched Kalliope walk out of the office. She then sat down in the vacated seat and swung her long legs over the arm. With all the patience of a hunter, she waited.

As Taegan headed down the halls, he was able to see firsthand how far and how outrageously word had spread. Students treated him coldly, which wasn't a surprise. Whether Kalliope was willing or not, he had betrayed all of their trust by crossing over a line he should never have gone near. A teacher was supposed to be their role model, and everyone had looked up to him.

It was no surprise to see Kienan in a loud argument with another student and shaking the other kid by his shirt. Kienan was a protector and his temper flared hot. It was, however, a surprise to see Mel almost at blows with another set of students. Mel wasn't known for his fast temper. Who would have thought it?

The entire council was already present when he arrived. "I was expecting this call," he said calmly as he shut the door behind himself. If he felt any discomfort or unease, it was well hidden.

"Have a seat, Taegan." The president leaned forward slightly when he had done so. "To be honest, we're not entirely certain we wish to believe these rumors. Your reputation is sterling and, by this point, the rumors are completely outrageous. Under the circumstances, we're also turning a blind eye to the fights your brothers and sister-in-law got into."

"Madelyne did?" His brows shot up. Madelyne was the least confrontational girl he knew.

One of the members cleared her throat slightly. "I believe that one began when another student referred to Kalliope Tavoularis by a very derogatory name in her presence." She saw the flash of fury in his eyes that was quickly hidden, and she knew that, regardless of the truth, the math teacher was seriously hung up on his student.

"The student who began the rumors is unable to be located right now. I think your brothers have the fear of God in him since they've threatened to murder whoever started this." The president cleared his throat. "Until we can determine his whereabouts and get the truth out of him, we have no choice but to suspend you from classes. You're not fired," he added quickly. "Think of it as a paid vacation."

Taegan took a little breath and asked quietly, "If I may make a request?" When the council nodded, he got to his feet and continued firmly, "Don't punish Kalliope for whatever may have happened. She does not deserve to be suffering for this. Please transfer her from my class to another, and don't let it affect her grade. She deserves to be valedictorian."

As the door shut behind him, one of the women on the council gave a soft sigh. Though he had tried to hide it, his suffering had been clear to anyone looking closely. "David, it's plain he's in love with her. How can we punish something like that? Are we so far entrenched in pomp and propriety that we can't bend the rules a little?"

Taegan wasn't surprised to find Audra in his office, sitting in the visitor's chair with her feet propped on the top of the desk. The afternoon sun slanted across her face and harshly illuminated the healing scar that started at her forehead and crossed down over her nose and to her chin. Whatever beauty she had once possessed had been marred forever by the vicious presence of the scar. It would forever scare and repulse most people.

He wasn't most people. He barely even saw the scar when he looked at her. If anything, looking at the scar brought nothing but respect, admiration, and love. He knew where she had gotten it, and he would forever be grateful for her dedication. He let her be while he packed up his things. But, after a few moments, he realized she was waiting for him to speak first. "Yes?" he asked dryly.

"I take it the council canned you?"

"No, they suspended me with pay. They want to get information from the source before they make a final decision. They don't entirely believe anything they've heard, which is good for me and Kalliope both." He shot her a sour look. "Damn it, you could have warned me a little more clearly! I couldn't control myself."

"Good. Rattling you up is the only way to get you anywhere." She swung her feet down and got to her feet. She flicked her hair back over her shoulder. "You want some advice?"

"From you? Always."

"You need to get away for the weekend," she informed him calmly. "Your family will support you, naturally, but you won't be able to stand seeing their happy relationships. Love that suffers always suffers more when it is around love that doesn't. And anyway, your brothers will nag you."

"You'd know," he murmured. "You've certainly been around us long enough."

She didn't respond to the bait. Instead, she turned and walked out of the office. As the door shut behind her, the oddly frightening and yet protective sense of her presence faded. He was well familiar with it. He could read energy, and hers was one he knew well. He would give things a try at home, but he didn't doubt his friend in the slightest. She knew his family as well as he did.

CHAPTER TWENTY

Kalliope knew the instant she walked in the front door of her house that her father had heard the news because she was immediately summoned to his office. She was hardly surprised. Word traveled fast around her.

Her exit from the campus had felt like a walk through a gauntlet. Half the students had been supportive, but the other half had been brutal and cruel. They had called her names, slung jokes, and made crude propositions. The battering of emotions on top of the highs and lows of the last few days was almost more than she could bear. The hotel looked more and more appealing.

Straightening her back, she walked into her father's office. Pride was all she had left, and she clung onto it with all her strength. She inclined her head slightly when he looked at her. "Yes?"

"What," he asked softly, "was the meaning of the phone call I received? You were found in a compromising position with a teacher? I raised you better than that."

For a moment, she could only stare at him in stunned hurt. "I can't believe you. You'd believe someone else before you even heard what I had to say." Her hands curled into fists at her side. "Yes, I was in Taegan Shaughnessy's office. I'm often in there because he's my friend and listens to me when I need someone to talk to."

"From the sound of things he's slightly more than a friend!" he snapped. He felt furious and betrayed. Taegan had crossed an ethical line that he found appalling. It made him begin to question the entire Shaughnessy family as a whole and rethink the idea of a merger. "I don't want you going near him again."

"You can't stop me." Her eyes glittered fiercely. "I won't bend my life to fit the whims of others."

"You'll damned well do what I say!" He got to his feet. "If you want to inherit this company, then you will do as I say!"

"Then keep your damned company!" The words exploded out of her on a wave of pain and fury. "I'm so *sick* of having to change myself to be good enough for you! It's never been about my skill or my intelligence! I've done everything you ever wanted to make myself be the best possible heir! But now, when I need you on my side, you don't even care! Fuck you, Dad!" She whirled toward the door so he couldn't see the tears trying to fall. "I'm going away somewhere for a few days. I'll come back when you've cooled down. And if you still can't apologize at that time, I'm leaving for good!"

The door slammed violently behind her as she left. Shaking, he slowly lowered his face into his hands and slumped down in his chair. How could she *ever* think that he didn't love and appreciate her? She was his pride and joy.

Mara slipped into the room and walked over to wrap her arms around his shoulders. She had wondered if it might someday come to this. "Neither of you seem to know when to pull back," she murmured softly.

He covered her hands with his. "Or when to leave well enough alone." He let out a breath. "I need to call Sullivan." He reached for the phone, but her hand covered his gently. He sighed and leaned against her. "I guess it can wait. I don't think I want to risk saying something else I'll regret."

Kalliope went upstairs and threw together, in a suitcase, the first clothes to come to hand. Her tears had gone away somewhere. She felt battered and bruised, pushed to the point of breaking. She drove on automatic and followed her car's navigator to get to the hotel Audra had suggested. It was on the other side of the town, big enough to get lost in, and oddly quiet for that time of day. Few cars were in the parking lot, and that suited her just fine. She was able to find a place where her car couldn't be seen in passing.

The manager who ran the place was behind the desk when he heard her walk in. He looked up automatically and was going to call a greeting when he realized her face was familiar. He looked down at the desk in front of him where a small photo sat. It was the same face.

His sharp eyes saw the remnants of grief and tears on her face. She was, indeed, in need of an escape. "Welcome to the Sanctuary Hotel," he told her gently as she came up to the desk. "Are you checking in?"

"Yes, but I don't have a reservation. Do you have a quiet room somewhere that I can hide for a few days?" Her smile was wan. "I'm having a bit of a family fight. I left before I and my father could kill each other."

The key was already sitting next to the photo though he said nothing about it. "Of course. There's a room on the top floor near the back. Only one other room is occupied, across from yours, so you should have plenty of quiet."

She went through the registration process in a sort of haze, signed the paperwork, and then accepted her key. She couldn't even argue when the bellhop insisted on carrying her one suitcase.

The manager watched her go before looking down once more to where there was another photograph and key waiting. He had stopped questioning Rhianna Taber and her odd ways of knowing things before they happened.

She found her room to be tranquil and quiet and just what she needed. She tipped the bellhop before he could try to explain things she already knew and he took that as his cue to leave. As the door shut behind him, she walked over to her bed and curled up into a ball on the top. She couldn't even cry. It hurt too much.

When Taegan got home, it was to a congregation in the kitchen. Mel was sitting on a stool without a shirt. Kienan was holding an icepack over one of his eyes, which was quickly turning black and blue. Madelyne was bandaging his knuckles, and Hiro was taking care of what looked like a couple of nasty abrasions on his upper arm.

The snippets of conversation indicated that he hadn't ducked in time nor had he made a proper fist. Taegan just sighed and kept going down the hall to his room. He dropped his things on the bed and turned to close the door when he realized that Aenya had been following him silently. She stared at him solemnly for long moments before moving closer and wrapping her arms around his waist in a fierce hug.

After all the upheaval of the day, her silent support was nearly his undoing. He lifted her up into his arms and held onto her tightly to take what comfort he could. He pressed his lips to her forehead. "I guess you heard."

"You could say that. It made its way to my high school, Taegan." There was no censure in her eyes or voice. Just steady support. "You want to tell me the truth? I've heard some interesting variations."

He put her down gently and sat on the side of the bed. "I'm in love with Kally, which I'm sure you're already aware of." His sigh was long. "I've been in love with her for years. It was fine when it was unrequited, but she seems to love me as well. Knowing it . . . I find I can't control myself any longer. A student walked into my office and found her in my arms."

"Kissing?" she asked calmly.

"Not at the immediate moment. If he'd been a minute sooner, yes." He smiled wryly. "I don't deny we shared an embrace, but I'm not telling anyone except my family that."

"We would have guessed anyway." She walked over to sit

beside him. Her hands covered his wrist softly as she wished with all her soul to make things better. "Where do you stand with the school?"

He studied her hands curiously. "Suspended with pay until they determine what really happened. If my reputation wasn't so solid, I'm sure I'd have been fired." Her hands were burning softly, hotter than usual. Oddly, the pain seemed to have lessened its chokehold. "Aenya . . ."

She lifted her hands with a smile. "I only recently figured out I could do that. I guess it's my gift."

"It suits you." He got to his feet as he heard Sullivan calling for him. "Thanks, Aenya." He brushed another kiss over the top of her head. "Your support means everything."

Sullivan was waiting in his office. When Taegan walked inside, Sullivan studied him intently. "Have a seat."

He shook his head. "I'll stand if it's all the same to you."

"Alright. You want to tell me what really happened?" Sullivan trusted his son to tell him the truth. He had raised Taegan, and he refused to believe any of the rumors he had heard. That there had been some sort of torrid embrace, he had no doubt. The wolf that had just snuck in the door behind him was proof of it.

"To be blunt, sir," Taegan ignored Stormy as she sat beside him in clear alliance, "I am in love with Kalliope and made the foolish mistake of kissing her. I had already released her, but she was still in my arms when the student walked in. Conclusions were drawn. As such, I am on suspension from the college until the council determines their next course of action. I have asked that Kalliope be transferred from my class. She won't suffer for my actions."

"Of course she will." Sullivan lifted a brow. "She loves you, I assume, or she would not have returned your embrace."

"Yes, sir, she does." He smiled sadly. "Her father will hardly approve of me now, not with the smear on my reputation. Pin your hopes for grandchildren on your other children. There will be none from me."

As he left the room, Sullivan got up and walked around the desk to kneel in front of Stormy. "I don't know what you are," he said softly. "I don't know who you are. But I've seen what you're doing for us. So, please, give him a happy ending, too. I can't bear my children to be so miserable."

She rose up to lick his cheek softly in comfort and ran lightly from the room. She caught up with Taegan halfway down the hall and followed him into his room. She sat in the doorway to watch while he packed a suitcase, looking for all the world like a wolf-shaped statue. It was clear she wasn't moving anytime soon.

He smiled wryly. "Alright. What is it you want me to know or do?" Her eyes flickered toward his desk and he walked over to glance at the top. There, printed neatly, were directions to a hotel on the edges of the city. "And if I don't want to go there?" She bared her teeth and he smiled. "I assumed so." He picked up the directions and quickly memorized them. It really wasn't a hard place to reach. "You do plan for everything," he murmured as he picked up his suitcase.

He had no idea how true that was, she thought wryly as she followed him down the hall again.

At the kitchen, he glanced inside to see his siblings. They looked at him expectantly but no one said anything. "No questions," he told them quietly. "I'm just not up to it right now. Kien, I'm borrowing the sidecar. I'm going to stay at a hotel for a few days. I'm hoping things will blow over quickly."

"Sure." Kienan tucked his hands in his pockets and watched as he left the kitchen. His eyes lowered to see Stormy following along in his tracks. He began to smile as he looked at his family. "What's that thing we say in 3rd District, Maddie?"

She smiled in return. "There's no such thing as coincidence."

Oblivious to that little fact, Taegan attached the sidecar to his bike and waited for Stormy to jump in before he put his suitcase in with her. He made sure she was safely secured before pulling on his helmet. A memory teased him of how Kalliope had felt so right riding on the bike with him, and his heart quivered. It would never happen again. He wanted to tell himself that things were better this way, but he couldn't really bring himself to believe it.

The hotel was blessedly large and isolated. He parked out front and saw no familiar cars. Suitcase in hand and Stormy at his side, he walked into the lobby. "Behave yourself," he murmured to her as he saw her eyeing a stray cat wandering outside. "Chicken. You handle Maddie's kitten just fine."

The manager was waiting for him when he came over to the desk. "Welcome to Sanctuary Hotel." His sharp eyes missed none of the strain in his face or the grief darkening his gaze. "Are you checking in?"

"Yes, but I have no reservation. And are pets allowed? I promise she's housebroken. I can get a leash for her as needed."

"Pets are allowed, and as long as she stays at your side while you are in the lobby, you don't need a leash." He would have said a leash wasn't needed at all, but then he would have to explain why the wolf was familiar to him. "We have a quiet room on the top floor. Only one other guest is up there. You'll have plenty of privacy."

"Do I look that bad?" he asked ruefully as he signed the paperwork.

"Worse," the manager admitted. He handed over the key. "If you need anything, just dial 0-4. We have a full room service menu."

"Thanks." He waved off the bellhop and carried his suitcase by himself as he headed for the elevator. Once on the top floor, it wasn't hard to find his room. The one across from him had a 'do not disturb' sign on the handle. He completely sympathized.

He opened his door and smiled with reluctant bemusement when Stormy leapt up onto the bed and laid down to claim a portion for herself. He ruffled her fur gently as he walked over to open the curtains. It was rapidly turning from afternoon into evening, the sun slowly beginning its descent. Sunset was coming quicker these days as winter took hold. If the weathermen were to be believed, it would be snowing in a few days. That suited his mood just fine. He felt cold and bleak himself.

Kalliope awoke to thin moonlight coming in the open curtains. Highly groggy, she staggered over and closed them. She hadn't intended to fall asleep but she wasn't entirely surprised that she had. She looked in a mirror, and she also wasn't surprised that her eyes were a little puffy. Her conscious mind couldn't cry but her subconscious was having no trouble.

There was no reason to repair the damage, and she hadn't brought any makeup anyway. She didn't care who saw her. She didn't feel overly hungry, but she knew she needed to eat. She raked a hand through her tangled hair and opened her door to step into the hall. She had just shut it behind her when she heard clawing at the door across from her.

"Alright!" Taegan exclaimed in exasperation as he opened the door to let Stormy out. "What the hell's wrong with you now?" He broke off in shock as he found himself staring at Kalliope. She stood motionless, staring at him in return.

He looked her over hungrily. He was dreaming. He had to be dreaming. You couldn't conjure someone by wishing for them. Her perfume reached out and curled around him, and he began to breathe again. "Kally," he managed to say.

"Oh my god." She took a quick breath as she saw he was about to go back into his room and shut the door. "No!" She leapt forward and reached for the door to stop it. Her foot caught on the rug in the hall, and she pitched forward without control. She landed safely in his arms as he caught her. On a soft sound, she burrowed closer. She clung on with a wild and desperate strength. "No, please," she whispered against his shoulder. "Don't shut me out."

"Kally." Trembling, he caught her even closer and lifted her off her feet to bury his face against her neck. "What are you doing here?"

"I fought with my father. We both said some pretty horrible

things so I left before it got worse." She wrapped her arms around him, afraid she would wake up and find it was another dream. "What about you?"

"My family is behind me one hundred percent, but I couldn't bear seeing Maddie and Kienan, or Hiro and Aenya. It was killing me because I couldn't have you." He eased her back and set her on her feet. "Go back to your room," he told her, his voice strained and aching. "If you stay . . . I don't know if I can stop myself from touching you."

She stepped back, and he closed his eyes tightly, his hands turning into fists at his sides as he heard the door shut. The sound of the lock turning had his eyes opening in shock. She stood just inside the doorway with the closed door at her back. She took a quick breath. "I don't want you to stop."

"I can't protect you." He held her gaze. "I don't carry protection around with me because it's not a game."

"No it's not." She walked toward him slowly. "I'm on the pill," she informed him, her voice calm. "I'm so irregular with my periods that I would get horrendous cramps. I went on the pill to help regulate them. I've only had two lovers, and both are as healthy as am I. Want my records?" It was said with an obvious hint of humor.

"You're making it very hard to tell you to leave." His voice was husky with desire as he lifted his hands to frame her face. It was easy to be gentle when she was finally his to hold as he had wanted for so long. "I love you so much," he murmured. He studied her face and tenderness filled his heart. He brushed at the skin under her eyes. "Were you crying?"

"Yes." She gave him a sour look. "I've cried more the last few days than I ever have in my life, damn you." Her words trailed off as he bent his head and began to brush soft kisses across her eyes and cheek. "We broke the rules already," she whispered. "What's one more?"

"Kally. My beautiful Kalliope." He lifted her into his arms and carried her toward the bed. He lowered her gently to her feet beside it. "I wish . . . if only . . ." He stopped as she reached up and pressed gentle fingers to his lips.

"Change nothing. Not you, not me, not this time. I don't want to ever regret anything." She began to unbutton his shirt slowly, her mouth going dry with every inch of skin she uncovered. He was more muscular than she had thought, more beautiful, and when his shirt was completely removed, she felt a small quiver of feminine fear as she realized how much stronger he was.

He felt the quiver in her fingers and brought them to his lips to kiss each tip softly. He eased closer and ran the kisses down the inside of her arm, up over her slim bicep, and around to the back of her neck. He breathed his love between every kiss. Her arms lifted to wind around him in a reverse hug and his hands settled lightly at her waist as he pressed his lips to her pulse.

Her eyes closed as helpless pleasure washed through her body. "You left a mark last time," she murmured huskily.

"I was too rough." He turned her in his arms and lifted her to her toes, his hands cupping her bottom warmly under her dress. His lips found hers and he sank into the kiss, lazily drawing it out until she softened and swayed against him. Still kissing her, he eased the dress up to her waist and skimmed his knuckles over the hot skin of her stomach.

He released her long enough to remove the dress and then held her hands at her sides as he looked his fill. She wore a pair of matching peach lace panties and bra that seemed only a few shades darker than her skin. The echoes of a tan from the summer were visible in places. He smiled as he realized she wore a bikini often.

She was soft and fragrant curves and long graceful lines. The urge to ravish surged at its chains, but he leashed it tightly. He knew it might be his only time to ever love her. He sank his fingers into her hair and drew her close again for another lingering kiss. The soft moan she gave was the sweetest sound he had heard.

She was floating, unable to breathe or think. She drowned in his caresses, and she couldn't have known his love more surely. When he lifted her in his arms and turned to lower her to the top of the bed, she had to say softly, "Too many novels."

"You disapprove?" He sat beside her on the bed and lightly skimmed his knuckle slowly over her ribcage and steadily higher.

"No, but you," her breath caught as his hand cupped her breast warmly, "are really ruining me for other men. I'll never have another lover. You're going to be," her breath broke again as his head bent and his lips teased her nipple through the lace, "going to be stuck with me."

She moved restlessly beneath him, arching fluidly into his touch as he eased the cups of the bra aside and took a bare nipple into his lips. He suckled softly, savoring the flavor of her skin that was the same no matter where he touched. A flick of his fingers opened her bra so he could drop it over the side of the bed.

She watched him through lowered lashes as she nudged his shoulders. He obligingly rolled onto his back and she rose to her knees beside him. She ran a hand slowly over his chest and thrilled at the knowledge this powerful male was hers. She seemed small and delicate beside him and it was a heady power to be given the freedom of his body.

She softly ran little kisses over his chest. She tasted him thoroughly and the little touches of her tongue made him shudder. Answering wild pleasure shivered through her own body. Her fingers skimmed lightly down the muscles of his arms and up again, and her lips curved against his as she kissed him softly. "Bad boy in disguise."

He turned suddenly and tumbled her onto the bed. He pinned her gently beneath him. "Hardly worthy of a princess." He ran his hand slowly over her legs and up over her hip. He couldn't stop touching her. His heart craved her as deeply as his body did. "But I love you."

She opened her mouth to respond but could only moan softly as his hand slipped under the edge of her underwear and slid downward to caress her slowly. He softly petted her and watched her face with rapt attention as she twisted against his hand, pleasure stealing her breath.

When ecstasy came, it rolled like a wave over her senses. It rocked her to her soul, branded her indelibly as his. Before she could catch a breath, he was kissing her deeply, building her hunger again as his hands stripped her underwear down her legs and away. "Taegan." It was all she could say.

"Kally. You're mine, Kally." He lifted her slightly into the kiss before lowering her once more and surveying her naked body with primitive satisfaction. Even if it was only once, she was his. She would belong to him as she had to no one else. Two lovers or two hundred, they both knew that what was between them was *only* between them. They would never find this anywhere else.

Her hands lowered as he continued to kiss her, and she began to unfasten his pants. He stopped breathing entirely as she slowly slid a hand inside his shorts and cupped him, learning him as completely as he had learned her. "Stop," he said a bit hoarsely. "You'll make me . . ."

"Good." Her voice filled with feminine welcome and delight. Secure in her power, she reveled in touching him.

"I'd rather be inside you." He dragged her hands up his body and kissed the palms with a little nip of his teeth. He released her only long enough to remove his clothes. He was heavy with desire for her, and the sight of her holding her arms out to him made him shudder with need. "I've dreamed of this," he admitted huskily as he sank into her arms. "Of you here, welcoming me. Reality is better than imagination."

She lifted a leg and curled it around his hip to hold him tightly as he braced his weight on his arms over her. Her hands lowered, and their fingers entwined securely as he slid into her in a single stroke. Her breath hitched in her chest and a shudder rippled through her body. It felt like homecoming. Belonging. "Taegan." Her hair tumbled around her shoulders as she twisted slowly beneath him.

If it was wrong, then why was it so very right? He drew their hands up until they were pinned to the pillow beside her head. He held her tightly as he began to slowly slide in and out of her. "Hold onto me," he urged huskily. "Don't let go of me."

Her arms wound around his damp shoulders and she held on tightly as the tension grew. She lifted her head to meet his kiss halfway and sank into the ecstasy of the union. They had to break apart only for air, and she buried her face against his neck, her arms tightening around his shoulder as he poured himself into her. She wished only that tomorrow would never arrive.

Long after she slept beside him, curled protectively into his arms, he remained awake and stared at the clock across the room as it steadily ticked away the seconds and minutes. As it began to grow closer to dawn, he turned and tucked her more firmly under the covers. She reached for him without waking, and he leaned down to kiss her softly and taste her dreams. She settled and curled into the pillow more firmly.

He called himself several kinds of a fool while he dressed. He scrawled a short note on the pad by the phone before ripping the page off and wrapping it around the stem of a rose he removed from the vase in the room. He set it on the pillow where he had slept and then gently brushed her hair from her face. Before he could change his mind, he left the room.

She knew she was alone even before she opened her eyes. She sat up and surveyed the silent room. His suitcase was gone. She noticed the rose belatedly, and she picked up the note to open it. The language looked completely foreign and unknown to her, yet just reading the words made them seem beautiful. She could only imagine how they would sound in Taegan's beautiful voice.

She held the note to her heart and closed her eyes tightly. Even if it was only one night, she couldn't regret it. She traced a finger over the petals of the rose and thought of the story of Cinderella again. It was time she played the tale through to the end. Ideas were forming, tumbling through her mind. Audra had been right. Suddenly she was thinking clearer and more steadily.

There had been a second party in one of the stories, hadn't there?

CHAPTER TWENTY-ONE

Kalliope spent the next few days at the Sanctuary Hotel. She felt secure and grounded once more and ready to take on the world. She was oddly peaceful, too. She refused to believe that she had been given such a wonderful chance at happiness, only to have it slip away. Her fantasies had been trumped by the reality of Taegan's love and desire for her.

The time wasn't spent moping. She made plans and lists and formulated ideas. She was going to have to play both sides. That Taegan had someone on his side was in her favor. She didn't know who it was, but she hoped they really had his best interests in mind.

By the time she was on her way home that Wednesday, she had made her plan of attack. The first step was to find out where she and her father stood. Despite what she had accused him of, she knew he only wanted her to be happy. He was just too entrenched in propriety and status.

She was disinclined to outright lie to him anymore. She was going to have another one of those conversations where they pretended they didn't know what was being said. She was getting rather tired of them. She preferred being blunt.

When she returned to her home, she parked in her spot and headed for the front door. Jiles was sitting on the front steps waiting for her. She warily slowed her steps, not sure what he was doing and thinking. He looked unbearably sad as if he had aged overnight. "Dad?"

He got to his feet, went down the steps, and pulled her into his arms. He rocked her back and forth and buried his face in her hair. "I'm sorry, baby," he murmured achingly. "Please forgive me. I *never* meant to make you feel as if I didn't love you. Of course I love you!" He eased back and gave her a trembling smile. "And I'm proud as hell of you. I couldn't ask for a better daughter."

She let out a little sigh and hugged him tightly, wondering why she was cursed in life to be surrounded by men who were convinced they knew what was best for her. "I know, I know. It's okay, Dad, really. Don't worry about it. Going away made me accept a few things." She walked into the house and set her suitcase down by the door. "Can we go into your office?"

"Of course." He led the way and shut the door behind her as she entered. "What's on your mind, honey?"

She settled herself into one of the chairs and waited while he sat down as well. Carefully, she asked, "Would you say that I'm a . . . fickle woman?"

"Of course not." His answer was swift. "You've always known your heart. It's why it's always been so vexing for me that you wouldn't marry for affection only, hoping for love to grow." He held up a hand. "And, I promise, I'm going to loosen up over that. Just don't wait forever. Retirement has been looking more and more appealing lately. I'm bored."

"Here's the thing." She crossed her arms. "I won't marry for less than love. And all your machinations in the world won't help your cause because I've already found the man I love. He danced with me in a moonlit garden." Her eyes met her father's. "It was a stolen moment, you see. He knew the outside world would never understand."

He opened his mouth, then slowly closed it. Oddly, he found that it made perfect sense of the entire scenario. The only thing he couldn't wrap his mind around was, "I could have sworn he was blond that night," he muttered.

She smiled. "Magic. But here's my question to you." Her eyes darkened, intense and serious. "Do you stand by my decision? I can assure you that he loves me as much as I love him. That he's suffered as much as I have."

"I would stand beside you if you decided to marry a trash

collector," he assured her. "You know I love you, but . . ." He sighed. "Things have gotten quite complicated, Kally. The entire city has heard about what happened." He tossed her a newspaper. "See for yourself."

"Hmm." She studied the article. It was devoid of a lot of details, but the author took gleeful delight in Kalliope being caught in a compromising position with a Shaughnessy, particularly one who was her teacher. "And yet they don't even say what really happened. At the *worst* anyone could say was that when that other guy walked in, he saw Taegan hugging me. Seriously."

Her father quirked a brow. "And if he'd walked in a minute earlier?" he asked dryly.

"That's beside the point." Her eyes twinkled for a moment before she grew serious again. "Here's what I want to do. Everyone knows about my birthday party and the mysterious man who caught my attention. I'm going to play this story out. The Palace is ours for another week. I'm going to have another party on Friday. All the same people from before will be invited. All of them. Invitations can go out tomorrow."

"What of the guards? Unless he shows up with a crowd, they will easily single him out and be able to determine who he is."

"We're not going to have guards this time." Her smile was all business. "The invitations will be keycards to the gate. You have to flash the card to even get inside. A body entering without a card is easily picked up. I wouldn't want to scare him away, you know."

"Are you that sure he'll show up?"

She barely refrained from touching the rose tucked delicately over her ear. "He won't be able to stay away. That I can be sure of."

It took Taegan longer to return home than his lover. He had gone further out of town with the hopes of discouraging her from following him. He couldn't even resent Stormy for deliberately forcing him to confront Kalliope. In many ways, he was deeply grateful. Even if he lived for centuries, he would never forget the woman he loved.

It was Thursday when he finally returned home. He wasn't in the mood to deal with his family just yet so he ducked around into the garden and tried to sneak into his bedroom. He wasn't entirely surprised, however, to discover Aenya waiting for him on the side of the bed. He sighed.

"Hi to you, too." Her eyes searched his face. Whatever she saw seemed to please her, because a little smile played with her lips. "Good thing you got here today." She hugged Stormy as the wolf leapt up beside her. "It would seem that Kalliope is fighting fire with fire. She's having another party tomorrow night. All the same people invited. Same elaborate masquerade."

"I see." His eyes flickered to Stormy who looked both slightly surprised and yet fully pleased. "Well, I can't go, obviously. I'm sure she's just trying to dispel the rumors."

"You could help with that," Aenya noted as she got to her feet.

"You have more confidence in my control than I do," he admitted ruefully. "Now scoot." He nudged her out the door. "Frankly, if I showed my face there, her father would probably kill me."

She contemplated the door as it shut in her face. Hiro's arms slid around her waist, and she leaned back against him. Companionably, she said, "He really had that look. I know that look. I believe it was on your face after we became lovers. And it was definitely on Kienan's after he and Maddie got together. I would bet my club on Kally being at that hotel too."

"Not on purpose," he murmured.

"Well, of course not. Nothing ever happens on purpose around here. At least, not by *our* doing." She blew out a quick breath. "So who is pulling the strings this time? I would have sworn it was Stormy, but she seemed slightly surprised by Kally's actions."

"Then it's no doubt Kally who is pushing things into place. This ought to be interesting."

The speed at which word spread was a double-edged sword. Even though it had made the rumor grow with beanstalk proportions, it also allowed for news of Kalliope's second party to make its rounds with time to spare. By Friday afternoon, she knew that every last person who had accepted an invitation before would be accepting again. Keycards were delivered to those who had given confirmation.

Still, Friday evening, she felt like a nervous wreck. She was taking a *huge* risk and crossing her fingers that not only would Taegan show up, but that he would also leave some sort of clue behind that she could use against him. It had to look as if she had forced Jiles to let her marry whoever she wanted or else he would never believe her.

This time she wore a red silk ball gown with rubies. She selected her jewelry with care to flatter her features, and she used bits of white for accent. Instead of a jeweled circlet, however, she wore a tiny circlet of roses with the one Taegan had given her at the very center. Even after a few days, it hadn't begun to wilt.

Two hours into the party, she was holding court and laughing away all the rumors and assumptions. It didn't take long before there wasn't a person left who honestly believed anything had happened, and all had plans to say so when they were back at school. It was to her advantage that several council members had attended as well. She sought them out deliberately.

"You look lovely, Kalliope," one woman told her.

"Thank you." She sighed. "Tell me honestly. Do you really believe that anything happened between me and Professor Shaughnessy? I mean, the school would say Big Foot was a gym teacher if someone started a rumor."

"True enough," another member admitted. "Are you saying nothing happened?"

"He hugged me." She sighed again as if it was more an

annoyance than heartbreak. "I was miserable and upset and you know how he hates to see a friend hurt. And he *is* my friend, thank you."

"That is also true," the woman of before murmured. Her eyes searched Kalliope's but saw nothing underneath the serene surface.

She just didn't know that the serene surface was a cover for a simmering boil of nerves and anticipation. Kalliope was watching the clock and waiting. It was getting later and later. He hadn't shown up with his family, and Mel hadn't known one way or another if he would show up at all. She still knew he would. They were both in over their heads.

It was a very restless and caged Taegan that paced through the Shaughnessy house as the time went by. He wanted to go, to see her just once, but he had given the mask back to Audra. Oh, he could scare up his own mask, but he didn't want to lay a chance on anyone recognizing him. That glamour was more than convenient; it was probably a lifesaver.

Since no one was there to see him, he picked up the invitation and keycard sitting on the kitchen counter. He carried both with him into his room. He hadn't personally accepted the invitation but Sullivan had said in his reply that 'the Shaughnessy family' would attend. Mathematically—and math was Taegan's specialty—that meant he got a keycard too.

The invitation clearly said there were no guards. Entry was via generic—not assigned—keycard. She had made it as easy as possible for him to sneak in. It was clear as day to him. The woman was too smart for her own good. "Damn it," he muttered as he buried his face in his hands, "where the hell are you when I actually need you?"

"Well," came Audra's voice from the balcony. "If you're going to be like that, I'll leave."

He leapt to his feet and turned quickly. She was leaning a shoulder against the balcony door. "Does the contract still stand?" he asked. He didn't bother to hide the desperation in his tone. "Please. I'd take even ten minutes to see her! But I don't want you to get into trouble, either."

"It's moot at this point. Don't worry about me." She held out the mask toward him. "This is the last chance, Cinder-boy. If you fuck this one up, you won't get another. Oh, yeah," she added, "don't forget your watch to keep track of the time."

Kalliope was beginning to think she had failed entirely when she felt the familiar sensation of being watched. Her heart began to pound and she felt her well-loved body throb in recognition of the eyes studying her so hungrily. She turned to see a familiar form standing at the top of the stairs. He had once more dressed to match her.

It took great control not to run across the room and fling herself into his arms. Instead, she walked slowly and met him at the base of the stairs. When he took her hand and brought it to his lips, her lips formed into a trembling smile. "You did come."

"I couldn't stay away. You knew I couldn't. Will you dance with me again, princess?"

Her answer was in her eyes, and he drew her onto the floor as the music began and the others parted to give them room. He twirled her gracefully into his arms, trying to let himself pretend that this was all that mattered, that he didn't crave more with every instant of his being.

From where everyone else watched, there wasn't a single person in that room who doubted that the two staring into each other's eyes were deeply in love. Kalliope glowed with a radiance that made her stunningly beautiful, and the man's hands were both possessive and protective as if he knew she belonged to him. The waltz was an intimacy, almost too intimate to watch. Many felt like they were voyeurs and seeing something never meant for their eyes.

The music came to an end amid applause, and Kalliope quickly escorted Taegan toward the gardens. People once more tried to follow, but they were brought up short by Aenya. She stood in front of the doors with a challenging smile on her lovely face. "Kally gets her privacy," she said pointedly. "Unless you want to deal with her." She pointed down.

Eyes shifted to see the slender gray wolf at her hip, and Stormy's teeth bared in a mockery of a smile. Everyone beat a hasty retreat.

In the garden, Kalliope threw her arms around Taegan's neck and reached up to kiss him. She had missed him more with every day, dying every minute she couldn't see his face or hear his voice. His arms tightened almost painfully around her waist before he loosened his grip and returned her kiss just as desperately.

When they eased apart, she asked, "What time is it? How much time do I have?" She spotted a glint of silver and plucked the pocket watch out of his jacket. She opened it and the clock sneered at her. It was eleven-thirty. "You took too long," she accused on a hitch of breath. "Now I have no time to be with you."

"My faerie godmother got stuck in traffic. Apparently it's hell on broomsticks at this time of night."

"Is she a faerie or witch?" Somehow she managed a smile.

"Sometimes," he said with feeling, "she's both." He framed her face with his hands and searched her features intently. "What did you hope to change, princess? Will this change your father's mind? Even if the rumor is dispelled, even if the council lifts the suspension, I was still your teacher. Your father will never forget that."

"He wants me to be happy. That's all he wants. He wouldn't care what your profession is." She saw the unrelenting expression in her lover's eyes and drew a ragged breath. He was too damn stubborn! "Why did you leave me?" She couldn't keep the pain from her voice. "I know I wasn't *that* experienced, but was I that bad?"

"I left because I couldn't get enough of you," he retorted harshly. "Before my pulse had calmed, I wanted you again." He flicked a finger over the rose in her hair. "The desire I have for you will never go away. And," he added softly as he dragged her against his aching body, "you're one hell of a lover. I've dreamed of you my entire life, damn it."

The sound of Mel clearing his throat caught their attention suddenly. "Mel?" she asked. She felt painfully cold as Taegan released her and stepped back.

"I'm pretending like I don't see anything out here. In fact, I don't because I'm looking at the ballroom." He kept his back turned to give the lie credence. "And because I am looking in the ballroom, I can see your father descending toward this area like Jackson taking Mississippi."

She covered her face with a hand. "Damn it, Mel! You know the Pantheon is in Rome, but you don't remember American history? It was New Orleans, you sieve-minded male!" She turned to speak to Taegan but realized with only a little surprise that he had already disappeared. She looked down at the watch in her hand and closed her fingers around it fiercely. It wasn't a glass shoe, but it would have to do.

She bided her time and brushed off questions until the party ended. She then spent the rest of the night on the internet. She had noticed that the watch was engraved with the same words that had been written on Taegan's note to her. She was desperately trying to find out what they were and what they meant.

She barely noticed the sunrise out her window. She had found and rejected dozens of languages, even some obscure ones she hadn't known existed. She knew Taegan was multi-lingual and a studier of classic language, but which one was the one so close to his heart that he would leave a note to his lover in it?

A soft scratching at her balcony door was so surprising it nearly sent her tumbling out of her chair. She looked over and saw a familiar wolf patiently sitting outside. She walked over to open the door and knelt down quickly. "What is it?" She realized the wolf was carrying a small bag and took it curiously.

She found three things inside. One was a very familiar mask. Another was a sheaf of papers. The third was a book. Her heart began to beat faster. It was a language book. Pages had been tabbed and she flipped to them quickly. And there, in those pages, she found the translation to the words in the note. "You sappy romantic," she whispered.

She closed the book and looked at the cover. Somehow she wasn't shocked. What else would have been the language of his heart? She turned her attention to the papers and began to read. A smile came slowly and spread across her face. It was a contract. It was a perfect contract and the answer to all her prayers. She now had all the ammunition she needed.

"I don't know who you are," she told the wolf, "but I owe you one!" She kissed the wolf very gently on the scar crossing its face. "Your heart is beautiful." Leaving the visibly bemused wolf on her balcony, she gathered up the things she needed and hurried downstairs to her father's office. It was barely after dawn, but he was always up early.

She walked right in without knocking. Jiles looked up in surprise and his eyes widened as he saw her. He had never seen her look quite so determined or triumphant before. Or exhausted. "Kally?" he asked warily. "Didn't you sleep?"

"I'll sleep when I have the man I love back." She slapped down the watch and the contract. "Here's the deal. He left this watch. It has an engraving in another language. I've since managed to figure out what it is and what it means. It's a very select language, Dad. I'd hazard a guess that of the people invited to the party, only one man would know it."

He began to smile slowly. "I see."

"And so here's the deal. I'm calling together everyone once more. Whichever man can translate, on the spot without help, the inscription on this watch can have my hand in marriage. This contract is a binding document and reads precisely as I have just stated."

Being a businessman, he picked up the contract and read it to be sure. It did, indeed, say precisely what she had. She would bring together all her invited guests for, again, he had entered with an invitation. She would give each *bachelor* a chance to translate, and the one that did would have her hand in marriage. "Are you sure?" he asked her. "Sure this will work?"

"I'm certain." She signed her name across the bottom of the contract and slid it to her father who also signed. She was a legal adult, but his signature ensured that he would not contest the contract, her decision, or her inheritance. "Everyone who was *invited* is invited again. I will personally track down everyone who *received* an invitation to make sure they attend." Her smile was a challenge. "Including my stubborn math professor. After all, shouldn't he be there when I get engaged?"

He leaned back in his chair as he watched her sweep from the room. He began to slowly smile to himself. His daughter was an absolutely brilliant woman, and he was going to greatly enjoy this unveiling. He picked up the phone and dialed. It was finally a good time to call Sullivan.

Monday proved to be a day of surprises, and it started when Kalliope arrived at school. She hadn't entirely been sure whether she would be able to stand going to math class, but as it happened, she didn't need to try. Someone was waiting for her in the parking lot and caught up with her as she reached the path leading toward the math and computer wing. "Hey, Kalliope," the boy called.

She waited for him to catch up and lifted a brow. "What?"

"You need to go to admin." He fell into step beside her as she changed her route. "Hey, I want you to know that the whole school is behind you and Professor Shaughnessy one hundred percent. You'd think this school had its own El Niño the way the wind changes so quickly. Your party was the kicker." He smiled. "And anyway, how can we think you'd be in a compromising position with the professor after we saw the guy you danced with last night?"

She coughed softly. "Oh, indeed. So I guess they found the guy who walked in on us?"

"He's *madly* jealous, Kal." He shook his head. "He's had a crush

254

on you for a while. He started the rumor out of spite. He went to the council this morning and admitted that all he saw was Professor Shaughnessy holding your hand. You were upset, huh?"

"He's a good listener," she said with complete sincerity, though she wondered why the student had suddenly turned the tale even milder than the truth. Still, she wasn't knocking her luck.

She discovered at the administration office that she had been transferred to a new math class. Her grades were not going to be affected and her position as valedictorian was secure.

Not that she had doubted her grassroots efforts, but she was beginning to be a smidge suspicious that someone *else* was pushing things around. She went directly to the computer sciences area and to the computer lab. The door was standing open. As always, the room was dark with only a computer to light it. Audra was definitely present, though, for her typing was audible. "Hey, Professor Alexandrios?" Kalliope called. "Can I talk to you?"

"Sure. Do you want me to listen?"

"Umm, yes?"

"Then wait a second." Audra typed a bit more and then stopped and looked up. "Okay. Now what? I've maxed my quota for good deeds today. In fact I'm going to be doing another one in a few moments so make it quick."

She just smiled. Audra was brash and blunt, but underneath it was a very giving heart. She was sure of it. "I was hoping you could tell me if Taegan is going to be alright as well. My reputation seems to have *mysteriously* cleared this morning. I was hoping his had as well."

Something that had to be a smile flitted across Audra's face though it was barely perceptible in the light. "Interesting timing." She got to her feet and shrugged into the leather jacket draped across the back of her chair. "I'm about to go make sure the council takes the sticks out of their asses and builds a nice bonfire so we can talk about that very subject."

"Professor," she murmured, "you didn't by chance have anything to do with the student's story, or with my grades being kept as is, or any of the other anomalies going on this morning, did you?"

Audra stepped into the doorway, a little smirk playing with her lips. Kalliope studied her face but felt no fear or revulsion. Audra sensed it and rubbed her knuckles over her head as she went past. "Go to class," she shot over her shoulder. "Don't let your grades drop like another Shaughnessy we all know."

"Bite your tongue," she retorted. She smiled, though. She trusted Audra. Leaving things to her, she headed toward her new class.

The thing about Audra was that, no matter where she went, she made her presence felt. So when she walked into the president's meeting room where the council was convening, she didn't bother to start with formalities. "Are you all just going to be asses, or are you going to open your eyes?" she asked bluntly.

The president himself had always been very wary of the tall woman with yellow eyes, and more so since she had been wounded. The scar was like the car wreck you couldn't look away from, unable to feel anything but horror and terror. "Professor Alexandrios," he began, "it's complicated."

"Look at my eyes for once," was her soft suggestion, the words almost a purr, "and try to explain." She walked slowly down the line of chairs. "Taegan Shaughnessy's reputation is gold. The student who saw them has since confessed he told the tale out of jealousy. Kalliope Tavoularis is in another math class, and," she added, leaning on the desk, "they happen to be in love."

"The student and Kalliope?" a woman asked. She shrank back as predatory yellow eyes landed on her face.

"Don't be stupid. It's unflattering." Audra's eyes flicked back to the president's. "To be frank, Taegan and Kalliope have belonged together for years. They withheld announcing an engagement because he really is the best teacher on campus and she needed the best instructor. He has never treated her with special care. Everyone knows that, don't they?"

"Of course." The president loosened his collar as he felt sweat sliding down the back of his neck.

"And since the engagement will be official tonight, you can hardly call things improper, can you?" she challenged.

He swallowed hard. "No, ma'am."

"And you would really hate to see Taegan's reputation ruined just because he can't resist his fiancée, wouldn't you?"

"Yes'm." He glanced along the seats at the rest of the council. No one wanted to cross her, and there was something so compelling about her voice that she had to be instantly believed. "Your opinion is good enough for me, and for all of us. Taegan Shaughnessy can return to teaching as soon as possible. The students will be quite happy."

She straightened and a smirk curved her lips. "Good boy." And turning on her heel, she walked from the room with the graceful and dangerous walk of a true hunter.

CHAPTER TWENTY-TWO

Taegan was crawling on the floor and looking under his bed when he heard his cell phone ring. Exasperated, he got to his feet. He couldn't find his Gaelic dictionary anywhere. He had been using it to write a letter to his grandmother in Ireland. He was only half-fluent at the immediate moment, but the language came so naturally to him that he had been absorbing it for years.

The school president's number glared at him from the screen. His shoulders braced as he answered the call, but the news was such a relief that he sat down hard at his desk. He was lifted from suspension and could return to work the following day. It had been bad enough to lose Kalliope, but losing his job would have been more than he could handle.

After hanging up, he reached for his watch only to belatedly realize he had left it with Kalliope. At the back of his mind stirred a bit of unease. He didn't *think* she could find a way to use it against him, but, really, he didn't put anything past her. She was too brilliant for his peace of mind.

It was quiet in the house. Everyone who had school was there. Sullivan was at work. Hiro was probably elbow deep in the latest case he was handling—he had shifted into primarily missing person's cases, particularly runaways. It made the whole family, especially Aenya, happy that he was less likely to get shot at.

Taegan wandered from window to window, restless and lonely. Until the day he died, he would never forget Kalliope. If he died an old bachelor, so be it. He wanted no one else. He would devote his attention to spoiling whatever nieces and nephews he might be blessed to have. Hopefully sooner rather than later. He kind of missed having kids around.

A muffled sound from the direction of the stairs had his brows pulling together. He quickly went to the second floor and toward Kienan's room. "Kien?" He could have sworn he was at class. He opened the door, and the sound identified itself as retching. Suddenly suspicious, he went to the adjacent bathroom.

Sure enough, Madelyne was bent over the toilet as spasms shook her slender body. He wet a cloth in the sink and knelt to press it to her forehead. Her startled gaze swung to his, guilt in her violet eyes. He just smiled. "When were you going to tell him? And when were you going to tell us?"

She sagged against him weakly, too tired to sit up straight. Morning sickness had hit hard and with a vengeance. "I was sort of hoping to wait until his birthday," she whispered, "but he'll worry now."

"He's good at that. Here, let's get you into bed, little sister." He gently lifted her into his arms and carried her into the bedroom to settle her on the bed. "Just rest, got it? No reason to overwork yourself. The first new generation of Shaughnessy needs to be properly cultivated to weed out Kienan's genes."

She gave a weak laugh. "I'll be fine by evening, promise." She regarded him for long moments and sadness filled her eyes. "Why can't you be happy? It kills me seeing you and Kally so lonely and hurting. You should have kids of your own."

He gently brushed her bangs from her face. "I know, but it's just not possible." He leaned over and kissed her forehead. "When you're feeling better, ring for some soup. It always helped my mother. Especially when she was carrying Kienan."

She groaned. "I hope it's not a sign. I can barely keep up with one of him! I don't need two!"

He laughed and tucked a blanket around her securely. He found himself oddly happy despite his internal grief; he envied his brother a great deal, but he loved him enough to be thrilled for him as well. He would have to talk to Aenya about planning a baby shower at the Faerie Club.

Rather than mope, he put himself into his own studies. Since he couldn't find his dictionary, he concentrated on what he did know, studying with the same intensity he asked of his students. It wasn't until it was close to evening that he realized he had been writing the same phrase over and over again.

"Damn it," he muttered as he put down his pen. He turned slightly and jolted as he saw his brother sitting on his bed. "Mel! For god's sake, don't sneak up on me."

"I didn't. I only just sat down." Something determined glinted in his chocolate eyes. "You need to come with us. Kally has called a meeting for everyone 'who received an invitation to her parties.' She didn't say who attended. She said who received an *invitation*. That includes you, bro."

"I can't go, Mel."

"You *have* to, Taegan. Kally jumped on my back out of nowhere earlier today and told me to tell you that if you didn't show up, then she was going to bring the party here so that you had no choice but to attend. She had that look in her eye. She meant it. And frankly? She terrifies me."

"What is she up to?" he muttered mostly to himself. "I left nothing behind that she would . . ." He broke off. The pocket watch with the engraving in Gaelic. She knew he was old-school Irish. Of anyone at the party, only the Shaughnessys would be likely to know Gaelic. If she had figured out that that was the language . . .

"Let's go." Mel grabbed Taegan's wrist as he saw a brief moment of surrender. He firmly dragged his big brother down the hall and into the kitchen where the others were waiting. "Let's get going before he tries to escape."

Taegan couldn't have escaped if he wanted. Mel was dragging him and Hiro and Aenya were shoving him. Kienan was escorting Madelyne since she was still tired, and the happiness on his face told its own story, as did the way Sullivan hovered like a hen around a chick.

His heart quivered. He wanted a child of his own. A child with Kalliope. A terrifying combination of his stubbornness and her brilliance. She would be an amazing mother and would blend all aspects of her life with ease. With all the flair and style she possessed, she would walk a boardroom with a toddler on her hip. If any woman could have it all, she could.

They were the last to arrive at the Glass Shoe Palace, and everyone had gathered in the ballroom. As they entered, it was clear that Kalliope wasn't taking chances. Several guards took roll and marked off every name. The fact that all names were marked made it obvious that everyone had sensed the seriousness.

There was very little room to stand, but they managed to find places. They even found a chair for Madelyne. Taegan was barely aware of anyone else, his eyes riveted to Kalliope as she stood at the top of the stairs and talked with her father. She was thinner, and there were dark circles under her eyes. He knew she was eating and sleeping no more than he was.

After a few minutes, she waved her hands to get everyone's attention. "Alright," she announced distinctly. "I'm sure everyone is wondering what's going on. Well, I'm going to be as brief and clear as I can. To begin with, as everyone knows that I've been in a Cinderella story lately, I've decided to play it out."

She came down the stairs very slowly. "I'm in love," she said very calmly. "I've been in love for four years. It was an unrequited love that I was sure would never come to be, but at my birthday party, the man I loved showed up incognito to steal a moment with me. And I knew he loved me, too.

"Then, of course, things went to hell. I thought perhaps he would be scared away, but when I threw another party, he came again." She took a deep breath. "He's a bit of a coward, you see. Even if I stood here and pointed to him right now, he would deny it. I could ask all of you, and if you were him, you'd deny it. He seems to think my father will hate him."

She paused briefly to let that sink in. Slowly, she pulled the contract out of her jacket. "You see this? It's a contract. I and my father have entered into it. My Cinderella made a slight mistake that last party. He left me with something that could only belong to him. And how do I know he has to be here? Because both times he entered by invitation." She pulled out the watch and let it dangle from her fingers. "See this? It has some words on it. If you can translate it right here and now, you can have my hand in marriage."

The room fell silent. Taegan barely kept his jaw from dropping, and he barely noticed when Mel and Kienan both elbowed him sharply.

"That being said, I'd like to have all the bachelors line up please." Her eyes looked as cool as obsidian. "And I want no arguments. If you do not get in line willingly, I have several guards happy to put you there."

Needless to say, the line formed quickly. Even Taegan got in line, though at the very end. He knew he didn't dare refuse. Really, how could he? It would give him away instantly. All he could do was brace his shoulders and prepare to lie to the woman he loved. Her father may have entered a contract, but that didn't mean he would be happy. He refused to tear apart her family.

Kalliope made her way down the line, giving each male only enough time to read the words. If he knew it, it would be clear on his face. Confusion reigned more than anything else. Mel had to admit to knowing the language somewhere but not being sure which it was or what it meant. Unknowingly, that very thing pointed the finger at his elder brother.

All eyes were watching as Kalliope stopped in front of Taegan and held up the watch. She knew damned well what he was thinking and what he might do. She would have done it too. "Do you know this?" she asked him, just as she had asked all the others.

"I don't read Gaelic," he lied.

"I see." She turned, walked two steps away, and smiled. She lifted her chin. "When did I say it was Gaelic, Taegan?" She turned around as everyone backed up quickly with lifted brows. "I believe this is what we call a Freudian Slip." She began to walk toward him slowly, and he took a step back. "If you know it's Gaelic, then you must know what it means."

"What makes you so sure?" He began to feel desperate. He could feel Jiles' intense gaze on the back of his head.

"Well, you see . . ." She pulled out a slip of paper from her pocket. "This was left on my pillow a few days ago, wrapped around a rose." The rose was currently over her ear. "And it's the exact same phrase. And, gee, it's in *your* handwriting. What man would go to the effort of leaving his *lover* a note he didn't understand?"

The entire room started to buzz softly. Kalliope wasn't pulling her punches. Jiles cleared his throat distinctly, and Taegan felt panic bubble up. He turned away and looked at no one. "It's just a coincidence."

He only took two steps before Kalliope snapped, "Taegan Shaughnessy!" He slowly turned back, and she held up the Mask of Illusions. She walked over to him and held the mask up in front of his face. The glamour flickered, but could not hold when the truth was out. Everyone recognized him in that moment.

"There's no such thing as coincidence in 3rd District," Madelyne murmured loudly enough that most heard her in the silence.

Kalliope hurled the mask to the side. Her entire body trembled, her eyes dark with longing. "Tell us what the note means, Taegan."

Very slowly, his hand came up to frame her face. He was trembling just as hard. "'To the one I gave my heart, I give a vow of eternal love.'"

"And will you love me eternally?" She turned her face into his hand helplessly.

He closed his eyes and gave in to the inevitable. He loved her too much to pass up a single chance, no matter how risky. He didn't care about his career or his family. He didn't care about anything except having the woman he loved. "Yes." His eyes opened, fierce and intent. "I've loved you for years. I'll love you until the day I die."

"And I love you." Her lips trembled. "I fell in love with a geeky math teacher, but the bad boy seduced me. I won't have any man but you, Taegan. I love you with all my heart." She looked up at her father. "My contract holds, and you signed it yourself. You can't deny me the right to marry Taegan."

When Taegan looked up at him, Jiles began to smile. "Why would I want to? I think he'll make you a fine husband. Perhaps he can keep you out of trouble!" His eyes twinkled merrily, astonishing everyone except Sullivan and Mara. "Welcome to the family, son. And God help you."

The entire room burst into cheers and applause. Everyone surged forward to congratulate Kalliope and Taegan, but the lights suddenly went out and plunged the room into darkness. By the time someone found the switch, the couple in question had disappeared from the dance floor. All eyes went toward the garden, but with every last Shaughnessy standing in front of the doors, no one was really inclined to go looking. Instead, everyone began to chatter excitedly. It was just like that fascinating family to give everyone another romantic story to talk about!

Kalliope and Taegan ducked swiftly around foliage in the garden until they were away from the doors. "Who killed the lights?" he asked.

"I don't know, but they get a medal!" She let out a little breath and glared at the man she loved. "Damn it, you son-of-a-bitch, you lied!" She leapt at him and beat at his shoulder with her fist. "It almost killed me! If you hadn't slipped up, I don't know what I would have done! Don't ever do that again!"

He caught her close in his arms, a shudder going through his body as he realized she was really his to keep. "No, I won't. I swear." He kissed her hard, then looked at her in puzzlement. "What contract were you referring to anyway?"

"This." She pulled it out of her back pocket and handed it to him. Her stomach fluttered lightly as he put on his glasses, and she decided not to mention that the geek side was very hot, too. He was too arrogant already.

No stranger to contracts, he found what he was looking for quickly. He smiled. That little disclaimer was almost a failsafe since it

provided loopholes of all shapes and sizes to ensure the contract was completed correctly. "Of course." He tossed it onto the bench near them and looped his arms lightly around her waist. "You know, I don't exactly recall being asked to marry you," he remarked lightly.

She smiled and linked her hands behind his neck. "Am I supposed to do that?"

"You've been doing such a fine job at playing the prince's role, I figured you would take over that as well." He ran his hands slowly over her back and savored the feel of her under his hands. "You wanted to play this story out to the happily ever after part, didn't you?"

As her smile spread across her face, it could have illuminated the entire District. "Will you marry me, Taegan Shaughnessy, and help me run a business and raise children? I want it all. I want to be a businesswoman, I want to be a wife, and I want to be a mother. I want to be your wife and the mother of your children."

"Yes, Kalliope Tavoularis, I'll marry you." He glanced to the side and wasn't surprised to see a familiar small box sitting on the bench. His faerie godmother was quite good at that sort of thing. "I have something for you," he told her as he picked up the box. "It's been in the family for one hundred and fifty years. It has been passed from firstborn to firstborn."

Lips trembling, she opened the box to see a delicate silver ring with a pearl set in the center. "Oh my god," she managed to say. "It's beautiful."

He removed it from the box and slowly slid it over her finger. "You know what? This ring has never belonged to any couple that didn't love each other for as long a time as they were given together. My family has been blessed, you see."

"I think I'm the one who is blessed!" She threw her arms around him happily and laughed as he spun her in a wild circle.

The contract on the bench glowed softly as the word 'Complete' appeared. Stormy picked it up with another contract she was already carrying and ran gracefully across the garden to leap over the fence without effort.

Kalliope stared at the sight. "That wolf . . . I know that wolf."

"That," he said, his voice warm, "was my faerie godmother. She's been pretty busy lately." He snorted very softly. "God help you, Mel. You're the last one standing."

His lover grinned. "He won't be for long."

CHAPTER TWENTY-THREE

Rhianna studied both completed contracts and added her notes before sliding them into the folder in front of her. The Mask of Illusions sat beside her on a chair. As she closed the folder, she looked across the room. "I gave you a lot more leniency than I'm supposed to. You know that, don't you?"

Audra watched as she slid the folder into a drawer labeled with the Shaughnessy name. She could have described every folder in there by heart. They were all engraved in her memory. "I know," she whispered.

"I can't lend you anymore props," Rhianna warned quietly. "You're going to have to do this one on your own, and it will be the hardest one yet. It's the last one, time is running out, and he's the most stubborn and willful Shaughnessy yet." She reached into her desk and pulled out a fresh contract. "Let's get started, shall we? Oh," she added with a smile, "make a note to remind me to have a nice gift picked out for Taegan and Kalliope."

"I'll add it to my To-Do list," was the waspish response. It wasn't like she had anything else important to do.

Status: File In Progress
Analysis: Pumpkins become coaches and commoners become royalty when love is the magic involved.

Folder Four
MEL

CHAPTER TWENTY-FOUR

If the saying that what goes up must come down was true, then it was also true that something continually going down eventually had to hit rock bottom—especially grades.

Mel was brushing his hair the following Saturday morning when his future sister-in-law stepped into the doorway and struck a dramatic pose. He didn't bat a lash. "Now what do you want?" he asked warily.

Kalliope began a pointed examination of her nails. "You're being summoned, Gibson."

"Must you persist in calling me that?" he muttered.

"Tell me your full name and I'll stop associating you with Hollywood."

"You *wish*."

She just smirked a little. "Suit yourself. But the fact remains that you are indeed being summoned. I do believe that *someone* around here has been watching his grades steadily nosedive. I think you're digging to China in fact."

The hairbrush hit the dresser with a thump as he glared at her. "Must you be so damned smug about this?"

She didn't hesitate. "Yes. And I believe that Taegan sent me to fetch you for the very reason that he knew I wanted to rub this in."

"Oh, god." He covered his face with his hands and scrubbed hard. "Taegan's in there with Dad? Now I know I'm doomed. Kally, for the love of God, have mercy," he pleaded. "Find some graciousness. Tell them I ran away. Or that I'm enlisting in the Navy."

"As cute as you'd be in uniform," she grabbed his wrist and began to drag him down the hall to the stairs, "they ain't going to buy it. Let's go, Shaughnessy. Suck it up and quit whining."

Having heard the commotion, Kienan stuck his head out of his room. "'sup?" he asked with a lifted brow. "You running away with Mel this time? You're not trying to make your way through the Shaughnessys, are you? Not that I don't think you're cute, but Maddie would kill you."

"Maddie scares me," she assured him gravely. "You're safe from my wicked wiles. As it happens, I'm not taking Mel away. I'm taking him to the Office." The intonation of the word was more suited to dramatic music than the cheerful radio playing somewhere downstairs. "Papa's going to chew on Mel."

"Does he need dental floss?" He grinned. "And can I watch?"

Mel flipped his middle finger at his brother and gave a startled yelp as Kalliope continued dragging him down the stairs. His stomach was sinking into his feet and his heart was somewhere in his throat. He knew what he was going to hear and it was the stuff of nightmares. "Where's Stormy when I need her?" he muttered.

She had been hanging around him for the last couple days, keeping him company amid a family full of recently, and happily, engaged or married couples. Ever since Taegan and Kalliope had formally announced their engagement, Stormy had attached herself to Mel.

It was a suspicious pattern. Everyone in the household was *positive* she had been behind the events lately, even though they had no way of proving it. She did things that defied all laws of reality and nature. Taegan seemed to know something but he certainly wasn't telling. It left Mel feeling oddly out of sorts, especially because Stormy had disappeared on Friday, and no one had seen her since. Was he that hard to play matchmaker with?

His thoughts stumbled to a halt as he found himself in front of his father's office. Kalliope threw the door open and shoved him in firmly. Despite being nine inches shorter and considerably smaller, she was terrifyingly strong. He found himself in the office before he could blink. Cheerfully, she called, "One boy sacrifice as ordered! Have fun." She winked at Taegan around Mel's shoulder as she left the room and shut the door.

Sullivan had to smile as he looked at his oldest son. "Taegan, the best thing you've ever done was bring her home."

Taegan laughed. "Believe me, I know." He was well aware that only Kalliope with her fierce and wild spirit would suit him. All the Shaughnessys had wild spirits, and whoever they loved needed to be just as wild. It had been more than a bit of a challenge for their 'guardian angel,' of that he was sure.

She would find Mel the hardest of all. Of all the Shaughnessys, his spirit was the wildest. The veneer of civilization was simply that— a veneer. He walked the line between modern man and ancient man, the edge where modern mentality could not completely dominate a primitive instinct to conquer and defend. It was why he was so much more suited to be the heir to the family company. And it was why he would be immensely difficult to match to any woman. Her spirit would have to be just as wild and primitive.

Mel barely withheld a fidget as his brother studied him. He summoned his best 'devil-may-care' smile and walked over to sit down in the visitor's chair. The hair on the back of his neck lifted as he sensed peril of some kind imminent. "So what holiday are we celebrating with a sacrifice? And why do I feel like I've been called to the principal's office?"

"Mel." Sullivan leaned forward and pushed a stack of papers across the desk. As his son picked them up, he said, "I asked Taegan to pull your records at college. You're scheduled for graduation in May. You didn't tell me your grades were this bad."

A bit weakly, he said, "A 'C' is one hundred in Roman numerals, and a 'D' is fifty, right? Does that make it a little better?" He got a narrow eyed look from matching pairs of golden eyes and gulped slightly. "Sorry."

Taegan put his glasses on and picked up the top page of the transcript. "You're going to hate me," he said calmly, "but I'm acting as a teacher, not a brother. I've been discussing things with Father and we are thinking of holding up your graduation for a year."

Mel leapt out of his chair in shock. "What! You can't do that!"

"We can, and we will," Sullivan said firmly. "Mel, you're not an idiot. None of my children are. But you're not putting any effort into learning. If," he continued in a hard tone, "you want to inherit my company, you will have to prove you actually want it. Otherwise, I may just name Kalliope as my heir."

"Oh great. Pick her over me." It was a matter of principle only because he liked Kalliope and knew she was a hell of a businesswoman. She would be taking over her father's company within a few weeks of her own graduation and marriage. "Come on, how about some familial leniency?"

"You've had too much leniency!" Sullivan leaned back in his chair on a sigh. "Mel, I'm sorry. I've made my mind up."

Before Mel could speak, something distinctly scratched at the glass doors leading into the garden behind Sullivan. All three males turned to see Stormy patiently sitting outside with a sheaf of papers in her mouth. Her tail wagged more with pent up energy than with canine happiness for her owners. In fact, no one in the family believed they owned her. She owned *them*.

"Salvation," Mel muttered.

Sullivan opened the doors with a smile and ruffled Stormy's fur gently. "What did you bring me this time?" He took the document from her and wasn't surprised in the slightest to see that it was a contract. He also wasn't surprised to see where it had come from. "Let's see." He put the contract on the desk and put on his glasses to read better. Taegan leaned over his shoulder.

Stormy pointedly walked over to where Mel was and sat beside him. The message was clear: she was on his side. Taegan looked up from the contract and smiled to himself as he began to turn ideas over in his mind. He had a feeling she didn't know what she was getting herself into.

"Alright, Mel," Sullivan finally said as he sat back. "I have a deal to offer you. I will withhold my threat to prevent your graduation if you can show marked improvement within the next week and begin to bring your grades up. You're in Winter Intercession right now. The classes are very short to begin with. Midterms are Friday. If you can score at least a B in two of your five classes, I will not hold up graduation."

Mel carefully asked, "And where's the catch?"

His brother grinned quickly. "You will be assigned a tutor for your five classes. She normally handles General Education, but she's adept in all fields."

The color drained from his face. "No. Oh no. Please no. Why do you hate me?" he pleaded.

"I don't hate you. She's the best we have. Starting Monday morning you will be reporting to Audra Alexandrios and she will be tutoring you. Since you will need a distraction-free environment, she has agreed to allow you to live with her for the next week."

"Can she do that?"

"You think the council would tell her no?"

He winced. "Guess not. But why does she care?"

"That's for her to decide to tell if she's inclined." Taegan held up the contract where Audra's curiously wild signature was visible. "As you can see, she has already agreed and signed. She's even doing this for no extra pay, Mel."

That she would help out of pity, just made him feel worse. He was getting pity from the beast of the campus. Just *great*.

"It comes down to two choices," Sullivan noted as he signed the contract. "You can either accept a tutor and work to pull your grades up, or you can just let things stand and be held back a year from graduation."

He sighed and slumped over in the chair. He really had no choice. Stormy nudged his hand and he glowered at her. "Couldn't you have found a better solution?" She lifted one canine brow and he sighed as he reached for the contract. It was a blur and he squinted at the bottom.

"Glasses," Sullivan and Taegan both said.

With a mutter, he put them on and brought the page into focus. He hated wearing glasses despite the fact that all the males in the family wore them. They felt too much like a handicap. He picked up a pen and scrawled his name across the bottom of the page. Dropping the pen again, he glowered at his family. "If I get eaten, I'm haunting all of you. No one who lives in 3rd District is normal, not even Madelyne. But she's not a beast like I've heard about Professor Alexandrios!"

Taegan glanced at Stormy, saw her faint smirk, and had to cover a smile. His brother had no idea. So who would their dear tutor be pulling onto his brother's path? It would be interesting to say the least.

Before Mel had even walked into the grounds of the college Monday morning, word had already spread. Students were waiting for him when he locked his car, and they tagged onto his heels with nervous chatter. His head began to be filled with all of their legends and rumors. One thing stood out to all of them as it always had: Audra Alexandrios lived in 3rd District.

Of course he knew that Madelyne was from 3rd District, too, but she seemed normal enough. He knew she had some kind of special gift, though not what it was. He didn't mind; so far, she hadn't turned anyone into any frogs or anything, and if she did decide to do it, the person probably deserved it. And, anyway, all the Shaughnessys themselves had special gifts. His lay in physical abilities. The simple fact was that he was ten times faster, stronger, and more agile than normal humans.

It was harder to hide than his siblings' gifts. He had to keep himself under strict control and withhold himself to what the proper limits of his body should be. As he walked slowly down the hall toward the computer sciences wing where his tutor had her office, he had the sinking feeling that he might need all of his extra skills. The school thrived on outrageous rumors, and try as he might, he was listening.

Professor Alexandrios graded fairly, but was intolerant of stupid mistakes.

She always wore black like she was going to a funeral.

She was tall and towered over people, making them feel like she was going to attack.

She was big and brawny, like a female football player.

She blew ice with her every breath. She could freeze computers by glaring at them.

Her eyes were like a demon's eyes, yellow and predatory.

Her nails were sharp like claws and could likely etch steel.

She always sat in the dark, never in the light. When she was in the light, she was horribly disfigured by a terrifying scar across her face.

She was a vampire. She was a demon. The rumors went on and on until his knees were almost knocking together as he walked. His palms were slick with sweat and his mouth dry. His footsteps echoed loudly down the hall of the sciences wing as he slowly approached where the computer room was situated.

There was no light in the room from the overheads, just the odd blue colored light from the computer across the room. The room was silent and he took a hesitant step inside, his heart thudding in his chest so loudly that it seemed to echo in the room. "Hello?" he whispered. Clearing his throat again, he called, "Hello? Professor Alexandrios? Are you here?"

The overheads came on suddenly and flooded the room with light even as a finger touched his shoulder. Strangling a yelp of fright, he leapt forward and whirled around as a sardonic woman's voice said, "Turning on the light usually helps with locating people, kid."

His heart still beating in his throat, he stared in surprise at the woman standing behind him. If this was Audra Alexandrios, then the rumors were grossly exaggerated. She was definitely wearing black, but it was just a black buttoned shirt and slacks, no more or less than any other teacher. She *was* tall, though, maybe two inches shorter than him and he was six-foot even. She was not, however, big and brawny. She was sleek and well curved, her muscles as nicely defined as her hips and bust.

Her eyes were yellow with a ring of amber around the pupil.

They didn't make him think of demons. They made him think of hawks and eagles and wolves. Of predators who were most beautiful on the hunt. They also held a deep and seemingly bottomless intelligence as if she had seen and done it all. Her nails definitely looked sharp. They were unpainted but well kept. Her hands were strong and somehow very feminine anyway. Her age . . . he couldn't guess at. She looked to be in her twenties, but she had been teaching for at least ten years.

The only rumor that held absolutely true was that her face was indeed marked with a scar. It had healed, thankfully, though it was supposedly recent. It was a shade of color that wasn't quite purple but wasn't quite rose either. It started at the scalp on the right side of her face and then traveled down over her nose and to her chin on the left side. It was at least an inch wide where it crossed over her nose.

Though behind the scar there was a strong hint of immense beauty, the scar somehow marred it entirely. It was impossible to look around the scar to what it so effectively hid. It brought a strong sense of menace to her face that was matched by her icy eyes. She truly looked as if she deserved the nickname the students had given her.

They called her a beast.

She examined her nails while she waited for him to get a hold of himself. She hadn't been able to resist the urge to scare him. He had been so obviously believing every rumor he heard that he had been expecting a scare. She would hate to disappoint him. He had also jumped much higher than anyone else, so that added to her amusement.

She watched him from under her lashes. He was quite typical of his family in many ways. For one thing, he was outrageously beautiful. His hair was only a few shades darker than Kienan's golden brown hair, and they shared the same chocolate colored eyes, but Mel's face was softer around the edges like Aenya's. It gave him an almost sultry appeal.

He was two inches taller than Audra, broad in the shoulder, and lean all over. He only occasionally lifted weights, preferring to get his workouts from playing sports—especially basketball. He had been team captain until his grades nosedived. She had always loved to watch him play. There was something about the way he moved, a sense of wildness, that she had always admired and respected.

Matching him was going to be a *bitch*. She had even seen strong-willed women intimidated by his hidden spirit.

"Professor?"

His voice startled her and she lifted a brow. "Yes?"

"I was wondering where the scar came from. It looks like you barely survived."

At the note of empathy, she felt her back stiffen. She flicked her hair over her shoulder as she went past him. Unbound, her hair fell to her hips in a black curtain. "I'm just a hard tutor to work with," she informed him. She dropped into her chair at the computer. "I often pull grades to see who is failing miserably. Congrats. You're the worst I've seen yet."

His back stiffened. She had no warmth in her at all. He had no idea what Taegan seemed to see in her. He had called her a *friend*. Like she knew what a friend was. In a frigid tone, he said, "I don't need your charity or your sarcasm."

"As a matter of fact, you do. If I kowtowed to you like everyone else, you'd think you could run roughshod over me." She glanced at him over the monitor, the blue light giving a frightening cast to the scar. "You're going to have to learn to not be in charge any longer. You'll do what I say, when I say it."

"You're just a tutor," he sniped. "Why should I bow to you?"

"Because I'm your last hope." He hissed through his teeth, and she smirked. "Don't like the truth? Well, get used to it." She began to type on the keyboard. "Your bags are being delivered to my place as we speak. We'll start with your language skills tonight. What language are you studying?"

"Japanese." The word was nearly a snarl, a distinct brogue beginning to color his voice.

"Good. That's easier for you to pick up after the others you're fluent in. Welcome to the real world, handsome," she added, seeing the boiling temper in his eyes. "Sometimes there are people who really do know more than you."

He seethed and snapped his back teeth together to refrain from the retort bubbling inside him. There was nothing appealing about her. He had begun to wonder for a few moments if her appearance was only an aberration, that there was something underneath that was worth knowing, but now he knew the truth: she really was, without a doubt, an utter beast.

Taegan, leaning outside the door, covered his face with a hand. If they didn't find some sort of harmony, Audra would never be able to help Mel with what he *truly* needed help in. She was his only hope of a happy ending—and he might just be hers.

If they didn't kill each other first.

CHAPTER TWENTY-FIVE

The day went downhill from where it had started. Mel found himself dodging sly comments and rude insinuations the entire day. It was clear that the entire college was taking some rather gleeful delight in his fall from grace. Most had known his grades were bad, but they hadn't known *how* bad until now.

His only reprieve came in the form of his family. Kalliope shared a class with him, and no one was smart enough to cross her. She made a point of sitting next to him, too. She was not yet a Shaughnessy, but she was still family. Everyone knew that the Shaughnessys stuck together.

He only had two classes on Mondays, so he bided his time while he waited for Audra. He was going to follow her back to the 3rd District since he didn't know where she lived. She taught three classes on Mondays, and he found himself hanging out in the parking lot near his car.

The snow laid thinly on the ground. It had finally arrived in New York, and since it was the first fall, it was already melting off. More snow was expected for the next few days, potentially enough to allow the kids in the city to build the snowmen they had been waiting for all year.

He sighed and tilted his head back to look at the sky. Even though it was only just starting to turn into evening, he could see the moon. It was nearly full. As always, the sight of it made something stir inside. Sometimes he snuck out of the house when the moon was full and let himself run across the acreage he lived on. He had never told anyone, though he was fairly sure that Sullivan had seen him once or twice.

The sensation of trouble caused the hair on his neck to stir and warned him he was no longer alone long before he heard the sound of boots crunching ice. His eyes slanted to the side to see three other young men swaggering toward him. All wore the familiar jersey of the basketball team.

If the smirks were any indication, they had also heard about what was going on. The one walking in the front was the ringleader. He had become team captain after Mel dropped out, but it was known around campus that he simply wasn't as good. When Mel had dropped out, he had never lost a game. Ever since joining the team, Steve hadn't *won* a game.

Steve sauntered forward with a nasty smirk. "So I heard this interesting rumor." His friends snickered and he grinned at them. It felt good to finally have one up on Mel.

"I'm sure you did." Mel kept his voice even with effort. "Rumors fly around this school faster than they do around the White House. Which ones are you referring to?"

"Oh, just an interesting story about a guy whose grades are so bad that he not only got kicked off the team, but his daddy might hold back his graduation."

Anger began a slow boil inside. "Actually," he countered pleasantly, "I wasn't kicked off the team. I dropped willingly. The coach was willing to overlook my bad grades because he knew the guy who would take my place wasn't half as good as I am." He paused before adding smoothly, "And it looks like he was right. How many games you won, Rutabaga?"

"Rudaveg!" Steve's eyes narrowed. "None of your business, Shaughnessy. You think you're hot shit because your daddy runs a big corporation and you're the little prince set to inherit. I doubt you could survive in the *real* world."

"Which world is that?" He crossed his arms. "Is that the world where I bully and terrorize other people to make myself feel better? Or the world where the only reason I don't have five DUIs on my record is because my daddy is a policeman? Or is it the world where my casual disregard for women has left at least two girls wondering if they're pregnant . . . or worse?"

Steve grabbed him by the collar of his jacket and his face twisted with a snarl. "You don't know shit about shit!"

Mel grabbed his hand and jerked it off his jacket without effort. He gave him a shove that, while appearing casual, sent the other male stumbling back several steps. "It's only fair," he retorted, his body tensed slightly, "as your breath smells like shit."

Steve lunged forward, fist raised, and Mel braced to duck. To his surprise, Steve's arm was suddenly thrown to the side, and his forward momentum had him hurtling onto the ground where he rolled a few feet before stopping. As his friends knelt beside him, Steve sat up holding his hand. "What the hell! Something hit my hand and numbed it!" It was already swelling up. He looked around swiftly and saw an innocuous rock sitting nearby. It hadn't been there before. "That hit me!"

"Be glad it only hit a nerve and not a bone."

The voice was so frigid and cold that the snow seemed to solidify further, defying the sun itself. Mel's eyes widened slightly and he turned to see Audra standing nearby with one hand propped on her hip. The other hand held another rock and she was lightly tossing it up and down. Her eyes looked as cold as her voice sounded.

Steve went several different shades of white before settling on a sickly pallor. "P-professor Alexandrios!" He scrambled to his feet as quickly as he could. "W-we were just talking. Right, Mel?"

"I had no idea you did your talking with your fists," Mel retorted. He linked his hands behind his head. Oddly, against all reason, he felt safe with Audra there.

"You . . . !" He broke off as Audra moved a step closer. He was taller and larger but there was no one in the world who terrified him more. His eyes fixed onto the scar on her face and couldn't tear free. His throat worked, but he couldn't swallow past the sawdust in his mouth. His heart pounded so hard it should have burst.

"I believe team rules indicate that brawling is just as bad as low grades." Her hair fluttered into her face as a wind blew softly. "Consider it part of my generous soul that I don't report you to the coach." Her eyes hardened. "Get lost."

The three males ran off so fast that they slipped and tripped over the snow as they scrambled to get out of the parking lot and to safety.

"Wow." Mel blew out a hard breath. "Hey, professor . . ."

"Save it. I don't need thanks, and I don't care if you thought you had it handled. They're assholes and I have a personal dislike of assholes." She turned and began walking across the lot toward where she had parked her black motorcycle. "Follow me, and don't get lost. I won't go looking for you."

Seething and snapping internally, he got into his car. It wasn't hard to keep her in sight as she was careful not to navigate in a way he couldn't follow. He didn't know if she simply didn't have a preference for splitting lanes of traffic or if she was conscious of him following her. Knowing her, it was probably the former. She had made her contempt quite clear.

Still, he was trying to look on the bright side. He was going to be staying in the 3rd District. There was just something about the place for him. No matter how different he felt from the rest of the world, sometimes, when he was in the District, he felt like he was home. He felt comfortable, normal even. If that was part of the magic, then he was a believer. If a real faerie had come and knocked on his window, he wouldn't have batted a single lash.

They said that no one who was born in 3rd District was normal. Audra lived there, certainly, but that didn't mean she had been born there. He wouldn't have been too surprised though. Like she could be considered normal!

But he *was* surprised when he saw where he was following her. The one residential area of 3rd District was, by most other standards, little more than a slum. The streets looked as if they needed repair and so did the buildings. An odd gloom hovered over the area as if the very air felt the weight of sadness and grief.

Her home was no more than a small two-story building. The driveway was only just big enough for her bike and Mel's car. Long before he had parked and turned off the engine, she had parked her bike and gotten off. And, before his fascinated gaze, he watched as a swarm of elementary school-aged children rushed toward her happily. Slowly, he got out of his car, something moving deep inside his heart.

She was smiling. He couldn't catch her words, but her voice sounded warm and gentle. Her hands were gentle as she ruffled hair. The love she had for the children came across clearly, and the children loved her just as visibly. There was no fear on their faces. No revulsion. Just a strong hero worship and acceptance of her for what she was.

Guilt filled him. He had to have misjudged her. No one who was truly nasty and cold to their core could have ever been so truly kind with children. Hating himself for judging on appearances, he shut his car door. He instantly found himself the recipient of many fascinated stares. "Hi. I'm Mel."

Audra murmured something low, and the kids ran off giggling. When she straightened and looked at Mel, however, her gaze had chilled once more. She turned and went up to the front door without a word.

He followed her and looked around with intense curiosity. It wasn't really a house. It was something that had been turned into one. It didn't look as if it had been renovated in at least one hundred years. All of the structure retained its original construction. As he stepped inside and saw his suitcases, he felt his stomach clench with more guilt. "Professor . . . I want to apologize."

"Ah, the prince speaks." She kicked the door shut and took off her jacket. She tossed it over the edge of a rickety looking banister that led upstairs. "Don't bother apologizing to a peasant, your majesty. I choose to live here willingly. The kids are orphans. I protect them from predators and tutor them so that they do not have to go to school where no one will understand them." As she went into the kitchen, she added, "Call me Audra, will you? We're not at school, and I loathe formality."

Feeling a little like he had missed something, he followed her. "Where are you from anyway?"

Her lips quirked. "Let's call it another time and leave it there." She poured a cup of cold coffee and stuck it in the microwave. "Take your bags upstairs. There's a guest room at the end of the hall. Get yourself comfortable, and we'll get down to business. This isn't a vacation, kid."

He felt his back stiffen slightly. Her kindness was clearly only for children. "Yes'm." The word was as clipped as a cold wind. He turned sharply and grabbed his bags to haul them upstairs. He cursed softly under his breath the entire way. Either he was more spoiled than he thought, or she had a serious personality problem.

Saying the guest room was at the end of the hall upstairs was a bit misleading. There wasn't much of a hall and it only had three doors. One was shut tightly and he assumed it was Audra's room. The second door led into a decent sized bathroom. The third door opened into an unoccupied bedroom.

When he walked inside, he saw it was quite sparse in decor; there was only a queen-sized bed, a dresser, a lamp, and a chair near the window. There was an exceptionally tiny closet as well. It didn't even have a door.

He began the task of unpacking and putting things away and hanging up things that needed to be hung. It was a welcome diversion that helped get his mind off his current situation and the maddening female downstairs that seemed to have a talent for getting under his skin.

When he opened a small drawer, he unexpectedly discovered a small painting. It looked like an old-fashioned family portrait from the mid to late 1800s, but the people in it told him it was probably just a commission.

It was a family portrait of what looked like seven siblings. One of them was Audra and she was distinctly the oldest. He couldn't guess how old she was in the portrait, but she was laughing and smiling. Several kids were climbing over her. A slender boy with eyes that seemed to be the same striking color as hers was caught in the circle of her arms. Mel found himself grinning as he looked at the joy in everyone's faces. It reminded him of his family. This was a family that would yell at each other and then turn around and play cards to decide who was right.

His smile slowly faded as he put down the picture. A little chill touched his skin. Something must have happened. She had given no indication that she had a family, and she lived alone. What had happened to turn such a vibrant woman into such a cold and remote one? He knew he couldn't ask. She would never answer. Still, it shifted his mind, yet again, about her. It seemed to have been shifting all day.

He changed into jeans and a sweatshirt and headed down the stairs slowly, his Japanese language book under his arm. He felt as if nothing was real anymore. In fact, he had a feeling he had left reality behind when he had entered the District.

Audra was waiting in the living room in front of a coffee table. Books and papers spread in front of her. When she sensed his presence, she said fluently, "*Konban'wa.*"

He almost dropped his books. She had no accent. She spoke Japanese as if she had been speaking it from birth. Her English was also without accent, and it was impossible to determine which she had been born speaking. He couldn't even put his finger on her ethnicity to begin with. "You're bilingual?"

"Multi," she corrected. "Like your brother, I speak several languages. I picked up Japanese a few years ago." It had been, precisely, fifty years since she had met a Japanese exchange student after World War II and been fascinated enough to learn the language. That wasn't something she could drop in casual conversation, though. "Have a seat."

He walked over to sit down beside her. When he did, he felt something quiver inside his chest. She seemed . . . smaller when he was up close. Not small, exactly, but he definitely felt bigger. It was a curious feeling. "You surprised me," he admitted. "You're really good with kids. Do you have siblings?"

He watched her face intently and saw the flash of ripe pain that flickered through her eyes. It was like seeing a glimpse of hell before it disappeared. She gave him a cool and steady look. "No." She turned back to the book and flipped it open. "Let's start here. Let's see what you've got down."

He proceeded to show her. His basic grasp of the language was strong, and his accent was as good as it was going to get for the time being. His pronunciation was actually quite strong, and he didn't mangle the trickier aspects. His vocabulary was minimal, but that could only come with practice. His true hang up, as it was with most learning the language, was grammar.

As she began to write out the various tenses and the way verbs used them, she asked, "Out of curiosity, what brought on the urge to learn *Nihon'go*?"

He sighed as he rubbed the back of his neck. "Well, I already know Spanish and French. Kally is trying to teach me Greek. The Shaughnessy Corp. has some strong connections with a company in Japan, and I don't want to always rely on a translator. It's not fair to make them learn my language if I can't learn theirs."

"You really want to take over the kingdom, huh?"

"Yeah." He found a smile. "Growing up, I was a little resentful of Taegan that he was the heir apparent. I knew he didn't want it, but he went along with things. When he became a legal adult and suddenly switched to teaching, I was so happy. For him and for me. I walked right into Dad's office, sat down, and told him that I wanted to take his place."

"You were only seventeen," she noted. "And you were sure?" The question wasn't just for form, though she suspected the answer. She had never been able to read him the way she read the others. He was amazingly resistant to compulsion abilities as well.

"I was definitely sure."

"Hmm." She slid the paper in front of him. "Alright, let's start here. You change verb endings to denote tense . . ."

As she talked, she made notes. It wasn't until she realized that he was too quiet that she knew something was off. She tossed her pencil down in annoyance as she looked at him. He was dead asleep on top of his books, his head on his arms like a child.

"If you keep falling asleep in class, I can see why you're flunking!" More disgruntled than genuinely annoyed, she leaned closer to take his shoulder and give him a shake. He couldn't sleep his way to a good grade.

Her hand stopped in the air as she looked at him. The lamplight slanted through his brown hair and turned it to the color of dark honey. It was soft and vibrant, as wild as its owner. A few locks tumbled into his eyes and more fell over his cheek. His skin was still lightly tanned from summer and his lips were sculpted in a way designed to devastate the feminine pulse rate. He was, without question, the most beautiful male she had seen in her long life.

Without thinking about it, she tenderly brushed his hair back from his face and tucked it behind his ear. Her lips curved as she saw the small earring he wore. It was such a tiny symbol of rebellion, but it spoke volumes about his personality. Even in his sleep, perhaps especially then, there was a hint of danger in him that was deeply seductive. He was a predator, a hunter, and that quality was magnetic to her.

Shock froze her still. She was attracted to him. No, attraction was too mild a word. As she looked at him, she was consumed with a steadily growing hunger to taste his stubborn lips and get her hands in the pelt he called hair. She wanted his hands on her, to savor the little calluses that proved he worked hard and wasn't afraid to get dirty.

She had always cared for the Shaughnessy family, but he was different. Terrified of him and herself, she yanked her hand back and got to her feet quickly. This was *bad*. She couldn't get involved, not like this. It could destroy her. Distance. She needed distance. She scrawled a note on the paper and then rushed to the front door. She ran out into the moonlight . . . and seemed to disappear.

The only reason he woke was because the door slammed. He leapt to his feet with a curse. "I'm so sorry, Audra!" he blurted quickly. He looked around but she was nowhere in sight and the house felt empty. He looked down at the table and saw the note; it was in Japanese, unfortunately. He frowned and crouched to squint at it. It was gibberish at first but as he broke down the structure and words, he realized it said she would be back later. With a sigh, he began to wander slowly through the house. He hoped he hadn't insulted her too badly.

The first floor was no bigger than the second. It had a kitchen, a small dining room currently being used to hold storage, and the living room. Something tugged at him, and he found himself going upstairs. He hesitated outside her door before slowly opening it and walking inside.

Sensitivity to emotions was more Taegan's forte than his, but as soon as he walked into the room, he felt the sadness buried in the walls. He could hear a cry in the back of his mind, a sense of despair and terror that rose in the air like a wail or a scream. It made the hair on his arms stand up.

The room looked barely lived in as if she spent little time there. There was even a bit of dust sitting on the dresser undisturbed. The light from the moon was strong enough to illuminate several details such as the battered wood floors, but it was the walls that truly caught his attention.

He walked closer and ran his fingers lightly over the marks he could see. It felt like a claw had ripped through the wall and someone had tried to plaster and paint over it. As his eyes adjusted to the gloom, he saw marks all over the room. His throat closed with rising pain. It looked . . . it looked like a war had been fought.

Deeply disturbed, he backed out of the room and shut the door. How could she bear to sleep in there? He couldn't bear walking in there.

The house was still empty, and he could feel it. Needing fresh air, he headed back downstairs to pull on shoes and a jacket. He opened the front door and stepped outside, but came to a stop as he saw Stormy sitting on the sidewalk watching him. She had been running hard if the little leaves stuck to her fur were any clue.

He sat down on the front step and held out a hand. She immediately came over and licked his fingers gently. He began to run his hands gently over her fur and removed all the leaves and twigs. "Played hard, huh?" he asked her softly. "I know that feeling. I do that sometimes, too. Just go running wildly." He glanced up at the sky. "When the moon is full, we can go running together."

She rested her head on his lap and he gently stroked her fur. He

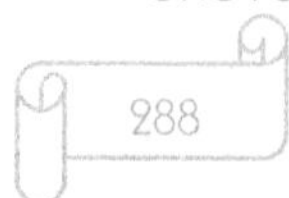

felt comforted by her presence. He always had been. In some ways he had been jealous of her attention to his siblings. He had always wished she belonged to him alone.

Sighing, he looked at the clouds drifting across the sky. "I royally screwed that one up." His smile filled with self-disrespect. "I let myself believe rumor and then let my first impressions cloud me. I know she was deliberately feeding them, but I really should have known better. Now she's pissed at me." He laughed softly. "She spends a lot of time pissed at people, I think."

He leaned his head back against the door, oddly comfortable to be sitting outside in the night with a wolf at his side. "She's not really all that bad." When Stormy lifted her head in surprise, he rubbed her ears soothingly. "Really, she's not. Oh she's prickly as hell, rude, and pretty darn mean when inclined, but she's *brilliant*. The kids love her, and she loves them so much. I think she's just been alone for too long. When I saw the pain in her eyes when I asked about her family . . . I think that's what clued me in. Maybe she just needs a friend."

He straightened with a wry laugh. "As if she'd let me try! I think I gave her just as bad an impression as she gave me. She thinks I'm a spoiled brat, just like everyone else does. And maybe I am a little spoiled. I grew up without a need for anything, and I've always had servants."

He fell quiet for a moment. "I don't take it for granted. I know how to cook and clean. We all do. If something ever happened and we found ourselves without means, we'd know how to survive. Hell, I could repair cars for a living. I'm good at it. Hiro swears that his bike has never run better." There was pride in his voice for a moment. "I guess it was the one class I really paid attention to."

Stormy cocked her head and there seemed to be a question in her eyes. He tilted his head slightly in response. "I don't hate school. Not really. I just have trouble learning from lecture. I listen and I listen but it never seems to stay in place. If I take notes, it helps a little, but if I lose my notes, I'm screwed. I need hands-on experiences. I kicked ass in Science because it was all about lab work.

"It's like . . . everything gets all crammed in my head and

dissolves. It's like because I have so many physical gifts, I didn't get any mental ones. Well, I guess." He frowned. "There are times when I've concentrated hard and made people believe me, but I don't think it's the same thing. I just wish there was someone I could explain this stuff to." She woofed softly and he smiled as he ruffled her fur. "Well, other than you. You're the best listener around, but you can't fix these problems. Maybe you can set me up with a nice bookworm," his voice warmed, "and she can teach me how to study better."

He got to his feet and glanced around, missing the brief flash of jealousy that flickered across her eyes. She was beginning to have deep suspicions about Mel Shaughnessy. All the little quirks that made him difficult to match were beginning to paint a familiar picture. Time would tell if she was right. If she was, it would to be harder than she thought to match him . . . especially when the thought of handing him over to another female seemed distasteful suddenly.

He sighed and drew her attention again. "I guess Audra isn't going to be back for a while. I *really* pissed her off. I hope she lets me apologize. Oh well, since she's not here, she can't argue if I have company over." He opened the door and gave a courtly bow. "After you, my lady."

Agreeably, she walked into the house and followed him as he headed into the living room. She watched as he put away the books and stacked the papers neatly. She wasn't surprised; he and his brothers were terribly meticulous about being organized. Aenya was the messy one in the household.

There was no predicting his actions ahead of time. He changed direction too easily. She followed him curiously as he headed upstairs. She had no idea what bedtime habits he had. She had never followed him into his room before. At first she had been focused on his siblings, and lately she had been trying to get the contract started. And, too, maybe she had been subconsciously wary of the intimacy of sleeping on his bed—in any form.

It was, therefore, with fascinated delight that she sat in the doorway and watched as he stripped down to his shorts. She wasn't going to argue with her current form when it gave her such a delightful free admission to view a body like his. He was strong and muscular from head to heels, sleek and so masculine that he would trip the signals of anyone with compatible hormones. Even in her current body, she felt her mouth go slightly dry, her heart beginning to skip a beat. He reminded her of a male wolf. She hadn't seen a body like that in a long time, but she had never forgotten.

He pulled on pajamas, blissfully unaware of her thoughts, then climbed into bed. He spotted her hesitating in the doorway and smiled suddenly. It was a slow and devastating curve of his lips, self-assured, and confident. It was a smile well designed by nature to serve as a lure to a mate, and he used it without compunction or knowledge of what it truly was meant to do.

She had always called it the Shaughnessy smile because it had been wielded by all men of the bloodline for as far back as she remembered. She just hadn't realized how lethal it could be when it got turned on a woman directly. She was not immune to it herself, not when it came from Mel. She padded across the room and jumped up to lay beside him.

He was holding a book, and she nudged at the glasses laying on the covers. He put them on with a wry smile for his own vanity. She genuinely had no idea why he was vain about them. They did many amazing things to an already stunning appearance.

She remained by his side until he finally fell asleep. He did so sitting up, his glasses sliding down his nose, and the book on his chest. She didn't want to wake him, so she softly slipped from the bed and left the room.

When Audra opened the door an hour later, he hadn't moved. She sighed wryly and walked soundlessly across the room to remove the book from his hands. She carefully removed his glasses as well and placed both items on the dresser. Then, gently, she eased him down so he was sleeping properly. She sat beside him for a moment and studied his face.

A friend. She lifted a hand and ran a finger softly down his cheek. She was afraid to let him try. Afraid to let him even closer. Already she could feel the haunting lure that was his eerie wolf-like persona and traits.

She was afraid she was falling in love with him herself, and that would only lead to tragedy for both of them.

CHAPTER TWENTY-SIX

Mel stumbled downstairs the next morning to the smell of bacon and pancakes. When he peered into the kitchen, it was to find Audra competently assembling two plates of breakfast. He sat down at the counter warily, not sure what to say or think. He had woken up lying down and distinctly remembered falling asleep while reading.

She put a plate in front of him and slid him a cup of coffee. "It's edible," she assured him. "The coffee might be strong, though. I prefer it that way."

He took a cautious sip but found nothing wrong with the taste. "Actually, this is the way I prefer my coffee." He picked up the syrup and poured lavishly over the fluffy cakes. "And this smells incredible."

She sat down at the counter across from him with her own breakfast and was just as generous with the syrup. "I figured that if I had to eat my own cooking, it might as well taste good." She bit into the bacon happily. She ate plenty of vegetables and grains, but she preferred meat to anything else. "Sleep well?"

"Yeah." He didn't bother to ask. She would never answer. Instead, he said carefully, "If I wanted to apologize, would you be willing to listen? I was an idiot. I've seen how stupid rumors get, but I still believed."

She said nothing for many moments. He wanted to be her friend. It couldn't hurt to try. Just as carefully, she said, "Mel, I'm a loner. I have been a long time. I'm not always good with people. Any blame also lies with me. I deliberately let you believe everything you heard. It seemed . . . safer."

"So, then." He offered a hand. "Let's start again. I won't act quite so spoiled, and you won't treat me like I'm a viral disease of some kind." Very slowly, as if it was foreign to her, she put her hand in his. He closed his fingers around hers and smiled. "There. Fresh start. Okay?"

"Okay." She slipped her hand free and picked up her fork. "Eat your breakfast," she ordered.

"Yes'm." Oddly, this time he didn't feel at all offended by her manner. He was starting to look under the surface, and what he was beginning to see slowly grew more and more intriguing.

His upbeat mood lasted until he got to school and parked on campus. From the minute he left his car, he found himself inundated with catcalls and whistles. Leering comments and sly looks were thrown at him the entire way to class. Some were subtle. Others were downright rude.

It didn't help any that when he walked away from his backpack for a second, he came back to a note pinned to it. The note read clearly *Beauty and the Beast* and there was a very disgusting, very lewd picture accompanying it. He threw it away instantly. Pride made his back straight as he walked, but embarrassment made his stomach churn.

Class wasn't even a reprieve. Students took turns kicking his chair or accidentally dropping more notes on his desk. He didn't bother to open any of them. He considered reporting the events, but he wasn't entirely sure the school could or would do anything. And, if he told, then Taegan would find out and he would probably get himself in trouble again.

It was one of the most confusing mornings he had ever experienced. By the time lunch came, he was left at a loss. The culmination of the day occurred when he sat down at a table and everyone else stood up and walked away. What the *hell* was going on this time? Was this just because he needed a tutor?

Kalliope suddenly sat down beside him with her lunch tray. "Assholes," she announced. She took a big bite of her pizza. "I'll explain after I eat. I'm starving."

"Me too." Madelyne sat down across from her with her own lunch, her violet eyes sparkling. "I usually am about this time of day."

"Well, you're eating for two." Kienan sat down beside her and dug into the paper sack he carried. "What'd you make anyway?" His voice was muffled as he stuck his head in the bag. "Smells like pasta."

"Get out of there," Kalliope scolded.

"You're not my mother," he muttered.

"No, I'm your new big sister. It's far worse and scarier." She grinned evilly. "You've never had one of those before. Maddie, better protect him or I'll run him ragged."

Mel felt the tension in his shoulders ease and he smiled as he listened to their bickering. He knew what they were doing. They were firmly aligning themselves on his side and showing the entire school that they would back him without hesitation. If you messed with one, you messed with all of them.

And because it was obvious they knew what was in the air, he leaned on the table and asked quietly, "Would someone tell me what's going on? Is this just because of my grades?"

His siblings exchanged a quick look. Kalliope, being the bluntest, finally cleared her throat delicately. "Well, as we all know, rumors fly around this school at light speed in a way NASA really should harness. And the newest rumor, currently ignored by teachers, FYI, is that you and Professor Alexandrios are lovers."

He choked on the water he had just taken a sip of. "What!" He stared at his sister-in-law as if she had grown another head. "Where did *that* come from?! She's just my tutor! We only met yesterday!"

"I did a little digging," Kienan admitted. "And I think the rumors originated with Steve Rudaveg. He's made no secret of the fact that he's pissed at Professor Alexandrios. Word is spreading that she stopped him from attacking you, and she never once laid a hand on him."

"It's like a puppy barking at a wolf," Madelyne muttered under her breath. "She'll eat him for lunch!"

"No kidding!" Anger filled Mel's eyes. "Guess that explains the comments all morning. I wouldn't repeat them to my brothers, let alone my sisters." He blew out a long breath. "Crap. Well, let him blow hot air. It'll all go away. No one would dare mess with Audra. She'd scare them silly."

Kalliope laughed. "Yes, she would!" She smiled and rested her chin on her hands. "So is Stormy still hanging around you? We haven't seen her lately."

"Actually," he frowned slightly, "I haven't seen her that often lately, either. But she did show up last night and hung around outside with me."

As casually as he could, Kienan asked, "Just you two? No one else showed up?"

"No one." Mel smiled wryly. "I know what you're implying, but she doesn't seem to be doing anything to try and introduce me to someone special. She's just there, keeping me company." His smile turned a little sheepish. "Funny as it is . . . I don't feel neglected. Her company is enough for me, I guess."

Something stirred inside Madelyne's eyes. Something that looked suspiciously like fear. Kienan, sharply attuned to his family let alone to his wife, turned toward her and his eyes darkened. "Maddie?" He put one hand on the back of her neck. His other hand rested protectively over her lower belly where their child slept. "What's wrong?"

"Nothing." She brushed a kiss over his lips and shrugged off his hands as she got to her feet. "I have someone I need to go talk to." She scooped up her backpack and hurried out of the cafeteria, her long hair fluttering behind her. She was terrified, her heart freezing inside her chest as she ran across to the computer sciences area.

"Audra!" She didn't wait for acknowledgement before opening the door to her friend's office and walking in. "What are you waiting for?" she demanded.

Audra looked up from her computer and scowled fiercely. "Do you think I'm enjoying this?" she snapped back. "This is harder than it ever was before?"

"Why?" Madelyne challenged. "Because it's the last? You should be scared! *I'm* scared! I don't want to lose someone else I love!" She took a quick breath and then threw out a hand as the room whirled on its axis. Audra promptly appeared at her side and gently eased her into a chair. "Damn it," she muttered. "Don't tell the family!"

A smile softened Audra's face as she gently touched Madelyne's stomach. "The stronger the will of the child, the more it affects the mother," she offered softly. "That's what we always said in my clan." Her nose flared slightly as she analyzed Madelyne's scent. "And I think you should be on your guard. It's a boy."

"I can't keep up with one of Kienan, let alone two!" The words were more exasperated than despairing. She sobered and covered Audra's hands with hers. "Why, Audra? Why is this one so much harder? You've always been so quick and sure, arranging scenarios so your chosen couple meets." She searched her friend's eyes intently, looking for a sign her suspicions were right.

"Mel is different." Audra got to her feet and walked over to the window. "Normally it's easy. I memorize the scent of my Shaughnessy. I search the city for his or her perfect match. When I find it, I either take advantage of current situations or arrange them to suit my needs." Her eyes closed. "I've been over this city thousands of times. I can't match Mel. He's so unique, so powerful. If his mate existed, then she should be here. It's simply how it is. If his scent is producing the call to a mate—and it is—then his mate is here."

Madelyne watched her for long moments. Then, softly, "And what about you? What about your scent?"

She laughed sadly. "Don't pin hopes on me for cubs to spoil, Maddie." She closed her eyes and pressed her forehead against the cold window glass. "As long as you are alive, I don't mind. When I'm gone, you'll be here with Kienan. To me that is everything. I'd give my life for any of you in an instant. It's the least of what I owe."

"You saved my life!" Madelyne shouted as she leapt to her feet. "You saved Kienan's life! And though we didn't know it then, you saved our unborn child! You almost *died* for us, Audra! I don't want you to die! The answer is there in front of you but you're too stubborn to see it!"

As she whirled and fled from the office, the door shutting wildly behind her, Audra slowly sat down once more. She tried to bring the monitor into focus but she was already thinking of her next course of action. She was well aware of the rumors around campus and she was equally aware of the source. She would be handling the problem without any effort; she had dealt with far more complex and powerful minds than Steve Rudaveg.

Mel had been hurt over the rumors. She had been unobtrusively watching him all day. He had lifted his chin and straightened his back with a warrior's pride, but she knew him well enough to see the pain underneath. It made fury boil in her heart. *No one* EVER hurt her family, especially not Mel.

She scowled at herself at the direction of her thoughts. She was there to take care of the Shaughnessys. She had loved all of them the same. Her feelings for Mel were no different than her feelings for Aenya or Sullivan.

Yet, as she lifted her hand, she was haunted by the memory of his skin and hair and how he had looked in the lamplight. She remembered his wild spirit and nearly wolf-like abilities. And she remembered a body that had stirred her own, raising desires stronger than she had ever before felt in her life. "Damn it," she whispered.

Classes were done. She turned off her computer and got to her feet. She had time before the end of the day. An elementary school sat around the corner, and the kids often came from it to play on the college campus where the snow always took longer to melt off. Even as other parts of the city looked clean, the college was still a winter wonderland.

What she needed was some time with some people who looked at her and saw inside. Both before and after the scar, children had always seen her as she was. They had never been afraid, never hesitated to show her they loved her. It was as if they knew she loved children more than she loved anything else.

As she walked toward the area where she could hear the kids playing, she let herself remember a time when she had always had children around. She had been young and whole, her existence bright. She had been looking at a future where she could hold a child of her own, to hear laughter around every corner.

The laughter had turned to screams. Blood had stained the snow. And her future had changed for all time. There would be no children of her own. No one to stand by her side. No one left to run across the land at midnight under a full moon. She was alone. She closed her eyes and pushed it aside as she went around a corner. It wasn't worth thinking about.

She got an unexpected reprieve from her thoughts in the shape of an immense snowball smacking her directly in the face. It sent her back a step with a curse and she swiped at her eyes, well aware of the giggling of kids. When she could see again, it was to immediately spot Mel standing with a bunch of kids, a look of mingled shock and horror in his eyes. "Mel . . ." she said warningly.

He coughed. "I was . . . well. The kids. Wanted to see if I could shoot a snowball like a basketball. I wasn't expecting you." He coughed again and this time it was clear that he was struggling against laughter. "Sorry."

She shook her hair vigorously to remove the remaining snow. It didn't help. A soccer ball struck the side of the building and sent more snow tumbling off the roof and onto her head. With a resigned sigh, she watched the kids and Mel laugh until they were holding their stomachs.

Her heart clenched as she listened to Mel. His laughter was . . . beautiful. Like his temper, his laughter carried the flavor of his Irish heritage, the brogue velvety on her sensitive ears. Striving for neutral territory, she bent and scooped up a snowball. He wanted friendship. It was worth trying.

He straightened with the intent of trying to apologize again, but a snowball smacked directly into his nose. The kids cheered. Pointedly, he wiped the snow from his face. His smile was as challenging as Audra's. "This means war, you know."

The kids were more than happy to split up between the two adults. Forts were built and lines were drawn. The kids could wildly chuck snowballs with more enthusiasm than aim. Audra and Mel had specialties. Mel could send a snowball airborne and bomb someone. Audra was a big league pitcher, sneaking out shots so fast that no one saw them coming. It wasn't long before they were the only two left standing.

Relying on her natural speed, she began to pummel him mercilessly until he lost his balance and fell into a snow bank. While the children cheered loudly, she gave a quick nod of satisfaction. "You're no angel, but you make a decent impression of one." She winked at the kids and sent them off into fits of the giggles.

A teacher began to wave for attention and the kids ran off happily. Mel managed to get to his feet and shot Audra a wicked grin. "You'd better run, teach, or I'll get you back so fast."

She knew she could outrun him, but the idea of a chase warmed her blood and stirred deep-seated instincts. "Try it," she challenged. She turned and took off running into the trees nearby, so fast and agile that her feet barely touched the snow.

Something also stirred inside him. In a blink he was chasing after her, without hesitation unleashing his natural speed and agility. A snowball was in his hand. He got a glimpse of her as she ducked around a large pine, and he hurled the snowball. She dodged gracefully, her yellow eyes alight. "Too slow," she taunted. As she ducked into the trees again, her laughter rose up and broke free.

The sound curled around him and raked at him with velvet claws. It lured and beckoned, an ancient call that he couldn't recognize consciously, but he felt it vibrate through his subconscious. The snowball fight was forgotten as he went after her again. This time it was something more. The change from playful to predator was instantaneous.

She didn't realize what had happened until she found herself pausing by a tree to determine his location. Quite suddenly, she realized he was behind her. His body barely brushed against hers, and his heat and scent seemed to sear into her nerves. His fingers brushed the nape of her neck so softly she almost didn't feel it. The velvety threat only belatedly registered. She immediately forgot the innocent game. She darted away from him agilely and threw a taunting look over her shoulder. Her body was heating, her heart pounding.

The game continued. She would hide, and he would find her.

Their bodies would brush. His fingers might skim her nape, the touch as sensual as it was threatening. She would deliberately leave herself open just long enough for him to get close, and then she would dance out of reach with a ripple of laughter.

It wasn't until she heard a soft rumble from his chest one of the times she got away that she finally realized what had happened. Without thinking about it, they had fallen into the mating hunt of a werewolf. She stopped in shock, her eyes widening as she felt the wild beat of hunger in her blood. Not only had he responded *instantly* to the chase, he was more than keeping up. With all the primitive dominance of an alpha male, he was *letting* her escape his grip just to prolong the chase.

He pounced on her from the shadows almost before she realized he was there. He caught her around the waist and tumbled her down onto the snow. She immediately tried to throw him off, but he flipped her over again and pinned her under his heavier weight. His hands caught her wrists and kept her held submissively beneath him. "Gotcha!" The word was almost a breathless growl.

Their eyes met and locked. She tested his grip and found it unbreakable. Despite the vulnerable position, she felt safer than she ever had in her life. Her heart beat hard, and her pulse throbbed in her neck visibly. The desire in his eyes as he gazed at her had hot fists of lust curling inside her body. She could feel the heated urgency of his arousal pressed against her. For wolves, the chase itself was an act of desire. Both had responded with all the savagery of those with wolf spirits.

But was it *her* that he wanted? She couldn't tell. She searched his eyes for any sign that he knew who it was he held. Would any woman have triggered his deeper instincts? She was torn between hunger for him to want her and for him to let her go. Alpha to alpha, he called to her in every way.

He stared down at her, his eyes raking hotly over her face. Halfway through the chase he had become conscious of what was happening, and he had let it go on. When she had danced away from him one of those times, he had looked into her and seen something he wanted. He still saw it. The scar seemed invisible to his eyes now. He wanted her more than he had ever wanted any woman in his life. His wildness commanded him, and she was just as wild.

As his lips lowered and the tip of his tongue traced the scar, her entire body shuddered with raw pleasure. To lick a wound was the act of a mated wolf. *He wasn't her mate*! Her mind insisted it even as her body and soul responded with eagerness to the tiny touches of his tongue. His mouth came to settle over hers and her mind went away entirely.

She arched her body to press further against his. Her mouth opened under his demandingly to accept the aggressive thrust of his tongue. His powerful shoulders trembled even as her body did, sparks leaping between them with such fury that their hair crackled in the static.

Hotter, harder, wilder. It wasn't enough. It went on and on until a low moan vibrated in her throat. She couldn't get enough of his taste or scent, that wonderfully unique flavor that was his alone and made it impossible to find his mate.

The thought made her stiffen as she realized what was happening. She tore her mouth free and gulped in the cold air. "Mel. Stop. Bad idea." A gasp caught in her throat as he buried his mouth against her shoulder and bit sharply in a warning little nip of possession. "Mel." She put as much command into her voice as she could. "Stop."

His head lifted, and shock exploded inside her soul. His eyes. His eyes carried the wild and feral soul of an alpha male wolf. A thin ring of amber had appeared around the rim of his pupil as a visible manifestation of the physical powers he possessed. If he didn't want to let her go, then she wouldn't get free. The worst part, the very worst part, was that she did not want to get free. Alpha to alpha. Male to female. He called to everything that she had ever been and might ever be.

"Mel." She said it again and exerted her will against his. Her only hope to stop the insanity was that he did not yet know the power of his mind.

He blew out a breath and looked away for long moments. It was a struggle to regain control of himself. He hadn't scared her away with what was inside him. If anything, she had responded back. He could feel the heat of her body and hear the thudding of her pulse matching his. Her scent was sharp and lush, a beckoning temptation. "Hang on," he managed to say roughly.

"Since I would appear to be pinned down," there was a touch of dryness in her voice, "I can't hold on to anything."

He released her quickly and moved away. As she sat up, he looked away in shame. "I'm sorry. I'm not sure what happened."

"Humans are animals, too. Chases spark primitive instincts, and you're a fairly primitive guy, I think." She kept her voice deliberately light. They were walking a thin tightrope. She would never have gotten free if he had been fully aware and cognizant of his own nature. To be honest, she probably wouldn't have tried.

"You may be right." He glanced at her. "But I have to admit that the more I'm around you, the more I want to know." He searched her eyes for any sign that she was still as shaken as he was. He saw nothing. Because he had never before felt anything like what had just happened, he let it lie. Maybe she was right. Maybe she was wrong. It wasn't the time to examine it, not when his body was aching so badly that even the cold snow was no help. "Well, let's pretend that didn't just happen, okay?" His lips curved. "But you're one hell of a kisser, Audra."

Her lips curved to match his. "Back at you, kid." She let him pull her to her feet and fell into step beside him as they began to head back toward the campus parking lot. He exerted a visible effort over himself and kept a foot of distance between them. She was grateful for it. He still smelled too damn tempting.

Deciding to put things back to normal, she said, "You fell asleep in the middle of lessons last night." From the corner of her eye, she saw his cheeks heat. Casually she continued, "I thought we'd try something a little different. Did you know there's a Japanese museum near here?"

Startled, he looked at her. "No."

"It's a very cool place. The entire tour is given in Japanese with a translator for those who speak English. All tourists go there, so you'd probably find yourself plopped down in a roomful of people speaking Japanese. Languages need to be learned by immersion so you'll do better there than my cramming verbs and tenses down your throat."

"I . . . hmm."

"Let's go by the house to drop off the bike, then take your car, okay?"

"Yeah. Sure." He rubbed the back of his neck, wondering at the timing of her decision and his conversation with Stormy the night before. Something tried to prod at his mind but he instinctively shied away. He wasn't ready to understand. "I guess it can't hurt to try." He searched his jacket and came up with his keys. The way they had tumbled over the snow, he had been worried he had lost them.

They parted at the parking lot so Audra could head for her bike. And though she was halfway across the lot and he made no sound, she knew instantly that there was something wrong. It came as a sharp slicing sensation through her heart. She was rushing back to his side before she was even aware of it. As she stopped beside him, she saw why.

Mel's beloved 1970 Mustang, carefully restored by his own hands, had been destroyed. The windows were smashed apart. The tires had been slashed. Gouges from some sort of sharp object had torn apart the paint on every surface. The hood wasn't resting properly, and when she lifted it, she saw that the engine had been covered in something dark and sticky. It smelled like tar.

It wasn't even dark yet; it was only evening. Nearly all the cars were gone except for the ones belonging to faculty. Her sharp eyes spotted Kalliope's car some distance away. She wasn't surprised; the young heiress had evening classes. Where she and Mel stood was isolated a little from any place that the crime could have been witnessed from.

She stepped closer to Mel. He hadn't moved an inch. "Well," she said. "Interesting." She looked at his face and the agony in his eyes made fury swell inside her heart. "You loved your car."

"I worked so hard. Months on end in every spare minute." He touched a cracked side window with trembling fingers. The side mirrors hung from their wires like broken arms. "I saved my allowances from the time I was ten to the time I was twenty. For my twentieth birthday, Dad gave me the last thousand I needed to have enough to buy and fix the car. I know it's old, but . . . I wanted this car."

"Can you afford to have it repaired?"

"If it can be repaired, yeah. I draw a paycheck from the company now since I'm already serving several roles. It's just . . . it's like . . ." He couldn't find the words, hurt and frustration welling inside him.

"It's like you were violated. I know." She would make sure the culprit was taken care of for him. Mel was *hers* regardless of whether or not her heart was involved. No one ever hurt her family. "Call a tow," she told him. "I'll go borrow Taegan's extra helmet." She took two steps away then stopped. She looked back over her shoulder. "I won't let anyone hurt you again, Mel."

He looked up in surprise and watched her as she walked toward the campus. His hurt blessedly diverted into admiration. She had, he decided, an incredibly sexy walk. Probably the sexiest walk he had ever seen on a female. It was like watching a predator or a hunter move, sleek and dangerous in a way that raised his pulse and reminded him just how she had felt under him. Her hips were definitely curved just right.

By the time she returned, a helmet under her arm and a very furious Taegan following her, the tow truck was just arriving to take the car away. Fury flashed in Taegan's gaze when he saw the sadness in his brother's eyes as he sat on a bench to watch. "If you don't handle things," he warned quietly, "I will. And I'm likely to get fired if

I do."

"It's handled." She flashed him a smile that showed her teeth. "They can't catch me." She walked over to Mel and knelt to hold the helmet out to him. "There's nothing we can do right now," she told him quietly. "So don't give them the satisfaction of showing how much this hurts."

He nodded and got to his feet as she stood. He pulled the helmet on and looked at his brother. "I'll figure out what to do later. Right now we're going to a Japanese museum." Taegan lifted a brow, and he smiled. "Hands-on learning for language. Maybe I'll do better if it's all I'm hearing."

"Good luck." Taegan's eyes missed nothing as Mel got on the back of Audra's bike. There was something in the way their bodies touched, in the way his arms went around her waist that spoke more than words. A smile curved his lips as the bike sped away. When he felt Kalliope slipping her hand into his, he glanced down at her. "Hands-on lessons indeed."

"Mmm. He definitely had that look." She leaned her head on his shoulder and smiled up at him. "When did you first expect this outcome? I admit I began to wonder when he said he hadn't met anyone else."

"From the beginning," he admitted. He drew her closer and swung her hand up to his lips as they walked back onto campus. "No meddling," he scolded lightly. "They can handle things fine, and," he added when she smiled innocently, "leave Steve Rudaveg to Audra. Trust me, she can handle him."

"Oh, come on. Just a little threat?"

"No."

She huffed. "Ever since we got engaged, you've been so bossy."

He swung her up into his arms. "That's because you get into trouble easily. In fact, you're getting into trouble right now."

She grinned. "I still think you need a couch in your office. That desk just isn't comfy."

At the museum, Mel found himself plunged into another world. As he and Audra walked along with the tour, he was inundated from all sides with the language. There were two tour guides, one for each language, and nearly everyone around them was speaking Japanese. It sounded like gobblygook at first, with only the words making sense and not the meaning.

But, slowly, he began to pick out the different verbs and tenses, using the English translator talking at the same time to get a better idea of the meaning. -Masu meaning present. -Masen meaning negative. -Mashita meaning past.

Audra watched him intently and could almost see the moment it clicked in his brain. She had wanted to see if he was right about his learning ability, and she knew now that he was. He really did learn better with a demonstration.

Tuning out the tour guides, she watched him instead, fascinated with the way he began to immediately speak in Japanese. Once it had unraveled, the syntaxes had connected and he was able to form proper sentences. He spoke almost as good as the natives, a feat that impressed more than one visitor. Several smiling looks were directed at him as he talked to the visitors in their own language.

He was also on a slightly euphoric high. They got outside the building and he caught her in his arms to spontaneously swing her in a quick circle. "You're the best tutor ever!" he announced with a grin.

For the second time that day, she felt extremely outmatched physically. She cleared her throat. "Mel. Put me down."

"Oh, sorry." He put her on her feet with a care that made her heart flutter. Unaware of it, he stretched his hands over his head. "It finally makes sense, you know? I can't wait to get to class. The dragon won't know what hit her!"

She coughed lightly. She really should tell him not to call

Professor Nobunaga bad names, but she really couldn't argue with the assessment. Even Audra was preferred as a teacher over Nobunaga, and that said something. "Since Japanese is fine, we can work on your history next."

He grimaced. "How do you have a hands-on lesson about history? A time machine?"

"Hardly. You just need someone who knows the subject well and doesn't mind talking about it." She pulled on her helmet, a slight smirk curving her lips. "Like me. I give a hell of a lecture, and I promise to draw you plenty of pictures and diagrams. I'll also," she added as he got on the bike behind her, "pour tea down your throat to keep you awake."

He felt a dull flush warm his cheeks. "Yes'm," he mumbled. As he slid his arms around her waist more firmly to hold on, he wondered to himself if he would ever fall asleep on her again. There was something about her now that he couldn't get out of his mind. It would fade if it was just the chase, but deep inside, he had the feeling it never would. If it didn't, he was going to have to figure out what the hell to do next.

CHAPTER TWENTY-SEVEN

Mel was still buzzing happily by the time they got back to Audra's place. Bemused at him, Audra went into the kitchen to start a pot of tea. It was a special blend that had no caffeine but the natural components made it even more effective. It also promoted clearer thinking.

While it brewed, she went upstairs and changed clothes. She was more aware of Mel's presence down the hall than she wanted to be. Her body still ached and throbbed. When she looked into the mirror, she could see the mark on her neck from his teeth. The little brand of possession was a stark reminder that for the first time in one hundred and fifty years she had met a male wolf that matched her.

She owned little to no makeup. Luckily, the one thing she did own was powder. She covered the mark to the best of her ability before going downstairs to pour the tea. As she was setting two cups on the coffee table, Mel came down the stairs. She tried to keep her eyes to herself, but she missed nothing of the way he moved fluidly, muscles rippling under jeans and t-shirt. How had she missed the signs for twenty-four years? And where had she been when he had been running under the moon? She would have run at his side.

"What kind of tea is it?" He sat down and picked up one of the cups.

"Drinkable kind."

"Well, I wouldn't want to bathe in it." He sniffed at the liquid but caught nothing familiar except mint. The urge to tease was irresistible. "You didn't put a witch's brew in it or anything, right?"

She rolled her eyes expressively. "Sure, I grow nightshade out back with the azaleas and moonflowers. Shut up and drink your damn

tea."

His grin flashed quickly. "Yes'm." He obediently sipped the tea. The flavor instantly spread through his mouth. Mint, certainly, but more as well. Things he couldn't identify but tasted good all the same. "Nice stuff." As if he hadn't discovered a hunger to learn everything about her he could, he asked casually, "Do you prefer coffee or tea?"

"Coffee in the morning, tea any time after noon." She sat beside him. "Both have to be strong. I have sensitive taste buds so I tend to be heavy on flavor. Never eat any spaghetti I might make. Madelyne says I could kill vampires at five miles."

"So you've known Maddie a long time? It wasn't until real recently she mentioned you were a friend. And I know Taegan calls you a friend."

Something warm moved inside her heart. She knew Madelyne knew what she was, and though he had never expressly said so, she was sure Taegan did as well. She cherished their friendship, especially Taegan's. If he ever knew what she had done, even his kindness might change. "I've known Maddie for many years," she said carefully. "I sometimes work with the Enforcers so I've known her through Rhianna Taber."

"Gotcha." He let it lie; he knew when to fight his battles. Little steps at a time, that was how to handle Audra. "So, history."

"Which time period?"

"Early 1900s America." His smile was all innocence. "You know, before women's suffrage and the world went to hell." He wasn't disappointed when she turned a slowly arched brow toward him. Deliberately, he said, "1930 was a bad year."

She leaned over and pinched his ear. "For one, I'm telling your sisters you said that. For two, you know full well it was 1929." She barely kept a smile hidden. The playful teasing was as thrilling in its own way as the more adult teasing of earlier. "Now then. Let's get started."

He scooted closer to watch and listen closely as she began to talk. She was *really* good at lecturing. Her voice fluctuated with dozens of nuances, her tone alone imparting as much information as her words. She used pop culture and modern references to illustrate moods and attitudes, giving his brain something it could easily comprehend. And above all, she talked as if she had been there. The information began to sink into his brain . . . and stay.

As she was flipping pages for information on World War I, he glanced at her face. "How old are you?" Her brows lifted over amused yellow eyes and he coughed. "Sorry. I know it's rude. But you look so young, and you know so much. I would swear you'd been there the way you talk."

"That's the mark of a good lecture," she countered calmly. "If you don't sound knowledgeable, then why should anyone care what you think? I've heard some bad lectures myself. In fact, I wasn't the first to walk out of the room. When I went to the cafe, I saw a stone gargoyle drinking coffee like his life depended on it."

He grinned at that. "Your sense of humor is as warped as mine."

"I'm not sure that's a compliment." After a few moments, she noted, "Fair's fair. My turn for a personal question. Why's a guy like you still single? You're handsome, smart, and rich. You ought to be at least solidly hooked."

"Gee, thanks." He fiddled with his pencil, gazing unseeing at his books. "I guess I never met anyone worth being serious over. And after what's happened with my family . . . well, I suppose I'm waiting now for that special someone to come my way."

"Oh?" She kept her voice casual. "What happened with your siblings?"

"Within a month, they've all either gotten married or engaged." He leaned back on his hands with a whimsical smile. "We have this family wolf. She's become a lucky charm for us, or maybe she's just a good faerie in disguise. She's been helping us all find someone. She hasn't been around me much, though. Maybe there's no one for me."

"There's someone for everyone," she whispered as she put her pencil down. Pain and sadness mingled inside her. It was her indecision that made him feel as if he was meant to be alone. He deserved so much better, and time was getting so much shorter.

"Even you?" She looked at him in surprise, and he smiled.

"You're pretty cool when someone gets to know you. Oh, you're still rude and blunt, but it's part of your charm, I think. And, frankly, under that scar is a really hot chick. Rumor says the scar is recent, so why aren't you married with a litter of kids to raise into hellions?" The question hung between them. He knew it was immensely personal and none of his business. It was almost a test of their friendship.

She very nearly found an excuse, but she just couldn't lie to him anymore. She took a deep breath. "I was engaged once. He was murdered. I guess I've never gotten over it." His hand covered hers gently and she looked down in surprise. It was the first time other than the incident in the snow where he had touched her of his own volition. "Mel."

"I'm sorry," he said softly. His heart hurt for her and for how much she must have loved her fiancé to still cling to his memory. Jealousy rose savagely for a moment, but he firmly shoved it down again. It, like the chase, needed to be examined when the event was well past. He smiled instead. "I'll introduce you to Stormy, okay? Maybe she can help. Taegan swears she is his faerie godmother."

She barely refrained from making a face. She was going to kick Taegan. The smartass. "He did pull a convincing Cinderella," she admitted. "The school is still talking about it."

A snicker was his response. "It'll get better. Kalliope is actually having glass shoes made so she can wear them at her wedding."

She bit her lip but a snicker emerged anyway. She adored that girl. Of all the mates she had given to the Shaughnessys, only Kalliope had ever worked harder than Audra. And thinking of her duties reminded her that she had something else to deal with. She closed the history book. "I'm feeling a little tired. It's been a stressful week. Why don't we make it an early night?"

"Sure." He watched her head up the stairs, his eyes lingering on her hips and legs with wistful yearning. He turned his attention to the notes and began to gather them up. He started to close his book but hesitated and opened it again. He squinted at the page.

From up the stairs came, "Glasses."

"How does she do that?" he muttered, but he obligingly put his

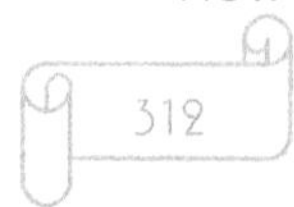

glasses on so he could read the book. The trick, he remembered her saying, wasn't to think of it as something that had happened, but something that could. Like a novel, or an interesting story. Think of a character, place them there, and build their world.

Taking it from that perspective, he began to read, shortly losing himself in the setting and the scenario. The facts he mentally filed away without notice. The opinions he mentally debated until he understood the value each had. He hit an interesting part that he wanted Audra to clarify and took the book with him upstairs. "Audra?" he called.

There was no response and he eased her door open carefully. There was no one inside and it looked as if she hadn't touched her bed. He frowned, wondering where she had gotten off to, if she was so tired. The woman needed a keeper, seriously. Shrugging slightly, he took the book with him and decided to read in bed. He was tired, too.

Steve Rudaveg was on his way home from a late game when he began to feel as if he was being watched. A chill went down his back and the palms of his hands began to sweat. His heart beat a little faster, his eyes moving restlessly around.

Danger. Danger was close.

Without even truly being aware of it, he began to walk faster. Though the nearly full moon had been bright, a cloud suddenly passed in front and plunged the street into a darkness not even the streetlights could penetrate.

Footsteps echoed eerily behind him. He turned sharply, but no one was there. His breath coming faster, he began to run down the sidewalk, desperately looking for where he had parked his car. When he stopped for a breath, a shadow moved in an alley and feral yellow eyes watched him. His voice emerged as only a strangled yelp. The wolf was nearly as tall as his hip, teeth bared, as low, menacing growls reverberated in the air.

He turned and ran the other way. He stumbled into a kid's playground and tripped over the edge of a sandbox. He landed with a thud on the ground and felt the wolf's breath near his ankle. With wild desperation, he clawed away to his feet and turned around. The wolf was watching him, slowly stalking forward. Taunting laughter seemed to ripple in his mind.

No escape.

The words echoed from the wolf's mind to his. He scrambled back and landed on his ass once more. "Get away from me!" The words were little more than a high-pitched squeal.

You called me here. Jealousy and rumor summon me like a hangman to the gallows. You knew you shouldn't spread rumors. You knew you shouldn't have ruined His car.

"Y-yes!" he stammered hastily. "I knew!"

And you're going to go to the college police and confess, aren't you.

"Yes!" he yelped. In that moment he would have agreed to anything. And when the wolf growled softly and crouched low, he threw his arms over his head in terror. "Don't eat me!" he wailed as the wolf lunged toward him.

Nothing happened. He slowly lowered his arms, his breath coming so hard and fast that it left a cloud of steam in the frigid air. There was nothing around him. No wolf. Nothing. The clouds were passing from in front of the moon. The night was quiet and still, crickets chirping cheerfully.

He ran the entire way home and didn't breathe again until he was in his room and under the covers on his bed.

Audra was still smiling to herself when she returned home.

There she had been, all set to 'convince' the punk with her compulsion powers to turn himself in, and instead all she had needed to do was terrify him. Not that that had been hard either. Chasing rabbits took more effort.

The house was silent, and she first went to Mel's room to peek inside. He was sitting up in bed, dead asleep, glasses slipping down his nose. Something warm moved through her as she slipped into the room and went over to his side. The man needed a keeper, seriously.

She gently removed his glasses and helped tuck him into bed. Her lips curved as she saw what he had been reading. If he set his mind to something, he gave it his everything.

He mumbled something and turned onto his side to snuggle into the pillow. Tenderly, she brushed his hair out of his eyes. He was as beautiful inside as he was outside. He was so wild and free, tugging at her in ways she hadn't felt before. She quickly left when he stirred again. The last thing she needed was to be caught there.

She went down the hall to her room and ignored the way chills always flowed over her skin each time she entered. It felt chilly enough that she pulled on an oversized sleep shirt. She usually slept in the nude but it truly was cold, colder than usual.

It was almost always difficult to fall asleep in that room. In many ways, she had always been almost pitifully grateful for the duties that allowed her to spend her time at the Shaughnessy home. There she could sleep. There she could rest. This night, however, she was so tired that she was asleep within minutes of her eyes closing.

And this time she dreamed.

The torches were burning. Children were screaming. The forests were ablaze with hellfire, the sound of guns firing, echoing loudly and bitterly. She ran as fast as her body was able, blood stinging her eyes and staining her skin where it slowly flowed from wounds of all shapes and sizes. She was praying. Praying with her every breath as she ran toward where the children had been hidden. There had to be hope!

There was none. Even before she ran into the shelter, she could smell the death. Claw marks lined the walls and gouged out chunks of wood and stone. Blood covered every surface. Bodies littered the floor.

Humans who had attacked and who had defended. Werewolves who had resisted death to the last moment.

Screaming for Kalin, screaming his name again and again, she tore up the floor and rushed down toward the basement. She could hear their screaming, hear their cries, the sounds imbedded in the very walls. And she knew they were already dead for she did not hear the sounds of their hearts beating.

The basement was covered with bodies. No one moved. No one breathed. Even the smallest, a child of barely two, lay like an abandoned doll with bullet holes riddling her body. Two figures struggled before a moonlit window, and she lunged forward to close her hands around the neck of the murderer. It snapped like a twig and he dropped. Kalin fell, and she held him tightly to her breast, knowing he, too, would be dead shortly. Even then, he did not move or breathe, his life bleeding away into her hands.

Her howl of rage and of grief shattered the night air as she vowed for vengeance against the humans who had done this to her people.

"Audra! Audra!"

Her eyes shot open and she saw Mel leaning over her. On a low snarl, she lunged for him with her hands hooked like claws. He caught her wrists and held her away with unthinking power, his grip gentle despite the strength. "Audra!" he said again, eyes dark with worry. "It's me! It's Mel!"

His voice finally penetrated the haze of her mind. The fight drained out of her, and she slumped against him weakly, tired to her very soul. Shaken, he wrapped his arms around her and pressed her head to his shoulder. "Wow. Jesus, you don't dream lightly, do you? Your scream scared the hell out of me. When I got here, you were thrashing like the hounds of hell were after you."

She said nothing as she turned her face into his shoulder. She had never been held after the nightmares before. It was an odd, foreign feeling, but the warmth and security of his arms slowly seeped into her body and melted the cold. His heart, though slightly unsteady, sounded strong and sure under her ear. She pressed closer unthinkingly, needing the feeling of safety that only this man had ever given her.

He felt his heart quiver. She had always seemed so strong, so unbreakable, but she was human, too, with fears and nightmares. His arms tightened, and he slowly ran his hand over her back soothingly. Without thought, he rubbed his cheek against her hair. Had anyone ever held her before? He didn't think so. "Want to talk about it?" he asked softly.

"No." Talk about it? She fought a shudder. She could barely accept that it had even happened. She slowly eased back from his embrace and looked at her hands. Though it had long been washed away, there were times she felt as if the blood was buried in her skin.

His hands suddenly slid under hers. Something quivered inside her soul. His hands were bigger than hers, his skin barely darker. She was only two inches shorter than he was, but he was so strong and powerful that she felt safe and secure. And when his hands slowly closed over hers, the touch was as possessive as it was protective.

"When was the last time you were held?" he asked softly.

"I don't remember," she admitted just as softly. "I never felt comfortable letting anyone close." Her lips twisted with a mockery of a smile. "It didn't matter. No one wanted to be close. I'm not talking about the scars. Something inside me . . . scares people."

"Not me." Her eyes lifted to his and he lowered his forehead to hers. "Not anymore. Yeah, you scared the hell out of me at first. You even admit to doing it on purpose. But . . . I'm not afraid of you. Not anymore. There's nothing you could say or do that would make me decide I didn't want to know you or comfort you. Or be your friend."

Her eyes closed. Though she knew he believed what he said, she knew he was wrong. At best, all she could say was, "Thanks."

"Hey." He eased back and smiled. "I know what you need. Come on." He got to his feet and held out a hand to her. "Come with me. When's the last time someone did something nice for you?"

"I'm not sure. Which century is this again?" Her heart soared when he laughed, his eyes twinkling in his handsome face. And though she knew it was stupid, she reached out and put her hand in his to let him tug her out of the bed. Something was happening. She had the feeling of freefalling without knowing where she would land.

He led her down to the kitchen and began to rummage in the fridge. Curious, she sat at the counter and watched him. He got out milk and then got a pan. "What are you doing?"

"Making some warm chocolate milk." He found the cocoa in a cabinet and added it to the milk in the pan. "It's what Dad always did when we had nightmares. He'd make us some warm chocolate milk and we'd talk until we were ready to sleep again."

"Oh." She rested her cheek on her arms as she watched him. She had forgotten that family tradition, and it felt odd to be part of it in this way. "What are we going to talk about?"

He contemplated how he wanted to ask what he wanted to know. When the milk was ready, he poured a mug and set it in front of her. She seemed oddly fragile as she sat at the counter in nothing but a giant shirt that did nothing to disguise her long and tempting legs. "I know you don't want to talk about the nightmare," he said carefully, "but will you at least tell me if the dream is connected to the walls?" When she went still, he gave a slight shrug. "Even I could hear the pain in this house. Why do you live here?"

"Because I have to. I can't explain." She sipped the milk and found that it was strangely soothing. "But I admit I do have trouble sleeping in that bedroom. Lots of nightmares. Usually I end up sleeping on the couch."

He sat across from her and let the subject lie. "Let's talk about something else." He smiled. "I'll tell you a secret if you tell me a secret. I'll even go first." He made a point of looking around and kept his voice low as if the secret was of grave importance. "My full name is Melville. I was named for my grandfather. But I *hate* my name. You'd only ever see it on my birth certificate."

She found a smile. She felt oddly trusted that he would tell her. Of course, she couldn't tell him that she had always known. "If Kalliope offers me enough money, I'm blabbing."

"Give me a chance to better the offer."

"Will do." Her eyes closed partially as the milk rested warmly in

her body and his companionship lulled her toward sleep. "I'm afraid of cats," she finally confessed, her voice drowsy. "Give me the willies something fierce. Whenever I see one, I sometimes can't help chasing them off."

"I could see you running after them with a broom," he decided. He grinned. "Yeah, I could see that. The tough computer sciences teacher that terrifies the campus. The beast of the college is afraid of cats and loves children. Your fan club would have a field day."

Her voice slightly slurred as her eyes closed, she mumbled, "I don't have a fan club. I fired them for holding parties and not inviting me."

He opened his mouth to find a retort when he realized she had fallen asleep at the table. Her lashes rested like dark crescents against her skin. A soft smile curved his lips and he went around the table to gently gather her into his arms. Her head fell against his shoulder, her breath softly feathering over his skin.

He let out a long breath as he carried her up the stairs. With the way everything she did or said seemed to make him want her more, he was growing strongly suspicious that her bullshit about the chase was purely that. Maybe it had shocked his eyes open, but it sure as hell wasn't the only reason. He didn't mind; he was willing to give it more time for her sake. She needed to believe it too.

He didn't take her to her room. He took her to his and settled her on his bed. He tucked her in tenderly and drew the covers up over her shoulders. She promptly rolled over and curled up on her side. "Kalin," she mumbled sleepily.

He hesitated but tucked in the blanket more securely anyway. He couldn't help wondering if Kalin was her dead lover. He also couldn't help his jealousy at the thought. He softly smoothed her hair back from her face and traced his thumb down the scar. With a soft sigh, he left the room to go downstairs. He was going to be the one on the couch that night, but he didn't regret it in the slightest.

She awoke the next morning to his scent surrounding her. She sat up quickly and looked around in shock. She was in his bed and in his room. His presence had permeated everything, blanketing her subconscious with its comforting energy. She felt more rested than she had in a century.

She warily got up and went downstairs, sure she was wrong, but when she went into the living room, she found him sprawled dead asleep on the couch. With that unquestioning generosity of his, he had given her his bed so that she would get true sleep. Once more, inside her soul, she felt something falling and hovering on the precipice of hitting . . . something.

A book dangled from his fingers and his glasses were falling off his face. She gently removed the glasses and picked up the book. It was his math book. She bit her lips and tried not to laugh.

She bent to tuck the blanket around his shoulders better and he gave a sleepy mumble that sounded like a math equation. Smiling, she shook her head and brushed his hair back from his cheek. His head turned and his lips brushed over her fingers. His scent lifted and curled around her, wild and wonderful . . . and that something landed inside her and brought understanding.

It was her.

It was her scent that matched his. *She* was his mate. All she had to do was close her eyes to find him in a room of millions. He could call her name from miles away and she would hear him. She was in love with him, this wild and untamed man who looked into her eyes fearlessly and gave his friendship unconditionally. No other would ever suit him. No other would ever suit her.

Pain and despair welled inside her as she buried her face in her hands. Her only hope for salvation was finding him true love, but if he knew what she had done, he would *never* feel for her as she felt for him. No matter if it destroyed her, she would have to try to find him another mate. Someone who was whole. Someone who deserved him. Someone who wasn't a murderess.

CHAPTER TWENTY-EIGHT

Mel awoke once more to the smell of breakfast cooking. This time he woke with a start and fell off the couch with a thump. As he sprawled on the floor, he realized there were feet standing in front of him. They were nice feet, attached to slender ankles that flowed into what he knew were exceptionally nice legs even though they were currently covered by black jeans. "Morning," he said.

Audra crouched down. "Morning," she told him gravely. She had decided to ignore her revelations until she could talk to the one person who could possibly help. "Sleep well?"

"I think the better question," he rolled over and got to his feet nimbly, "is whether or not *you* slept well." He searched her face. There was something behind her eyes that he couldn't catch, but there was indeed more rest to her face. "I'm glad," he said softly.

"Food is in the kitchen," she informed him.

"So I smell." He stretched and covered a yawn. "I'll go grab a quick shower and be right there." A thought occurred and he frowned. "How am I getting to school?"

"You can go with me, but I'm just dropping you off. An emergency came up that I have to take care of. I've called a substitute in to my classes today." She headed into the kitchen. "So hurry up. We haven't got all day."

Smiling a little to himself, he went upstairs.

After dropping him off at school, she made a beeline back to the 3rd District and the immense skyscraper that served as the Enforcers' headquarters. It was thirty-six floors high and sleek and elegant in its design. It had undergone many renovations over the centuries to keep up with the times, and currently it was glass and metal. When the sun was rising or setting, it reflected in the windows and made them glow like fire. It was one of the most beautiful sights in New York.

The Enforcers had been formed when the District had, and they maintained the buildings and protected the people. They had alliances with multiple large corporations, and the mutually beneficial relationships ensured that the Enforcers were never without an edge in any market. Some suspected they even had federal backing, but it could not be proven.

Audra was a regular in the building. She had been there so often that she didn't even wear her badge. The guards merely waved her in. However, the top few floors were under strict access, so she had to use her badge on the elevator to go all the way to the very top floor. As she rode upward, she let herself remember a time when she'd had to take the stairs. Thank god for modern conveniences.

Without waiting to knock, she walked right into Rhianna's office and said, "For the love of God, Rhianna, tell me you have five minutes."

Rhianna's elegant brows rose slowly toward her red bangs. She smiled and closed the document she had been reading. She was a shorter woman with a thick mane of red hair and vibrant black eyes. Beautiful by any standards, she also had a regal and commanding air. Her powers were immense though the extent of them was unknown to all, even her partner.

She studied Audra intently, well aware of the clock slowly ticking away in the back of her mind. "If this is about Madelyne, I'm already aware. Imagine." She gave a little laugh of delight. "Me, a grandmother, after all this time. Eric says I need to learn to knit."

Audra didn't bother to sit down. She stood behind the visitor's chair, her fingers wrapped around the back so hard that her knuckles were white. "You're old enough to be someone's *ancestor* but that's neither here nor there." She took a quick breath. "I need an extension. Please. Anything."

Sadness clouded Rhianna's face. "I can't, Audra. It's too close. There's nothing I can do now. I can't amend a contract this late in the process." She began to frown. "Why? What's wrong? I knew he would be difficult, but surely . . ." Her voice trailed off as she saw the agony in Audra's eyes. "Oh. I see." She ran a hand through her hair, not sure what to say. She had hoped this would be much easier. "When did this occur?"

"I realized it this morning." Audra shook her head quickly. "What am I supposed to do, Rhi? He's a Shaughnessy. If he knew what I'd done . . ." Her voice broke as a shudder ripped through her body. "My god, he would hate me! *I* hate me for it!"

Rhianna got up and walked around the desk to help her into the chair. She knelt down beside her friend. "Audra, you know that if you don't find him true love . . ."

"I know." She closed her eyes, tears beginning to slide down her cheeks. "But how can I find him someone else when I know that his scent only matches mine?" She drew a deep breath. "Rhianna . . . he's a wolf. It should be impossible, but somehow the District blood in the Shaughnessy line has manifested wholly inside him. He's a werewolf. He's an alpha male, no less."

"If you are meant to be his mate," Rhianna noted mildly, "he could be nothing less. Has he shifted or compelled?"

"His mind has *tried* to compel; he said he felt as if he had influenced someone. As for shifting, no. But he could. If he needed, he could. The Amber Mark is in his eyes now. If he finds himself with a great need, he could shift." She lowered her head. "I can't even tell him what he is," she added softly. "Not without telling him what I am. And if I do . . . he'll hate me for that, too."

"Then be as open as you can. Give him a side of you that you've never given anyone else. Know that you gave the man you loved everything. Just that alone can ensure you have no regrets." Rhianna tilted her head slightly. "Have you any idea how he feels about you?"

"He wants me." She shrugged one shoulder. "At the least, he seems to. The Amber Mark appeared because he was chasing me. We fell into the mating hunt of werewolves and it got to us both. I played it off as just primitive instinct, and he bought it."

"You don't suppose he might actually want you, do you? To

begin with, he wouldn't have fallen into that hunt if there was nothing inside to spark it. For another, I might add, once you get past a cactus' bite, its flesh is sweet."

"Thanks. Thanks a bunch." She gestured at her face. "Trust me, I know my lack of appeal. Even before . . . I scared people." She didn't scare Mel anymore, she remembered then, her heart skipping a beat.

"You're a tad overwhelming, dear." Rhianna got to her feet. "Very few humans know how to deal with a true hunter. Try as you might, you can't hide what you are. Oh, you can pretend for a while, but you're no civilized pet in the slightest. Humans have survived so long because they can feel when a predator is close." She paused before adding smoothly, "Which is partly Mel's problem, I believe. His predatory nature is barely concealed as a wild spirit only."

Audra slowly got to her feet. "I can only play things by ear now. I don't . . . I don't think I'll be able to do it, Rhi." Her smile was sad but accepting. "Wolves mate for life. I can't hand him over to another woman." She let out a long breath and pulled a letter out of her pocket. She dropped it on the chair. "When it's done . . . give that to Mel."

The door shut behind her and Rhianna picked up the glass statuette on her desk. She hurled it furiously at the wall where it shattered into millions of pieces.

Softly, a male voice asked from another doorway, "What do we do?"

His partner looked at the fragmented remains of the statuette. It was like seeing how her heart felt inside. "Whatever we have to." And though soft, her voice was hard as steel.

Mel had braced himself for another day of snide comments and trouble, but it was as if the day before had never happened. Students greeted him cordially. Others waved at him across the quad. Teachers asked with genuine concern about his ruined car.

He went looking for Kalliope at the first available opportunity. He caught her as she was coming out of a class and promptly grabbed her around the waist. He lifted her off her feet and stalked down the hall. "You're coming with me."

"I hadn't noticed." She braced an elbow on his shoulder and ignored her dangling feet. "Are we having some issues, Gibson?"

He put her down when they were out of hearing of other students. "Okay, talk," he ordered. "You have ears like a damn alley cat and you know *everything* happening on campus. So what the hell is going on?"

She lifted her brows. "Oh, you mean the 24-Hour flip-flop. Well, it would seem that Steve Rudaveg went to Administration this morning and confessed to not only spreading the rumors but also vandalizing your car. He was escorted off campus by some very nice policemen just before you got here. You'll probably get a call tonight. And since the student body blows with the wind, everything's fine now."

"What did you do to him?" he accused.

"Me?" She scowled. "Why must you always blame me?"

"Because you're usually at fault."

"Damn it." She hated when he was right. All of the Shaughnessys had her number now. "As a matter of fact," she said with dignity, "I did nothing. In and amongst his ramblings, Rutabaga mentioned an encounter with a wolf. In the middle of NYC at night. If you want answers, look to Stormy. Where's she been lately anyway?"

"I've seen her once or twice lately." He sighed wryly. "I think I'm causing her difficulty." He waved it off with a shrug. To be honest, he wasn't minding it that much anymore. Somehow he couldn't miss Stormy if he had Audra around. "How are things at home?"

"Kind of boring. It's like a deck of cards that's missing an entire suit." She gave his arm a light punch. "Hang in there. Two days to midterms, and everything will be fine. We're pulling for you."

"Thanks." He watched her walk away and then headed for his own class. He decided to go with the flow and pretended like nothing had happened, opting for the high road instead of ignoring his fellow classmates for their two-faced attitudes.

To his surprise, within a few minutes of being seated in class, an attractive young woman dropped down onto the seat beside him. Since she sat down without any books, he lifted a brow. "Can I help you?"

"I'm new on campus, and I'm just here to hit on you," she said with a laugh. She offered a hand. "Kate Willowby. I don't suppose you're free this evening."

He studied her. She was assuredly attractive with short brown hair and lively blue eyes. Shorter than average, around Kalliope's height, and with a lovely, shapely figure. She carried herself well and there was a definite humor inside her. He made his decision easily, wondering if she might finally make sense of everything. "Sure. I have a tutoring session, but it could be ended early. How does dinner sound?"

"It sounds like a date." She scribbled her address on his notepad. "I live a block or two away from 3rd District, so I'm not hard to find. You're staying with Professor Alexandrios, right?" When he nodded, she gave a little shiver. "She's a bit scary." She smiled. "But I guess she isn't so bad."

"Agreed."

She hopped to her feet. "See you later, Mel."

"Later indeed." He waved when she disappeared into the hall and turned his attention to the front as the teacher called for roll. He put his cute date out of his mind and settled in to learn. Much to his immense shock, he was ahead of his class. It was History, and he had always lagged behind. He was now several chapters ahead, and even the teacher noticed.

The same thing happened in both his Math and Japanese classes. By the time lunch came around, he was beginning to seriously think he would be able to fulfill his end of the bargain. He was even whistling lightly as he joined his family for lunch.

"Well, you're cheerful," Kienan remarked. "Where's my brother, and what did you do with him?"

"I'm not that bad," he muttered as he sat down. "I," he announced, "happen to be ahead of my classes, and I have a date. I'm entitled to be cheerful." He watched Kalliope and Madelyne exchange a quick look. "Problem?"

"No. Who's the date with?" Madelyne asked it casually, but her stomach was clenching in a way that had nothing to do with morning sickness.

"Kate. New girl. Really cute."

"Hmm." Kalliope said nothing more than that.

He was the first to finish lunch since the others took their time. As soon as he had left the table, Kienan muttered, "I didn't think new students could start at midterm time."

"They can't." Madelyne frowned.

"Stormy?" Kalliope wondered.

"No." Madelyne pressed her hands to her stomach, her fingers shaking. Not even Kienan's arms wrapping around her could take away her trepidation. "Something else is going on." She couldn't even say whether it was good or bad. Time was running out.

Audra was waiting for Mel outside when his last class ended for the day. As he approached whistling, she lifted a brow. "Are we cheerful for no good reason today?"

"You and my family." He sighed. "Am I always grumpy?"

"Yes."

"At least *pretend* like you don't agree." He stuck his tongue out at her but still smiled. He liked it when she was teasing him. "As it would happen, I have a date tonight. Can we make the tutoring a short session?" While he spoke, he pulled on his helmet and got on the bike behind her.

The knife that drove into her heart was sharp and serrated. It was almost a physical blow, driving the breath from her lungs. Her

nails curled into the handlebars of her bike as she fought for control. *Hers.* Everything inside her seemed to snarl at once, feral with possessive rage.

He felt her body quivering slightly but said nothing. When they got home, however, he pulled off his helmet with a frown. "What's wrong?"

"Nothing." The effort of fighting for control made her voice cold and clipped. "Heaven forbid school come in the way of hormones. Have your date. In fact, why don't we skip tonight altogether?" She jerked her helmet off and tucked it under her arm.

He caught her arm as she started to walk away. He felt a little shocked. It had been a long time since she had acted that way. It hurt more than he had imagined. "Audra, what's wrong?"

She turned on him, her eyes nearly as feral as she felt. "Seeing someone gamble with their future pisses me off." The words were almost snarled. "Some people don't even have a future!" She jerked her arm free and disappeared into the house.

He waited a few moments before going into the house as well. Somehow he wasn't surprised when he checked and found no sign of her. There had to be a secret door somewhere that he didn't know about.

The entire time he was getting ready, he bounced back and forth between whether or not he still wanted to go out. Ever since the 'chase,' he had felt more sharply attuned to Audra. He was sure that her lashing out was the result of pain and not anger. He wanted to track her down and find out what was wrong so he could make it better. The only thing that stopped him was knowing she would go for his eyes if he did.

He killed time by reading a book. When it was time to leave, he put on his jacket and left the house. Kate really didn't live far away. It would be easy to walk to her place and then to the restaurant where they wanted to have dinner.

To his surprise, he found Stormy sitting outside on the sidewalk. He instantly brightened. "Hey, there you are." He knelt and ran a hand over her head as she nudged his leg. "Where have you been? I was feeling a little neglected." He rubbed his cheek over her fur, comforted with her presence. "I missed you." He straightened with a smile. "I might be usurping your job, but I might have met someone on my own."

When he started to step forward, she planted herself in his path. Her ears were laid back, and her teeth almost bared. If he tried to step to either side, a low growl vibrated from her throat. He wasn't stupid. He got the point. "Stormy, I can't just stand her up. I know what you're telling me, but I'm not that much of a jerk. Now come on. You can come with me."

Her fur didn't lie flat, but she stopped growling as she fell into step beside him. She would have dragged him back by the seat of his pants if she could have, but he wasn't two anymore. *Really* wasn't two anymore, she thought, glancing over him wistfully.

The silence held for a few moments until he murmured, "I hurt Audra. I didn't mean to, Stormy. Really. I'm not even sure how I did. I guess she just doesn't want me to fail. She's very odd about it, but she cares for me. Last night . . ." He trailed off for a moment. "It was different to have her lean on me. I wanted to protect her. I still do."

She looked up at him in shock and he rubbed the back of his neck. "Yeah, I know. She's the least likely person to need protecting. She's such a strong woman. But she's been hurt too much, I think. I don't want to be another one on the list. If I could, I'd keep her safe from everything."

He stopped walking as he realized he had reached Kate's door. He took a breath and then walked up and knocked. The door opened instantly and Kate smiled at him. In a long sleeved blouse and black skirt, she was even lovelier than he remembered. Her eyes sparkled. "Good evening!" A low growl caught her attention and she looked down. "Umm, Mel? Tell me she's yours."

"Stormy!" He caught his wolf's collar and pulled her back. "Stop that!" He knelt down and caught her face in his hands. He held her eyes intently. There was something oddly familiar about them, but once more his mind shied away. "Be nice or go home."

Stormy stopped growling but didn't fully relax. She sat down

obediently, and even let Kate pet her head gently. Her eyes measured her rival intently. She looked like a ball of cotton candy compared to a prime piece of steak. Fluffy and insubstantial and not nearly enough for an alpha male. As she watched them walk away, she laid down with her eyes narrowed. She didn't like her one bit. She didn't even *have* a scent.

Mel and Kate walked to the restaurant they had chosen earlier via text message. It was a sit down place, but it wasn't terribly formal. Once they were seated and had appetizers, they looked over the menu. "I want something with vegetables," she decided. "How about you, Mel?"

"I'm eyeing the rare steak." He smiled wryly. "I've been craving red meat lately."

"You carnivore you." Her voice was teasing.

As dinner progressed, he found her to be a lively companion with a sharp wit and clever mind. He enjoyed himself, and her company, but it didn't take long for him to start wishing it was Audra there with him instead. She could have walked into a fancy restaurant in her black jeans and been treated like a queen.

The longer the evening drew on, the more certain he became that his desire for Audra was not a result of primal instinct. He didn't want Kate, no matter how lovely she was. She didn't have thick black hair like a mane, and she didn't have a hunter's yellow eyes. She was too short for him, and she wasn't that strong. She was too nice, not acerbic enough.

She wasn't Audra, and Audra was the only woman he wanted.

Stormy was still lying on the sidewalk when they returned home, and as Kate turned to unlock her door, she said cheerfully, "That was fun, the three of us."

"Three of us?" Mel blinked.

"Yes. You, me, and the woman you were wishing I was." Dull color filled his cheeks and she gave a sigh. "Oh, well. The good ones are always taken. It was fun anyway. If you want her," she added as she went into her house, "go after her, okay? If I'm going to lose out on a great guy, I want to lose him to a great woman."

"I will." He had to smile. "Thanks, Kate. I really am sorry." The door shut and he let out a long sigh. He walked over to where Stormy was waiting and knelt down to run a hand gently over her head. She looked up at him expectantly, and he sighed again. "Okay, you were right. Just don't gloat." He stood and began to walk down the sidewalk with his wolf walking companionably beside him. "I don't want Kate." He tucked his hands in his pocket. "I want Audra."

She stopped dead in her tracks for long moments. She shook it off quickly and hurried to catch up. Once she had, he said thoughtfully, "It hit me pretty hard the other day. When I kissed her . . . god. There's no way to describe how *right* it felt. It was the hottest kiss I've ever had the luxury of experiencing, and my hunger for her hasn't gone away. It just keeps growing. The scent of her skin is maddening. The curve of her neck . . . I have the almost unbearable urge to bite her there. I want her like hell on fire, and I have no idea what to do about it.

"She doesn't think she's beautiful, but she is inside. There's something about her . . . something different. Once I got past the scar and her surface attitude, I began to look at her as a whole. And there's a whole lot to Audra. She's rude, and brash, and she's definitely mean. But . . . that's Audra. I like the way she is."

The house was dark when they arrived. He could only assume Audra was still out. He held the door open for Stormy and shut and locked it behind them both. As he headed up the stairs, he began unbuttoning his shirt. "I'm not sure what to do," he mused. He dropped his shirt on the chair in his room. "Maybe if I sleep on it, I'll get a clue."

She had stopped listening. Her eyes were riveted to the back of his left shoulder. There, right where the muscles of his back rippled when he moved his arms, was the telltale wolf's head. The black tattoo was a birthmark that differentiated between regular werewolves and alpha ones. A regular wolf had a black claw. Only an alpha had the wolf's head.

If put under enough pressure, he would not be able to resist the urge to transform. The first change was demanded by nature, but he would have perfect control after it. She could only be glad she had left the knowledge behind for him. Even when she was gone, the wolves would continue.

She leapt up onto the bed and laid down to watch as he changed into sweatpants. He was so beautiful to her eyes. He always had been. When he got into bed, she couldn't resist moving closer to rest her head on his lap. His fingers moved softly over her head but couldn't wholly soothe her. Being told that a man wanted you like hell on fire was murder on self-control.

She stayed beside him until he fell asleep. Once he had, she leapt down and ran through the house to her balcony. She leapt over the side and landed gracefully on the grass outside. She was going to run until she was too tired to drop. If she did, perhaps the unbearable urge to change back, strip naked, and climb into his bed would go away. It would be stupid, but it was tempting.

Still, for the time being, it was enough to know he wanted her. It had been a long time since anyone had.

CHAPTER TWENTY-NINE

Mel awoke the next morning to a mind that was crystal clear. If he wanted Audra—and he assuredly did—then he needed to make the first move. It was a move that had to be made when there was no excuse she could use for his behavior. She couldn't have any reason to push him away.

"Primitive instinct, my ass," he muttered as he got out of bed. It was early, barely dawn, but there would be no better time.

He headed down the hall and walked right into her room without knocking. Cheerfully he called, "How can a man apologize if you keep running off and then sleeping the morning away?" He flicked the light on, and she sat up instantly, cursing sleepily in another language he had never heard. At that moment, he wasn't sure he remembered his own name.

She was naked. Wonderfully, gloriously, naked. The blankets had fallen to her waist and he could see every inch of her silky skin. Her strong shoulders flowed down into breasts that were high and shapely and perfectly formed to fill his hands. Her ribcage was elegant, and her stomach was trim. He saw her only as a whole at first, but then his eyes truly focused and he began to see the smallest details.

Her body was riddled with scars. Small ones all over her ribcage as if she had been shot. There was a vicious one across her lower belly in the same color as the one across her face; it too was still fairly new. Pain ripped him apart inside as he wondered how she had survived whatever had happened. "Audra."

Sleep finally lifted. She realized he was staring at her and she hastily grabbed a sheet to cover herself. She tugged it up to her chin and narrowed her eyes warningly. "Your father failed. He seems to have missed one."

"One what?"

"A gentleman!" She threw her pillow at him. "Get out of my room, you bastard. This isn't a peep show, and I want my sleep!" She rolled over and jerked the sheet over her head. It was promptly jerked down again and whisked away entirely. Cursing, she sat up and crossed her arms across her breasts. "Mel!" She glared at him fiercely.

"Well, it was already too late," he said reasonably.

She tried to hit him, but he was faster. He caught her wrist and yanked her off balance. She tried to twist free but by the time the dust settled, she was pinned underneath him entirely with his weight keeping her prisoner. Her hands were once more cuffed over her head. "This is getting to be a bad habit of yours!" she almost snarled.

Softly, he said, "You're beautiful, Audra."

She went very still, her eyes widening. Something that was shock and panic moved in her yellow gaze before anger spiked once more. "The hell I am. Put your glasses on and look again." Her stomach quivered as he continued to gaze at her, his chocolate gaze melting her. "I'm scarred," she reminded him curtly. "There's no way that could possibly turn you on."

He said nothing as he looked her over. The scars went all the way down her legs as well, more small marks where something had ripped through flesh. Thin lines from a blade. The worst was the ragged mark across her stomach. He shifted his grip on her wrists to one hand and slid his freed hand under her. His fingers found a matching scar on her lower back and more small scars all over her upper back. She had been *run though the stomach* at some point in time.

She closed her eyes tightly and turned her head away. She felt exposed and ripped raw. She could fool herself into believing her body was attractive as long as she had clothes on, but if she was naked, every flaw was laid bare. No man in his right mind would ever want her and she knew it. Something hot landed on her shoulder and she looked up quickly to see tears in Mel's eyes. Suffering had turned his eyes black. Her own eyes slowly widened. "Mel . . ."

"God, Audra." His voice was strained. "How did you survive? It destroys me to think of how much pain you must have felt!" He lowered his head for a moment, struggling for control. He wanted to kiss and caress every mark, to remove even the memory of pain. His eyes fell on the little black birthmark on her hip, and it was a welcome distraction. He skimmed a knuckle over it softly. "Nice. A tattoo?"

"Birthmark," she admitted. It was hard to lie to a man who had you naked in his arms. It only added another layer of guilt as she remembered all the other lies she had told. She tugged lightly at her hands, but he had her held firmly. Heat began to slowly roll through her blood as she saw that he was still only in sweatpants. His chest was broad and powerful, and her mouth watered just looking at him. "This is a bad idea," she whispered, her eyes lifting to his. Her toes curled as she saw darkness in his eyes that was no longer pain but pure, raw, hunger.

"So what?" He lowered his head, his lips teasing hers. "I'll show you," he murmured, "how much I want you. I'd never lie to you about that."

But I've lied to you, she thought in despair. A shudder went through her body as his mouth touched hers, and she struggled between acceptance and denial, resistance and surrender. He wanted her. Despite all odds, he wanted her.

A child's scream rent the morning air. His head jerked up in shock. He released her and rolled to his feet. She was only a step behind him as they ran down the stairs, and she yanked on a shirt over her body as she went. She followed him outside and they rushed around the side of the building. She took in the entire scene within moments.

A man had a small girl by the wrist and was dragging her down the street. She resisted fiercely, small wings on her back fluttering madly, she tried to pull out of his grip. "Let go of her!" Mel shouted.

The man looked up and light glinted off the blade in his hand. Something moved inside Mel and awoke with a rush. Audra sensed it and knew that he was about to forcefully change for the first time. She couldn't let him put himself in danger. Her decision was made in a second. She lunged forward with a snarl, and her body glowed and shifted as she changed into the form of the wolf.

She struck the man's chest with all fours and took him flat to the sidewalk. The child was set free, and she rushed over to fly into Mel's arms. He barely noticed. He could only stand still in shock, staring at what he was seeing, disbelief and dim horror filling him. He knew the wolf. How could he not?

Audra was Stormy.

The shock was enough to open his mind to all the little things he had never wanted to understand. Anger began a slow boil and grew into a simmering rage as he realized how badly he had been lied to, how badly he and his whole family had been manipulated. He put the child down. "Call a policeman," he ordered quietly.

"Audra will protect us." The girl popped her thumb in her mouth. "She always protects us. She'll make him go away."

He observed the way 'Stormy' was growling with her teeth inches from the man's throat. He half expected her to eat him, and he couldn't really begrudge her that at the least. Yet she wasn't attacking. Her eyes were locked with the assailant, and Mel could almost feel a conversation happening. After a few moments, she backed up a step and the man got to his feet before turning and walking away with a dazed look in his eyes.

"Audra!" The child lunged forward and wrapped her arms around the wolf's neck. "You saved me!" She held on as Audra changed back and found herself clinging to the woman's neck. She held on tighter and snuggled close. "Thank you."

"Do not," Audra said firmly, steel in her voice, "ever go outside unescorted again, Nell. I will beat you until you can't sit for a month!" She turned her face into the child's hair and knew her entire body was trembling. It wasn't just from fear at nearly losing a child, but with dread for the coming confrontation. Mel was furious.

She put Nell down and watched her run into the orphanage again. Then, hiding as much of her trembling as possible, she turned to Mel and gestured to the house. "After you."

He turned and walked into the house, his body stiff with anger, and she tried to brace herself for when he unleashed it. She wasn't sure she could handle it.

He let it loose the instant the door shut behind her. "My god," he said through his teeth. The words were clipped and came out with the full force of his accent. "You really played me for a fool, didn't you? You've been manipulating my whole family, playing at the family pet . . . you listened to me babble about my dreams and things I've never told anyone else! Faerie godmother, my ass!"

She kept her voice even with effort. "If you had asked me, I'd have told the truth."

"How was I supposed to know?!" he shouted. He turned and began to pace furiously. He raked his hands through his hair. "God," he muttered, "I've been lusting after the family pet. My siblings will have a fit."

The blow was well placed, and she tucked it where it couldn't be seen. "Yes," she said coolly. "I am a family pet. I was once the alpha of a proud werewolf clan that was destroyed. I was their greatest warrior. Now I'm a pet, only here because I am guiding your family on its path."

He snapped, "Don't sound so ill used. You've had it good for a long time now. What? Were you bored and in need of a hobby? Pity for the lowly human family?" His head snapped to the side as her palm cracked across his cheek.

"It's not a hobby!" she shouted. "It's my life! And do you think it was any easier on me?! I've wanted you for so long, and I knew I would never have you if you knew the truth! For a few precious days, you looked at me as if I wasn't what everyone has always known me to be. You knew from the beginning, Mel Shaughnessy! You knew I was a beast! In your own mind, you condemned me and you *were right*! Get out of my house. Don't come near me again!"

She ran up the stairs faster than any human ever could and a door slammed so hard that the building shook. Shaking slightly, he slowly sank down to sit on the side of the couch. He felt like scum and lower than dirt. Like an idiot, he had lashed out to hurt because he was hurting. It was an unfortunate family trait that he had thought he didn't have. His temper began to cool, and he began to see things through her eyes. And as he did, he realized nothing had truly changed.

He still wanted her. Human or werewolf, he wanted her. Where was the difference in his telling her his secrets and dreams while she was a wolf than while she was human? Wasn't that part of getting to know someone? Also, she had her self-imposed job to find them all a true love. If she wanted to match him, then she needed to know him.

He had known he was making things hard for 'Stormy,' but now he finally understood why. How was she going to find him true love when he was all tangled up with her in her human form? The simple answer was . . . she wasn't. He didn't want anyone else. He wanted her. Were his feelings love? He didn't know. But he knew, absolutely knew, that he could not let her go. They had a chance at something special.

He climbed the stairs slowly. He could hear the shower running and somehow he heard her crying though not a sound emerged. He paused outside the door for long moments and then nodded once. Burning his bridges, as they said.

She stood under the pounding water and let it wash away her tears. It couldn't wash away her pain, and it welled endlessly inside her, hurting more than any bullet or sword could. She just wished it was all over with already, that the pain was gone. Freedom didn't matter anymore. She just wanted to be away from the pain.

She didn't blame Mel. She had been expecting his reaction all along. It was just so much worse coming on the heels of the morning's events. For the first time in a time longer than she could remember, she had felt desired. Someone had wanted her despite all odds. Even though it had only happened once and would never happen again, she held the memory close.

His scent unexpectedly seemed to sear into her lungs. The wolf mark throbbed softly. Her head jerked up in shock. She hadn't heard the door open, but strong masculine arms were suddenly wrapping around her waist and drawing her back against an equally strong body. She couldn't breathe, too afraid to hope. "Mel?" She twisted enough to look up at his face.

"I'm sorry." He pressed his lips to the curve of her shoulder and tasted the freshness of her skin. "Forgive me, please. I was an ass. Don't close me out."

A shudder of pleasure rippled through her body. Her neck was the most sensitive place on her body, and she was unable to resist his touch to begin with. Her eyes closed and her head fell back weakly as his hands slid slowly over her body to learn her curves. "This is a mistake," she whispered.

"It doesn't feel like one." He could feel each little pucker under his fingers as his hands glided over her stomach. He wished he could take them all away and erase even the memory of pain. "I want you until I can't breathe." His lips curved. "But I already told you that."

"No, you don't." She gasped as he drew her hips firmly back against him so that she couldn't mistake his arousal pressed against her.

"How old are you again?" he teased softly, catching the rim of her ear in his teeth lightly. "That's not a cell phone in my pocket."

"You," her breath broke as his hands closed over her breasts and rubbed slowly, sending fire flicking through her veins, "you don't have pockets. You're naked."

"So are you. And you're very beautiful naked." He turned her in his arms and his hands sank into her wet hair to tilt her head back. Before she could voice the protest he sensed, he covered her mouth with his. He kissed her as deeply as he could, drinking from her wildly, his tongue tangling with hers.

She fisted her hands into his hair on a low moan and met the kiss with an equal passion. She couldn't fight any longer. She loved him, and he was her perfect mate. If she didn't hold him inside her body soon, she would go mad.

He dragged her closer with one arm and turned off the water with his free hand. Still kissing her, ravenous for her taste, he boosted her in his arms and left the shower and bathroom. She expected to find herself on the bed in her room, but to her surprise he went down the hall into his room instead. "What are you doing?"

He tumbled her down onto the bed and kissed her so deeply that her body arched helplessly toward his. "No ghosts," he muttered as he raced his lips over her face. "No bad memories, no nightmares. Nothing but us." His lips traveled the length of the scar. "Thank you," he whispered. "You gave me my brother and sister, and my baby nephew."

"Madelyne is my friend." She shuddered as the tip of his tongue once more caressed the scar. The little healing touch seemed to reach all the way to her soul. She quivered helplessly in his arms as his lips buried against the curve of her neck, right where he had said he was so interested. His teeth nipped sharply in a wolf's love bite, jerking a ragged moan from her throat.

Ravenous for her flesh, desperate to remove all bad memories, he slowly made his way down her body, his lips and tongue tracing and soothing every scar. She was wild in his arms, wonderfully free and uninhibited. He knew he was out of control, felt nothing restraining him as his teeth nipped at her hip right over the birthmark. She responded as if she had been made for him.

As his teeth nipped again, almost playfully this time, pleasure flooded her body and left her feeling clean. The cold had been banished in fire, and she reached for him eagerly. She wanted to know that wonderful body, to leave her own mark as a warning to any female who dared look at her mate.

He caught her hands and held them at her sides. "Not yet," he murmured, and closed his lips over her nipple and sucked strongly. Her response was a muffled cry, and she arched against him desperately.

He was relentless in his pursuit to drive her out of her mind. Her breath was almost a sob as she struggled to free her hands. "Stop, too much!" His hot breath washed over the sensitive skin of her inner thighs and she stopped breathing entirely. "Let me loose, you fiend!"

His husky laughter was as seductive as his touch, and his lips touched her in a thrilling caress. Her entire body shuddered. He was gentle but ruthless and drove her higher and higher until the tension shattered and left wild ecstasy behind. It wasn't enough. His grip loosened just a fraction, and she broke her hands free with a wild twist of her body that had desire gleefully stabbing through his body.

Rolling quickly, she pinned him beneath her and her hands locked with his. "I want you crazy," she muttered against his shoulder. She bit sharply, unable to control the instinct urging her to mark him as her own. He shuddered, his eyes as feral as hers as he looked up at her. Power flooded her wildly and hotly.

Hers. Even if only for a little while, he was hers.

Hungry to imprint him on her very soul, she petted and caressed him from head to heels, her lips tracing hot designs across his skin. His muscles knotted with desire, and she dazedly felt the rise of her own need. She felt drunk on him as if she couldn't get enough. A little purr of pleasure in her throat, she rose over him, her lips seeking his. Her fingers slid down his body, curled around his erection, and his control broke.

He dragged her hand up to curl around his neck and rolled swiftly to pin her. He caught her hips and dragged her up against him. Before she could catch her breath, he was sinking into her, stretching her completely, desperate to feel her pulsing around him. When he was in her to the hilt, he stopped and buried his lips against her throat to taste her pulse. Seamless, perfect. Audra. She was *his*.

She strangled a cry in her throat as his teeth closed sharply over her neck. He sucked softly on the skin to soothe it and flames licked over her nerves, making her writhe beneath him wildly. "Mel, please!"

He dragged her closer, his mouth sealing hers as he began to drive in and out of her quickly. He was going out of his mind; he would never have enough of her soon enough. The pleasure grew to unbearable heights but wouldn't end; it felt wilder and hotter than anything before. It slammed into him without warning and a low groan ripped from his chest as he surrendered to the wild ecstasy.

It was too much for her to bear, and she clung onto him as wicked waves of pleasure washed over her. His arms locked around her tighter, and she felt inside as the part of her that was the wolf, the part that had never been tamed, calmed and quieted. It brought a sense of completion and peace that she had never thought possible.

And when his body shuddered, his weight pressing her deeper to the mattress, she knew he, too, had felt the joy of finally finding his perfect match.

She didn't bother to move for a long time. She simply lay peacefully in his arms and listened to the clock tick softly in the background. He stirred finally and slowly lifted himself onto his arms. His eyes swept over her face possessively. "Hey," he said huskily, his lips feathering over her face. "You going to sleep on me?"

"Under you." Her voice was drowsy with satisfaction. "There's a difference." She found the energy to open her eyes as he shifted to lie beside her. "It wasn't a complaint." His hand moved slowly over her skin, and when it slid down to rest over the scar on her stomach, she closed her eyes. "Mel," she started, but stopped when his hand moved up to touch her lips. His thumb traced their shape and then down along her scar as if it was just another part of her body for him to caress.

"I know. I'm so sorry." He gathered her closer, his eyes closing as he thought about the unfairness in life. Someone as giving as Audra, someone who loved children so deeply, deserved a chance at children of her own.

"I've learned to accept it," she admitted softly, her hands stroking slowly over his shoulders. She turned her head and glanced at the clock. She promptly sighed and turned her face into his shoulder. "You need to get ready for class, and so do I."

"I don't wanna." He smiled down at her. "Wanna play hooky?" He kissed her softly, but the way her lips clung to his made hunger stir anew. The kiss turned carnal quickly. He eased back enough to huskily tease, "I'm not worried about my grades. I have this really good tutor. Mind you, she's kind of bitchy, but she's really hot."

She snorted lightly and twisted to pin him to the bed instead. "Who's bitchy? I'll have you know I'm a paragon of good graces." She sighed and rested against his chest. One day. She already knew how it was going to end. She could steal one day. "Oh, give me the phone," she finally sighed. "I'll call in." She tasted his pulse softly, liked it, and lingered there. "Want a hands-on lesson, kid?"

"Depends on what subject." He skimmed a knuckle down her ribcage, fascinated by her skin. She was utterly beautiful. Scars and all. There was something inside her, some purity that shined through any surface imperfection.

"Mmm. How about a time in history when women walked around half naked?"

"I like my women completely naked. And, hey, convenient, you are." He grinned as she braced herself over him. "As always, I'm glad to learn. Am I going to be graded?"

Her lips curved as they met his. "Maybe you are."

The next time she felt compelled to move, it was only because he rolled onto his back and dragged her over on top of him. He had, once more, managed to get her pinned. She was finding she really liked his dominant side. Then again, it *was* to be expected. He was her perfect match. Alpha to alpha. Male to female. At some point during the day, she was going to have to teach him how an alpha female dominated her male. He would greatly enjoy it.

Thinking about it made her realize that there were still secrets she was keeping. She couldn't tell him all of it. One of the secrets could yet make him hate her. She also could not tell him that she was his perfect mate. If she did, he would never find the will to love again. More than anything, she wanted him happy in the end. She could at the least tell him what he was, though. "Mel?"

"Hmm? Going to give me my grades now?"

Her lips curved against her will. "What's higher than an A+?"

"I'm not sure. We can invent something." He tucked his hands under his head as she slid off his chest and rose to her knees beside him. He could feel the seriousness in her mood. "Is there more you need to tell me?" he asked quietly.

"Yes." She lowered her gaze and let out a little breath. "The

Shaughnessy family . . . the first Shaughnessy I aided was a man named Kay Shaughnessy. He was the founder of the Shaughnessy Corporation."

He blinked. "That was one hundred fifty years ago."

"You remember when you asked my age? I think the proper response is roughly around one hundred eighty-nine."

"I can handle that. Older women are sexy. And you look amazing for your age." He skimmed a hand over her hip. "Is that supposed to scare me? Hell, Audra, you're a werewolf. If that doesn't scare me, nothing will."

"How about the fact that you are also a werewolf?" He went very still and she lowered her gaze. "Kay's perfect match was a young woman from 3rd District named Raven. Her blood, though thinned over the years, has given each Shaughnessy child a gift. All of you knew you had a gift. It manifested in small ways as was to be expected of thin blood. But you . . . you are different."

He let out a long breath as things finally began to make sense. "My strength and speed. My agility. The feralness inside me that you so revel in. My dominating personality and the wildness that scares most people. When did you realize?"

"When you were chasing me."

He snorted softly. "Primitive instinct, my ass!"

"It was technically true. It just happened to be primitive *wolf* instinct. You fell so naturally into the mating hunt of a wolf that it shocked me. Then when you pinned me, when you nipped at my neck, I saw your eyes." She lifted her gaze to look into those same eyes. Beautiful chocolate brown with the amber rim. "The Amber Mark. It's in your eyes, too, now. I'm surprised you didn't notice it. Only a wolf has that mark."

As she took a breath, he let his out. "And there's more."

"A little bit." She drew his hand to the birthmark on her hip. "This is the mark of an alpha. I am an alpha female wolf. It means I am the strongest and fastest of all female wolves born. I am the leader of all female wolves should there be any others. There is only ever one alpha per gender per generation for the clan."

His eyes slowly widened. "I don't have a mark."

"Yes, you do. It's on your back shoulder. I saw it the other night. It is the proof that you are an alpha male werewolf. Given enough pressure, you will change into the wolf for the first time. After that, you will be in control."

There were dozens of things he could have said. He could see she was waiting for rejection or fear, but all he felt was a curious sense of understanding. "It makes sense," he finally said, "of everything about me. Everything about you and me. The way we come together." A flustered look suddenly crossed his face. "I bit you."

She lowered her lashes to hide a smile. "Repeatedly. And have you noticed you're a bit, hmm, dominating, shall we say, with me? It's the alpha instinct. You have to be on top. Especially of me, because you *know* instinctively that I could take control."

He reached out and tumbled her onto his chest once more. "Any time you want to return the favor," he tugged her down so that he could feather his lips over her neck, "feel free. I think I can handle letting you take charge. You being so much older and wiser."

As his lips found hers, she let herself sink into him. Tears burned her eyes but never fell. He might never love her, but he accepted her. He wanted her. She could do nothing but give him everything. As Rhianna had said, it meant there would be no regrets.

She wanted to regret nothing about him.

CHAPTER THIRTY

Friday was midterms for Mel's classes. Audra had given her midterms the day before so she stayed home while he went to school. It was one of the hardest things he had ever done to leave her sleeping in his bed. He had grown addicted to the way she felt and tasted, to the way her scent always seemed so *right*. And as a lover . . . as a lover, she was something else.

She was as wild and free as he was, unafraid of the volatile passion that exploded between them. No matter how out of control he got, she matched him. He didn't have to fear hurting her. He didn't have to fear that whatever was inside him would terrify her. He was, however, a little wary to see what reactions he got at school. He felt different. He was different.

It was a visible difference. Males and females alike watched him a little warily when he approached. Once he spoke to them, showed he was the same Mel, they relaxed and the wariness went away. Mostly. The wolf inside him was close under the surface and humans were instinctively attuned to predators.

It made him realize just how long and lonely Audra's life had been. It was little wonder she had spent so much time as a wolf with his family. They loved her unconditionally. She still didn't talk about herself, but he knew he had all the time in the world to get her to open up. He had moved her into his room with him, and she hadn't had another nightmare since.

All his midterms were in the morning. He actually liked it that way because it meant he could go home early. He had a rather cranky alpha female who would be waiting impatiently to hear the results of her hard work. Even being lovers hadn't stopped her from shoving as much information in his head as possible. He kinda suspected it was making her *more* determined. She had a bigger interest in his well-being now.

The first class for the day was Japanese. It was clutch time, do or die. He finished his paper well ahead of the rest of the class and could only sweat out the results. When the teacher walked past his desk and placed his test on it upside down, he almost didn't want to look. He carefully peeked up the edge and a cheerful 'A-' at the top seemed to stare up at him. He looked up in shock and found Nobunaga smiling at him.

An A. Him, Mel Shaughnessy, with an A. It nearly made him giddy. It also drove him to do his best in all his classes. With every A or B, his spirit rose. It couldn't even be diminished when he got a C in Geography. He *hated* Geography, no matter how many cities and states and countries he was forcefully fed.

He had borrowed Audra's motorcycle to get to school, and on the way home, he stopped to buy a bouquet of flowers. A little spring was in his step as he entered the house. "Audra, I'm home! Guess what?"

There was no response. With a frown, he dropped his bag by the door and climbed the stairs. "Audra?" To his surprise, he found her curled in a miserable heap on his bed. She was coughing weakly as if she didn't have the strength for anything else. "Audra. It's okay, baby." He walked over and sat beside her to gently press his hand to her forehead. She was burning up. "Got yourself a bug, did you?"

"Yes. Go away." She jerked the covers over her head, cranky and miserable. They were immediately jerked down again and a shiver roughened her skin. "I'm cold," she complained.

"You've got a really high fever." He scooped her up into his arms and carried her down to the bathroom. He ran lukewarm water in the tub and gently stripped off the borrowed shirt she wore. "Thief," he teased gently. "That's my best shirt."

"It was there. It smelled like you." She let her head drop onto his shoulder.

"It looks better on you than on me." He gently lifted her into

the tub and felt his heart ache when she bit back a whimper of pain. "I know, honey." He gently began to wash her, soothing her heated skin with a soft sponge. "Why didn't you say you were sick?"

"I didn't know until I woke up." She leaned weakly against his shoulder. She couldn't tell him, had no way of explaining, what was truly happening. Her body was beginning the process that would end her contract with the Enforcers. It felt so good to be taken care of, so wonderful to have him caring for her. She could only revel in his tenderness.

He gently lifted her out of the tub and held her steady as he dried her. Her skin was already cooler and she wasn't shivering violently anymore. He gently tucked her back into the shirt and carried her back to their bedroom. As he slid her under the covers, he asked, "Do you feel well enough for some good news?"

"Good news is always welcome." Her eyes had fallen half closed but they opened again as she saw the flowers he was holding out. Her heart thumped painfully. Only the children had ever given her flowers before. "For me? What for?"

"You're one badass tutor, Professor Alexandrios." He grinned at her. "Guess who aced his midterms."

She began to smile. "You did? That's wonderful. Now you won't have to worry about your graduation at all." Tears burned her eyes suddenly as she realized she wouldn't be there for it. "I'm . . . really happy." She turned her face into his shoulder and held onto him with a desperate sort of strength. "Sorry."

"You don't feel good. You're entitled." He tucked her in securely. "I get to pamper you for a while now," he informed her gravely. "You're going to have to lie there and take it like a good little wolf." To take the sting out of the words, he leaned over to steal a kiss. "And if I get sick, you can boss me around."

"I don't need an excuse." She didn't argue as she laid there and watched him tidy up the room. His presence was so soft and comforting that she felt herself sliding toward sleep. She would always cherish how safe he had made her feel. How wanted. With a little sigh, she curled up and fell asleep.

He glanced over and a smile softened his face as he walked over to sit beside her. He gently brushed the hair back from her face, his fingers smoothing down her cheek. He didn't like seeing her sick, but he liked being able to take care of her, especially because no one else had. He wouldn't mind doing it for the rest of his life.

His hand froze as he realized where his thoughts had gone. A little breath shuddered out his lips. Well. That was unexpected. He was in love with her.

He began to smile. Truthfully, it wasn't so unexpected. Stormy had attached herself to him with the intent of finding him true love, and she had done exactly that. It just happened to be her personally. But, really, even the logical part of his brain could understand why. Who would suit an alpha male wolf better than an alpha female wolf, and vice versa?

She might not believe him but he was determined to convince her and make her stay with him. When she went home with him, as she damned well would, she would not go home as a pet. She would go as his lover and future wife. Wolves mated for life, and it was time she truly claimed the place in their family that she had always owned.

He started to reach for her shoulder to wake her and tell her, but the phone rang and startled him. He quickly grabbed it before it could wake her. "Alexandrios residence."

"Mel!" It was Taegan, and there was a trace of panic in his voice. "Thank god! We've been trying to call you all morning but your cell was off!" He drew a ragged breath. "You have to come to the hospital. Dad's had a heart attack. He's in surgery right now. We don't know how bad it is."

The color drained from his face. "Oh, shit. Okay, yeah, I'm on my way! I'll be right there." He hung up the phone and turned to look at Audra. She was in no shape to go anywhere, but she would understand. He would just come back on Saturday after he was sure Sullivan would be fine. That he would be fine was not up for debate in his mind.

He wrote her a note and packed his things. He wasn't leaving them there. When he came back tomorrow, he was going to convince

her to come home with him where she had always belonged. She needed family, and the Shaughnessys were the only one for her. His siblings and his dad would love her true self even more than they had loved her as a wolf.

That done, he called for the family chauffeur. He needed to get to the hospital and refused to wait for a cab. There was no way he was going to lose his father.

When Audra awoke not long later, she knew she was alone in the house. She carefully got out of bed and walked on rubbery legs to where she could see a note sitting on the dresser. The room, she noticed, carried no sign of Mel except for the shirt she still wore.

The note was short and simple. *'Dad's in the hospital. I'll be back tomorrow afternoon if everything's okay. Get some rest.'*

Tears slowly welled up in her eyes and slid down her cheeks. Gathering all her strength, she went into her bedroom and simply pulled on jeans under his shirt; she couldn't bear to let go of that tiny connection to him. It was all she had left. She picked up the phone and began to make calls. She had been planning for this for so long that everything was done on automatic.

When Mel got to the emergency room, he saw his entire family was already there. Aenya was on Hiro's lap, sobbing in his shoulder, and Taegan was pacing like a caged animal. Kalliope was curled up on her chair, her face streaked with tears, and Kienan was holding Madelyne. Mel's stomach clenched. "Is he okay? Do we know anything?" he asked.

Taegan shook his head. "Not yet. It caught us all off guard. He

was arguing with Kienan about something, like always, then he suddenly went gray and collapsed. The paramedics think Kienan doing CPR saved his life, but we don't know that yet for certain."

"Stupid old man," Kienan said roughly. "The doctors told him to watch his heart!" Tears slid slowly down his face. "He can't die. He's too young to die."

It was close to ten o'clock that night before the doctor came to them. He surveyed the drawn faces in the room then looked at Taegan who was clearly the eldest. "He'll make it," he announced.

Taegan sagged against the wall as Kalliope gave a little cry and flew into his arms. Kienan and Madelyne nearly fell out of their shared chair. Aenya just cried harder, this time in relief, as she clung to Hiro. He held her tighter, his face as raggedly relieved as the rest. Mel felt so lightheaded so fast that he had to hastily sit down.

"How is he?" Taegan asked. He held onto Kalliope with all his strength, his entire body shaking.

"We had to do a bypass since one of the arteries was completely clogged. A stent took care of the other one." The doctor checked his notes. "He had a lower than average vitamin count and his iron was borderline. His blood pressure bottomed out at one point but we got him back." He let out a little breath, exhausted to his core. "We're going to keep him in CICU overnight. If he's doing this well tomorrow morning, we can probably move him to a regular room." He found a smile. "Go home and sleep, kids. He's not ready to give up yet."

"He's going to make it," Mel repeated softly as the doctor walked out. "Thank god." He raked his hands through his hair, already thinking of everything that needed doing. The most important thing on his list was calling his lover. "I should tell Audra as soon as I can."

All eyes swung toward him. They had all noticed the difference inside him but there really hadn't been a time to say anything about it. Naturally, it was Kalliope who went right to the point. "You're in love with Professor Alexandrios."

"Yeah." His smile softened. "She matches me in every way. I love her so much, guys. If I've ever made fun of you, you have my utmost apologies right now."

"Accepted," Kienan said promptly. He found a grin. "I never believed she was that bad a person." He felt the trembling in Madelyne's body and frowned as he held her tighter. "What's wrong, nightingale?"

"Did you tell her?" she demanded of Mel.

"No, not yet. I was going to, but she was asleep." She leapt to her feet and rushed into the bathroom, and he rubbed the back of his neck in confusion. Her mood swings lately had been just flat out strange. "Does anyone know what the hell is wrong with her?"

"Impending motherhood?" Kienan offered, but he was frowning at the bathroom door. "Aenya, Kally . . ."

"We're on it." Kalliope was already heading for the bathroom with Aenya on her heels. "You! Maddie! Talk, damn it!" They disappeared into the bathroom and the door swung behind them.

Mel didn't wait to find out whether or not anyone found out what was wrong with Madelyne. They all decided to go home, and he was the only one who didn't need to wait for one of the women, so he left by himself. The chauffeur was more than happy to pick him up, and he was just as relieved to hear that Sullivan would be fine.

It wasn't until Mel was standing in his bedroom that he realized how lonely it seemed without Audra. His bed was big, but he missed having her wrapped around him like a breathing blanket. She had a tendency to wiggle on top of him and sleep draped over him. It was very cold without her warmth. He needed to bring her home, and soon. She had always belonged to him and he to her, but they had never known. Knowing it now, he refused to waste more time.

Sullivan was moved into a regular room Saturday afternoon, and everyone took turns visiting him in the hospital. Mel went last and made sure he brought his midterms with him. He was fairly sure where the conversation was going to go.

He started it by walking in the room and saying, "If you wanted to hit on pretty nurses, there are better ways of going about it, Dad."

Sullivan smiled wryly and moved his bed enough he could sit up slightly. "Well, I hardly intended to do it." He fumbled slightly as Mel hugged him. It had been a long time since his boys had hugged him. "Stop that. The women were bad enough."

Mel pulled over the visitor's chair and sat with a smile. "Kally is going to make you miserable. She's already planning a meal schedule, and Maddie is helping find tasty but healthy alternatives to the things you dislike. God help you now, Dad."

"Maybe they can keep me here longer," he agreed on a grimace. He loved Kalliope but she was hell on wheels just like the rest of his kids.

"You wish," his son retorted dryly.

Silence fell for a few moments as Sullivan gathered his thoughts. He finally sighed softly. "Mel, I'm going to be retiring when you graduate. This has seriously made me realize my mortality, and I'm ready to turn the reigns over to you and focus on being a grandfather. And, of course, until I'm out of here, I'm counting on you to handle things at the company."

"Absolutely. If it makes you feel any better, by the way," he dropped his midterms on Sullivan's lap, "take a look. I graduate in the spring, as planned."

Sullivan felt his recently battered heart swell with delight and relief. "Mel, I'm so proud of you." He cleared his throat slightly and tried to find a subtle way to ask. "Is there . . . you know, anything else you'd like to tell me?"

Mel laughed. "Don't be subtle. Yes, there's something else. I've decided to get married."

"Wait, call it a hunch . . . the tutor?"

"Good hunch." He tried to find a way to explain. "Audra is a werewolf, Dad," he finally said. "And she's been . . . rather involved in our lives, if you take my meaning. Stormy won't come home if I bring Audra."

It took Sullivan a second to understand. "I see." He cleared his throat. "Well." A werewolf. Well, Madelyne wasn't human either, so he could take it in stride. It was just a little unnerving to think that a wolf he had called a pet at one point was about to be his daughter-in-law. "How does she feel about things?"

"She's hurt. Badly. Or rather, she's been hurt. I don't know the details, but her entire body is riddled with scars. It's made people turn her away, and made them turn away in revulsion." He lifted his gaze, his eyes stark. "But I love her. No matter how rude and brash she is, I love her. Her heart . . . if you get close enough to her, her heart shines through it all. She's so beautiful inside."

"Then why haven't you brought her to me, boy? Go and find her and bring her to me so I can meet her properly." He watched intently as Mel left the room. His stomach was tight with dread. Just before he'd had the attack, he had been looking at the contract. It had been flashing red, but the word hadn't been 'Complete.' It had been 'Void.' Something was wrong.

Something was very wrong, Mel realized when he arrived at Audra's house. Her motorcycle was gone, and the curtains were drawn in every window. His mouth dry with fear, he ran up the stairs and unlocked the door to rush into the house. "Audra!"

In growing shock, he looked around the room at all the sheets that covered every piece of furniture. He raced up the stairs and found more of the same. There was no sign that she was there or had ever been there. She was gone.

His heart shattering in his chest, he slowly sank down to sit on the steps and wondered what the hell was going on. She had been sick, so how could she have done all this? And why? She knew he was coming back. What the hell was going on around here?!

His cell phone startled him by ringing loudly in the silence, and he slowly pulled it out of his pocket. He didn't know the number but still answered. "Shaughnessy."

"My name is Rhianna Taber. We've never met," a woman's voice said quietly, "but I work with your father, and soon I will be working with you. I need you to come to Enforcers' Headquarters. Immediately. Bring your contract when you do. This is, literally, a matter of life and death."

His heart began to pound dully in his chest. "Whose?" he managed to ask.

"Audra Alexandrios'."

CHAPTER THIRTY-ONE

There was a guard waiting at the doors of the Enforcers when Mel arrived. The guard escorted him to the elevator and rode with him all the way to the top floor. "Second door," he said and then left him alone on the floor.

Mel headed quickly down the hall and opened the second door. "Ms. Taber?" To his utter shock, he found himself looking at Kate Willowby. "Kate?!"

"Not exactly." She reached up and pressed the blue earring she wore. Her image wavered, shifted, and then splintered. It left behind a woman with rich red hair and deep black eyes. She wore a blue visor that she removed and tossed onto a chair. "A modern variation on the Mask of Illusions that your brother borrowed. You needed a push, so I gave it."

He sagged against the door as she went around behind the desk and sat down. "I'm afraid I don't understand."

Rhianna folded her hands on her desk and inclined her head at the free chair. "Sit down. There's not much time left." When he had complied, she studied him with eyes that were haunted. "May I see your contract?" He handed it over and she studied it intently. Her stomach rolled threateningly. "I see." She took a deep breath and reached into a drawer. She pulled out a scroll and passed it across to him. "This is the contract Audra Alexandrios has with Enforcers. It completes tonight, at midnight."

He didn't open the scroll. His fingers were shaking too hard. He simply put it on the desk again. "And?" Try as he might, his voice still shook. Terror choked him. Something inside howled in pain and denial. "What is all this? What is Audra? What happened to her? Why was she with my family? Ms. Taber, please tell me!"

She pressed her fingers to the bridge of her nose. "Little over one hundred and fifty years ago, there was a clan of werewolves living here in 3rd District. Audra was one of them. She was, beyond a doubt, their greatest warrior and most beloved member. She had a full family with six younger siblings. Kalin, the eldest, was her partner on the hunt."

So that was Kalin. "What happened?"

"A raid was raised by humans and they went into the forests that used to be nearby, the place where the clan lived. It was a slaughter. A massacre. Audra led the defenses, but even she can't outrun bullets. By the time she had killed the enemy, her entire clan was decimated.

"The house where she lives? It had been her family's home. She returned there, but it was in shambles. I'm sure you've seen the marks that remain. The blood and death . . . it was horrendous. The children of the village had been hidden there, and she went to find them. Unfortunately, a human had found them first. They were all dead. Kalin died in her arms not long after."

He closed his eyes as he thought of the screams in the walls and Audra's nightmares. Rhianna didn't look up, the story pouring out of her as if she had been holding it too long. "Audra went mad. Vowed vengeance on the humans who had arranged the slaughter. Among those she attacked was a Shaughnessy, one of your ancestors. She killed both husband and wife, and she was going to kill the child as well when soldiers caught her. They were going to kill her then and there but Enforcers stepped in.

"She could have been justified in her actions except that she had acted blindly. The Shaughnessys had been innocent. So, in an effort to stave off her execution, Enforcers offered a contract. She would stay with the family for as long as it took to make one hundred Shaughnessy children find love. A clock started from the day your ancestor came of age. She would have one hundred and fifty years to help his descendants, and if she could, she would be free of her execution. If not . . ."

"She dies." His voice was as stark as his eyes as he leaned forward urgently. "You said her contract completes tonight at midnight. You mean she's failed?"

"You're the hundredth," she said simply.

"But I love *her*. Doesn't that count for anything?" he shouted as he leapt to his feet.

Her composure cracked and she shot to her feet as well. "No!" she shouted back. "Feeling it isn't enough! You have to tell her! The words only have power if you say them! Audra loves you more than you know! She would be furious if she knew I had told you any of this now!"

"I have to find her!" He flattened his hands on the desk. "You have to tell me where she is!"

"I've looked! I can't find her anywhere!" She let out a ragged breath and drew a letter out of her desk. "She told me to give this to you tomorrow. I'm giving it to you now. Please, Mel. For the love of Zeus, help her. I've done all I can. You're the only one who can find her now!"

He took the letter and opened it quickly. He had recognized Audra's handwriting instantly. His hands shaking, he pulled out his glasses so he could read.

Mel,

If you're reading this, I'm gone. I'm sorry. I'm so sorry. I should have told you, but I didn't want you to feel obligated. It would have been so simple if you'd been anything but the wonderful man you are. I fell in love with you. You wondered why Stormy couldn't match you. It's because 'Stormy' let herself get involved.

I'm a werewolf. I was bound to protect your family and took the wolf's form to do it. Don't hate me, please. If I hadn't fallen for you, it would never have mattered. But I did. You're so unique, Mel. You're a human who is truly a werewolf. If you let yourself, you'll be able to access all of the skills that are yours by rights. You'll need to change under pressure the first time to gain control of your wolf form. When you feel it rise inside, just reach for it. It's that easy. I know you'll be fine. You have more strength and courage than any man I have ever known.

Remember me when the moon is full. And remember that I love you.

P.S. Study, damn it. Don't waste my hard work!

Tears slowly slid down his cheeks. Classic Audra. He folded the letter to tuck it safely in his pocket. "What time is it?" he demanded.

"Six."

"Only six hours," he whispered. "You have my cell number," he shouted as he ran toward the door. "Call me if you hear anything! I'm going to find her if it's the last thing I ever do!"

He tore the city apart in his quest to find her, but no matter where he went, who he asked, the response was always the same. No one had seen her. No one knew who she was. It was as if she had never existed. Yet Mel, with his sharpened senses growing slowly sharper, recognized the signs of compulsion. She *had* been through; she was erasing her presence.

Something inside had stirred and was raging. He was a werewolf. Her scent was seared inside him. Alpha to alpha. He reached without hesitation for that something inside and let it take him. It took only a moment to change to the shape of the wolf. It was a welcome and comforting change, familiar and warm.

His nose was thousands of times more acute in that form. He rushed through the city tracking her scent, seeking her with the single-minded determination of a mated male. In the end, he only found himself back at her home. It was where her scent ended and began. He shifted back and went inside, but she still was not there.

It was close to midnight and despair wrenched his heart and soul. He climbed the stairs to her bedroom and sat on the side of the bed as the walls cried their grief. Helplessly, his gaze sought the clock and the time.

11:55.

His eyes closed on a wave of pain, but a sound made him instantly look up. To his shock, he saw a young boy standing in the doorway. He was insubstantial and pale, and Mel realized in disbelief that he had to be staring at a ghost. The boy had Audra's eyes.

"Kalin?" he whispered.

The boy nodded and ran out of the room. Mel raced after him and followed him down to the living room. The boy pointed at the floor, and he began to pull up the torn carpet. "Of course," he muttered. "They hid the children here!"

The carpet came up and revealed a trapdoor. He yanked it up and descended the stairs as quickly as he could. He rushed down the cold hallway toward where he could see a spot of moonlight ahead of him. His mate's scent was rich and strong down there, summoning him to her side. He burst into the underground room and felt the walls scream.

Audra stood by a window that faced the full moon in the sky. She was pale and visibly weak but she was alive. "Audra," he managed to whisper.

Her head swung toward him in shock. "Mel!" Coughing wracked her body and she lost her hold on the window. He caught her before she fell on the floor, and she closed her eyes helplessly. "I didn't want you to see me like this!"

"Why didn't you tell me?" he demanded roughly.

"You deserve more than me. I killed your ancestors." Her eyes closed as tears spilled down her cheeks. "Innocent blood is on my hands. You deserve so much more! A woman who is whole, who is worthy of you!"

He heard in the distance as a clock began to toll the hour and desperately clutched her closer. "No!" he shouted. "No! I don't want anyone else! I love you, Audra Alexandrios! I don't care what you look like or what you've done! *I love you*!"

The bell stopped tolling midnight and she was motionless in his arms. Gut wrenching pain boiled up, and he lowered his head as sobs shook his body. It had never mattered. Nothing else had ever mattered. All he had ever wanted was her all along, and he hadn't known until too late!

A sudden light startled him, and he straightened up quickly as her entire body began to glow. Before his stunned eyes, the scars that marked her body began to glow with light one by one and disappear.

He began to count them as they disappeared, and as the last scar, the one across her face, began to glow, he realized that she had been bearing exactly one hundred scars. The same number of Shaughnessys she had helped to find love.

The glow faded and he held his breath as he prayed to every deity he knew. She drew a sudden sharp breath, as if her lungs had been too long without air, and her eyes opened. She stared up at him without comprehension for long moments and then slowly lifted a hand to touch her face. "The scars," she whispered. "They're gone."

"I never saw them." He framed her face with his hand. "I love you, Audra. Werewolf, huntress or," his lips curved, "faerie godmother. I don't care. I love you exactly as you are."

Tears slowly slid down her cheeks as she wrapped her arms around his shoulders. "I love you too," she whispered, and she saw over his shoulder the young boy watching them from the stairs. *Thank you, Kalin*, she thought. *Goodbye.*

The spirit lifted a hand in farewell as he disappeared. And, as he did, the walls slowly stopped screaming as if all those who were gone were finally able to rest.

EPILOGUE

Rhianna sat in her office and stared pensively at the two contracts before her as she heard the clock slowly tolling its merciless melody outside her window. Both contracts flickered . . . and the word 'Complete' appeared across both of them.

The first laugh startled her as it slipped through her lips. It continued as she scrawled notes across the bottom of both contracts and slid them into a folder that glowed softly as the word 'Complete' appeared. She opened her drawer, slid the folder inside, and closed it. It only belatedly dawned on her that she was laughing *and* crying. She leapt to her feet joyously. "Riku!" she called to the office next to hers. "Get out a bottle of champagne!"

"Hot damn!" was the response. "Are we celebrating what I hope we are?"

"Damn right! Hurry up!" She knelt and locked the drawer beside her, her heart swelling happily as the drawer sealed itself and the word 'Finished' appeared across the front in bold red letters. Yes, the Shaughnessy File *was* good and finished.

She caught movement from the corner of her eye and stood to look. Her gaze softened as she saw the ghost standing inside the window. "Thank you," she said softly. "I owe you one, Kalin."

The little boy just smiled and waved a hand before disappearing into the waning moonlight. She watched him go and then turned with her hands on her hips to demand, "Where's my champagne?"

Status: File Complete
Analysis: The beauty wins the beast when the beast shows the beauty inside.

*Turn the page for a bonus story about the first Shaughnessy, and for
a peek into another world . . .*

Bonus Folder
KAY

CHAPTER ONE

A little over one hundred and fifty years ago, America was entering an industrial revolution following the end of a bitter civil war. Inside New York, a second revolution was also occurring. It was a revolution of religion. Sides split and formed their own new units. And, caught in the middle, used as cannon fodder by the insanely fanatic who chose neither side, was the 3rd District in New York City.

The massacre took place in the dead of the night. Humans armed with weapons of all kinds plunged into the woods near the District and laid to waste the entire werewolf clan that had called the trees home. Men, women, and children were thoughtlessly slaughtered. Viewed as unspeakable, horrific, and inhuman, innocent blood was spilled. Only one werewolf survived.

The leaders and protectors of the 3rd District, the Enforcers, were enraged. Rhianna Taber's displeasure was felt when her powers erected an impenetrable barrier around her District. Eric Mason's fury was felt when his elemental powers ripped a river from its bed and sent it tearing through the homes of the murderers.

Rhianna and Eric were co-owners, partners, and best friends. They worked in tandem without thought, often by thought alone, and shared a single-minded determination to protect their people. When they heard that the surviving werewolf had attacked the Shaughnessy family, the Enforcers were quick to act. They argued her case before the governor himself, and then even to the President. Both distinguished gentlemen considered Eric and Rhianna friends. The werewolf's sentence was commuted so long as the Enforcers took her on. They agreed.

A new law was signed shortly thereafter by the governor. If any

ever dared to harm a single denizen of 3rd District, they would be immediately arrested and brought before the Supreme Court. An uneasy sort of acceptance began as the 'normal' people came to grips with the unique beings within 3rd District. The people of 3rd District accepted the tentative truce, but they always watched warily when a stranger arrived.

There was one woman in particular who was truly terrified. Some people who were 3rd District born, like her, were finding their marriages annulled for every reason possible so that the person they were wed to didn't find themselves attached to the stigma. This woman held a very, very powerful position and was very well cared for. She was also pregnant.

She feared that if her husband learned she was 3rd District born, he would strip her of her position. And what would he do if he found out his child was therefore also an 'unusual'? Out of fear for her own security, she fled out of the city to the mountains by professing a fear of losing her child.

When the child was born, it was a lovely little girl. Her eyes and hair were pitch black, strong evidence of her paternal bloodline. Her mother despised her, for the child also had a small wave birthmark over her hip that declared her maternal water elf bloodline. If that mark had been gone . . . her mother would have never needed to worry.

The mother stood at the window with her child in her hands and considered hurling her to the ground and killing her. Only a fear of retribution for murder made her hesitate.

"I wish . . . I wish you'd turn into a raven and fly away!" she shouted.

To her shock, the child began to glow. She turned into the shape of a baby raven and flew away out the window on a mournful cry. The mother was fearful at first, afraid the child would die and she would be a murderess, but then she told herself that it was out of her hands. Anything that befell the child now would not be her fault.

Hugging the information close, she returned to her husband and tearfully told him the child had died in childbirth. He believed her, and she felt no fear for her position. Unfortunately, or perhaps fortunately, it turned out that life itself did not look kindly on what had occurred. She discovered very shortly that she would have no other children.

The raven flew and flew, crying the whole time. Rhianna Taber heard the cries and went looking for the child, wondering what was causing it to be so afraid. When she found her, she knew. She took the baby home personally and tried to determine what she should do next. It was her partner's suggestion to form a contract for her to hopefully dispel at least some of the curse. She agreed, and the child became known as Raven Childrose.

Over the next few years, the people of the state learned to be more lenient with the 3rd District. It was still a slightly uneasy truce, but the hostility had dimmed. Most were certain that within a short amount of time no one would even remember the coup at all. Rhianna personally knew that by the time a century was past, no one would even know the 3rd District was more than a rumor.

Indeed, only a handful of people remembered the coup by the time summer rolled around nineteen years later. Even the young survivor of the Shaughnessy family, now twenty-one, had trouble remembering. It was to his advantage in some ways, most thought. What person would want to remember something so terrifying?

Kay Shaughnessy didn't find it to be terrifying. He had no memories of his parents, so he couldn't miss them. And he certainly had no memories of the werewolf that had tried to eat him, so he had no reason to be afraid of wolves. In fact, his dearest friend was a wolf and always by his side. He called her Stormy.

As he tended to the repairs of his small boat, he glanced over to the side where Stormy was lying in the sunlight. She seemed to be asleep, but he knew better. He smiled. "You always look so lazy," he told her. He always talked to her as if she understood. It made him feel less lonely. "If a cat ran by you *might* be stirred to action, but only then."

Her tail thumped on the ground in agreement and she opened one eye to regard him. He turned back to what he was doing and

ignored the sweat rolling down his face and back. It was sweltering hot, but if he went home without repairing the crack, then his adopted father would beat him.

It didn't take too much to set him off, as it never had over the course of his life. His 'parents' had taken him in on the premise that they hated the idea of a child being without a family, but within the first two years of his life they had squandered his family's money and begun treating him little better than a slave. By the time he was ten they had progressed to forcing him to work for his keep, beating him whenever he didn't make the 'proper' amount.

Now at twenty-one, he was indebted to them. He couldn't go to school and learn a trade, and he could not make enough money to pay back what they declared was his fair amount. Some nights he wished to simply curl up and die.

He felt a nudge at his elbow and looked down to see Stormy sitting beside him. She had the bucket of water. He gratefully put the tools down to lift the dipper and take a drink. He never asked how she did things like that. He simply believed in the magic.

As he stared at his reflection in the water, he said softly, "There are days when I wish that werewolf had eaten me."

She huffed softly. He smiled and ran his hands through her fur. "I know. Then you'd be alone. I guess if we're going to be alone, at least we're alone together." He hugged her tight for a moment before turning back to his task. A leaky boat was a disaster waiting to happen with his job.

He ferried people up and down the river to take them wherever they needed for a few coins. Some people even gave him tips because they liked his handsome face with its white-blond hair and brown eyes. His soft Irish accent claimed he was of immigrant blood, but he was kind and friendly, and people admired him regardless.

It took him an hour, but the boat was finally repaired, and he was able to get underway again. He wore a hat to shield his eyes from the harsh glare of the river, and his clothes were sturdy even if they weren't in the best of condition. Many a head was shaken over the sad state of the Shaughnessy heir.

It was mid-morning, and he had a full day of sailing ahead. He set out immediately with Stormy riding along as both mascot and protector. Some of the types who got on the boat were questionable, but a single look at her exceptionally sharp teeth made them behave properly.

By the time evening came around, his bag of money felt refreshingly full. He began to sail his way home and watched the moon rising in the distance. It was cool and peaceful, and he felt his shoulders begin to relax a little.

As he approached a bridge, he saw, much to his surprise, a young woman sitting on the rail and staring into the distance. Her hair shined ebony black in the moonlight with silvery highlights. He couldn't guess at the color of the dress she wore, but it looked pale with cherry blossoms scattered across it.

A shiver went down his back. "A ghost?" he whispered, and he heard Stormy snort softly. He glanced at her with a smile. "Well, she might be."

He realized shortly that she wasn't a ghost when a couple of men crossing the bridge began to harass her. He couldn't hear their words, but her body language said she was frightened. He began to frown as he got off on the shore and tied his boat. His motions were automatic, and his eyes were on the scene.

One of the men suddenly made a grab for the girl, and she jerked backwards instinctively. Her feet slipped off the edge of the bridge, and she fell into the river with a little shriek. The men ran off, and Kay swiftly raced to the shore and dove in. It wasn't hard to find her under the water with her pale clothes, but she wasn't strong enough to kick to the surface with all the material weighing her down.

He seized her under the arms and propelled them both to the surface. "Are you okay?" he asked urgently.

She clung to his shoulder with one hand and used her other to sling her wet, and now unbound, hair out of her eyes. "Yes. I'm dreadfully sorry about this. I can't swim," she apologized. "My foster mother said learning to swim would interfere with my destiny."

"I'd like to know how." He was exceptionally strong from his years on the river, and he found it easy to carry them both back to the shore. They staggered out of the water and then collapsed onto the grass.

Both were silent for a moment before she gave a muffled giggle. He tried to hide it, but he snickered. It took only a moment to have them both laughing, and he pushed himself up into a sitting position. "Well, that was certainly the most interesting way I've ever ended a day." He smiled, and it was a swift and devastating curve of his lips that fluttered the pulse of all the females he had ever met. It was all the more lethal because he didn't have a clue about its impact. "Shall I take you home?"

"Oh, no." She shook her head swiftly and stung her cheeks with her wet hair. With a sigh, she caught two handfuls and began to wring out the river water. "I will be fine, I promise." She gave a little grimace. "If I can just get some of this water out first. I look like a wet dog."

He tried not to stare, really he did. He couldn't help it though. Even though it was night, the moon was full and the light was strong. He could see that his 'ghost' was not only almost unbearably lovely in her features, but her dress also molded to her body like a second skin. He could see every curve, and every curve was worth seeing. "I've never seen a wet dog look like you," he admitted honestly, and then felt his cheeks warm. "That is . . ."

She gave a little cough, her cheeks darkening in a way that indicated she, too, was blushing. "Thank you, I think." She got to her feet and blinked as she realized she could feel the grass. She looked down and frowned. "I lost my shoes."

He opened his mouth to offer to go find them when his wolf—his very wet wolf—suddenly sat between them and dropped the shoes on the ground. "Stormy!" He stared for a moment, then, with characteristic humor, said, "This is a wet dog. She is not to be confused with you."

The girl giggled softly as she took her shoes and carefully put them on. Stormy, with a touch of indignity, shook herself enthusiastically and sprayed fresh river water everywhere. Kay laughed as he got to his feet. "Alright, alright! I know when I'm beaten! Ladies always stick together, don't they?"

The girl smiled. "I wouldn't call myself a lady."

He looked at her in surprise. "I would."

"Thank you, I think." She reached out and took one of his hands. She turned it over to place some coins there. "This is for rescuing me." When he started to protest, she shook her head quickly. "No, I want to. You're a good man, Kay Shaughnessy."

He frowned. "How did you know my name?"

She smiled. "Just because everyone does." She hesitated for a moment before rising on her toes and kissing his cheek. "Thank you again." She gave him a graceful curtsey. "You make an incredible hero."

He touched his cheek with his free hand and looked down at his hand to discover he was holding several dollars. Shocked, he jerked his head up. "Wait!" he said quickly, but he was not entirely surprised to realize she had disappeared into the moonlight.

At first, he didn't want to accept such a gift, but then he realized how late it was and that his father would be horribly furious. The money might allow him to escape intact. Holding his breath, he hurried up through the streets and back toward the farm where he lived. Not to his surprise, his adopted father Richard Johnston was standing on the steps in an aggressive stance.

Kay quickly dropped to his knees. "Please! I know I am late, but I was escorting a high-class lady to her home after she had a mishap on the river. She paid me well!"

"Really." Richard's tone could only be called menacing. "Then where is the money?"

Kay tossed the bag to him and it landed at his feet. As he sorted through the funds, Kay held his breath. He was praying, praying with everything he was, that this time he would be okay and would make it through.

Richard gave a little grunt. "This seems to be more than enough. There are scraps in the barn waiting for you." He went back into the house and slammed the door hard enough that the entire structure rattled.

Kay's breath unraveled slowly. Stormy whined and nuzzled him, and he wrapped his arms around her neck tightly. "We're okay," he whispered. "We'll be okay this time. Are you hungry? I am."

He got to his feet and hurried to the barn that he called home. He found the plate of scraps near the lantern, and it had been covered to keep out bugs. For that he was dimly grateful. He could only assume they didn't want him getting sick because it meant he could not work.

He carried the plate with him as he climbed into the loft. Stormy was very agile and followed him up the ladder despite the sharp angle. He always made sure her bed was aired, and he fluffed the straw for her with a smile. "There. Fit for a queen."

He only had two different changes of clothes, so he took off his still wet clothing and put on the dry ones. He could hang the wet ones to dry overnight. He picked through the scraps to find the edible ones and made sure that he and Stormy both had a share. She almost balked, but since he wouldn't eat until she did, she reluctantly gave in.

Finally, exhausted, he curled up on his bed of hay and straw and went to sleep. He had a tattered blanket to cover him but he fell asleep before reaching for it. Instead, a woman with yellow eyes gently tucked it around him and brushed his hair from his eyes. He was hers to protect, by god, and protect him she would.

Now she needed only to figure out how to arrange his happiness as well.

CHAPTER TWO

Kay's days were always the same. He would wake early in the morning and go down to the pump to get cold water to wash his face. Sometimes another plate of scraps would be sitting on the back porch. Whenever it wasn't, he would go into the city early and ferry a food merchant down river as a payment for some breakfast.

After that, his day would really begin. He would work his way up and down the river by ferrying people wherever they needed to go. Stormy was always with him, and it eased the lonely times to talk to her. There were times when he would look longingly at the school where the children of good families attended and wish to go himself. His reading skills were minimal at best.

One afternoon that week, while he was taking a break, he was surprised when a woman sat beside him on the bench overlooking the river. She was almost stunningly beautiful with vivid red hair and piercing black eyes. He knew immediately that he looked upon a woman of very high standing. He felt grubby and outclassed sitting beside her.

Her dark blue dress had a design around the bottom of what looked like patterns he had seen in a book. He thought they had been from a country far beyond even England. She was *tiny* too. Maybe not short, but she was very slender. As he stood slightly taller than average, he felt like a giant. He swiftly stood. "I'm sorry," he apologized. "I'll move."

"Why?" Her eyes smiled at him.

"I smell like the river," he admitted shamefully. "It must be distressing to you."

"Not at all. Sit down, please." When he had done so, and very

warily, she turned to take stock of his appearance. She was *not* pleased with what she saw.

It had nothing to do with his looks. He had outrageously beautiful features paired with unusual and stunning coloring. Even among the blonds of the world, his hair stood out. His eyes held a wild spirit barely kept in check, and it gave a mischievous sparkle to the golden color. If there was one thing Rhianna Taber appreciated in anyone, it was a mischievous, wild spirit. She certainly had her own.

No, what displeased her was the state of his clothing, and the fact that he seemed too thin for his size. A young man of his height should not have been so slender that it was a wonder his bones supported his muscles at all. There were shadows under his eyes, and his cheeks were more hollowed than thin.

Little sparks that her partner liked to call her 'temper sparks' appeared in her eyes. "May I make a deal with you?" she asked. When he frowned thoughtfully, she smiled and touched his hand. "You look like you are in need of a good meal. I need a ride upriver. How about a trade?"

He thought of a real meal and his stomach clenched. He always felt hungry because he never got to eat his fill. There were times he wondered if his body ran on sheer stubbornness. "Well . . ." he hedged.

"No arguing," she ordered briskly. She got to her feet and pulled him up as well to tug him along with her as she walked. "I don't take no for an answer from anyone." Sensing his astonishment, she smiled. "My name is Rhianna Taber. I'm co-owner of the Enforcers."

He stopped dead in his tracks which forced her to stop as well. His jaw had fallen open. He knew the Enforcers as well as anyone else did. They were the biggest company in New York and they rivaled the governor for power. They protected a section of the city known as the 3rd District.

The 3rd District was where magic lived. It had been there that the werewolves had lived, and it was there that the bloody massacre had occurred. He did not fear the District or those who lived there. He was fascinated. If Rhianna was the leader of Enforcers, then she was probably really old. It never even occurred to him that a woman shouldn't be in charge of a large company, though it had often been thought by others. Of course, they had shortly changed their minds when they met her.

Without thinking, he blurted, "You look so young!" Indeed, she looked to be barely out of her twenties.

Her smile came quickly. "I do like you. Come along, Kay. I intend to feed you a proper meal for once." Since he seemed to have lost his resistance, she found it very easy to pull him along behind her.

She took him to a restaurant nearby and ordered them both large dinners. With satisfaction, she watched as he began to eat. His manners were impeccable, but he made short work of his meal. She was satisfied to see some of the haunted look fade from his eyes as well. "Talk to me," she offered.

"About what, ma'am? Er, miss." He corrected himself hastily as he remembered the rumor that she was unwed.

"About you." She smiled. "I was there that night some nineteen years ago. I'm curious how you're doing these days. I see being attacked by a werewolf does not give you a fear of wolves." She indicated Stormy lying patiently outside in the sun.

He smiled as he picked up a piece of bread. "I don't fear wolves. Why should I?" he asked curiously. "The werewolf who attacked my family was entitled to her fury, even if we were innocent. It wasn't like she was a murderer."

She considered that. "Then you don't hate the 3rd District?"

"No." His lethal smile flashed quickly. "I envy you who live there."

Hiding a smile of her own, she had to wonder if he had any idea how stunning his smile could be. She hoped it would carry on down through future generations. "Envy?" she repeated. "How so?"

"You belong," he said simply. "It's your home. You belong there. Everyone there supports each other. I envy that. I've never had a home."

"No?" She began to drum her fingers on her leg under the edge of the table. "Then where have you been living?"

"With my adopted family." He opened his mouth to say

everything was fine, but something in the ancient black eyes watching him made him change his mind. He couldn't lie, not to her. "I live in the barn," he admitted softly. In a rush he added, "It's truly not so bad. They give me scraps to eat, and I have clothes. There's a roof over my head, and I have a blanket for when it's cold."

The sparks were in her eyes again. "I see. And the money you make?"

"I'm indebted to them for raising me. I have to make enough money to pay them back." He blinked as he saw her eyes. He had never seen a literal manifestation of temper before. "It truly is okay. Mr. Johnston only beats me when I don't make enough. Oh!" He covered his mouth quickly.

She did not normally anger easily, but it took all her considerable willpower to remain seated and not go knock down Richard Johnston's door. "I won't tell," she promised. "Are you full, Kay?"

He looked down in surprise. He had eaten everything on his plate, and he felt very full. "Yes, thank you. I've never gotten to eat my fill before. I'll ferry you wherever you need, Miss Taber."

"Thank you very much." She let him escort her out of the restaurant and back to where the boat was waiting. She smiled as she watched him navigate the river. When Stormy nudged her hand, she ruffled her fur lightly. "Well," she murmured softly for her ears only, "I wouldn't call this interfering. It's more like watching over one of my own. He does have a contract, after all." And it was beginning to look like Richard had heavily violated it.

When Kay assisted her out of the boat, she smiled at him. "I wish you well, Kay." She waved merrily as he sailed back down the river. She felt someone join her, and her smile faded as the sparks in her eyes came back. "If I asked you to shove a lightning bolt up someone's ass, would you do it?"

Her partner looked the direction Kay was sailing, and his eyes were as displeased as hers. "Quite gladly," Eric Mason murmured softly. "Quite gladly, indeed."

The shock of the morning's events lingered with Kay, and he couldn't figure out what exactly had occurred. It made the day pass much quicker than ever, having his stomach full, and he wasn't nearly as tired as he normally was when he tied his boat off that evening. He even had enough time to count the money he had made.

His full stomach lurched, however, as he counted the coins. He hadn't made enough for his weekly share, and he was short by a dollar or so. The day was done, and there was no time for him to find a quick job. His throat tight, he made his way toward home.

Richard stood on the porch, his entire body ready to do battle. Terror made Kay's palms slick but his back was straight as he walked over and put the bag of money in his hand. He backed up a step and waited.

Richard counted the coins and turned a narrow eyed gaze on him. "You're short by two dollars. Were you goofing off on the river today instead of working?"

He had learned over the years that denying and fighting it would only make it worse. He said nothing. Instead, he kept his chin high and his back straight. He refused to cry and show the weakness that Richard always claimed he had.

Richard's face tightened. He had always hated this boy. He had taken him in for the money that came with him, but there was something so innately proud about Kay that he despised. He wanted to break him. "No arguments?"

At that point, Kay figured that things couldn't get worse. "Why waste my words when they fall on deaf ears?"

Fury lit Richard's eyes, and he came down the steps swiftly with his fist lifted. The first hit knocked Kay backward as the punch landed on his jaw. Though he had always taken the beatings without an argument, something inside him snapped and he leapt at Richard with both fists.

Richard was stunned enough that Kay managed to get in several good shots. Then, with a snarl, he grabbed Kay's shirt and hurled him into the side of the house. In a rage, he went after the younger man with fists and feet, mercilessly beating him with all his strength.

Kay curled into himself and bit his lower lip hard to bite back sounds of pain; dying couldn't hurt that bad. Sometimes he wished he *would* die so that it all went away. He couldn't even feel pain anymore. It had all turned white hot and numbing. His breathing was labored, and he suspected that maybe something had been broken. A particularly sharp kick landed in his back and rattled his ribs with a pain he hadn't known existed. He couldn't stop a whimper.

There came a low and vicious snarl on the night air, and Stormy lunged out of the darkness at Richard's throat. He cursed and staggered back away from Kay as Stormy braced herself in front of him, snarling in a way that showed all of her sharp teeth.

Richard backed off, breathing hard. "He brought it on himself."

She didn't move, and he slammed into the house. As soon as the door shut, Kay tried to move. He couldn't, though. Not without pain screaming through his body. He was bleeding too, from his skin splitting under the force of the blows. He dug his nails into the dirt and dragged with all his strength to pull himself onto his knees. His eyes focused blearily on the barn. It could have been a mile away instead of twenty feet. He could do it. He had done it before.

Stormy whimpered, and he thought for a moment she was sympathizing with him. A rustle surprised him, and he was surprised more when he realized someone had knelt beside him. As if moving through mud, he turned his head and saw that the young woman from earlier in the week had joined him. "You . . ."

"Shh." Her lips were thinned with anger, and her eyes filled with concern as she glanced at the quiet house behind them. "Let me help." She wasn't very big, but she knew she could do at least enough to help him walk. She would drag him if needed to get him away from there.

She had never met anyone so unthinkingly kind before. He

hadn't known her, and yet he had dived into a river to save her. There was no calculation in him, no fear. He accepted Stormy readily despite what had happened to him. He was as rare as a diamond in the rough, and just as precious.

He tried to get to his feet, but it hurt too badly and he fell to his knees. "Sorry," he managed to say.

She set her chin. "I'm not giving up. Stormy, help me." She took hold of him under the arms, and Stormy grabbed a mouthful of his shirt, and together they struggled and dragged him toward the barn.

It hurt like hell, but he gritted his teeth and tried to help. They staggered into the barn, and he looked at the ladder toward the loft where his bed was located. He knew he would never make it. Instead, he collapsed onto the nearest pile of hay. "Leave me here," he groaned. "I've imposed enough."

He didn't hear anything else for a moment and assumed that she had left. She had repaid his kindness and had no reason to linger. He was so sure of it that he was doubly startled when he felt her kneel beside him on the hay and begin opening his shirt. His eyes popped wide in surprise. "Wha?" She was leaning over him, her hair falling down, and the scent drifted toward him like rain. It was beautiful. "Who are you?"

"My name is Raven Childrose." She took a sharp breath as she saw the marks across his chest. It infuriated her. It was an incredibly beautiful body and a sin to mark it, and the idea of anyone at all being hurt like that made her mad.

Scars of older wounds marked his smooth skin, and the newest ones from that night were open and bloody welts. There were rapidly darkening bruises everywhere, and she could tell from the way he breathed that at least one rib was cracked. Tears welled in her eyes. "How can you stand it?" she whispered.

"I don't have too much of a choice." He watched as she got to her feet and left the barn. When she came back, she was carrying a pail of water that she set down before kneeling beside him again. "You don't have to do this," he told her quietly. "I've gotten through this before."

She shot him a quick look. "I don't like it." She ripped a long strip of material off the end of her petticoat and dipped it in the water. "Even if you hadn't helped me, I'd still do this. I can't stand seeing someone be hurt. I would be a doctor if they would let me learn. I must settle for reading books, I suppose."

He braced himself for the cold water but, to his amazement, it was warm. He frowned. "How did you do that?"

Red color climbed her cheeks. "Do what?"

"Make the water warm. The pump is always cold." His eyes closed tiredly as she continued to clean the wounds. "Are you from 3rd District?"

She hesitated before she resumed gently cleaning the wounds. "Yes," she admitted softly. "I have water elf blood. I can manipulate it to some extent, like changing the temperature." She gingerly touched the bruises dotting his flesh. "I cannot believe someone would be so horribly cruel."

"I suppose I am used to it." He continued to watch her, fascinated with the way she moved and the gentleness in her features. She was unbearably lovely, and he wanted her more than ever. It had been sparked that night by the river, but now it was getting more powerful. He knew her to be incredibly beyond his reach, that it would always be hopeless, and it broke his heart. "You must be a nobleman's daughter."

She flinched slightly and turned to take the bandages Stormy was holding. She didn't ask where she had gotten them, and neither did Kay. "Why do you say that?" She scooted closer and tried to help him sit up.

He pushed himself upright and had to wait for a moment to let the dizziness pass. He carefully shrugged out of his shirt and held his arms up as she began to wrap the bandages around his chest. He tried not to notice, he really did, but his eyes couldn't miss seeing that her bodice was partially unbuttoned. He could see the gentle swell of her breasts underneath.

Raven was not like most women. She had, after all, been raised in the 3rd District by the entire community, including Rhianna Taber.

She had been given an understanding of men and women that wouldn't be commonplace in young adults until another century had passed. It was because of that understanding that she noticed within a few moments that he was distinctly attracted to her. In fact, she would have had trouble missing it with how she was leaning over him and all but sitting on his lap. She swiftly sat upright, her eyes wide. "You can't want me," she blurted.

He stared at her as if she was insane. "Why not?"

"Because . . . just because!" She felt flustered, and she knew she sounded it, too. "Men don't . . . I mean . . . they've never . . . I'm not . . ." She gave up and covered her burning cheeks with her hands. "Oh this is going so wrong!"

He tested the bandages, found they were snug, and tried to breathe a little more normally. It still hurt, but not quite as bad. He took the pail and material and began cleaning the wounds on his arms and legs himself. "Try at the top," he suggested with a smile. "Because I know I like you."

Her pulse fluttered wildly in her body at the sight of his smile. She had never seen anything that lethally beautiful before. "Alright." She took a long breath. "I'm not a noblewoman. I was thrown out by my mother. I was raised in 3rd District by everyone. And I . . . well, I just have nothing to offer a man."

He tossed the material aside where it landed with a wet plop on the barn floor. Anger churned inside his heart. How could anyone as kind and beautiful as her not have a hundred suitors? He had no idea who had put such a stupid idea in her head, and he wouldn't have minded giving them a kick of their own. "I think you're incredible," he told her honestly. "If I wasn't just a poor river ferryman, I'd be courting you."

She frowned. "No."

"Yes."

"You don't know me!"

"I want to." He smiled. "But since I can't court you, will you be friends with me instead?" When she eyed him warily, he held up his hands with a sad smile. "I think I could fall in love with you, Raven, but

you're so far beyond my reach. I know that I can't ever have you, so will you at least be friends with me?"

Her heart clenched in her chest. He had no idea how wrong he was. It wasn't that he wasn't good enough for her; it was the other way around. She didn't deserve a man as wonderful and handsome as Kay. "I've never had friends," she whispered. "Not real ones."

"Me neither." He couldn't stop himself from reaching out and threading his fingers through her hair. It felt as soft as feathers. If it could have been woven into cloth, it would have been the finest of silks. "Will you visit me?" He smiled. "When neither of us are in life or death situations?"

She had to smile even though she fought a fierce urge to go into his arms. She wanted to be held, just once, by someone who thought she was beautiful. "I have, umm, things to do during the day. I can only visit at night."

"Me, too." He felt battered and tired, but oddly more at peace than he ever had before. With a little sigh, he almost fell over. She caught him and gently eased him down onto the hay. "Guess I'm just tired," he apologized.

"You have reason." She took the blanket Stormy had fetched, and she gently tucked it around him. He was asleep a few moments later, and she watched him for a long time. When she felt dawn was a mere hour away, she got to her feet and walked out of the barn. Stormy tried to stop her but she shook her head. "You have your contract," she said softly, "and I have mine. He deserves more than me."

Stormy highly doubted that, but kept the thought to herself as she went back into the barn and curled up next to Kay. The first few lights of dawn eventually spilled in the window and she watched quietly. A few moments later, a black raven flew across the face of the sun on a mournful cry.

Every Enforcers' contract had a clause or condition to be met. Stormy knew it for a fact. She just had to figure out what Raven's was, and use it.

CHAPTER THREE

Kay awoke a little after dawn to a body that was stiff and sore in every muscle. He painfully got to his feet and forced himself to go to the pump for cold water. He barely spared a glance for the house. He knew there would be no scraps.

He was almost tempted to think it had all been a dream, but his wounds were definitely bound, and he could still smell the scent of Raven's skin and hair if he breathed deeply. It hadn't helped any that he'd had a particularly vivid dream about kissing her. He had never kissed any girl before, but his dream self certainly seemed to know what he was doing.

His feelings puzzled him in a way. They had only met twice, and yet she had become incredibly important to him. Those brief two meetings had taught him everything he needed to know about her. She was sweet and shy, gentle and caring, and she was also strong-willed, smart, proud, and beautiful. She had an independent streak that he found more alluring than alarming.

"It's so odd," he murmured. When Stormy tilted her head, he smiled at her. "Love at first sight. I think I know what it is now. It's Raven." A particularly smug look crossed her face and he laughed even though it hurt. "I thought that would please you. Don't think I don't know what you're up to!"

He got his drink of water and walked carefully back into the barn. He changed his clothes because his current ones were both dirty and muddy, but it was not easy. With an inner pride that nothing could break, he squared his back and began to walk painfully toward the river in the distance.

It hurt. Every step felt like torture, and he couldn't turn without hurting from head to heel. On top of that, his stomach was growling loudly with painful hunger. He carefully climbed onto his boat and began to check all the parts to be sure everything was in working order. He never went out without a onceover.

Stormy began to sniff the deck in a search for something. He let her be and sat down heavily on the floor. He tried to convince himself that it didn't really hurt as bad as he thought, but it didn't work. Then, suddenly, Stormy sat beside him with something in her mouth. He turned his head carefully and found she had a basket.

He was further shocked to find it packed with food. Hot cakes, sausages, bread, and potatoes. It looked as good as it smelled, and his mouth watered. A pink ribbon tied around the handle caught his eye, and the gentle scent of rain drifted to him over the food. It must have been Raven who left it for him. He removed the ribbon and tucked it reverently into his sleeve for safety.

He had enough time to eat, and he made short work of the food. It felt wonderful to eat his fill again. Everything tasted incredible, and he didn't think it was just because his taste buds were underworked. He liked the idea that Raven had made it for him. He just wished he could do something to take care of her in return.

Once he was done, he forced himself to get to work. It was painfully difficult to navigate the river turns, but Stormy stood directly beside him and helped keep him from falling over. She also helped grab the pole and pull it through the water, giving his arms a much-needed rest.

The day seemed to drag on but he focused only on his work. His passengers all noticed the bruise on his chin, and the way he moved carefully, and they suspected they knew what had occurred. There just wasn't anything they could do for him.

During a rough patch in the river, he almost lost control of the boat and one of the passengers hastily stepped over and grabbed the pole before it went flying. "Easy," he told Kay with a smile. He seemed older than Kay, though it was hard to determine by how much, and there were wings of white in his brown hair. He stood not much taller, but he was distinctly bigger, because Kay was not at his full potential.

"Thank you," Kay said shamefully. "I'm just a little clumsy today."

"Little wonder." The man studied him knowingly. "Cracked a rib, did you?"

"I fell out of the barn loft," he lied automatically. He started to reach for the pole again when the ribbon in his sleeve got free and tried to fly off. "Oh! Grab it!"

The man moved as fast as the wind and snagged the ribbon before it could get far. He offered it to Kay with a smile. "A gift from a lady friend?" When the boy's cheeks flushed, Eric Mason felt almost amazingly old. Thinking it, he promptly heard Rhianna's laughter in his mind. He ignored her. "Have you given her something in return?"

"Well, no." Kay frowned. "I don't have any money of my own. Everything I make goes toward my living."

"Ah." Eric took his hand and dropped a few coins in his palm. "Consider this a tip. Buy something nice for your lady. I think she'd be pleasantly surprised."

He wanted to argue, but Eric had already walked away. Even though he knew he ought to save the money for the future in case he ever came up short, he really, really wanted to buy something for Raven. He tied the money into a handkerchief and tucked it safely in his pocket.

As the day wore on, it got harder and harder to steer. Even Stormy's help did not fully help. The pole was clumsy enough under good circumstances. It wobbled too much at the top, and it nearly bobbed out of his hands more than once. One particularly bad dip found him being unexpectedly saved when a raven flew up and landed on the top of the pole. Her weight was just enough counterbalance that his work became instantly easier. He smiled and ran a hand down her soft feathers. "Thank you." A little frown touched his lips as he looked at his fingers. Oddly, the raven's feathers were as soft as, well, Raven's hair.

He put it out of his mind and took advantage of the help from his companions to finish the day with enough money to keep Richard happy. He even finished a little ahead of schedule. As soon as he tied the boat, he hurried quickly into a nearby square where some shops were located.

The raven had flown off at the first sign of sunset so it was just Kay and Stormy browsing the shops. He had no idea what he wanted to get, but when he saw the store selling jewelry, something caught his eye.

It was a matching set of cameo and ring. The cameo was carved from pearl and had the relief of a woman's profile. The ring was also pearl, and little silver threads wrapped around it. He was certain he wouldn't have enough, but when he checked the price it was exactly the right amount. He bought it immediately and tied it safely inside his shirt where it couldn't be found.

It had gotten dark, and he hurried home as quickly as his injured body would let him. Richard again waited on the porch, and Kay handed him the bag of money without a word. That done, he turned and headed toward the barn.

Richard snorted derisively. "Where do you think you are going?"

Kay stopped but didn't look back. "The money is there. And even if it weren't, if you beat me again, I could die this time. You wouldn't want that, right? Then you'd be out your source of funds. I know there are no scraps waiting for me. Right now, I don't care."

Richard snarled, "Do you want me to kill you, you little upstart?!"

Kay looked at him. "Sometimes, yes. Go ahead. I can't stop you." When Richard only slammed into the house, he let out the breath he had been holding. "I'm an idiot," he muttered under his breath. "What was I doing, provoking him like that?"

He made his way to the barn and climbed one step at a time into the loft. He lit the single lantern he had and then just sat there for a few moments to let his muscles stop yelling at him. He eventually pulled out the single book he owned and tried again to go over the passages. It had been a gift from a passenger when he was a child, and it alone had taught him what little he knew how to read.

The scent of vegetables and chicken reached his nose

unexpectedly, and he frowned. Maybe the meals lately had made him start to hallucinate. He eased to the edge of the loft and peered downstairs just in case he was wrong. He wasn't. Raven had just set another basket on the ground and steam wafted from it gently. Stormy pranced around her ankles happily and Raven shushed her softly. "He'll hear," she whispered.

Stormy, naturally, chose to bark at that moment and Kay laughed. Raven looked up swiftly and her cheeks turned as pink as the cherry blossoms on her dress. "I didn't mean to disturb you." She bit her lip nervously. "I was just going to leave this and go."

"No." He shook his head. "I was hoping you would come see me. Would you come up here?"

She hesitated visibly but finally picked up the basket and carried it with her as she went up the ladder. He helped her onto the loft. He studied her for a moment before smiling and reaching for the ribbons in her hair. She swatted at his hands, flustered. "No, stop!" She could only sigh as her hair came down. "It's not proper to take your hair down around people."

"I'm not people. I'm your friend. You like it this way more, too. I can see it on your face." He reached eagerly for the basket. "What did you bring?" He happily purveyed the small feast waiting for him. "I saw the breakfast this morning and enjoyed it very much. Thank you."

Her color deepened. "I just . . . wanted to make you something. I know you don't get to eat much." She watched with deep pleasure as he began to eat contentedly. Though Rhianna had told her time and again not to be bound by the rules of society and to strive to be more than 'just a wife,' she knew that she would never be happier than when she was trying to take care of the people she loved.

She supposed it was her own silly fault, falling in love with Kay. It had happened so quickly that she hadn't even seen it was a danger. When she had seen him get beaten . . . she had wanted to unleash a flood on Richard. And then, today, she hadn't been able to help herself from following Kay. She had even helped him steer but when sunset had come she had been forced to leave.

Something would happen that night. Something to change her life. Somehow she knew it. She had tried to sneak in and out to avoid it, but she hadn't truly been surprised that Stormy would thwart her attempts. She also knew what the wolf was doing. She pushed it aside for the time being. "How old are you, Kay?" She wanted to know everything.

"Twenty-one." He set the basket aside. His happy tummy was full yet again. "What about you?"

"Nineteen."

His eyes widened. "And you're not married." He remembered her words of the night before and still could hardly believe it. "I can't believe that some man hasn't swept you off your feet. You're incredible."

"I'm not." She closed her eyes and tears glimmered under her lashes. "My mother tried to kill me when I was born because I was visibly of the 3rd District. It was right after the coup, and people were scared still. Rhianna of the Enforcers saved me, and the whole district helped raise me."

His face tightened with anger. "If I ever met your mother, I'd probably hurt her, and I hate the idea of hurting women." She looked at him in shock, and he reached out to run his hand down her cheek. "I lied to you, Raven," he said softly. He smiled. "I'm already in love with you."

She tried to jerk backwards in shock but Stormy bumped her firmly from behind and sent her flying into Kay's arms. He gave a soft grunt as his ribs protested but his arms instinctively closed around her tightly. He had nothing to base his feelings on, yet something inside told him no other would fit so perfectly in his arms.

Her eyes slowly closed and she pressed closer without thought. Joy seemed to blossom inside her heart at the feel of his arms. She felt . . . safe. Cherished. And yet, there was an odd hunger moving inside her body as well. Her lashes lifted to see his slightly open shirt, and the revealed skin made her tempted to press her lips right there.

The unusual emotions rioting through her heart and body in no way distracted her from whatever was poking her in the shoulder. She tried to pull away and his arms tightened. "Don't move away," he protested. "I like holding you. If I get my courage back, I'm going to kiss you."

She blushed. "I wouldn't protest but there's something digging into my shoulder."

He remembered suddenly and released her. "Oh!" He reached into his shirt and came out with the handkerchief he had wrapped the gift inside. "Here." He held it out with a smile. "I wanted to get you something, and someone gave me a tip, so . . ."

With trembling fingers, she opened the handkerchief to discover the cameo and ring. Her mouth opened soundlessly and then closed several times in sheer disbelief. "I can't accept this!" she protested.

"Yes, you can." He took the cameo and leaned in closer to fasten it to the edge of her bodice. Her scent curled around him, and he gave in to the urge to bury his nose against the curve where her neck met her shoulder. "I love how you smell," he murmured softly. "Like fresh rain." Not even fully conscious of his actions, he moved lower and his fingers unfastened some buttons so his nose could nuzzle into the opening in the bodice.

Her heart began to beat harder, and her breath hitched in her lungs as she felt his hot breath on the sensitive skin between her breasts. "What're you doing?" she managed to ask. "Kay."

He straightened up quickly. "I . . . I don't know. I'm sorry, did I scare you?" He felt both sheepish and embarrassed for having given in to such a shameful urge. It didn't help any that his body ached in an entirely new way as desire gleefully ripped through his blood. He was a healthy young man who had been interested in a pretty girl once or twice. Never like that, though. Never to the point of forgetting himself.

"No." She reached up and touched the cameo with a smile. "It's beautiful." She made a startled sound as he picked up her hand and slid the ring over her finger. "No, don't do that. It looks . . ."

"I know." He smiled almost shyly. "If I could, I would give you a real ring. But I don't deserve you."

"Stop it!" She shook her head swiftly and her hair flew around her shoulders. "It's not you, Kay, it's me! I don't deserve *you*, don't you understand? I'm 3rd District born, and I have no family. I don't even have a place to call home! My parents . . . at least your parents loved you!" Tears ran down her cheeks. "Do you think I don't want a home? A husband and children? If I could, I would marry you the minute you asked!"

He almost stopped breathing. "Are you in love with me, too?"

"Yes." Defeated, her shoulders slumped. "But we both know it's hopeless." When his hands framed her face, she met his golden colored gaze and felt as if she was sinking into the promise it made. "Are you going to kiss me?" she whispered.

"May I?" he whispered back. He drew her closer until she was sitting on his lap. The pain in his body had faded as if it had never been. The only pain he felt was a longing to hold her as close as he could.

"You shouldn't but . . ." Her lashes fluttered closed. "Please."

He wasn't going to ask twice and lowered his head toward hers. Unfortunately, lack of experience for both meant the embrace was a little awkward and their noses banged smartly together. "Ouch!" He pulled back, askance. "Raven, are you okay?"

She wiggled her nose. "Yes, but, ouch." Her eyes met his and she tried not to, honestly, but a giggle escaped anyway. "You missed."

He started snickering too. "I'm sorry. I've never kissed a girl before." The sound of her laughter enchanted him. It just seemed impossibly beautiful. Before he could stop himself, he bent his head and caught her smiling lips with his own.

She even tasted like rainwater. The taste of her spread through him like a wave and made the arousal he had been ignoring since she had arrived all the more painful. His hands lifted to frame her face, and he remembered in his dream how he had kissed her. He glided his tongue over her lips, trying to tempt her into opening her mouth.

She had taken a startled breath when he kissed her, and she couldn't get it back. Heat radiated from his body, and every nerve she possessed was tingling deliciously. Her body felt hot and achy, and she shifted closer without conscious thought to wind her arms around his neck.

She felt his tongue teasing her lips and parted them without hesitation, eager to know his taste. It was rich honey, and it went to her head faster than the wine she had once secretly tried. His tongue touched hers and startled her for a moment before she gave a little sigh and returned the tiny caress. She was more than willing to be seduced by this man.

The kiss lengthened and unraveled in silence until a little whimper escaped her when he lifted his head. Their eyes met and she trembled as she saw the hunger swirling in his eyes. "Again?" he asked softly, his voice rough.

"Please." Her hands slid up into his hair and tugged to urge him closer. When he complied, she trembled with need as the kiss erupted between them. His confidence had grown, and he kissed her with an edge of desire that stole her breath. In the space of a moment, the soft desire inside sharpened into raw lust.

He couldn't get enough. Hunger deepened the kiss until it was nothing but a tangle of tongues and lips. He had to touch her, to know her in every possible way. His hands lifted and plucked at the buttons on her dress until the bodice was unfastened entirely. The edges of the dress opened instantly and slid over her skin like a hungry lover. He could only wish it was him who touched her so intimately.

She couldn't muffle a soft moan as his hands slid under her opened dress and curved around her waist. Even through her thin corset, his heat burned her. She twisted toward his touch, begging silently for more. It was only when she felt his lips leave hers and bury against the pulse racing in her throat that she realized what was going on.

"Oh!" Her voice was nothing more than a breathless sound. "Stop. Kay, stop!"

He stopped, but it took him several moments to find self-control. He had never wanted anything in his life more than he wanted her. He released her slowly and clenched his hands into fists at his side. He didn't look at her as she got off his lap and fixed her clothes. If he did, he would not be able to keep himself from touching her again. "You really have to marry me," he decided with as much humor as he could.

She smoothed her dress with trembling fingers. Her stupid corset already made it impossible to breathe without adding the recent events to things. "Why?" Even as she asked it, she knew it was a stupid question. They were friends, they were in love, and they had almost set the hay on fire. Rhianna had called it one of the perfect combinations for a lasting relationship, and Raven could no longer doubt her. It felt as if the entire world hovered beyond her reach.

"Because." He looked at her with eyes that burned. "I've never felt that before. I know you haven't either. And I'm *sure* we never will again unless it's together. So, we ought to marry."

"Kay . . ." She caught sight of the moon starting to wane and realized it was no longer late and instead very early. "I have to go!" She hurried down the ladder and out of the loft. "Kay, I'm so sorry! Just . . . just forget it, please!"

He could not forget it, nor could he forget the pain in her eyes. He sat watching the night sky and waited for the dawn to come. The sun began to rise with all of its splendor, and he thought he saw the form of a raven flying across the sky. Her sad cries ripped at his heart and soul.

He thought he might be starting to understand, and understanding brought determination. So much in his life had been taken away before he was able to fight for it, but not this. Not Raven. He would fight to the death for her if needed.

First, he needed advice. There was only one person he trusted and that was an old priest who lived very far down the river. He didn't hesitate as he hurried to his boat and set off to go visit. He would be pushing it to have enough time to make his daily quota, but this was more than worth it.

"Father Evans!" he called as he got off the boat and hurried toward the church not far beyond. "Father Evans!"

The old priest was sweeping the steps of the church and smiled as he saw Kay. "Ah, I wondered when you would arrive, young man. Come, sit with me. I will give you a drink to ease the pain of your wounds, and you can tell me of the woman who took your heart."

Kay smiled as he followed Father Evans and shortly found himself sitting on the steps with an odd herbal concoction in his hands. It tasted sort of bitter but he trusted Father Evans' medicines implicitly and drank the entire thing. The pains and aches almost immediately began to fade. "Thank you, Father Evans."

"You are very welcome, son." Evans sat down on the stairs beside him. "Now, tell me of this woman who captivated you."

"Her name is Raven Childrose." He looked in the distance thoughtfully. "I met her by accident, and then she happened to be near my home when I was beaten the other night. We became friends, but I've been in love with her the whole time, I think."

Evans tugged on his long beard. "A coincidence, Kay?" When Kay nodded, he smiled. "There are no coincidences around those of 3rd District. This was meant to be." He crossed his arms inside his sleeves and studied the sun rising in the east. "In some places," he murmured, "it is whispered that there are two beings who watch over the fate of lovers. I've always thought it was so. Perhaps one, or both, is watching over you."

Kay smiled. "I like that." He studied the ground intently. "I think Raven is cursed, Father Evans. She says no man has ever wanted her for a wife. But I do. I want her to belong to me, and I want to belong to her. But . . . if we marry, Richard would have to approve before anyone would ever perform the ceremony."

"I do not answer to Richard Johnston," Evans countered serenely. "I answer to God for my morality, and I answer to the government for my legality. You are an adult, and you are not a slave—no matter what you may think. If your lady agrees, I will perform the ceremony and take care of the paperwork that goes with it."

"Really?" Kay looked at him in surprise.

"I would be honored."

"Then I'll find the courage and ask her," he decided firmly. He leapt to his feet as he heard the birds beginning to sing. "I have to go, but thank you!" With a wave of his hand, he hurried back down

toward his boat, hoping only to make it through the day. If he could survive to seeing Raven again, then everything would be alright. He was sure of it.

CHAPTER FOUR

Kay was not entirely surprised when the morning passed without the raven showing up to join him. Somehow he just knew that the raven was *his* Raven. She probably didn't think he would understand. Maybe he didn't, but he did accept it. He would find a way to fix everything.

The morning stretched on and he continued to work. Much to his terror, he realized Richard was in town that day and keeping a close eye on him. Kay tried to ignore him and focus on his sailing but it was very difficult. His passengers noticed everything, and fury rose among them all. They just couldn't do anything!

Evening finally arrived, and he began to think everything might be okay. It all took a nosedive when a sudden fire caught life at one of the shops along the shore. People scrambled to safety, but almost not in time. An explosion from the fire getting into gunpowder sent flaming bits of roof and wall flying everywhere.

Kay could not steer fast enough to get away, and one of the massive chunks struck the small boat with enough force to punch a hole in the wood. Flames swiftly began to eat through everything. Because he knew it was either abandon the boat or possibly go down with it, he dove over the side and swam away with Stormy close behind.

He got to the opposite shore and pulled himself out in time to see the boat beginning to sink. Terror choked him suddenly. He had no way of making his living without the boat. His eyes shot across the shore and he saw Richard walking toward the nearest bridge with a nearly inhuman look of rage on his face.

Kay felt sick. If he stayed there, he was dead. He scrambled up to his feet despite the pains his chest gave him and took off running into the woods nearby. He had youth and agility on his side, and running over grass would make him impossible to track. Even knowing it, he didn't let it lull him into a false sense of security. He kept running and praying for nightfall. He could hide in the darkness.

Dark eventually fell and he huddled behind a tree to catch his breath. A step nearby had him leaping to his feet instinctively. Instead of the raging madman he expected, it was actually Raven that ran out of the bushes. She flung herself into his arms desperately, and it staggered him a step. His arms closed around her fiercely and he buried his face in her hair. "Raven."

"I saw the wreck!" Her entire body shook as she clung onto him tighter. "And I saw Mr. Johnston coming after you! I knew . . . I knew he'd kill you if he found you! Kay, please! You can't go back there!"

"I won't, I promise." His fingers found the ribbons in her hair and plucked them out so that the chignon came down and unraveled. He immediately buried his face in the strands and breathed in the scent of rain. "I'll find somewhere safe, I promise."

"I know somewhere." Her lips trembled as she eased back. "It's horribly improper of me to do so, but I can take you home with me. I live just inside 3rd District, in a home under an oak tree." She tilted her head. "Does that alarm you?"

He shook his head. "I've always believed in magic. If you told me you lived in a palace on top of clouds, it wouldn't surprise me." He took her hand tightly and followed her through the trees toward the 3rd District.

He felt it the instant they entered. His entire body seemed to prickle with awareness of power. He watched curiously as she fit a key into a hole in a tree and then smiled as the tree crawled by its roots to the side to reveal a staircase. "I think I could like this place."

She felt her shoulders relax, and she smiled. "I'm glad." She went down the stairs with him close behind, and the tree moved back into place overhead. Blushing, she lit a lantern and hung it safely out of the way. "It's small," she said in a rush, "but you're welcome to stay as long as you need."

The small house was more like a one-room living space. There was a stove for cooking and strange plants sitting beside it that he assumed were something like firewood. Lanterns hung from the ceiling and she lit one of them for more light. There was a fireplace as well, and a hand carved bed of immense proportions.

Seeing his curious gaze, she went over to the bed and sat on the edge of it. "It was a gift for me from Rhianna. She said that I deserved to have something spectacular for my sixteenth birthday. Even a king wouldn't have something this grand."

He studied the height. "I'd be afraid of falling out of it." The intimacy of the place struck him all at once. They were completely alone, and she was sitting on the side of a bed piled with blankets and pillows. His body tightened on a surge of desire. "Raven . . ."

She swiftly got to her feet, her heart pounding madly inside her chest. She knew she wouldn't have been so nervous if she hadn't been so sure that the next time he touched her she wouldn't be able to stop him. She wanted him so terribly. "Well . . . you could probably use a bath. I know you must be uncomfortable."

He looked down and realized he was covered in river water and mud. He grimaced. It didn't make him want her less, but it made it easier to find control. He would sooner cut his hands off than touch her while he was that dirty. "I don't have clean clothes," he apologized.

"That's okay." She smiled. "Riku, that is, Eric Mason, gave me some clothes for you the other day. I just never got a chance to bring them to you." She got them out of a trunk at the end of the bed and held them out. "Here. I'll wait outside while you bathe."

He would have liked her to stay but knew it would be improper as long as they weren't married. He watched her use her powers to fill a large copper tub with hot water before disappearing up the stairs. He had never seen a tub quite like it before, but it looked plenty big enough for him. He swiftly stripped off his ruined clothes and grabbed the cake of soap nearby. It felt good to scrub off all the dirt from his skin and hair though it also felt quite strange to be that clean. He normally just got a river bath once a week or so. It really wasn't the same thing.

When he was done, he got out and dried off with a thick blanket that had been set out with the clothes. He then turned his attention to the clothes themselves. He felt almost embarrassed with how fine the material was, but he liked the warmth. The coat and slacks he liked even more with their blue-black material and little lightning bolt stitching at the cuffs. He pulled on new socks and sturdy boots, stood up, and his mind was boggled when he looked at the mirror.

He began to smile after a moment. He felt overdressed, and yet he was only dressed properly for once. He quickly climbed the stairs to find Raven and complained as he went, "I feel overdressed."

She muffled a giggle from where she was sitting on a rock watching the stars. "I know the feeling. I very rarely wear a bustle, and I only reluctantly wear a corset if I'm going outside. Every time I do, I feel rather odd."

"I think you're beautiful no matter how you look," he told her honestly as he sat beside her.

She smiled, secretly pleased. "Thank you." She took a quick breath as she saw him, and her eyes widened slightly. Dressed so properly, he looked like the prince of her secret fantasies there to rescue her. "You look handsome," she said softly.

"Good." He turned toward her more fully and lifted a hand to catch her hair and thread his fingers through it. "I want you to find me irresistible." He tugged her closer for a light kiss. "Then maybe you'll agree to marry me."

Her eyes closed as despair welled. "I can't," she whispered. "You know what I am, Kay. I know you do."

"Not entirely. Tell me what happened, please." He pulled her into his arms and held on tightly.

She sighed. She was sure he would change his mind when he knew, but for that moment she savored the feel of his embrace. "When I was born, my mother hated me, so she cursed me. I turned into a raven. Rhianna found me, and Enforcers were able to make a contract for me, changing the curse a little. By day, I have to become a raven. At night, I am a woman." She closed her eyes and waited.

He thought about it for a few moments. "So?"

Her eyes opened in surprise. "So? What do you mean 'so'? Kay, no man in his right mind wants a woman who is cursed and can't run his house during the day! And there's no guarantee I could ever have children either!"

"Well, I don't care!" His brows pulled together in a scowl. "As long as I could hold you at least at night, I would be happy. I can cook and clean during the day if needed. Or . . . or I can become nocturnal. We can sleep during the day and live at night. I don't mind. As for children . . . well, I don't have a legacy to pass on. I just love you, Raven."

She shook her head sharply. "You don't believe me!"

"I do, but I still want to marry you!" His expression grew determined. "I'll prove it. Come on." He pulled her up to her feet and began heading with purpose toward the District proper. He was sure someone would lend them a carriage. "We're going to get married."

She stopped so sharply that he stopped for fear of hurting her arm. Shocked, she stared at him. "B-but . . . if you changed your mind . . ." Her voice dropped to an anguished whisper. "I couldn't bear it!"

He turned and caught her arms to lift her off her feet until their eyes met. "I love you," he repeated firmly. "I'll say it over and over again. From the moment I pulled you out of the river, I loved you." He smiled. "Someone told me there are no coincidences around those from 3rd District. That means this is destiny."

"Well spoken." Father Evans smiled when Kay hastily put Raven down and both turned quickly. He lowered a hand and patted Stormy on the head. "Stormy came and fetched me. I now see why."

Raven felt as if the floor had fallen out from under her feet. "B-but . . . !" She looked up at Kay, and his golden eyes shimmered with an endless well of sheer determination . . . and love. He meant it. Wonder began to fill her heart. He truly wanted her. He truly wanted to marry her. How could she ever deny him? "Alright," she conceded shyly. "I'll marry you, Kay."

His breath released on a rush of air. "I was getting scared," he said under his breath. He held her tightly for a moment as he looked

at Evans. "You said you would marry us if we wished. Please, Father Evans."

Evans smiled. "I would be honored, Kay."

And so, they were married. It seemed rather astonishing to Raven; she had always thought it would be very complicated, but it wasn't, not really. Before she knew it, Kay was kissing her, and she was his wife. A little thrill went through her as she threw her arms around him. He was hers, too. Her husband. Now no one could ever take him away.

"Good luck," Father Evans told them both. He wandered off further into the woods, and Stormy followed him. He smiled though he did not look at her. "These eyes are old and have seen a lot," he murmured. "Sometimes they even see things that will come to be. Guard this family well, young wolf. Your destiny is tied to them."

She snorted softly under her breath. No, really? She wouldn't have guessed.

"We're married," Raven told Kay, the astonishment still on her face. "I . . . I can't quite believe it. I never thought it would ever happen . . ."

His grin could have lit the forest. "Me neither, but now you're mine." He drew her closer and rocked her in his arms. Now no one could ever take her away. "We'll make a home somewhere."

"We can stay under the tree for now." She smiled shyly. "It's *our* home now, not just mine." Her heart fluttered a little as he took her hand and began walking back through the trees. She felt a little nervous, but it couldn't stop her heart. Even if, somehow, things ended badly, she wanted to belong to him.

She used the key once more and the tree shifted to the side. Before she could go down the stairs, her husband scooped her up into his arms and started down them personally. She clutched his shoulders, eyes wide. "What're you doing?"

"I thought it was a tradition."

"Well, yes, but . . ." Flustered, she fell silent. It was almost unbearably romantic, and her heart fluttered wildly. A prince, she thought again, but one in disguise. Or perhaps a fallen prince because his kingdom had been taken away.

The romantic moment was thoroughly ruined a few moments later as he stubbed his toe on the tub and tripped. She muffled a shriek as they tumbled, and her breath whooshed out as they hit the floor.

To her astonishment, she realized he had wrapped his arms around her so that her head was protected. He was still sprawled over her, and her pulse began to pound in her body. He was heavy, but something inside wanted to purr with delight. Her fingers itched to touch him and find out what he felt like.

Despite the jostle to his ribs, he was more mortified than injured as he lifted his head. "Are you okay?" The words died as he saw the look in her eyes. It was the same helpless, longing look he knew was often in his own gaze whenever he looked at her. The desire he had been determinedly ignoring roared back hotter than ever before.

She licked her lips at a touch of nerves. "I should bathe," she whispered. "Prepare myself."

"And stall for time?" he whispered back.

"That, too." Her eyes closed helplessly as he freed one hand and cupped her cheek. His fingers were warm, and the heat shivered through her softly. "I love you, Kay."

"I love you too, Raven." His smile spread. "Raven Shaughnessy. It has a nice sound to it."

She turned her face into his hand. "I've never had a family before."

"Me neither. We'll make a new family together." He lowered his head to brush soft kisses over her face and tasted her skin tenderly. "I need to warn you. I have no experience at this. It's all instinct. You'll have to tell me if I'm doing something right."

She softly slid her hands up around to the back of his neck. "So far I like it." She smiled as her nerves seemed to fade away. There just wasn't any room for them. "I'm a terrible hussy, and probably completely improper for suggesting it, but since I don't have any experience either, can I explore you, too?"

His breath hitched at the idea of having her hands all over him. "Please do." He rolled off her and winced vividly as his body finally protested painfully. He saw her frown, and he shook his head. "I'm fine."

"No, you're not." She helped him stand and urged him over to the bed so that he sat on the side. "Take off your jacket and shirt. I want to see the wounds." Fully expecting him to follow orders, she went over to where she kept medicines and began rummaging inside. When she turned around again, her breath came in sharply.

He had indeed removed his jacket and shirt. He also hadn't rewrapped the bandages after his bath, and she could see every wound clearly. There were fist-sized bruises of mottled purple and red, and the places where his skin had been broken open were dull and partially scabbed over.

His body was full of tempting, sculpted lines. All his years of hard work had given him much muscle, and the recent meals had helped fill out the lines of his face and body more. Rather than thin, he seemed sleek. To see such imperfections on his perfect body . . . she entertained a brief idea of pecking out Richard's eyes.

Her hands were steady as she fetched a bowl of water and some cloth. She crossed over to her husband and sat beside him on the bed. Tenderly, she began tending to all the wounds by cleaning them thoroughly and carefully rubbing herbs into the bruises to bring down the swelling. "I could kill him for this," she whispered fiercely.

He watched her under lowered lashes, taking great enjoyment in having her hands running over his chest. He didn't know if she realized it was arousing him to have her tending to him but he thought they might both enjoy it if he returned the favor. "I'm used to it." There was a shrug in his voice as he said, "He used to whip me."

Her head shot up sharply. "What?" Her black eyes were fierce as she tugged at his shoulders, and he obligingly turned around so his back was towards her. Tears welled in her eyes as she saw the old scar marks across his back from where a whip had been laid. She fiercely wrapped her arms around him and pressed her lips to his back. "I hate him for this."

He shuddered at the feel of her lips. Pleasure seemed to radiate from his back outwards as she began to press soft kisses over all the marks. "Raven," he managed to say. "You ought to stop."

"Why?" She nuzzled his shoulder. "You're my husband."

"Yes, but it's not fair." With a grace and speed that surprised her, he suddenly turned around and caught her into his arms. "I want to touch you, too."

The heat of his skin was shocking, and the feel was electrifying as her hands flattened on his chest over his heart. Without giving herself time to be embarrassed, she leaned forward and darted her tongue over his collarbone. He shivered, and delight filled her. "I can't believe I'm here with you."

He buried his hand in her hair and tilted her head back. "I can't either," he admitted softly. Unable to hold himself back any longer, he bent his head and kissed her deeply, his tongue slipping into her mouth to tangle with her own. She tasted like fresh rain. It was addicting.

On a soft sound of need, she slid her hands around the back of his neck and drew him closer. She was beginning to feel feverish, her clothes too hot and confining. By the time his lips released hers, she could hardly breathe for the hunger to feel him touching her. "Kay," she whispered. "Please."

He slowly unbuttoned her bodice and dropped it over the side of the bed. The corset was next to be unlaced. He found nothing beneath the silk material except even silkier soft skin. He gently tugged it away and then lifted her to her feet. They unfastened the skirt together and it fell to the floor. Her petticoats and pantalets went next. In moments she wore nothing but lamplight as she eased once more onto the bed beside him. Shadows partially concealed her from view in a tempting tease.

He had nothing to compare her to, but he felt as if she was somehow perfect. Her trim figure needed no corset, and her curves were gentle and supple. Her skin was pale from lack of sun, and a soft flush made her radiant. He couldn't resist slowly running a finger across her collarbone, and he watched her face intently as he did.

Her eyes closed as she waited in an agony of suspension for him to truly touch her. Her body ached, and her breasts felt hot and heavy. Everywhere his fingers touched there was a wave of fire left behind. His hand suddenly cupped her breast and the lash of pleasure shocked her. She arched toward his touch helplessly on a low moan, the nipple swelling on a rush.

Encouraged, he began to trail kisses over her neck and shoulders, delighted at her taste. He slowly worked his way lower, and his hands trembled with the force of his need. He had dreamed of this, dreamed of touching her. Reality was better than he had dared dream. He closed his lips hungrily around the tip of one breast and thrilled at the whimper she gave as she twisted against him.

Suddenly ravenous, he caressed her with lips and teeth, his hands rushing over her sides and up higher to cup her breasts. He raced his kisses over her chest and tasted every inch of her flesh. She began to tremble, and a fierce throbbing began between her legs. Instinctively, her legs shifted to press together.

He barely noticed as he laid her back on the bed. He simply looked his fill for a moment, feeling his body throbbing lightly with the wild urge to possess her. She was so beautiful! The sight of black curls at the apex of her thighs was tempting, and his fingers skimmed over her stomach and lower.

When his lips covered hers, she went into the kiss eagerly. Her hands skidded over his shoulders and her nails scraped lightly. She felt wild for him, as if she couldn't get enough. She unexpectedly felt his fingers sliding through the curls shielding where she was most vulnerable, and she made a grab for his wrist in embarrassment.

He didn't let her deter him, and his fingers slid lower until he was cupping the heart of her. She was hot and wet, and his fingers slid through her folds to caress her intimately. She gave a little cry that thrilled him, and he used his free hand to drag her closer for another kiss as his fingers explored her softly.

Tension gripped her body and she whimpered thinly as she felt the pleasure getting stronger. Desire drowned her nerves and she released his wrist to clutch his shoulders. One of his fingers slipped inside her again, and she couldn't control a desperate arch of her hips. It wasn't enough. She needed something more. "Kay," she pleaded. "Something's wrong."

Somehow he was certain something was *right*. He continued to caress her and felt a greedy thrill as she surged against him, her body calling to him with a lure he couldn't resist. "Touch me," he urged against her lips. "I want to feel your hands."

She couldn't have stopped herself if she had tried. Her hands eagerly lifted and explored his chest with a sensuality she hadn't been able to release when tending to him. Her fingertips brushed over his nipples, and he shuddered. Encouraged, she did it again, and she was delighted when he moaned softly. She felt drugged on pleasure and her nails bit into his shoulders lightly when his fingers stroked her softly.

With a little surge of strength, she twisted her body and sent him tumbling off her. His eyes almost crossed as she almost pounced on him, and her lips and fingers caressed his skin. It didn't hurt. Nothing could hurt when she touched him.

She had been tipsy once in her life, when she had tried wine for the first time a year or two before. Now, for the first time, she understood what it meant to be drunk. She drowned in her lover, and there was no room for shyness inside, not with how his presence filled her. She helped him remove his pants without hesitation and then simply stared at him.

She had been raised by an open-minded community. She knew full well about sex and babies, and the differences between men and women. It had always seemed so clinical before, but now it was a little unnerving as she beheld the vivid evidence that he wanted her. Her curiosity overrode her nerves and she reached out to touch him with a soft finger.

He hissed softly and bit back a groan; the small touch was like a lightning bolt. He grit his teeth and fought his body, trying to keep from losing control as she explored him. Finally he couldn't take it anymore and rolled her over to pin her beneath him as his mouth devoured hers.

"Your ribs!" she protested breathlessly. She whimpered as he settled between her legs and she felt his hot flesh rubbing against her. Instinctively, her legs wound around his hips. "Kay!"

"Forget my ribs." His mouth rushed over her face, and one hand held her tightly to him. "I can't wait. I need to be inside you." He reached between them with his other hand and caressed her, needing her breathless cries to know she wanted him just as terribly. His erection nestled against her, and as he flexed his hips, he pushed slowly inside. "Raven?"

"If you stop," she warned thickly, "I'll be forced to do something drastic!" Her breath caught as he pushed slowly deeper, and her body slowly stretched to hold him. It hurt a little, but it stirred something deeper inside. She craved having him as close as possible.

On a groan, he buried his face in her hair and surged into her fully. She was hot and wet, and the feeling was electrifying, drawing his body taut with desire. Terrified he might have hurt her, he lifted his head and rained kisses over her face. "Did I hurt you?"

"No." She trembled and returned the kisses almost ravenously. It was what she had wanted, but . . . she needed something more. She didn't understand it but felt it beckoning her. Without conscious thought, her hips arched against him, and it sent off a shockwave through them both. Helplessly, she twisted beneath him. "Kay, do something, please!"

Instinct took over, and his lips sealed hers as he began to slowly slide out of her only to drive deeply back in. Again and again, until he felt as if he might break from the tension, he drove into her, hungry for everything he could have from her.

Her fingers clenched into his hair as the pleasure grew and grew until it suddenly erupted with a force that stunned her. Ecstasy rolled over her without stopping, and she muffled a cry against the side of his neck as she clung onto him. She felt the shudder that ripped through his strong body, and then he was buried in her to the hilt, his head thrown back as he gave in to their pleasure. She had never seen anything more wildly beautiful.

He managed to not collapse on top of her, but he was

exhausted. He was also stunned. There was, he realized in vague surprise, a difference between knowing the mechanics of something, and experiencing it firsthand with someone you loved. He turned his head and kissed her deeply. "Are you okay?" he asked softly.

Her eyes opened slightly and a smile curved her lips. "Yes." Her arms slid more fully around him, keeping him close when he would have moved. "I can't think of a word to describe how I feel except 'happy,' but that isn't even close." Her eyes opened wide suddenly. "Oh! Your ribs!"

"They're fine." He felt them twinge in argument but ignored them. He carefully rolled to the side and tugged her closer so that she was protectively tucked against him. "You're my wife now, completely. I'm never letting you go."

Tears burned her eyes as she burrowed closer. "I just hope you feel that way tomorrow morning," she whispered, "when you wake and find that your wife has become a bird."

"Watch me." He held her securely and closed his eyes. He knew that nothing could possibly change his mind.

He awoke hours later to the realization it was after dawn because there was sunlight filtering through the pipe where the stove went above ground. Raven wasn't in his arms. He frowned as he realized he had wanted to wake with her beside him. A soft sound reached his ears, and he looked around swiftly to see a raven sitting on the trunk. She was crying softly.

He immediately got out of bed and lifted her into his arms. He rubbed his cheek over her feathers, and she stopped crying. Her black eyes looked at him in despair. He tightened his hold on her protectively. "I don't care," he said softly. "You're still my wife. You're still my Raven. I'll find a way to free you, I swear it. Just promise never to fly away."

She sighed softly and rubbed her head against his chin in acceptance. He continued to tenderly stroke her feathers and knew that nothing mattered except that they were together. Bird or woman, she was the one he loved more than anything. He would protect her from everything. "I love you Raven," he vowed quietly.

She closed her eyes and nestled closer. She finally believed that he meant it. Perhaps someday everything would be alright. She wanted to believe in the happily ever after Rhianna had always told her belonged to true lovers. She had found her true lover. They deserved a happy ending.

CHAPTER FIVE

Kay gently set Raven down on the end of the bed and looked for his clothes. Once he was fully dressed, he sat down and frowned thoughtfully. "I suppose the first thing I need to do is to find somewhere I can work." His stomach rumbled loudly, and he cleared his throat. "Sorry."

She flew over to the stove and flapped her wings to get his attention. He walked over with a tilt of his head, and his brows lifted. Breakfast sat waiting on the top of the stove, and it was still steaming warm. She had taken the time to make him something before her change. He tenderly caressed her feathers, love making his eyes soften. "I don't deserve you."

Pleasure filled her heart and she landed on his shoulder so that she could be close to him. It made her very happy to watch him devour his meal, and she really hoped that she could bring him breakfast in bed someday. He was long overdue to be pampered by someone who loved him!

Perhaps a bit amusingly, he was thinking the same thing about her. He deeply liked the idea of completely and thoroughly spoiling his lover as soon as she could be human during the day. Barring that, he would spoil her mercilessly at night instead.

Content in many ways, he put the plate back and smiled. "Let's go into town. I'm not going to be afraid anymore. I know I still owe him money, but he can't force me to be a slave anymore. I can just pay him back in installments."

She frowned mentally but nuzzled his cheek. She didn't think it right that he should have to pay Richard anything, not after how he had been treated his whole life. She could only hope that Stormy was on her way to talk to Rhianna and Eric and tell them what was going on.

It was not yet mid-morning when they got to the city center nearby, and the townspeople greeted Kay with smiles and laughter. Several waved cheerfully. Kay had no idea what had happened, but he got his explanation when one gentleman stopped to greet him, "We all heard from Father Evans that you got married yesterday!" His smile was wide. "We're all happy for you. Where's your bride?"

"Resting." Kay smiled in return. "She's a very delicate woman. Ow!" He rubbed his ear as Raven pecked at it with her beak. He barely hid a laugh; he did not find it surprising that she disliked being labeled as delicate. "Thank you," he said to the man. "Your support means a lot."

"We've always liked you, Kay," the man told him seriously. "If we could have found a way to get Johnston off you, we would have. I know today is a day to rest for you, but tomorrow come see me, and I'll find you a job at my shop." He smiled. "You'll need to support your family."

"Thank you very much!" Surprised, Kay watched him walk away and wondered if the entire city had been on his side without his knowledge. It was an oddly freeing feeling. Deeply curious, he wandered down to the river and sat on a bench to study it. Now that it wasn't his prison, he was able to admire it. "It feels odd to simply stop and relax."

Raven agreed but wished fiercely that she could be sitting there beside him and holding his hand. She gave a startled chirp as he suddenly lifted her off his shoulder and onto his lap, and his nimble fingers smoothed over her feathers. It was akin to when he ran his hands through her hair and very pleasurable. She snuggled under his hand contentedly. How had she been lucky enough to find this particular man?

His hand stopped and she felt tension fill in his fingers. She swiftly looked up and saw Richard Johnston standing less than twenty feet away with an inhuman sort of fury on his face. In that moment, she knew she was looking into the face of evil. She bristled and prepared to do whatever it took to protect her husband.

Kay felt curiously unafraid. He had known the confrontation was inevitable. Because he needed the leverage, he got to his feet. His confidence began to grow more as he realized something he never had before: Richard was the smaller man. He stood at five-seven, at most, and he had more fat than muscle on his frame. Kay stood taller and the steady meals lately had been adding more weight to his already present muscle.

He began to smile. "Good morning, Richard." A soft wind ruffled his hair, and the soothing sensation felt like someone stood behind him in support. Raven's little trill of greeting implied it might not be just his imagination. He gently put her down on the bench. "I assume you're here to congratulate me on my marriage."

Good boy, a familiar woman's voice murmured in his mind. *Keep him talking. Let him hang himself.*

Richard's face twisted with rage. "What woman would want a nobody like you?"

"A wonderful woman," he countered. "One I love very dearly. She is a true lady."

"A whore no doubt." Richard spit at the ground near his feet. "You deserve each other."

Never one to flare with quick temper, Kay found he had to fight for control. He could handle insults to himself, but *never* to Raven. "Actually, we do." His faint accent thickened slightly in warning. "And I really do not care what you have to say." He lowered a hand and rubbed his fingers over Raven's head to comfort her rising distress. "May I assume we have your well wishes?"

"I own you!" the older man roared. "You owe me for raising you all of these years!" He seemed completely unaware of the crowd that had gathered around them. More than one man was armed on the chance that things turned physical. "You owe your life to me!"

Since it seemed he didn't want to keep the truth hidden, Kay didn't feel alarmed at the idea of it all coming out. "Is that why you beat me nearly to death whenever I didn't make what you deemed was the right amount?" His voice was bland and without inflection.

"A boy like you has no idea of his betters! You deserved to be beaten! And who would care if you died?! A homeless, useless child with no family! No money of his own!" Richard took a step closer. "You owe me!"

"For what? Living in the barn my whole life? For working like a slave? For being beaten? For knowing that you were wasting my family's money when there was nothing I could do about it?" Every word made nineteen years of suppressed fury rise hotter and hotter. His hands clenched into fists at his sides. "You're a disgusting, pathetic old man!"

"How dare you?!" Richard lunged forward on a roar, beefy fists raised in warning.

Raven shot into the air on a screech, and her talons raked across his face. Blood flew as he shrieked in fear and pain. He grabbed her out of the air and hurled her violently aside. She landed safely in a familiar man's arms, but she looked distinctly dazed.

Kay saw red. "Don't ever touch her again!" He took a single gliding step forward, and his fist cracked across Richard's jaw so hard that he was sent flying into the river beside them. "I owe you nothing," Kay warned in a dangerously soft voice, "except contempt!"

"Indeed." Eric walked forward, and he had Raven securely held in his arms. His ice blue eyes were dispassionate as he watched the man struggling to stay afloat in the river. "Richard Johnston, did you not sign a contract with Enforcers that stated you would care for Kay Shaughnessy as if he were your own son?"

Rhianna walked up to stand beside her partner and took Raven from Eric to hand her to Kay. "I believe he did, Riku," she countered calmly, "and in light of the evidence, I believe this is a breach of contract. What did the stipulations state?"

"An eye for an eye, Rhi." He reached down to haul Richard out of the river. Eric was not much bigger than Kay but he was immensely stronger. "Let's take him to the sheriff, shall we?" He smiled at Kay. "Consider any debt you *might* have owed to be completely null and void."

Stunned, Kay stood holding Raven and watched Eric head off

down the road, all but dragging Richard by the seat of his pants. A little shiver touched his skin for a moment and he held the raven in his arms closer. "He won't make it to the sheriff, will he?" he asked Rhianna softly.

"No," she told him gently. She lowered a hand and scratched Stormy behind the ears as the slender wolf came up and sat beside her. "Richard has been destroyed by his own greed. There is nothing but evil inside him. Part of the Enforcers' role is to destroy evil. Riku will handle things." She smiled. "Now come along with me. We're going to the Enforcers' office to talk."

"Alright." He gave her an odd look as they began walking down the road toward the carriage waiting. "I thought . . . for a moment, I was sure I heard you in my mind. And that wind . . . it felt as if it came from Mr. Mason."

Her smile spread. "Perhaps. We of 3rd District are . . . singularly blessed." She had to laugh softly as he quickly beat her to the carriage and offered a hand to help her up. "Blood will tell. You're a true gentleman at heart." She let him assist her and then took a seat as he joined her. Stormy and Raven sat on the seats beside them.

The Enforcers' building was the largest in the District and in fact the largest in most of the city. It boasted an impressive number of stories and the architecture rivaled the capitol building. Kay loved it on sight, and the entire 3rd District. Where parts of the main city were beginning to be modernized, the styles starting to change, 3rd District was still the same as it had been for centuries.

Rhianna ushered them straight up to the top floor where she and Eric had their offices. Once inside, she took the pins out of her hair and shook out the thick red mass so that it swung around her shoulders. "I do hate those." Rubbing her scalp, she went over to her desk and had a seat behind it. "Sit down, Kay."

He did so, still looking around curiously. Everything in the office had been made from hand carved wood with an eye for detail and design. It was clearly made by the same craftsman who had made Raven's bed. His color climbed as he remembered how comfortable that bed had been when he had been lying in it with Raven snuggled beside him.

Rhianna covered a smile. She truly liked him, this kind boy with dreams in his eyes and a wild spirit in his heart. They were traits she hoped were passed down through the generations along with his beautiful smile. "Well," she started, "to begin with, congratulations on your marriage."

He smiled and smoothed his fingers over Raven's feathers when she landed on his lap. "Thank you." His face grew serious. "Miss Taber, please, tell me. Is there any way to break this curse on Raven?"

"Call me Rhianna." She toyed with a pen. "What would you do if I told you there wasn't?"

His face tightened. "I'd find a way to support us by working during the day, and I'd spend every minute of the night with her. I love Raven," he vowed intensely. "I don't care what she is!"

She smiled suddenly. "I see why your paths crossed. You are truly meant for one another." Perhaps things would be just fine for Stormy after all. Well, if they could all go this smoothly, of course. "There is a way to break the curse," she announced.

His eyes widened. "Really? How? I'll do anything!"

"First . . ." She held up a hand. "Let me explain something, alright? About the 3rd District and its origins." She folded her hands on her desk. "It started many, many centuries ago, before I was born." She tilted her head. "If I told you there were other worlds out there, worlds that cannot be seen by the naked eye, what would you think?"

He thought about it. "I'd think that doesn't sound very wrong," he decided. "I believe in magic, Rhianna."

"Good, good." She settled back in her chair. "There *is* such a world out there; one that lies parallel to this one. It is known as Mirage. Have you ever, on a truly hot day, thought you saw something there but got closer and discovered it was gone?" He nodded and she smiled. "You were seeing a piece of the world known as Mirage, a place of magic. A century or two before I was born, it drifted too close to Earth and became stuck."

"Stuck?" He cocked his head. "How does a world get stuck?"

"Simply because the River Styx runs like a band around the

world, right under New York in fact, and Mirage consists entirely of magic. The two got meshed together. The river is now a gateway between worlds." She swirled a finger in the air. "This district is built directly over where the Styx is closest to the surface."

"Magic," Eric added from the doorway, "is literally born here. It affects all of New York, really, but much more thinly. It took a long time for people to evolve as they did. Rhianna's and my generation was the beginning of the truly powerful and visible changes. We chose to build our district on this location so that the magic was always cycling. Now any child born here, even to normal parents, will be gifted."

"So why call it the 3rd District?" Kay wondered. "Why not give it a real name, befitting it?"

Eric's smile spread as he walked over to sit on the edge of Rhianna's desk. "What makes you think we didn't? You see, Kay, when you hear us say '3rd', you are hearing the number three."

"As if it were the third district built," Kay agreed. "It's not?"

"Actually, it was originally named 'thierde,' which is pronounced the same way. It is a word in the language of Mirage that means 'sanctuary of magic.'" Rhianna spread her hands as his eyes widened. "As time went past, people forgot the meaning. We let them. This world is not . . . comfortable with magic. We had thought that most had forgotten, but the slaughter of the werewolves proved us wrong. In a hundred years, I'm sure we'll be nothing but a myth once more."

"Let it happen." His voice was firm. "If it keeps everyone safe, then let it happen." He smiled as Raven nuzzled his hand. "How does this matter to Raven's curse?"

"It's very simple, Kay." Eric crossed his arms. "To break the curse, her feathers must be changed from black to white, and the only way to do that is to immerse her in the River Styx. It is the river that not only connects to Mirage, but sailing along it will also take you to the afterworld where we all go when we die. It is a river of life, death, and rebirth."

Kay leapt to his feet. "I'll do it! I'll take Raven there and break

this curse!"

Rhianna smiled. "Good boy. Stormy knows the way, so she will take you there. And, Kay, remember: you cannot touch the river yourself. If you fall within it, you will die."

He nodded firmly. "I won't. I'll come back as soon as I can, and Raven will be walking beside me no matter what time of day it is." Holding an astonished Raven close in his arms, he left the office and followed Stormy as she hurried down the hall.

The door shut behind him, and Rhianna looked at Eric. "Well?"

"He's gone." He didn't elaborate on the details but there was a hardness in his blue eyes for a moment before disappearing. "When I spoke to the governor to tell him how the Shaughnessy heir was doing, he was delighted to hear of his marriage. He wants to meet Kay and Raven once the curse is lifted. The only trouble is that his ex-wife looked . . . a bit alarmed."

"As I imagine she would. If her sin is exposed, she will be labeled as an attempted murderess." She drummed her fingers on her desk. "My only concern now is that *all* the people from 3rd District know how to find the River Styx."

He studied her. "Rhi, have I ever told you that I often think you manipulate people and the only reason there are no coincidences in 3rd District is because of you?"

"Daily."

"Just thought I'd mention it again for good measure."

Raven could not fight a bundle of nerves and huddled against Kay's shoulder for security; was this really going to work? Kay had his own nerves, but he was damned determined that he would make things work out. Nerves turned to puzzlement as he followed Stormy down below the first floor of the building into what looked like a basement. They then went down another set of stairs into a dungeon.

"Where are we going?"

Stormy pawed at the wall. He touched it, and a door appeared. Startled, he jerked his hand away and the door disappeared. He touched it again curiously and the door once more appeared. With a quick breath, he pushed on the door and it swung outward into blinding white light.

Stormy nudged him through the door, and he hastily covered his eyes against the brightness. The door silently swung shut behind them, and he slowly lowered his arm as he felt the light fading.

He discovered he was standing on the edge of the world. At the least, that was how it felt. He stood at the top of a sharp cliff, and he could see a series of more cliffs ahead that slowly dropped downward as if they were a giant's stairs. The last one in the distance seemed to drop off into nothing at all.

Wildflowers bloomed everywhere in a riot of colors. He knelt to pick one, and it turned into a butterfly. Another flower was left in its place, and he ran a hand over the top of several blooms. A curtain of butterflies swirled into the air and toward the sky, and it was then that he finally noticed the most spectacular part of that beautiful place.

The sky seemed to be a relatively normal blue, but in the middle, suspended like an illusion, was the appearance of another world. He could see forests and rivers, lakes and towns. It looked like nothing he had ever seen before, and certainly nothing like New York. Castles dotted the landscape and he could almost hear the trumpets. It was grand and beautiful. "Is that Mirage?" he asked softly. "It's amazing."

Stormy took off running down the field, and he hurried after her with Raven flying along beside him. When he had first stood there looking around, it had seemed like such a long distance. By the time evening fell, he knew that they would reach the end the next day. Perhaps time moved at a different rate there.

They were all tired so they stopped where they were to rest for the night. The sun also set in that magical place, and he watched it slowly sink in a fiery blaze of color. Just as it disappeared beyond the horizon, he realized Raven had started to glow softly. The light swirled up and around her, and as it faded away, she was once more a woman. She was also naked, and she blushed profusely as she wrapped her arms around herself.

"Now you know why I always hid," she whispered. "Unfortunately, my clothes never change with me. I turn back and I'm naked." She looked up in surprise as she felt him wrapping his jacket around her shoulders. "Thank you."

He knelt beside her and drew her into his arms as his lips sought hers. He had craved her taste and touch every second of every minute. "Welcome home," he murmured. He slowly lowered her down until she was lying in the flowers. "I missed touching you."

Stormy, being a wise and rather discrete wolf, took off. Neither Raven nor Kay noticed. She tenderly ran her hands over his face and savored the feel of his skin. "It was the hardest thing I've ever done, leaving your arms this morning." She burrowed against him on a soft sound of need. "I've never needed anyone like I need you. I love you so much!"

He caught her close and kissed her deeply, his body shaking with the force of his emotions. He knew how she felt. He knew, precisely, how she felt. If he lost her, he would be willing to jump into the Styx to find her again.

"So that's Mirage," she murmured drowsily hours later as they were snuggled together watching the sky. Her head was tucked on his shoulder and they were using his jacket as a blanket. She had never been more content. "It's beautiful. I always knew it was there, but I'd never seen it."

"I didn't even know it was there." His hand stroked over her back slowly. "It seems so odd to me, in some ways, to think of everything that has happened. But . . . but I like it. Let's make sure that our children always believe in magic."

She straightened up, startled. "You want children with me?" He looked at her oddly and she shook her head. "But we can't be sure I can have them." Blushing furiously, she whispered, "I've never . . . my body hasn't . . . monthly I don't . . ."

He frowned. "I'm still not following."

She bit her lip as her cheeks turned pink. "Women . . . monthly . . . well, they bleed. And that's how they know that they can have children, but aren't pregnant." She shook her head. "I'll teach you to read and then give you a book on it. It's so embarrassing!"

He felt slightly embarrassed himself, and also quite sympathetic for women of the world. "Basically what you are saying is that since you've never . . . you know . . . you can't be sure your body is capable?"

"Yes," she whispered.

His lips firmed. "We'll figure it out. I think if we wish for anything hard enough, we can have it." He rolled over and tucked her protectively underneath him. "Rhianna and Eric are old and wise. They might know something. And if not . . . then maybe we can adopt." He smiled. "We would do much better than the Johnstons."

She smiled and pulled him close. "Yes," she agreed softly. "We would."

As dawn was beginning to rise, she left his arms. He awoke instantly and sat up with a frown to watch as she walked a few steps away. Somehow he heard her tears inside his heart, and he knew this was why the raven cried every morning. He quickly got to his feet and wrapped his arms around her. "Don't cry," he urged.

She trembled and closed her eyes as her head fell back against his shoulder. "I'm alone."

"No, you're not. Not anymore." He held onto her tightly and felt the rise of her power inside. Light consumed her and swirled around them both as the sunrise washed over them. Moments later, he was holding nothing but air, and the raven was sitting on the flowers in front of him.

She took a breath as if to cry but he knelt and lifted her into his arms. "Don't cry," he said again, rubbing his cheek over her feathers. "I'm here with you always." He eased back and smiled. "I love you."

She nuzzled her head against his shoulder and finally let go of the pain she had endured her entire life. No, she wasn't alone. She would never be alone at dawn again, not as long as she had him.

Stormy rejoined them not long after he had gotten dressed again, and they all continued on their way toward the canyon that

marked the western edge of the River Styx. When they reached it, Kay carefully got down on his knees and peered over the side. His eyes slowly widened.

The River Styx was nothing like any river he had ever seen before. It wasn't blue at all, and it wasn't even a clear color that reflected blue. It looked visibly, richly, silver and white. It flowed gently and steadily, and he felt his stomach quiver as he saw a small boat sailing down it. A cloaked person was pushing it along and he gave a nervous laugh as he saw the skeletal hands holding the steering pole. "I do not want to know who that is."

He straightened and smiled at Raven as she landed beside him. "Are you ready?" He heard Stormy suddenly growl softly with menace and turned his head sharply to see several soldiers approaching them quickly. He got to his feet and braced his shoulders. "What are you doing here?"

"Orders from the First Lady." One of the men drew a bayonet. "We're here to kill you and the bird."

"No!" He stepped in front of Raven defensively. "You won't touch her!" Even when the soldier aimed the tip of the weapon under his chin, he didn't back down. "Go back to where you came from! You don't belong here!"

The blade was pressed harder, and it drew blood. Raven gave a chilling cry and shot at the soldier's face with her talons extended. His scream of agony echoed everywhere and sent butterflies in mad flight as she clawed at his eyes and ripped flesh. The other soldiers were too horrified to move.

The first soldier managed to grab her and twisted her wing sharply. Bone and cartilage broke loudly in the eerie silence. With a shout, he hurled her over the side of the cliff.

"Raven!" Kay lunged for the edge and dove over the side after her. A broken wing meant she could not fly. She would never survive the fall into the river unless something bigger broke the surface first.

"Well." The solder could barely see as he swiped at his bleeding face. "That's that."

A low, menacing growl rose on the air, and they all turned to see the wolf glowing. Hearts stopped dead as the wolf's body stretched up and became a familiar figure. Everyone knew who she was and what she had done. The scent of their terror filled the air as she slowly walked toward them. They knew their lives were done.

Raven had closed her eyes to prepare for the impact, but they flew wide again as she felt one of Kay's arms close around her. She flapped her good wing and struggled wildly, but he drew her closer with a tender smile. "If we die, we die together." The words came from him with absolute calm.

They plunged into the River Styx. Kay's half-dive managed to break the surface enough to keep them from dying on impact, but it still nearly knocked him out. His arm loosened and freed Raven, and she had suffered no ill effects from the landing. The water surged around her sharply, and he watched dazedly as her feathers turned to white. She would be okay.

The light engulfed her as it always did at sunset though it was only the middle of the day. The transformation had never hurt until that moment when it stitched her broken arm back together and healed it. The light slowly faded, and she found herself staring at her hands. The curse's heavy presence had lifted from her soul. All she had to do was kick her legs and she would float to the surface and be free.

She turned her head and saw Kay suspended in the middle of the river. He would die if he remained there for much longer, and yet there was no way to free him. He was normal. Normal people could not go into the river lest they never leave again.

Without hesitation, she kicked her way over and wrapped her arms around him. He started to struggle then, shaking his head adamantly, but she just smiled and leaned up to kiss him softly. She didn't want to live without him, curse or no curse. If he was doomed, then so was she. "If we die," she mouthed tenderly, "then we die together."

His eyes softened and he moved his arms enough to pull her close. The weight of the river covered them both and dragged them deeper, compressing their lungs until the last bubble of air was forced

from their lips.

The bubbles merged together over their heads and began emitting a soft golden light. The light swept down over them, severed the ties the river held on them, and held the waters back. Fresh air that carried a soft scent of peaches surrounded them and both breathed it in deeply. Neither knew what was happening though they were grateful.

The light swirled around them and carried them up toward the surface, and then it carried them even further up to the top edge of the cliff. It set them down gently amid the flowers. Raven pushed herself up to a sitting position and shoved her wet hair out of her eyes. "Why?" she asked softly.

"Because," a man's voice answered just as softly from within the light, "those who are willing to die for love are the ones who truly deserve to live."

The light faded away and the scent of peaches disappeared. Shivering, she wrapped her arms around herself and looked aside to see Kay carefully sitting up. She threw her arms around him on a surge of joy and nearly knocked them both over again.

His arms closed around her fiercely, and he buried his face in her hair. "We did it," he murmured. "We really did it."

"Idiot!" She pressed her face to his shoulder, her shoulders shaking as she began to sob. "You were going to die! How could you think I'd ever want to live without you?!"

He gently framed her face and leaned down to kiss her. "You'd do the same for me." He held her close and looked around, but there was no sign of the soldiers. He spotted Stormy sitting not very far beyond them, though, and there was blood from a gash across her front haunch. She looked relatively intact overall.

He just smiled. He had always suspected he knew who and what she was, but it was her secret to tell if she ever wanted. He felt honored to call her his friend. "Thank you," he told her softly, and saw her surprise. "For everything."

CHAPTER SIX

By the time they got back to the Enforcers' entrance, both Raven and Kay were desperate for clean clothes. He was wearing only his shirt and pants, and she was wearing his jacket. The clothes were stiff from drying in the sun and slightly dirty from being used as blankets at night.

The only bright spot that either had found was the morning they had woken together at sunrise with her still safely curled in his arms. Even as dawn had washed over them, the only glow inside her had been the happiness she felt. She had always hated the dawn, but now she loved it and the way it made Kay's white hair shine brilliantly.

Stormy limped along at their side, and her wound had been dressed by a makeshift bandage torn from the edge of the shirt. She was just as happy to see the exit as they were. Kay opened the door, and she ran in on a loud bark. Her claws skidded on the floor as she ran up the stairs.

Moments later, Eric came down the stairs with her yanking him by his pant leg. "Yes, I'm hurrying," he told her. "Impatient thing." He spotted Kay and Raven and had to smile. "Ah, so the heroes return triumphantly. Well done, children."

Raven felt horribly embarrassed standing there in nothing but Kay's jacket, and she hid partially behind her husband. Never mind that Riku was like an uncle or surrogate father to her. It was still embarrassing! "Thank you, but . . . is there somewhere we can bathe and get clean clothes, Riku?"

Rhianna came down the stairs with two blankets over her arms. "Naturally." She gave one to each of them and then smiled as they wrapped themselves up firmly. "Once you have bathed and rested, come and see me. There's much we have to discuss. And you," she added to Stormy, "come with me to get bandaged up. Troublemaker."

Kay and Raven were shown to a guest room on the second floor and both were more than happy to take advantage of the private bath attached to it. The water was cold, naturally, since no one had known when they would return, but Raven used her powers and had it steaming hot in short order.

She shamelessly admired her husband as he stripped off his dirty clothes. He truly was as beautiful inside as out. The wounds had wholly disappeared after the trip into the River Styx, and even the scars had faded more. Perhaps in a few years they would fade entirely.

He caught her gaze and was warmed. He liked knowing she found him attractive. He smiled and reached over to begin unwrapping her from the blanket and jacket. "You're so beautiful," he told her, "that it seems a shame to cover you up now that I can see you in the daylight."

"It feels so odd," she admitted, holding onto his shoulders as he lifted her and carried her into the tub with him. As he sat down and held her on his lap, she slid her arms around his neck and studied his face intently. "Would you have truly stayed with me if the curse could have never been broken?"

"Yes." He tugged her down for a kiss. "I love you exactly as you are." He eased her back and picked up the cake of soap to begin gently washing her. "And I'm going to warn you now that I'll do everything in my power to spoil you entirely."

"Oh." It was the best she could manage as his hands sent ripples of pleasure through her body and stirred her senses. "I think you're taking advantage of my weakness for you." She shuddered as his fingers slid between her legs.

He smiled. "I just can't keep my hands off you."

"Can we . . . in a bathtub?"

"I know a water elf. She won't let the floor get wet."

When they walked into Rhianna's office an hour or two later, Stormy sniffed at Raven and gave a happy bark as her tail began wagging enthusiastically. Rhianna and Eric both hid smiles as they got to their feet. "Feeling better?" Rhianna asked blandly.

Kay and Raven both blushed profusely. At least there was no evidence. The water had stayed off the floor, but Raven still couldn't figure out how she had been able to concentrate at all. "Yes, thank you." She smoothed a hand over her cherry blossom dress. "Where did you find this? I left it at home."

"I know an elemental master," Rhianna noted dryly. "He has his way with trees."

"Hush, you."

Kay smiled. "You seem like brother and sister."

"Heaven forbid I be related to this shrew." Eric didn't deny the charge though, and neither did Rhianna. They had been best friends for centuries and were very much like family in many ways. Truthfully, they *were* family, in all the ways that counted. "Have a seat. We want to hear what happened."

"Alright." Kay sat down on one of the chairs. Raven took the seat beside him and he automatically laced their fingers together. "Everything went normally until we got to the river. These soldiers came from out of nowhere and told us they were there under the First Lady's orders to kill Raven and me."

"One of them threatened Kay and cut him." Raven lowered her gaze. "I attacked him with my talons. He broke my wing and threw me over the cliff. Kay dove after me and we both went into the river."

Rhianna lifted a brow slightly. "And yet you both sit here alive."

"Well . . ." Kay frowned. "Raven had thought to stay there with me, so that we died together." His hand tightened around hers for a moment. "But there was this light, this golden light. It gave us air and we could smell peaches."

Rhianna went very still and drew Eric's puzzled gaze. "And?" she asked softly.

"It carried us out of the river and to safety. A man's voice told us that only those who are willing to die for love truly deserve to live." Raven frowned as she saw Rhianna's fingers tremble for a moment on her teacup. "Are you alright, Rhianna?"

"Yes." She firmly blocked Eric out of her mind and told herself to get a grip. Still, her heart beat hard within her chest. "Well, clearly, this light was someone with a soft spot for true love." She found a smile and it was natural. "As for the soldiers . . . well, we can explain that."

"Can I make a guess?" Kay asked.

"Certainly."

"Raven is the governor's daughter, isn't she?" He felt her incredulous gaze and looked at her with a smile. "It just seems to add up. The First Lady shouldn't have cared one way or another about you, unless she was afraid that your existence would prove she was a murderess."

"A *very* sharp young man," Eric murmured for Rhianna's ears only. Louder, he said, "You are correct, Kay. When Raven was born, her mother feared for her position if her husband knew she was from the 3rd District. So she cursed her daughter and pretended the child was stillborn."

"She has paid a price," Rhianna murmured. "She can have no more children. More importantly, her husband eventually divorced her to marry a woman he loved far deeper. Rumor says he could not bear to remain with his first wife because of their lost child. I strongly suspect he at least senses something."

"I still don't know why he let her stay on as First Lady after the divorce," Eric muttered.

"Pity," Rhianna told him.

"I . . . ." Raven slowly shook her head. "I can't be the governor's daughter!"

"Why not?" Eric asked. "As a matter of fact, this is quite opportune timing. The governor wanted to meet Kay and see how he is faring since the incident nineteen years ago. I think it only fitting that he meet his firstborn child." When he saw the distress on her face, he smiled gently. "Raven, I think you will be surprised. Your father will love you, I'm sure of it."

She wasn't nearly so sure, but she was willing to give it an attempt. She put on a thick and enveloping cloak to hide her features from sight until Eric deemed the right time to reveal her. Kay was the only reason she held any courage, and she clung tightly to his hand as they were shown in to see the governor.

The capitol was grander than she might have ever imagined. Kay was no less stunned, but he was fascinated as well by the architecture. He had always been fascinated by buildings and the ways they could be made. He liked secret passages, too. He had always wanted a home with one or two.

Eric seemed perfectly comfortable as he walked into the governor's office and bowed deeply. "I have brought Kay Shaughnessy and his wife." He heard a slight strangled gasp from where the First Lady stood, and he slid a cold blue gaze toward her. "Is something wrong, my lady?"

"No, no!" She averted her gaze swiftly.

Looking at her, Raven felt nothing but anger. This was the woman who had given birth to her, and this was also the woman who had tried to kill her. Objectively, she could see where she had gotten her looks. Her mother still looked quite beautiful at her later age, but the similarities were purely superficial. Her mother's eyes were narrowed and cruel, and little lines at the corners made her look far older than she was.

In stark contrast, the governor's second wife had soft features that no doubt made her seem deceptively youthful. Kindness edged her face and time would always sit gently on her shoulders because she treated others gently in turn. She stood closest to the governor and had a hand resting on his arm. Hiding just behind the folds of her elaborate dress was a little boy no more than five years old.

Raven's breath hitched as she looked at the governor. There was no denying that this man was her father; they possessed the same black eyes and dark hair. He seemed a bit plain, yet some inner beauty made him larger than life. He had been only a prominent lawyer at the time of her birth, and he had worked his way up the ladder over the years. He was now a well-loved governor that always thought of his people first.

Eric gently placed a hand on Kay's shoulder. "This is Kay," he said to the governor. "He is twenty-one years of age now. He was raised by Richard Johnston."

The governor frowned. "Mr. Johnston has not been seen lately."

"He breached an Enforcers' contract." Eric's voice was almost gentle. "He let himself be eaten away by evil. He abused Kay and treated him worse than a slave. He squandered all of the Shaughnessy wealth and forced Kay to work like a dog to make more. Regardless, Kay has become a man among men."

Kay knew he was blushing but couldn't help it. The governor smiled; the handsome young man's manner was refreshing and endearing. "So I see. Tell me, Kay, is there anything you would ask from me? I feel I owe you a service for not noticing all these years how you were treated. I helped get the approval to you entering that household."

"Hold onto that thought," Eric noted when he saw how speechless Kay was. "You see, I have some advice to ask from you. Let me tell you a tale, and you tell me what should be done."

"Very well. You have my undivided attention, Riku." The governor smiled as his son climbed onto his lap. "Most of it anyway."

"This is the tale: A woman feared for her own safety because she was 3rd District born. Out of that fear, she cursed her newly born child and condemned it to become a raven. This child was given a contract by us, and she was allowed to be a woman by night and a raven by day. She grew up to be a wonderful young woman, well loved by all she met. She eventually fell in love and got married. Her husband loved her in spite of the curse but sought to break it. They looked for a solution together.

"The mother heard of this, and she feared her secret would come out. She sent assassins to kill her child and son-in-law so that the secret could not be revealed. Now, the woman and her husband survived this ordeal and the curse was lifted. Quite a happily ever after, isn't it? My question is about the mother. Thrice attempted murder, lying, child endangerment . . . the list could go on. What ought to be her punishment?"

The governor was thinking, and he did not notice his first wife's agitation, or the nearly deadly look Eric sent her. His second wife did, and she glanced immediately to the cloaked figure standing just behind Kay. It did not take much to guess the tale was a true one, not when the 3rd District was involved. Her heart ached, and she fought an urge to scoop up the lost raven and promise everything would be fine.

"Well," the governor finally said, "I would not want to argue my feelings in court, of course, but if the evidence was heavy enough, I would say the mother had earned herself a life in prison or worse."

The First Lady began to weep softly, and Eric walked over to stand behind Raven. "Well said, sir. Tell me then, do you know this young woman?" And before she could stop him, he whisked her cloak off and revealed her to one and all.

The governor's breath lodged in his chest painfully as he found himself staring into his own eyes, set into a face as beautiful as his first wife's had once been. He *knew*. Fury swelled in his heart, and he turned toward his ex-wife. "Explain yourself," he said menacingly.

"I'm so sorry!" she burst out on a sob. "I was so terrified you would throw me aside! I didn't want to live on the streets or go back to my family! I was certain if you learned I was 3rd District born that you would toss me aside, and I would have to work so hard again! I had no choice!"

"Everyone in 3rd District is under government protection!" he roared as he got to his feet. "I am *honored* to call Riku and Rhianna my friends! How dare you! You tried to kill our daughter! You do not deserve to even associate yourself with the people of that District! Be gone from my sight! I let you keep your duties all these years only because I thought you grieved over our child. You are relieved of every single one, and with much relief, I might add!"

Security guards hurried inside and took the sobbing woman away to await her fate within the local jail. Kay could not bring himself to care one way or another. All he cared about was Raven. He gently pulled her into his arms and buried his face in her hair. "It will be alright," he said softly. "I promise."

The governor straightened and crossed his arms. "Come here,

child." When both looked at him, he beetled his brows at them. "Come here, Raven Shaughnessy. I am your father, and I command your obedience!"

Her knees shaking, she slowly crossed the room to stand before him. She would have curtseyed but she was terrified that she would fall on her face. He stepped toward her, and she squeezed her eyes shut. To her shock, she felt his hands gently framing her face, and his fingers were trembling. Her eyes flew open.

His smile trembled too, and tears glimmered in his eyes as he studied his child. "Look at you," he breathed. "You have my eyes, but you have your mother's beauty. My daughter. I thought . . ." His voice broke and he gathered her close against his heart. "I thought you lost to me forever."

She began to cry softly and held onto him tightly. "I thought you didn't want me!" she sobbed.

"No, never that!" He eased her away and wiped at her tears. "I'm honored to call you my daughter." He looked to where his true wife stood. There were tears in her eyes as well. "What say you, madam?"

"Raven," the proper First Lady said softly as she stepped forward. "I can have no more children. My son is the only child I may ever have. I always wished, so hard, for a daughter. I would be honored to be your mother, if you would let me."

Raven's lips trembled. "I have no idea how to handle parents."

"Mostly we will simply be bossy and interfere with your life," her stepmother teased gently. She reached out and hugged Raven close to rock her gently. "I wished for a daughter. It seems I got my wish. Our District miracle."

The governor pulled his son forward from where he had been hiding and nudged him toward Raven. "This is your big sister," he told him gently. "Go and greet her properly."

The little boy walked forward and wrapped his arms around Raven's leg in a happy hug. She buried her face in her hands as she sobbed harder. She whirled around and nearly flew into Kay's arms.

"Why is she crying?" the little boy asked Eric.

"She's happy," Eric promised him. He smiled at the governor. "Now, as to Kay . . ."

"Yes." He retook his seat and studied Kay intently. "Whether you intended to or not, you seem to have married my daughter. Her dowry is quite considerable, and if you wish it, a part of my land is yours."

"I thank you for your generosity," Kay told him, "but all I want is Raven. I would ask simply for the means to get any sort of training I might need in order to support her. I'm afraid I do not read very well as I never attended school."

He tugged on his beard lightly. "You do not wish for land and money?"

Kay smiled. "Not that I do not earn myself."

The First Lady leaned down and whispered in her husband's ear. He listened closely and began to smile. "Then this is how it shall be. You will accept Raven's dowry. Ah!" He held up a hand as Kay tried to protest. "Your father-in-law is speaking, boy. As I said, you will accept Raven's dowry. But you will return it to me as payment for a parcel of land. I will then give to you, as a wedding gift, a fine house. It will be built on your land. And, as my wife's gift to you, you will be sent to the finest master of whatever craft you wish to learn."

Eric covered a smile as Kay and Raven both stared at the governor in shock. "Well, Kay?" Eric asked. "What do you wish to learn?"

"I . . . well, I would be interested in learning accounting." Kay was still highly puzzled. "I always dreamed when I was much younger that I would learn how to make money, and then I would invest in others' dreams so that they could do it, too."

"And are you good at this?" the governor asked curiously.

"I learned many things listening to the passengers of my boat trips. Richard may have hated me, but he always invested in what I suggested. It doubled the profits."

He nodded firmly. "Then you will attend the best of schools, and when that is done, I will give you my own personal funds to invest. And who knows? Perhaps you will even be able to make a fine company out of your dreams." Almost pointedly he added, "One to pass on to your children?"

Eric laughed. "Don't worry. You'll have your grandchildren within a few months." Raven and Kay stared at him, and he winked. "Why do you think Stormy looked so pleased with herself?" Leaving them to have that sink in, he bowed deeply. "Good day, all of you." Without another word, he walked out.

Because the governor insisted on having Raven stay in his manor so he could get to know her better, Kay and Raven found themselves being shown to a grand bedroom where they could stay. High quality clothes were laid out for them, and she fingered the material of one of the dresses. "It seems too fine for me."

He slid his arms around her waist. "I like you in this dress best anyway. We should save it for our daughter or granddaughter."

She turned and wrapped her arms around him with a smile. "What if we only have boys for many generations?"

"I'm sure we'll find ourselves a female descendant somewhere." He lowered his forehead until it touched hers. "I love you, Raven Shaughnessy."

"And I love you." She framed his face with his hands, memorizing his features. "I never dared to dream for someone like you. I was so certain I would always be bound to the night, never able to embrace the dawn. You brought me the day, Kay. You rescued me."

"Does that mean we'll live happily ever after now?" he teased her softly, his heart swelling inside. He loved her more than anything in the world. When she smiled, he felt as if there would never be anything wrong again.

"Yes." Her eyes shimmered with love as she gazed at him. "Yes, I think it does." Her happy ending was right there in his arms. Her emotions welled up inside like a wave, and she rose on her toes to kiss him. Every faerie tale with a happy ending always ended with a kiss powerful enough to build dreams on, and she wasn't about to change the pattern there.

And if their kiss was truly the power for their dreams, then their dreams would never fade. They would never be broken down again.

EPILOGUE

Eric looked into Rhianna's office as he went past. "Everything is taken care of."

"So I see," she murmured as she looked at the two contracts she held. Both of them glowed suddenly, and the word 'Complete' appeared on both. With a smile, she added some notes to the bottom and slipped them into a folder. She then opened an empty drawer to put the folder inside. On the outside of the drawer she carefully wrote 'Shaughnessy File.'

"There." She glanced toward the figure standing on the other side of the room. "One down, ninety-nine to go."

"Good for me," a woman's voice muttered.

"You enjoyed it," she scolded her lightly. "I won't hear otherwise." Well satisfied with the events, she stretched her arms over her head. "I think that someday Kay's company will be one of the biggest in New York. And I see a lovely young woman with blonde hair and the Shaughnessy eyes wearing a cherry blossom dress."

"Are you looking into your crystal ball again?" the woman asked dryly.

She shook her head. "Call it a hunch."

The woman groaned. "I hate your hunches. They always mean more trouble for me."

She thought of the visions she'd had and just smiled.

Status: File Begun
Analysis: A man poor on wealth can be rich on love

Author Notes

I hope you enjoyed this first visit to my magical 3rd District! There's so much more to come in the future as the series continues! If you love this, be sure to get THE CARMICHAEL FILE, the second book in the series, now available on Amazon. THE DEASE FILE, third in the series, is scheduled for Fall 2016.

If you loved this story, or any of my stories, please leave me a review on Amazon! Reviews are the bread and butter of an author's life, and even a simple "More, please!" will keep us going.

You can keep up with me on www.facebook.com/stacyjgarrett or www.stacyjgarrett.com or follow my blog at stacyjgarrett.wordpress.com. I sometimes lurk on Twitter (@stacyjgarrett), and Tumblr as well (stacyjgarrett.tumblr.com).

I can't wait to see you again within my magical District! Until then, keep looking for those happy ever afters!

Stacy J Garrett

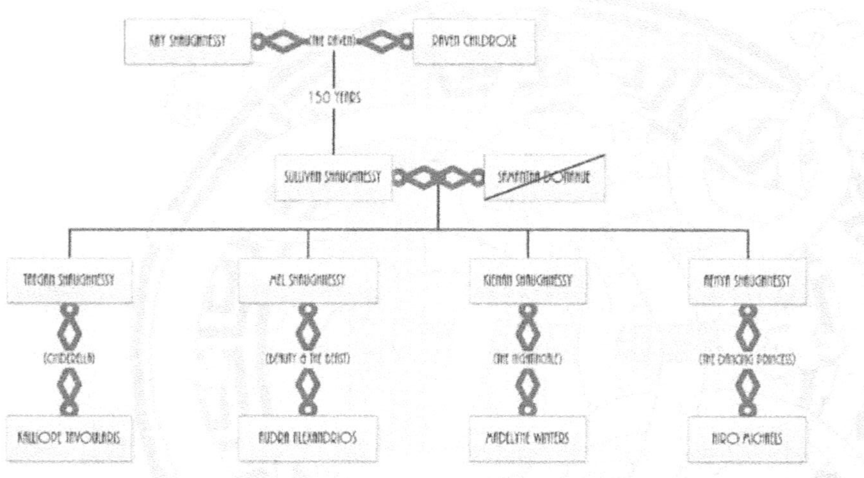

SHAUGHNESSY FAMILY
KAY SHAUGHNESSY
(THE RAVEN)
RAVEN CHILDROSE
150 YEARS
SULLIVAN SHAUGHNESSY
SAMANTHA DONAHUE
TEAGAN SHAUGHNESSY
(CINDERELLA)
KALLIOPE TRIVOULARIS
MEL SHAUGHNESSY
(BEAUTY & THE BEAST)
AUDRA ALEXANDRIOS
KIERAN SHAUGHNESSY
(THE NIGHTINGALE)
MADELYNE WINTERS
REMYA SHAUGHNESSY
(THE DANCING PRINCESS)
HIRO MICHAELS

MARRIAGE
ADOPTION
DIVORCED
FWB

Stacy J. Garrett was made in England but born in Sacramento, California, and like the redwoods of the state, her roots have dug deep. Her destiny as a bard was somewhat inevitable. Little else can explain how she constantly told her mother tall tales so outlandish that she couldn't even get grounded for them. Her mother and grandmother had her reading by age three, and that love of a good story propelled her through so many books that Scholastic Books gave her a medal. A love of worlds created by others eventually brought out the desire to create her own, and she has never looked back.

Stacy has seen both good and evil in her life, and her stories, like life, have no half measures. Even in a fantasy world of dragons and faeries, even in a modern city where magic abounds, she knows that the constants of real emotion never change. Dreams come true, love can be found at first sight, princesses can rescue their princes, and maybe there really can be happily ever after. Her happy endings never come without cost, though, for she truly believes we can't appreciate the good and the joy without the bad and the pain along the way.

Her current haunt is a comfy house in her beloved Sacramento where she wrangles four feline fur-kids and consumes peppermints like mana in order to balance a calendar filled with more creative venues than a sane person should realistically undertake. If she's not chained to her desk, she's stomping through the scenery in search of equally fantastical photographs.